EPIC ZERO

Books 4-6

Epic Zero 4: Tales of a Total Waste of Time

Epic Zero 5: Tales of an Unlikely Kid Outlaw

Epic Zero 6: Tales of a Major Meta Disaster

By

R.L. Ullman

But That's Another Story... Press

Cover designs by Yusup Mediyan
All character images created with heromachine.com.

Published by But That's Another Story... Press
Ridgefield, CT

Printed in the United States of America.

First Printing, 2019.

ISBN: 978-1-7340612-0-8
Library of Congress Control Number: 2019916284

For Matthew,
my Meta 4

GET MORE EPIC!

Don't miss any of the Epic action!

Get a **FREE** copy of
Epic Zero Extra: Tales of a Superhero Screw Up
only at rlullman.com.

TABLE OF CONTENTS

EPIC ZERO 4: Tales of a Total Waste of Time   1

EPIC ZERO 5: Tales of an Unlikely Kid Outlaw   167

EPIC ZERO 6: Tales of a Major Meta Disaster   339

You Can Make a Big Difference!   520

Get More Epic FREE!   521

Meta Powers Glossary   522

Do You Have Monster Problems?   531

About the Author   532

Epic Zero 4: Tales of a Total Waste of Time

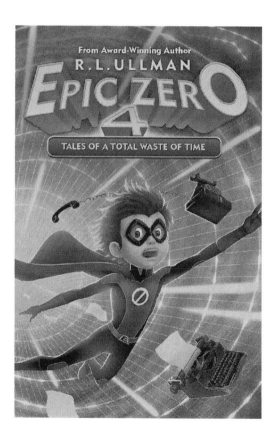

ONE

I TANGO WITH A T-REX

There's a rabid T-Rex on my tail.

Yep, you heard me. A gigantic, kid-eating Tyrannosaurus rex is stomping through Keystone City, and he's penciled me in for his next meal! Yeah, I know what you're thinking. How does a super-smooth hero like me always end up in ridiculous situations like this?

Honestly, I have no idea. But I guess it comes with the territory. After all, sometimes a hero's gotta do what a hero's gotta do. Even if he'd rather be doing *anything* else—like algebra or going to the dentist.

I hang a right at the corner bakery and make a beeline for Keystone Police Station. Why the police station? Well, it's not because I'm trying to stuff this Godzilla wannabe into a human-sized jail cell. That's impossible, although it sure would be nice.

No, I'm heading for the police station because that's where TechnocRat told me to meet him. He said he had a big solution for our not-so-little problem. And he better be right, because we're coming in fast, so I hope he's ready to deliver on his end of the deal.

THUMP!

My feet fly off the pavement. Every time that over-sized lizard takes a step, it's like a mini earthquake throwing me off balance. But I can't stop now. I mean, I've seen all the Jurassic Park movies. I know exactly what'll happen if that thing catches up to me.

I slide across the front hood of an abandoned car. The only good news here is that the city was evacuated hours ago. That means there's no one crazy enough to be traipsing around town in this dangerous situation.

Well, present company excluded.

Suddenly, I hear a SWISH.

Instinctively, I duck just as a telephone pole whizzes over my head and punctures the street like a giant spear.

Now he's throwing things?

Just. Freaking. Wonderful.

Maybe he should be called a 'T-Wrecks?'

Bad puns aside, there was one little snag to our plan. In order to seal the deal, TechnocRat said he had to go back to the Waystation to get what he needed. You know, our secret headquarters way up in (gulp!) outer space.

So, yeah, I'm hoping he makes it back in time.

I hit Main Street and keep on booking. I can see the police station in the distance. It's a straight shot from here, probably six long blocks away. I'm winded, but if I stop to catch my breath, I'm toast.

Speaking of toast, I wonder what Dog-Gone is up to? When TechnocRat asked for a volunteer, that mutt stepped four paws backward, basically leaving me on my own. So much for man's best friend!

And unfortunately, it's not like the rest of the Freedom Force are around to help. They're handling their own dinosaur problems all over the globe.

Dad and Makeshift are stopping a squad of Velociraptors marching through Mexico. Shadow Hawk and Blue Bolt are halting a herd of Triceratops in Tokyo. Master Mime is wrangling a Megalodon in the Atlantic Ocean. And Grace and Mom are fighting a gaggle of Pterodactyls in Europe—try saying that one three times fast!

So, that leaves TechnocRat, Dog-Gone, and yours truly to take down this dino-sore right here in Keystone City. This would have been a whole lot easier if the T-Rex was a Meta and I could simply negate his powers. But he's not, which means I'm powerless against him.

Not a great feeling.

We're three blocks away.

That rat better not let me down.

ROOAARR!

The hairs on the back of my neck stand on end.

Peering over my shoulder, all I see are teeth—giant, super-sharp teeth! He's right behind me!

Time to motor! But I've been running for so long I'm losing—

SMACK!

Suddenly, I slam into something solid and find myself sitting on my backside. My nose is throbbing, and I wipe it with my sleeve. It's bloody. Marvelous.

What happened?

That's when I realize I'm staring at a pair of dark, green boots. But I thought the city was evacuated?

"Who are you?" comes a frantic voice.

Who am I? Sheesh, I really need to hire an agent. I look up to find a man staring at me with wild, brown eyes. He's wearing a cone-shaped helmet and a green jumpsuit with an hourglass insignia on his chest. I know I've seen his Meta profile before, but I can't place him.

Then, it clicks.

"You're the Time Trotter!" I say.

The Time Trotter is a Meta 1 villain with a magical watch that allows him to travel through time. He's mostly a small-time crook who likes to pop up in history where he can profit the most—like when he stole the first truckload of gold headed for Fort Knox. He's had countless run-ins with the Freedom Force, but every time we're about to catch him he slips away through the timestream.

"Y-You're wearing a costume," he says, sounding

strangely desperate. "Are you a hero?"

"The name is Epic Zero," I say, getting to my feet and dusting myself off. Even though I've single-handily saved the world three times, why is it that no villain has ever heard of me? "I'm on the Freedom Force."

"The Freedom Force!" he says, grabbing the front of my uniform. "Please, help me! I'm in danger!"

"Whoa, back off, buddy," I say, knocking his hands off the merchandise. "What danger?"

Then, I remember the T-Rex.

Where's the freaking T-Rex?

I glance over my shoulder to find the behemoth leaning over me, jaws wide open for the kill. I jump, but the T-Rex doesn't move. It's like he's... frozen?

"Don't worry," the Time Trotter says. "I've isolated time around him so that every second is moving a million times slower. I-I can do that now."

Wow, that's how I feel whenever Grace opens her mouth. But something is wrong. In the Meta Profile I read, the Time Trotter can only manipulate time around himself. It never said anything about him manipulating time for others. But if he can do that, then...

"Um, you wouldn't happen to be responsible for bringing all of these dinosaurs here, would you?" I ask. "Because as far as I can remember, you can't do that."

"I-I didn't think I could either," he says, talking rapidly, "until he made me do it. But it hurts so much I-I can't bring any more."

"Whoa," I say. "Slow down. First off, who is this 'he' you're talking about?"

"Please," he begs. "I don't have time. The connection was severed, but I don't know for how long. Get me out of here. He's coming for me!"

"I'll try one more time," I say. "Who is 'he?'"

FWOOM!

Without warning, something powerful blows me backward, throwing me to the ground. I land hard on my left shoulder, but that's the least of my problems. Because hovering above us is the giant head of a man!

But it's no ordinary man. This guy has red skin, pointy ears, and three orange eyes! I drop into a fighting stance, but then the man's face flickers and I realize he's not actually here. He's an image being projected from somewhere far away.

"No!" the Time Trotter screams, totally freaked out.

I study the red guy's face, but I don't recognize him.

"Time Trotter," the three-eyed man rumbles, his deep voice rattling my bones. "The distance is great, but I have restored our link. Yet, you disappoint me. I did not offer you a kingdom only to watch you play with toddlers."

Hang on. Did he just call me a toddler?

"P-Please," the Time Trotter pleads, holding his head in his hands. "I can't bring any more. It's too painful."

"I am afraid it is too late to renegotiate our bargain," the three-eyed man says. "You have a job to do. Now, where is the Key?"

"I-I don't know," the Time Trotter says. "I can't find it. None of them can find it. Look, I'm sorry, I don't want a kingdom anymore. Just leave me alone. Please…"

"Enough!" the three-eyed man commands. Then, the eye in the middle of his forehead turns green. "I enhanced your power. But clearly, I erred in putting my trust in you, for I see you have already failed me. Your world's champions have already stopped your prehistoric pets before they could locate the Cosmic Key."

The Cosmic Key? What's that?

"It's not my fault," the Time Trotter says. "They're the Freedom Force. They're heroes."

"When I rule the universe," the man says, his third eye transforming back to orange, "there will be no more heroes. Or failures."

"Please!" the Time Trotter begs. "I-I'll ignore the pain. I'll go back in time and get more dinosaurs to search for the Cosmic Key. I-I can—"

"Silence!" the three-eyed man orders. "At least your creatures are more disciplined than you. They have spread far and wide across your pathetic planet, allowing me to conduct a proper scan. And while I no longer detect the presence of the Cosmic Key, I do sense its latent energy. It was here at one time but has since been removed."

Okay, this is getting weird. And why is he so determined to find this key?

"I imagine my greatest enemy is laughing at me now," the red man says. "He probably believes he has tricked me. He is probably expecting me to begin searching the universe anew. But the final laugh will be mine. For with your unique powers, we will indeed 'go back in time,' just as you suggest, and we will find the Cosmic Key on this very planet—before it was removed! Isn't that right my loyal subject?"

Then, the man's third eye turns green again.

"No!" the Time Trotter begs, but before he can run away, his body goes rigid and his eyes emit a faint green light. "Yes, master."

Master? Is he being mind-controlled? I've got to—

But before I can act, there's a huge flash of white light and I'm blinded. It takes several seconds to stop seeing stars, but when I do the Time Trotter and his three-eyed friend have vanished. But if the Time Trotter is gone, does that mean—

CHOMP!

The T. Rex!

Suddenly, I'm lifted into the air, my legs dangling above the ground. My costume tightens around my neck, strangling me. I can't breathe! The T. Rex is reeling me into his mouth by my cape!

I've got seconds to act. I reach into my utility belt, pull out my pocketknife, and begin sawing away at the fabric of my cape. As the left side gives way, I feel something slimy run across the back of my neck! Was that his tongue? So gross!

I move into overdrive, frantically cutting away the

right side of my cape until I rip through and drop to the ground. I hit the pavement feet first and let my forward momentum carry me into a somersault. If I survive this, I'll have to thank Shadow Hawk for teaching me that one.

I pop up and start running, my knees feeling like jelly.

STOMP!

He's chasing me again!

I'm two blocks from the police station.

Up ahead I see movement on the front steps. There's good old Dog-Gone prancing back and forth. And next to him is a tiny, white dot scampering over a gray object.

It's TechnocRat! He made it back!

And it looks like he's got his solution all right. It's some kind of a contraption, but why is he jumping off of it? If I didn't know better, I'd say he's looking for something on the ground—like he's lost something?

O. M. G! He's not ready!

One block away.

Suddenly, the area around me darkens, which can only mean one thing—the T-Rex is on top of me!

"Shoot it!" I yell.

"I need a second!" TechnocRat shouts back. "Stall!"

Stall? Are. You. Freaking. Kidding. Me?

Fifteen feet away.

"Hit it!" I yell.

"I can't," TechnocRat yells, "I'm missing a screw!"

"You're darn right you're missing a screw!" I yell. "Now shoot it! Blast it! Do something high-tech to it!"

Five feet away.

The T-Rex is nearly on top of me!

"Found it!" TechnocRat says, proudly holding up a silver screw in his pink paw. Then, he looks my way and whispers, "Holy guacamole."

I look up to find humungous, razor-sharp teeth over my head. Newspaper headlines flash before my eyes: *Unknown Superhero Kid Swallowed by Hungry Dinosaur.*

The T-Rex closes his mouth.

"Auuuuuuugh!" I scream, diving to the pavement.

VZOOM!

A neon green beam shoots straight over my head and slams into the dinosaur. The creature staggers backward, caught in a dazzling vortex of green energy. The T-Rex ROARS as it spins round and round, sinking deeper and deeper into the ripples of the cyclone until he's no longer in sight. And then, the vortex is gone.

What was that?

I look back to find TechnocRat still holding his screw, and Dog-Gone's nose pressed against a red button on the cylindrical machine.

"Well, go figure," TechnocRat says, "I guess I didn't need that screw after all."

I'm gonna kill that rat.

"G-Good boy," I mutter to Dog-Gone.

And then everything goes black.

Meta Profile
The Freedom Force
Captain Justice
Ms. Understood
Glory Girl
Class: Super-Strength
Meta:
Class: Psychic
Meta:
Class: Flight
Meta:
Shadow Hawk
Epic Zero
TechnocRat
Class: None
Meta:
Class: Meta Manipulator
Meta:
Class: Super-Intellect
Meta:
Blue Bolt
Master Mime
Makeshift
Class: Super-Speed
Meta:
Class: Magic
Meta:
Class: Energy Manipulator
Meta:

TWO

I SEE DEAD PEOPLE

There's pressure on my stomach. It's hard to breathe.

I open my eyes, and all I see is a black nose.

Then, I'm slobbered to death.

"Get off, Dog-Gone," I say, wiping my cheeks. "You're too heavy. I can't breathe."

Dog-Gone lifts his big paws off my body and I see my parents standing over me, their expressions changing from concern to relief.

"Take it easy, son," Dad says, putting his hand on my arm. "You need to rest."

"Rest?" I say. "Why? And where am I anyway?" I'm lying in some sterile-looking room I've never seen before. Everything is white—the ceiling, the walls, the floor. I try sitting up, but my left arm is hooked into a tube.

What's going on?

"Relax, Elliott," Mom says. "You're back on the Waystation in our new Medi-wing. TechnocRat worked all night to get it finished."

TechnocRat? Hang on, there's something I wanted to say to him. I just can't remember what.

"Hey there, Elliott, old buddy!" TechnocRat says with unusual gusto. He's standing at the foot of my bed, perched on a steel railing. He looks tired, with droopy whiskers and tiny circles under his eyes. "I'm so happy to see you up and alert. Here's the bad news. You passed out from exhaustion so we're going to have to shut you down for a while. But there's also good news. We learned you're faster than a T-Rex."

T-Rex? T-Rex!

Without thinking, I pop up and swipe at the rat.

"Elliott!" Dad says, holding me back. "What's gotten into you?"

"Ask him," I huff, slumping back into the bed.

"TechnocRat, what's he talking about?" Mom asks.

"Well," TechnocRat says, running his claws along the railing, "Don't be mad at the kid. He's right. I… messed up. I got so caught up trying to complete my device that he nearly got eaten by a dinosaur. At least the mutt had enough sense to save the day."

Dog-Gone scratches his hindquarters.

"I'm… sorry, Elliott," TechnocRat says, his paws

behind his back. "I guess I can't always expect everything to be perfect. It's a technical flaw of mine."

Wow, TechnocRat apologized. He never, ever apologizes—for anything. Part of me still wants to yell at him, but he looks so pathetic I can't.

"Elliott?" Mom says, nodding towards TechnocRat.

I'd love to let him stew a while longer, but I decide to give in, even though I'm still not happy about it.

"Apology accepted," I mutter. "By the way, what did Dog-Gone zap the T-Rex with?"

"Oh, that's my Time Warper device," TechnocRat says. "It's a portable time machine capable of opening a temporary distortion—otherwise known as a wormhole—in the space-time continuum. I invented it years ago but never use it because altering time is risky business. If you travel back into the past and change it in any meaningful way, it could have a ripple effect that significantly compromises the present."

"Influencing events from the past is a major 'no-no' in the superhero rulebook," Dad says. "You should never mess around with time."

"Correct," TechnocRat says, "I didn't want to use the Time Warper, but since dinosaurs are extinct, I figured sending them back to the Jurassic era posed little risk to our current timestream. Fortunately, I was right, but we got lucky. When you're dealing with time you never know what could happen, which is why I keep my Time Warper safely tucked away in my lab. But I guess I pulled it out in the nick of time—get it?"

Everyone laughs but me.

"Too soon, huh?" TechnocRat says, looking at me nervously. "Well, um, I think I've got an electro photon lightbulb to fix somewhere. I'll check in on you later."

Then, he scampers off the railing and disappears.

"Elliott," Dad says, "You're being way too hard on him. He did the best he could."

"Yeah," I say. "With my life hanging in the balance."

"His methods aren't always conventional," Mom says. "But you know he's a hero through and through."

Suddenly, I feel guilty. I do know he's a hero, that's for sure. Maybe I was too hard on him.

"Sorry," I say. "The whole T-Rex thing was just so intense. Plus, I ran into the Time Trotter and—"

"The Time Trotter?" Dad says. "He was in Keystone City? But he's a Meta 1. He couldn't be responsible for those dinosaurs. He doesn't have that kind of power."

"Well, that's what I thought too," I say, "It's kind of a long story." I'm about to launch into my whole ordeal with the Time Trotter, his three-eyed friend, and the mysterious Cosmic Key when...

"Alert! Alert! Alert!" the Meta Monitor blares. "Meta 2 disturbance. Repeat: Meta 2 disturbance. Power signature identified as Where-Wolf. Alert! Alert! Alert! Meta 2 disturbance. Power signature identified as Where-Wolf."

"Where-Wolf!" I exclaim, throwing off the covers.

"He's an Energy Manipulator who can teleport all over the place. Not to mention, he's got a terrible dandruff problem. We'd better get—"

"Hold on, hotshot," Dad says, putting a hand on my shoulder. "You're not going anywhere. You need to recover. We'll handle this one with the rest of the team."

"But…," I start.

"But nothing," Mom says, pulling on her Ms. Understood cowl. "Rest up, Elliott. We'll talk more about your 'long story' when we get back. And please, don't go wandering off this time. Got it?"

"Sheesh," I say. "Fine."

"Dog-Gone," Mom orders, "keep an eye on him. Sit on him if you have to."

Dog-Gone barks in agreement.

"Love you," she calls out as she leaves the room.

"Clearly," I mutter.

Dog-Gone and I stare each other down while the Freedom Flyer disembarks from the Waystation.

We're alone.

Okay, so I didn't get to tell them about the weird three-eyed guy yet, but there's no reason I can't find out more about him myself. I carefully remove the IV from my arm, pull down the covers, and step out of bed when my not-so-loyal companion growls in objection.

Seriously?

"Listen," I say, "we're not doing this."

Dog-Gone blocks the door with his big behind.

"Look, when Mom told me not to go wandering off, she didn't mean I couldn't leave my bed. She just meant I shouldn't leave the Waystation."

Dog-Gone growls again, but I really don't have the energy to go into a full negotiation with him.

"Okay, let's cut to the chase. If you move, I'll give you an entire bag of doggie treats and you can get as sick as you want. Does that work for you?"

Dog-Gone's tail starts wagging.

"I thought so. Follow me." We head into the hallway when I realize the Medi-wing is next door to the Galley. Well, that's convenient. I grab a bag of doggie treats from the pantry and pour all the contents into a metal dog dish.

"Knock yourself out," I say, as Dog-Gone starts crunching away. "But if I were you, I'd pace myself. You're cleaning up any invisi-barf."

With Dog-Gone busy gorging himself, I head up to the Monitor Room. If I'm going to find any information about that three-eyed villain, it's going to be here. I hop into the command chair and punch a few buttons on the keypad. The Meta Monitor lights up.

The Meta Monitor is the most extensive database in the world for Metas. If a bad guy used a superpower anywhere, it'll be captured in here. I type in a few search queries: *Red Skin. Three Eyes. Male.*

Then, I wait. I sure wish I grabbed some popcorn. Thirty seconds later, the Meta Monitor spits out:

No Matches Found.

Huh? That's weird. Why isn't the Meta Monitor showing anything? Hang on, it seemed like he was projecting his image from a distance. I add an additional search term: *Alien*.

The Meta Monitor does its thing, and up pops:

No Matches Found.

That's strange. I don't understand how someone could use a Meta power, but not register in the Meta Monitor's database. I try figuring out an explanation, but I can't come up with one. I guess I'll ask Dad when they get back. Maybe he can think of something.

Well, this was a dead end. I set the Meta Monitor back to autopilot and slide off the command chair. My legs are crazy sore, so I decide to stretch them out with a long walk.

As I stroll down the hallway, I hear faint footsteps behind me, followed by a low whimper.

"You ate them all, didn't you?" I ask.

Dog-Gone is moving slowly. He looks up and his guilty expression says it all.

"I warned you," I say. "You know, you have absolutely no willpower. I hope you've got a fast metabolism."

We walk in silence for a while, me trying to solve the mystery of the three-eyed man, and Dog-Gone trying not to yack, when we enter a dark corridor.

Suddenly, I get the feeling we're not alone. Like, we're surrounded!

"Who's there—," I start, but as soon as my eyes adjust to the darkness I'm embarrassed. We're surrounded all right, but not because there's a team of bad guys waiting to attack, but because we've wandered into the Hall of Fallen Heroes.

The Hall of Fallen Heroes is a memorial space dedicated to honoring former members of the Freedom Force who gave their lives in the line of duty. Each hero is represented by a life-sized, bronze statue depicting them in full costume.

There are five statues in all.

I flick on the light switch, triggering spotlights that illuminate each one. Honestly, this area of the Waystation creeps me out. When we were younger, Grace and I would play tag all over the Waystation, but we would never come up here. We both agreed it was off limits.

Mom, however, comes up here all the time. She says it gives her perspective whenever she needs to make tough decisions.

There's a giant inscription carved into the wall. It reads: *True Heroes Give So Others May Live.*

I walk down the row of statues.

First up is Rolling Thunder, a Meta 3 Energy Manipulator with the ability to shape and magnify sound. He had a handlebar mustache and wore the insignia of a sound wave stretched across his barrel-shaped chest. Dad said Rolling Thunder was a character and his laugh sounded like a sonic boom.

Next up is Madame Meteorite, a Meta 3 Flyer who wore the symbol of a comet across her bodysuit. She was an astronaut who passed through a strange dust cloud, giving her the ability to defy gravity and glide through any atmosphere, including outer space.

The third statue is of Robot X-treme, a Meta 3 Super-Intellect who was part-man, part-machine. Robot X-treme was a genius with a rare disease that attacked his own body. So, he transferred his brain into a seven-foot-tall indestructible robot with built-in weaponry. Dad says Robot X-treme had the most brilliant mind he's ever known, which always sends TechnocRat into a tizzy.

Then, there's Dynamo Joe, a Meta 3 Strongman with long hair, a thick beard, and the insignia of a boxing glove on his chest. Dad said Dynamo Joe was not only a former boxing champ but also a hippie—whatever that means. Dad always brags about how he once beat Dynamo Joe in an arm-wrestling match. But based on the ridiculous size of Dynamo Joe's biceps, I'm not sure I'm buying it.

Finally, I reach the last statue, which always gives me chills. That's because it's of a girl about my age. Her name was Sunbolt, and she was a Meta 2 Energy Manipulator with the power to harness solar energy. She wore pigtails, a cape, and had the image of a sun on her top. Mom said she was brave and wanted to learn everything she could to be a great superhero.

She was also Dynamo Joe's daughter.

I stare into her determined eyes, and for some

reason, I can't look away. Maybe it's because she was just starting out—sort of like me.

I've never really spent time with the statues before. I guess I can see why Mom comes up here so often. It's a great reminder that playing superhero isn't a game. It's life or death every time you put on the cape.

I mean, these guys sacrificed their lives being heroes. Could I do that? Would I do that?

"C'mon, Dog-Gone," I say, heading back the way we came. The poor mutt is starting to look green.

Then, I remember all these fallen heroes have something in common.

They were all killed in the battle with Meta-Taker.

The battle that created the Freedom Force.

Thankfully, that monster is out of our lives now.

Well, I'm no closer to solving the mystery of the three-eyed man. I'm wiped, so I head back to my room, drop my utility belt and mask on my desk, and climb into bed. I'm so tired I can't even change out of my costume.

As I lie down on my pillow, I catch a glimpse of the photograph on my nightstand. It's a picture of my family all together in costume. Of course, Grace's shoulder is blocking half of my face.

Nevertheless, I'm thankful my parents survived that battle with Meta-Taker.

I close my eyes, and as I drift off to sleep, I hear the not-so-sweet sounds of Dog-Gone barfing in my bathroom.

Meta Profile

Name: Time Trotter
Role: Villain   Status: Active

VITALS:

Race: Human
Real Name: Harlan Ticker
Height: 5'9"
Weight: 204 lbs
Eye Color: Brown
Hair Color: Brown

META POWERS:

Class: Magic
Power Level:

- Limited Time Manipulation powered by a mystical watch
- Can only transfer self through timestream

CHARACTERISTICS:

Characteristic	Value
Combat	25
Durability	65
Leadership	15
Strategy	46
Willpower	34

THREE

I FREAK OUT

Have you ever woken up more tired than when you went to sleep? Well, that's how I'm feeling right now.

There's drool running down my chin, and I can't even lift my head off the pillow. I don't know how long I've been out but based on how heavy my body feels I'm guessing it's been a while.

Mustering my strength, I roll over and squint at the alarm clock. It reads: *3:23 p.m.* Wow, I've slept in all day! I don't remember ever sleeping this late. I mean, Grace sleeps in all the time, but she's a teenager, that's her job!

My stomach is rumbling, which isn't surprising since I've missed breakfast and lunch. And speaking of food…

"Dog-Gone?" I call out to the bathroom.

The last thing I remember is hearing my poor pooch getting sick. Ugh, I can't imagine what's waiting for me in there. I wish dogs had manners, or at least better aim.

"Dog-Gone?" I call again. "Are you okay?"

I wait for a signal—a bark, a groan, the waving of a white flag, but there's nothing. Since it's so late, I bet Mom let him out of my room so he wouldn't wake me up begging for his breakfast. After all, no matter how bad he's feeling, Dog-Gone never misses a meal.

Then, I notice something weird.

The picture on my nightstand is… different?

Instead of my family, there's a photo of a black cat wearing a blue mask. I have no clue whose cat it is, or how it got there.

I bet Grace is playing a prank on me. After all, I'm always busting on her for streaming hours of mindless cat videos. I bet she snuck in here while I was sleeping and swapped out my picture.

Why are sisters so annoying?

I pull down the covers and throw my legs over the side of the bed. With herculean effort, I trudge over to the bathroom, hoping beyond hope that Dog-Gone didn't leave me too huge of a disaster. But as I peek inside, I'm shocked. The floor is sparkling clean!

How is that possible? I swear I heard him barfing up a storm last night. Did Mom or Dad clean it up? Whatever happened, I'm counting my lucky stars.

I catch my reflection in the mirror. My hair looks like

a bird's nest and I'm still wearing my costume. Well, most of my costume anyway. My mask is on my desk and I can't help but notice I'm minus one cape.

Stupid T-Rex.

I think about showering, but my rumbling stomach objects. So, I decide I'll grab a bite first in the Galley. Maybe I'll catch Shadow Hawk making one of his famous peanut butter and banana sandwiches.

I exit my room and pray I run into Dad. No one gets costumes cleaner than Dad. Plus, he's such a stickler for detail I can count on him to sew on a new cape. I just hope he'll do it without his usual lecture on the proper care of Meta gear.

I enter the Galley to find Grace bent over, rummaging through the fridge. I also hear loud munching coming from beneath the dining table, which can only mean one thing—Dog-Gone is back on his furry feet.

"I see you're feeling better, huh?" I say, patting the tabletop. "That's great news because you looked so stuffed, I thought you were going to pop."

But instead of a bark, he lets out a high-pitched hiss.

Okay, maybe he's not feeling better.

Grace is still digging around the refrigerator, so I lay a hand on her shoulder and say, "Nice try with that cat picture, but I knew it was—"

Then, she wheels on me, chicken drumstick in hand.

And I realize it's not Grace at all.

Her eyes are red instead of blue. And her hair is

black instead of blond.

"Who-Who are you?" I stammer.

"Funny," she says, her voice deeper than my sister's, "because I was wondering the same thing about you."

Just then, I notice her costume isn't crimson red with white shooting stars. It's all black with a big skull on it!

"You're not Glory Girl," I say.

"Nope," she says. "I'm Gory Girl." Suddenly, a red aura emanates from her hand, and the meat on the chicken drumstick melts away, leaving only the bone!

"Where's the Freedom Force?" I ask.

"The Freedom Force?" she scoffs. "We kicked those losers out years ago. Now this place belongs to us—the Freak Force."

The Freak Force?

"Um, I think I woke up on the wrong side of the satellite," I say, backing up to the entrance.

I don't know what's going on, but I can tell she's sizing me up to be her next chicken drumstick. Time to make my exit. I bang on the dining table. "C'mon, Dog-Gone. Let's go."

But instead of a German Shepherd, out steps a black cat wearing a blue mask. The thing is huge and fluffy, nearly the size of Dog-Gone. Then, I realize it's the same cat that's in the picture by my bed!

"Stick him, Scaredy-Cat!" Gory Girl commands.

Scaredy-Cat?

The next thing I know, the cat's claws extend to a

ridiculous size and the feline jumps me! I flail my arms just in time, knocking it back towards Gory Girl. The cat smashes into her, and they both crash into the refrigerator in a tangled mess of hair and paws.

Suddenly, I feel a sharp pain on my right side. I look down to see my costume is ripped from my armpit down to my waist. The cat got me! I've got to get out of here!

I bolt down the hallway.

"Get him!" Gory Girl screams.

What the heck is going on? I'd like to think I'm dreaming, but my side hurts so much I know I'm not.

Something has gone totally bonkers here.

I mean, where's my family? She said the Freak Force kicked the Freedom Force off the Waystation years ago. How is that possible?

I head for the Monitor Room to see if I can find a familiar face when I hear—

"Don't let him get away!"

That was Gory Girl again! And it sounds like she's rallying her troops! How could I be home, but everyone inside my home is from bizarro world?

And then it hits me. The three-eyed man!

He said he was going back in time.

He said there would be no more heroes when he ruled. Did he somehow alter the course of history?

But if that's the case, how am I still here?

I reach the Monitor Room stairwell and I'm about to go up when I see a pair of boots coming down.

"I'll find him!" comes a voice.

Gotta move!

I book down the hall. If the Freak Force are the only Metas here, then everyone on the Waystation must be a villain.

Just. Freaking. Wonderful.

Well, if that's the case I know one thing, I can't stay here. So, the question becomes, what's the fastest way off of a satellite orbiting Earth?

It's useless heading for the Mission Room or the Combat Room because they're both dead ends. I could go for the Hangar to nab a Freedom Flyer or Ferry, but what if they're all gone? Another option is the Transporter Room, but if the timestream *is* screwed up I could be trapped in a world filled with villains or worse.

Then, I get a terrifying thought.

What if going anywhere is useless?

I mean, if my timestream *is* screwed up, the only way to fix it is to go back into the past myself. But how?

I sure wish TechnocRat was here. I know I gave him a hard time, but he'd whip up something in his lab and… and…

That's it!

I've got a plan!

I double back the way I came, running past the Galley and sprinting towards the West Wing. I spot more villains out of the corner of my eye, but I'm not planning on dropping in for a chat. Instead, I huff and puff to my final destination.

TechnocRat's laboratory.

Even though the Freedom Force isn't here anymore, it looks like the lab still is. But the doors are closed and there's yellow cautionary tape on the outside that reads: DANGER. DO NOT ENTER.

Danger? That's weird.

But I'm not going to let some warning tape stop me, because my only escape route is inside that room. At least, I'm hoping it's inside. Of course, if I'm wrong, I've just made the worst decision of my life.

I reach for the keypad when I notice it's covered in dust. Wait a second, Gory Girl said they kicked the Freedom Force out years ago. So, is it possible no one's been in TechnocRat's lab since then?

I read the warnings on the yellow tape again.

Then, I notice the carpet next to me is singed black.

Suddenly, it clicks!

No one on the Freak Force knows the passcode to TechnocRat's lab. And just like the Vault, TechnocRat boobytrapped the entrance if you input three incorrect codes. Fortunately, I know what the code is.

I'm about to start typing when I hear a high-pitched HISS. I turn to find a black cat sitting in the hallway, licking his paws, and watching me through the narrow slits of his blue mask.

What was that superstition about black cats again?

"Listen," I plead. "I'll give you all the doggie—I

mean, kitty snacks you want. Just let me go, okay?"

But Scaredy-Cat just keeps on licking, his tail swaying back and forth like a cobra preparing to strike.

I need to up the ante.

"Okay," I say. "How about you let me go, and after I solve this little mix-up, I'll bring you a tasty rat from my timestream. He might be a little bitter going down, but he's totally worth it. Deal?"

But Scaredy-Cat just stands up and arches his back.

What's he doing? Is he going to pounce?

And then, he tilts his head back and lets out the loudest, most ear-piercing MEOW known to cat.

"No deal!" I say, ducking just in time to avoid Scaredy-Cat's sharp-clawed lunge.

I quickly type in the code: C-A-M-E-M-B-E-R-T.

Bingo! The doors swoosh open, splitting the yellow tape in half. I dive through the entrance seconds before the doors shut closed behind me. I made it!

But when I turn around, my stomach drops.

The lab looks exactly like I remembered it, and that's not a good thing. Beakers, test tubes, and vials line the walls, and the tables are covered with microscopes and machine parts. Clearly, TechnocRat didn't clean-up before he left—not that I expected him to. The guy is a packrat to the core.

Well, this is going to be like trying to find a needle in a dozen haystacks. But I can't give up. I've got to find my ticket out of here.

I've got to find the Time Warper device.

I remember TechnocRat saying he kept the Time Warper tucked away in his lab. But where?

I race around, looking under tables, throwing open cabinets, and turning over boxes. Everything is covered in layers of dust, making me sneeze. Clearly, no one's been here in years, but I still haven't found it. I'm pretty sure I know what I'm looking for. I remember it being gray and cylindrical, with a big red button on top.

How hard could this be?

Apparently, a lot harder than I thought.

I'm starting to regret not going for the Hangar.

BOOM!

I jump. They're pounding on the door!

I know it's made of tungsten steel. But I'm not sure how long it can withstand Meta 3 punishment.

I try a few more cabinets, but I can't find the Time Warper anywhere. Then, I have a horrible thought. Why am I even assuming a Time Warper exists in this timestream? Maybe it doesn't. Maybe this was a huge mistake. Boy, wouldn't that be a kick in the pants?

BOOM!

Suddenly, a fist pops through the door.

I'm running out of time! Sweat pours down my forehead as crazy thoughts race through my brain. Maybe I should give myself up? Maybe they'll take it easy on me? Maybe I'm delusional?

Then, I notice a door in the back corner.

Could it be?

I slide across a table, knocking all kinds of doodads to the floor, and yank open the door. It's a closet—a deep closet—filled with giant crates stacked three levels high. I grab the end of one and pull with all my might, but it doesn't open. It's nailed shut! The crates look big enough to hold a Time Warper, but I've got no time to open—

BOOM!

Nope, no time at all!

I'm about to give up when I notice the crates are labeled. Thank goodness someone is organized around here! I read the closest one. It says: *Camembert Cheese.*

Wow, that's a lot of cheese. I scan a few more crates: *Swiss Cheese. Cheddar Cheese. Mozzarella Cheese.*

Ugh! They're all cheese!

This isn't good.

Then, I realize one crate in the back is not like the others. Instead of brown, it's purple. That's peculiar. It's sitting on the top layer, and I can just read part of its label, but not the whole thing. I stretch up on my tippy toes as far as I can go.

All I can make out is: *--arper.*

No! Way!

My heart is racing. These things look too heavy to bring down, so I guess I'll have to go up. But then I realize that even if I make it to the purple crate, I have no way to open it. My eyes dart around the room before landing on a crowbar. Score! I tuck it under my arm and scale the tower of cheese crates.

By the time I reach the top, my arms and legs are shaking. I go into army-crawl mode, moving across the crates until I reach my goal—the purple crate!

I stretch down to read the label. The words are upside down, but it clearly says: *Time Warper.*

Yes!

BOOM! CRASH!

No! They've busted down the door!

"Search the room," Gory Girl says.

There's no time to lose. I take the crowbar, jam it into the purple crate, and push down with all my might. The top pops open and falls to the floor.

CRASH!

Uh-oh.

"What's that?" Gory Girl asks.

I dig inside the crate and pull out a cylindrical device. Yes!

My hands are shaking as I hold it. There's a yellow label on the side that reads: *Warning: This is a portable Time Machine. Before operating, please ensure all parts are securely...*

Yada, yada, yada. I don't have time for this!

I set it on top of a neighboring crate and point it at me. Then, I notice a keypad and counter on the side. The keypad reads: *WHERE*, and the counter reads: *WHEN*.

Where and when? Two very excellent questions.

What should I enter?

Just then, I notice something strange.

Taped to the red button is a small, handwritten note that says: *For Elliott.*

For… me? What the…?

I unfold the paper, it's crinkly and yellowed at the edges like it's been here a long time.

It reads: *WHERE: Keystone City, WHEN: -30 years, 3 months, 10 days.*

That's weird? I scratch my head when it dawns on me that someone is telling me where to go!

But who?

Unfortunately, I'll have to figure that out later.

I shove the note into my pocket and type K-E-Y-S-T-O-N-E-C-I-T-Y into the keypad and set the counter to -30 years, 3 months, and 10 days.

Then, I hear a HISS.

I turn to find Scaredy-Cat's face peering over the top crate! They found me!

It's time travel time!

I punch the red button.

"Hey!" Gory Girl yells. "Stop right—!"

But I never hear the end of her sentence, because I'm spiraling into a wave of green energy.

And then I'm gone.

FOUR

I GET GROOVY

I think I'm gonna hurl.

I've never been a big fan of amusement parks, and my Time Warper experience was like a teacup ride on steroids. In fact, it kind of felt like I was being sucked through a million bathtub drains. But finally, after what seemed like an eternity, I crashed to the ground.

I've got no clue where I am, but at least I managed to escape the Freak Force—so hooray for that. Now for the big question. Did the Time Warper deliver me to the right place?

Well, I seem to be sitting between two buildings and staring at a bunch of garbage cans. So, I'd say I've landed in an alley. But how do I know it's the right alley? Then, I notice a crumpled newspaper in the corner. I crawl a few feet over and pick it up. Gross, it's totally soggy and nearly disintegrates in my hands, but I recognize it as the Keystone City Gazette. So, I'm in the right place.

Then, I pull out my scrunched-up note and re-read it: *-30 years, 3 months, and 10 days.* Wow! This seems to match the date on the newspaper. But I need to know for sure.

Even though I'm still feeling dizzy, I get to my feet and step onto the sidewalk when I hear something loud approaching. I dive back just as a van motors past. It looks like one of those old-fashioned VW vans—with a white top, blue body, and whitewall tires. It even has a peace symbol on its side.

But then I realize something. That van wasn't old-fashioned. In fact, it's just right for the time period I'm standing in. I peer around the corner and my eyes bulge.

This is Keystone City alright, but it's the Keystone City of the past. Everything is different, from the cars to the streetlamps to the buildings. Other than the bakery and the bank, I don't recognize any of the other shops, like the Keystone City Record Store which is offering two-for-one vinyl deals on Mondays.

What the heck is vinyl anyway?

Just then, a group of teenagers walks past and I pull back. The girls are wearing plaid pants, colorful sweaters, and headbands in their hair. The guys are wearing turtlenecks, striped sweaters, and polyester pants. Okay, no kid from my school would be caught dead dressed like this.

So, that seals it—I made it!

Inside I do a happy dance. The Time Warper worked! I mean, what are the odds of that? Now all I need to do is find the Freedom Force, fix my timestream problem, and jump back home, which hopefully will have returned to normal.

This should be a piece of cake. Not.

I'm about to set foot into the street again when I suddenly hear TechnocRat's voice in my brain: *If you travel back into the past and change it in any meaningful way, it could have a ripple effect that significantly compromises the present.*

I stop myself. What am I thinking? I can't go wandering around Keystone City like this! I'm still in costume!

This is bad news. I mean, I'm a kid from the future! If anyone sees me, it could cause a chain reaction that screws up everything! I've got to get some normal clothes so I can explore the city without attracting attention.

But how? Then, I spot a miracle.

Directly across the street is a clothing store! I read the awning. It says: *Groovy Threads Clothing Store.* Bingo!

Except I've got one problem. I don't have any money. Usually, I keep twenty bucks in my utility belt, but I left it in my room. Genius move.

So, how can I pay for new clothes? All I have to offer is child labor. Maybe if I beg hard enough, they'll let me sweep the floor?

But first things first. I need to get across the street without being seen. I look around, but there aren't any blankets or towels to cover me up. In fact, I can't even find a freaking cardboard box!

So, there's one option left. I position myself at the edge of the alley and wait for traffic to die down. What I wouldn't give right now for Blue Bolt's speed or Dog-Gone's invisibility power.

It takes forever, but when my moment comes, I hustle across the street and bound through Groovy Thread's front door. As soon as I enter, a bell RINGS announcing my arrival. So much for stealth mode.

Fortunately, the store is empty.

There's music playing in the background. It sounds like that old disco music Mom plays on the Waystation. She tries to get me to dance with her, but I never give in.

Well, I probably shouldn't say 'never.'

Anyway, I scan the merchandise until I find the boys section. They have a wide selection of shirts and pants, but they're nothing like I'm used to. The shirts are all flowery-patterned button-downs with huge collars, and the pants are super slim with bell bottoms.

Seriously? People actually wore this stuff?

"Hey, dude," comes a voice from behind me.

I nearly jump out of my skin. I turn around to find a big man with green eyes, long brown hair, and a beard staring at me. His arms are so big they look like they're bursting out of his shirt. Where'd he come from?

"What's your bag, man?" he asks.

My bag? What's he talking about?

"I mean, what can I help you with today?" he asks.

"Oh," I say. "I was hoping to try some things on."

"We don't sell Halloween outfits here," he says.

Halloween outfits? What's he talking about? Then, I realize he's referring to my superhero costume.

"Oh, yeah," I say. "Good one. No, I was looking for regular clothes."

"Groovy," he says, looking me up and down. "Are you from Keystone City?"

"Y—," I start, but then change direction. "I mean, no. I'm from out of town. Just passing through."

"Oh, okay," he says, nodding. But he looks at me suspiciously. "No problem. What do you need?"

"Um, a shirt," I say. "And some pants. And socks. And a belt. And—"

"Got it," he says, stopping me. "I'll hook you up with everything. Why don't you chill out in the fitting room?"

He guides me into a small room behind a beaded curtain. I sit down on a stool and look at my reflection in the mirror. I'm such a mess I'm surprised the guy is even letting me stay in his store.

"Here," he says moments later, pushing a stack of clothes through the curtain. "Try these on."

"Thanks," I say. I put on underwear, black socks, a blue-and-white plaid shirt, brown bell-bottom pants, and a pair of red-and-white Converse sneakers. Strangely, I've never been so excited to see underwear.

"So, where are you from?" he asks.

Oh, jeez! If I say I'm from somewhere he knows, he might start asking me detailed questions. Better to stay vague. "Um, here and there. My parents move a lot."

Please, please, stop asking questions.

"I see," he says. "Do the clothes fit?"

"Yes, thanks," I say, checking myself in the mirror. Surprisingly, everything fits perfectly. I roll up my superhero costume and tuck it under my arm. Now comes the hard part. How am I going to pay for this?

"Um," I say, stepping out of the fitting room. "Sorry, but I just realized I don't have any money. Maybe I can sweep the floor for you? I'm happy to stay all night."

I brace myself for the worst.

But the man just smiles and says, "Nah, it's on me."

"What?" I say. "Are you serious?"

"Sure," the man says. "Styles change fast around here, and that outfit will get more use on you than on one of my mannequins. Just do me a solid and if anyone asks you where you got your look, tell them you came to Groovy Threads. Deal?"

"Sure," I say, stunned. "Thanks."

"Would you like a bag for your costume," he says pointing to my Epic Zero outfit under my arm. "I mean, your Halloween outfit, of course."

"Um, sure," I say.

The man goes behind the counter and brings out a plastic bag with the Groovy Threads logo on the side.

"Here you go," he says. "Be careful out there."

"Gee, thanks," I say.

"No sweat," he says with a wink. "See you around."

I step out of the store still in shock. Well, that was lucky. Weird, but lucky. At least I look normal enough to blend into the crowd. Now I've got to find the Freedom Force.

Just then, I see a dog walking on the opposite side of the street. It's a German Shephard, just like Dog-Gone, but its fur is gray-and-black instead of brown-and-black. Boy, I really miss my partner-in-crime.

Suddenly, my eyes get all watery and it hits me. If I don't solve this time-traveling mess, I may never see him again. I rub my eyes and look for that dog again.

He's stopped at the bakery in front of a basket of baguettes. He's not wearing a collar, and his owner doesn't seem to be around. The poor fella must be lost. He's probably tired and hungry, just like me. I wish I had some doggie treats to give him.

But then, the pooch looks left, then right, and then disappears into thin air! I blink hard. Are my eyes playing tricks on me? The next thing I know, a baguette is magically lifted out of its basket, and takes off down the street!

No! Way!

He can turn invisible! And he stole the bread!

I take off after him. He's really fast, which isn't surprising since he has a two-leg advantage. My mind, however, is racing faster than my body.

First of all, that can't be Dog-Gone. He's the wrong color. Besides, I'm, like, thirty years in the past.

"Stop!" I yell.

Without breaking stride, I see the bread point towards me, then go even faster. He knows I'm chasing him! Okay, calling out to him was a huge mistake.

As we pass by, strangers point at us and I realize how nuts this must look. I mean, it's not every day you see a goofily dressed kid in hot pursuit of a runaway baguette. But I need to stop that mutt no matter what. After all, he's a Meta, which means he's my best shot at finding other Metas—like my family!

But the dog has the advantage and he knows it. He's staying low, cutting around people, bicycles, and park benches. I'm doing my best to keep up, but I'm losing ground every second. Then, he flies across the street, barely avoiding an oncoming car.

I stop at the crosswalk, look both ways, and pick up the trail. He's way ahead now. If I don't do something, he'll get away for good.

I hop up on a bench, concentrate hard, and cast my negation powers far and wide. If I can negate his powers, I can remove his invisibility. But I don't see him anywhere. He's gone.

Well, it was probably pointless anyway. Even if I

could see him, I couldn't do anything to stop his natural speed. So, there goes my only hope. Now what?

I step off the bench when—

CRASH!

Shards of glass come flying at me. The next thing I know, two guys in all black leap through a busted store-front window. They're wearing stockings over their heads and carrying big sacks over their shoulders. I look up at the sign on the building. It reads: *Keystone City Jewelers.*

It's a robbery! And it's happening right in front of me! My first instinct is to stop these guys, but then I remember I'm not supposed to do anything. The last thing I want to do is cause a timestream disaster.

Suddenly, I hear SIRENS.

Great. The boys in blue will handle this.

The crooks pull out guns as a fleet of police cars screech into view, blocking all escape routes. Car doors fly open everywhere, and the next thing I know, dozens of pistols are pointed our way.

"Drop your weapons!" an officer shouts through a megaphone. "You're surrounded!"

"What now, Weasel?" the bigger goon asks.

I want to say, 'now you get arrested, numbskull,' but apparently, 'Weasel' has other ideas.

"Easy, Moose," Weasel says. "It's time for Plan B."

Plan B? I wonder what these morons came up with for Plan B? Then, I realize they're looking at me!

"Grab the kid!" Weasel orders.

Uh-oh.

Before I can move, Moose grabs me and puts me in a headlock. Then, Weasel presses his gun to my temple! I try pulling free, but I can't. And to top it off, my Meta powers are useless against these guys because they're Zeroes!

Somehow, by trying not to interfere, I've put myself in the worst situation possible. I'm a hostage!

Just. Freaking. Wonderful.

"Release the child," the officer demands.

Did he call me 'child?' Seriously?

"Get lost cop and maybe we'll think about it!" Weasel shouts back, pulling back the gun's hammer.

Then, I get a weird thought. Can I die in the past?

"Stand back, officers!" booms a male voice. "I've got this situation under control!"

Just then, a masked figure lands ten feet in front of us. He's wearing a red, white, and blue costume with a giant American flag across his chest. He has long blond hair, blue eyes, and a square jaw. At first, I'm elated that I'm about to be saved. But as I take a closer look, I realize he looks like he just graduated from high school.

"Liberty Lad!" Moose yells. "Get lost!"

Liberty Lad? I've never heard of...

"Sorry," Liberty Lad says. "But it's Fight Time!"

Fight Time! Fight Time? Hold on, there's only one Meta I know who says that. I study Liberty Lad's face more closely and my jaw drops.

O.M.G!

It's… Dad? But way younger!

"Back off," Weasel orders. "Or we'll waste the kid."

"Let's talk this over," Liberty Lad suggests, sounding surprisingly nervous. "Don't make any rash decisions."

"Step aside!" comes a female voice. "Let a real hero handle this!"

Suddenly, a masked girl appears. She's wearing a red bodysuit with a lightning bolt on the front. She has a brown ponytail and brown eyes. She looks as young as Dad, but I'd know that voice anywhere.

It's Mom!

So, that can only mean one thing.

The three-eyed man failed!

The Freedom Force is still together!

"I *am* a real hero," Liberty Lad says, clearly annoyed. "And I don't need your help. So why don't you take your mind tricks somewhere else, Brainstorm."

Brainstorm? I didn't know she called herself that.

"Really?" she says mockingly. "Then tell me, why is the innocent hostage here still a hostage?"

"Because I was just about to act," he says. "Until I was assaulted by your rudeness."

Hang on a second, are they… arguing?

"Rudeness?" she says. "You're one to call me—"

But as they bicker back and forth, it dawns on me.

My parents aren't together at all.

In fact, they hate each other.

Meta Profile

Name: Liberty Lad
Role: Hero   **Status: Inactive**
- Currently operating as Captain Justice

VITALS:

Race: Human
Real Name: Tom Harkness
Height: 6'3"
Weight: 205 lbs
Eye Color: Blue
Hair Color: Blonde

META POWERS:

Class: Super-Strength
Power Level: ▮▮▮
- Extreme Strength
- Invulnerability
- Enhanced Jumping
- Shockwave-Clap

CHARACTERISTICS:

Combat	85	
Durability	90	
Leadership	65	
Strategy	70	
Willpower	86	

FIVE

I MUST BE DREAMING

I can't believe what's happening.

I mean, I'm not even supposed to be here. The only reason I traveled into the past is to fix my present, which somehow went completely bonkers! And I suspect it has everything to do with that mysterious three-eyed man and his plan to find that Cosmic Key he was mumbling about.

But that's not even my biggest problem right now. Both Dad and TechnocRat told me the number one rule for time travel is never to interfere in any way. Yet, here I am, being held at gunpoint by a couple of petty criminals.

So, I pretty much flunked that one.

But then, just as I'm desperately searching for the Freedom Force for help, my parents show up out of the blue as young adults with completely embarrassing superhero names. You'd think my job was done, except they're way too busy arguing with each other to bother saving me.

You know, their kid from the future.

I've got a headache.

"Sorry, Brainstorm," Dad says. "But I work solo. That means alone."

"Gee, thanks for the vocabulary lesson, Captain Grammar," Mom scoffs, "but I know perfectly well what 'solo' means. In fact, it's how I prefer operating as well."

"Well, feel free to leave," Dad says. "Because I don't team-up with Metas I can't trust. Not with everything that's been going on."

Wait, what's he talking about? What's going on?

"My thoughts exactly," Mom says. "So, let's just say I'm keeping an eye on you."

"Me?" Dad says. "You think I'm responsible?"

Oh, jeez. Here they go again.

"Weasel," Moose whispers. "Let's get out of here."

"Yeah," Weasel says. "Follow my lead."

The two morons tiptoe backward, taking me with them! And my parents are completely oblivious!

"—not infringe on my territory," Dad says.

"This isn't your territory," Mom says. "I don't see the words 'Inflated Ego" on any street sign anyw—"

"Hey!" I interject. "Sorry to bug you in the middle of this enlightening conversation, but are either of you 'superheroes' actually planning on doing anything super?

You know, like helping me out?"

"Shut it, kid," Weasel says, digging the tip of his gun into my temple. "You heroes back off! And that goes for all of you cops too! Drop your weapons or the kid gets it!"

My parents look my way, their jaws hanging open. They were so caught up arguing, they forgot we were even here. And the cops can't do anything but lower their pistols. So, this is pretty much going from bad to worse.

"See, Moose," Weasel says, puffing out his chest. "I told you I had a—yeooow!"

Suddenly, I feel an intense burst of heat, and Weasel grabs his right foot like it's on fire.

"Ahh!" he screams, hopping around before falling to the ground, his gun rattling on the pavement.

"Weasel!" Moose says, letting go of me.

I drop hard to my hands and knees.

"What happened?" Moose cries, but as soon as he raises his gun, the barrel melts into a gloppy mess.

"Sorry," comes a female voice, "but I guess that's too hot to handle."

The next thing I know, a girl with red pigtails and a yellow cape blazes out of the sky and lands with her back to me. Moose swings at her but misses badly. The girl socks him in the gut and then kicks him squarely in the jaw, sending several of his teeth flying. Moose topples over and doesn't get back up.

"M-Make it stop!" Weasel begs, his foot smoking.

"Not a fan of a hot foot, huh?" the girl says. She waves her hand, and the smoke subsides.

"T-Thank you," he says, relief washing over his face.

Just then, the police come charging in. They slap handcuffs on the crooks and yank the stockings off their ugly mugs.

"Well, I think the good guys have this one under control," the girl says.

Then, she turns to face me, and I do a double take.

She's around my age, with bright green eyes and a big smile. For some reason, I feel like I've seen her before, but I can't place her. And then my eyes land on the yellow sun insignia on her costume.

O. M. G.

It's... It's...

"Sunbolt," Mom says.

Sunbolt? B-But, she's... she's...

"In the flesh," Sunbolt says. "Sorry to barge in like that, but it looked like the kid needed help."

"You did the right thing," Dad says, then he walks over to me and reaches out. "Sorry about that, kid. Can I help you up?"

I reach for his hand but then stop myself.

What am I doing? I mean, how can I ask them for help without revealing who I am? It's not like I can just say: 'Hi there, I'm Elliott, your son from the far-flung future.' That could affect the past in such a dramatic way it could change everything! I need to think this through.

"Are you okay, kid?" Dad asks.

"Um, yeah," I say. "I'm fine." I clasp his hand and he pulls me to my feet, but I keep my head down. The last thing I want is to make eye contact. I can't let him get a good look at my face.

Then, Mom comes over.

"I'm so sorry," she says, putting her hand on my shoulder. "I guess we got so distracted we forgot what we're here to do. But I have to say, you were really brave back there. I'm impressed."

"Oh, thanks," I say. I've got to stay low key. The worst thing that could happen right now is for Mom to read my mind. "Anyway, I guess I'll be going now."

"You dropped your stuff," Dad says, leaning over.

My heart skips a beat.

My Groovy Threads bag is on the ground—and my Epic Zero costume is sticking halfway out of the bag!

"No!" I yell.

Dad stops in his tracks.

"Sorry," I say more evenly. "Thanks, but I'll get it." I scoop up the bag and shove the costume back inside. "It's just a silly Halloween costume."

"Well, thanks again, Sunbolt," Mom says. "It's nice to know there are some heroes you can still trust."

"Now what's that supposed to mean?" Dad asks.

"You're a smart guy," Mom says. "I'm sure you'll figure it out. Later, Sunbolt. Glad you're okay, kid."

Then, she runs off.

"Well," Dad says, "she's got some nerve. See you around, Sunbolt. And be careful out there. These days you can't be sure which Meta's are on your side."

Dad departs and Sunbolt and I are all alone.

"Are you okay?" Sunbolt asks. "You look like you've seen a ghost."

Well, how am I supposed to look? I mean, the last time I saw Sunbolt was in the Hall of Fallen Heroes. And that was her memorial bronze statue!

Yet, here she stands, completely alive and breathing. I feel totally awkward talking to her. After all, I know she died in the battle with Meta-Taker. But it's not like I can tell her that.

"Hey, it's okay," she continues. "I can imagine this was overwhelming for you. Most people never come face-to-face with Metas."

Oh, if she only knew.

"Um, yeah," I say, smoothing out my wrinkled shirt. "You're probably right. Thanks for saving me."

"No problem," she says. "That's what heroes are for. Do you need a lift home? I can fly you there."

Home?

For some reason, the word hits me hard. Believe me, I'd love nothing more than to go home. Except my home is in another time and place. Here, my parents don't even know I exist. And apparently, they'd be fine if the other one didn't exist either.

Suddenly, I feel kind of … lost.

"What's wrong?" she asks.

Ugh, I'm tearing up. This is so embarrassing!

"Nothing," I say, wiping my eyes. "I'm good."

"What's your name?" she asks.

"El—," I start, but then stop myself. Am I crazy? I can't tell her my real name! "I'm... Eric."

"Are you homeless, Eric?" she asks. "Is that why you're so upset?"

Great question. Now, how am I supposed to answer that one? "Yeah," I say. "I guess."

"I'm so sorry," she says. "Look, you're probably hungry. Why don't you come with me for a bit? I've got some friends that can help you out."

Well, I know I can't do that. I mean, I'm supposed to be laying low while I'm here. But as soon as she said the word 'hungry,' my stomach rumbled. I never did get food back on the Waystation and it feels like I haven't eaten in days, which may actually be the case.

"What do you think?" she asks. "It's good stuff."

My head says 'no,' but my stomach rumbles 'yes.' I wonder if Dog-Gone makes his decisions this way?

"Sure," I say, shocking myself. "Thanks."

"Great," she says. "But first, I'll need to blindfold you."

"What?" I say

"Trust me," she says. "It's safer for you that way."

Safer? Then, I realize if she wants to blindfold me, she must be taking me somewhere secret—like to her headquarters where I can find other Metas.

"Okay," I say. "Let's do it."

"Great," she says. "I just need a blindfold." She scans the ground and picks up one of the goon's discarded body stockings. "This should do it."

She doubles the stocking and covers my eyes, tying it tightly behind my head. I can't see a thing.

"How's that?" she asks.

"Surprisingly effective," I say.

"Great," she says.

Then, she wraps her arms around me and takes off. But as my feet leave the ground, I get a funny feeling in my stomach, and I know it's not air sickness.

I mean, I feel so totally out of place here. I may be in Keystone City, but it's not my Keystone City. And the way Mom and Dad were arguing made it seem like something strange is going on in the Meta community.

"Sunbolt," I call out, "can I ask you something?"

"Sure, Eric," she answers. "What is it?"

Eric? Why'd she call me... oh yeah.

"Why did D—, I mean Liberty Lad, say that these days you can't be sure which Metas are on your side?"

"Well," she says, "some Meta's have gone missing. But it's nothing to worry about. I'm sure they're fine."

"Oh, okay," I say casually, but my alarm bells go off.

Metas are missing? That's not good.

I wonder if it's related to why I'm here. But before I can give it serious thought—

"We've arrived," Sunbolt says.

My feet touch down gently.

"Wait here," she says.

I hear latches unlocking and then a door screeches open. Sunbolt takes my hand and leads me inside.

Music fills my ears. It's disco music, just like I heard at Groovy Threads. Man, I guess this stuff was hot back then.

Then, she stops me, and the door slams shut behind us cutting off the music. I hear latches being relocked.

"Okay, Eric," Sunbolt says, "meet my friends."

As my blindfold comes off, I see three people seated at a table in front of us—two men and one woman.

And they're all wearing costumes!

But why do they look so familiar?

[Greetings, tiny Meta Zero unit,] comes an automated voice, startling me from behind.

But as I turn around, I take a step back.

A giant robot is staring down at me.

Wait, I've seen him before!

Then, I look back at the people.

Hang on.

I-I know these guys!

They're the other dead members of the Freedom Force!

Meta Profile

Name: Brainstorm
Role: Hero   Status: Inactive
- **Currently operating as Ms. Understood**

VITALS:

Race: Human
Real Name: Kate Meyers
Height: 5'5"
Weight: 124 lbs
Eye Color: Brown
Hair Color: Brown

META POWERS:

Class: Psychic
Power Level:
- **Extreme Telepathy**
- **Extreme Telekinesis**
- **Group Mind-Linking**
- **Long-Range Capability**

CHARACTERISTICS:

Combat	70	
Durability	40	
Leadership	82	
Strategy	76	
Willpower	89	

SIX

I CAN'T BELIEVE MY EYES

I'm in shock.

I mean, I'm standing in front of a room full of heroes who are supposed to be dead! But because I've traveled into the past, they're all still alive!

"Come in," says a large, masked man with a handlebar mustache. He's wearing a green costume with the image of a sound wave across his chest. "Any friend of Sunbolt is a friend of mine. I'm Rolling Thunder."

I want to blurt out: 'Yeah, I know exactly who you are because I just visited your memorial in the Hall of Fallen Heroes.' But I manage to keep my mouth shut. No need to open that can of worms.

"Please sit down," says the woman, who pulls out a chair. She's wearing a red costume with a comet blazing across her top. "I'm Madame Meteorite, and I'm guessing you could use something to eat."

"I'll fix him something," says the second masked man. He has long brown hair, a beard, and is wearing a purple costume with a red boxing glove on his chest. I already know who he is, but he introduces himself anyway. "I'm Dynamo Joe," he says. "Please, come in. Don't be shy. And don't let that bucket-of-bolts scare you. He gets cranky when he hasn't had his tune-up."

[I am not cranky,] the robot says. [I am Robot X-treme.]

I look up at the metal monolith. He certainly looks intimidating, with his massive robotic hands and rocket-powered legs. And then I remember that inside this tin can is an actual human brain.

"Go ahead, Eric," Sunbolt says. "Sit down."

I'd love to, but I hesitate. After seeing these guys, I feel like I've made a big mistake coming here. But I'm also in way too deep to back out now. Plus, I'm starving. So, I guess I should just eat something and try not to screw anything up—like the entire future, for instance.

"Um, thanks," I say, sitting down. I pull up to the circular table and take in my surroundings. Monitors lining the walls project images of famous landmarks like the White House, the Statue of Liberty, and the Grand Canyon. Giant computer consoles occupy every corner, studded with buttons, radio dials, and flashing lights. A dizzying number of cables crisscross the ceiling, all connecting into a centralized power source.

"We call this the Nerve Center," Sunbolt says, taking the seat next to me. "It's where we monitor the globe for trouble. Robot X-treme designed the whole thing. It's super-advanced."

"I can see that," I say. I'd love to tell them about the Monitor Room TechnocRat designed, but I can't. That would blow my cover. But maybe if I play dumb, I can collect some information. "So, where are we anyway?"

"Nice try," Sunbolt says, "but we can't tell you that. Remember the blindfold? It's safer for you if the location of our headquarters remains a secret."

"Right," I say. Well, that didn't work.

"Here you go," Dynamo Joe says, placing a plate of fried chicken, corn, and steamed broccoli in front of me.

The smell hits my nostrils and I salivate.

"We hope you like it," Rolling Thunder says.

But I can't respond because I'm stuffing my face.

"I'll take that as a 'yes,'" Rolling Thunder says.

"Mmmhmm," I mumble, gobbling a drumstick. Man, I didn't realize I was this hungry. I probably look like Dog-Gone when we found him inhaling our holiday ham.

"Glad you like it," Madame Meteorite says. "Rolling Thunder made it. He's quite the chef."

"It's a hobby," Rolling Thunder says.

After I polish off my plate, I lean back in my chair, totally stuffed. Okay, I ate that way too fast.

"Well, if he were a Meta, I know what his power

would be," Rolling Thunder says.

"Chill, Thunder," Dynamo Joe says, reaching for my plate. "Glad you dig it. Would you like more, Eric?"

I look around for Eric, when I remember, that's me!

"Oh, no," I say quickly. "That was great, thanks." But as he takes my plate away, I stare into his green eyes and get a strange feeling that I've seen him before.

"Groovy Threads?" Dynamo Joe asks, admiring my bag. "That's a happening place, isn't it?"

Then, it hits me!

He's the guy from Groovy Threads!

"Yeah," I say. "Very happening."

"So," Madame Meteorite says to Sunbolt. "How'd you two meet?"

"Well," Sunbolt says, "I rescued him from a hostage situation. Liberty Lad and Brainstorm were both there, but they couldn't get the job done."

"Good work," Dynamo Joe says. "And I'm glad Eric is okay, but you have to be careful around other Metas. We talked about this."

"Da—," Sunbolt starts but then stops herself. "I mean, Dynamo Joe, the bad guys had him at gunpoint! What should I have done? Let the kid croak?"

"Of course not," Dynamo Joe says. "But some heroes aren't who they claim to be. And that could be dangerous."

Dangerous? Wait a second, is he calling Mom and Dad dangerous?

"I had it under control," Sunbolt says.

"I'm sure Blue Bolt and Master Mime thought the same thing, but now they're missing," Dynamo Joe says.

Blue Bolt and Master Mime are missing?

The room is silent. I can feel the tension.

"Um, sorry to interrupt," I say, "but what exactly happened to Blue Bolt and Master Mime?"

"We think they were ambushed," Rolling Thunder says. "Word on the street is that they were on a mission with some other 'hero' who probably betrayed them. Who knows? It could have been Liberty Lad or Brainstorm."

What?

"Hang on," I say. "Everyone knows that Liberty Lad and Brainstorm are heroes."

"Are they?" Rolling Thunder says. "Or is one of them the Trickster?"

"The Trickster?" I say. "Who is that?"

"That's what the hero community is calling the traitor," Madame Meteorite says, flashing an annoyed look at Rolling Thunder. "But don't worry about it. Some people just like being dramatic around here."

"Am I being dramatic?" Rolling Thunder asks. "Or a realist?"

"Anyway," Dynamo Joe interrupts, "everyone should just remember that all of the people we trust are right here in this room. We're the real heroes."

"But so are Liberty Lad and Brainstorm," I blurt out.

"They're real heroes too. I mean, they're part of the Freedom Force."

"The Freedom Force?" Rolling Thunder says. "What's the Freedom Force?"

Whoops! Clearly, the Freedom Force doesn't even exist yet. Now I've really stepped in it.

"Power Alert!" screams an alarm, accompanied by flashing lights.

What's that?

"Power Alert!" it repeats. "Power Alert! Meta Powers Detected!"

The heroes jump up and congregate in front of a squat, round computer. The monitor screen looks like one of those old-time radar screens. Every time the pulsar sweeps over the United States, it flashes. This must be their version of a Meta Monitor!

"Who is it?" Sunbolt asks.

"Not sure," Dynamo Joe says, punching a few keys, "but there's a lot of them."

The image changes to video and we're looking at Mount Rushmore. It's the national monument where sixty-foot high faces of former presidents are carved out of granite. I've never been there, but it looks pretty cool.

Suddenly, a strange creature blocks the camera. Whatever it is, it's absolutely ginormous, with huge wings and a long, pointy beak. We watch as it circles the mountain and then comes back around into view.

My eyes go wide.

I-I can't believe it.

It's a... a...

"Pterodactyl?" Madame Meteorite says.

The creature flies straight towards the camera and then veers off at the last second.

Then, it's joined by another. And then another.

But that can only mean...

"How did those things get here?" Madame Meteorite asks. "They must be millions of years old."

[You are correct, flying Meta 3 unit,] Robot X-treme says. [Based on scientific evidence, Pterodactylus antiquus lived approximately 201.3 million years ago. Therefore, we can conclude with one hundred percent certainty they must have traveled through the timestream.]

"The timestream?" Rolling Thunder says, scratching his head. "So, these dingbats traveled through time?"

[Yes, mustached Meta 3 unit,] Robot X-treme says. [A Meta disturbance caused a ripple in the timestream, triggering the Nerve Center's alarm.]

"But how did that happen?" Sunbolt asks.

I want to tell them all about the Time Trotter and what happened in my time period, but I know I can't. I mean, I've gone too far just by being here. But then—

"Power Alert!" the monitor blares again. "Power Alert! Meta Powers Detected!"

"What now?" Sunbolt says.

"More prehistoric problems," Dynamo Joe says, typing into the keyboard. "Right here in Keystone City."

Then, up pops an image that gives me the chills.

It's a T-Rex. My least favorite dinosaur.

"It's in the woods," Dynamo Joe says. "Near the ArmaTech Laboratories building."

ArmaTech? I know ArmaTech. That's a weapons lab. And it's also where TechnocRat was injected with some secret brain serum that turned him into the world's smartest creature.

"Isn't that a private company run by some rich, mad scientist?" Madame Meteorite asks.

"That's the one," Rolling Thunder says. "The mad scientist's name is Norman Fairchild. He's a billionaire who develops dangerous weapons and sells them to the highest bidder. I wouldn't exactly call him a good guy. And ArmaTech isn't the best place for a T-Rex to be stomping around."

"Let's split up," Dynamo Joe says. "Madame Meteorite, you take Rolling Thunder and Robot X-treme to Mount Rushmore and knock those Pterodactyls out of the sky. Sunbolt and I will stop the Tyrannosaurus Rex."

"On it," Madam Meteorite says. "Take care, Eric."

[Farewell, Meta Zero unit,] Robot X-treme says.

"Be good," Rolling Thunder adds.

"You too," I say.

And then, they're gone.

"Here's the blindfold, Eric," Sunbolt says, wrapping it around my head. "Time to go."

She takes my hand and leads me back through a

door. I hear that wild disco music again as a series of latches close shut. Then, we're airborne.

"Are you sure you don't want me to drop you off somewhere?" she asks.

"No," I say. "Anywhere is fine."

A few minutes later, we touch down and she removes the blindfold. But as I open my eyes, I can't believe where we're standing.

"The police station?" I ask.

"We figured this was the best place to bring you," Dynamo Joe says. "They help runaways like you."

"But I'm not a—."

"Good luck, Eric," Sunbolt says, shaking my hand. "But we've got to get to ArmaTech to stop a T-Rex."

"Take it easy, dude," Dynamo Joe says with a wink, "And don't lose that cool Halloween costume."

I was right! He was the guy from the store!

But before I can respond, Sunbolt takes off and Dynamo Joe follows with a tremendous jump.

They're gone.

I look back at the police station. Maybe I should go inside. After all, I am sort of a runaway. But I already know that no one inside that building can help me.

Nope. I need to help myself.

And I can start by finding the Time Trotter. Which means it's time for a second date with a T. Rex.

So, I tighten the straps on my Groovy Threads bag, stretch out my legs, and head for ArmaTech.

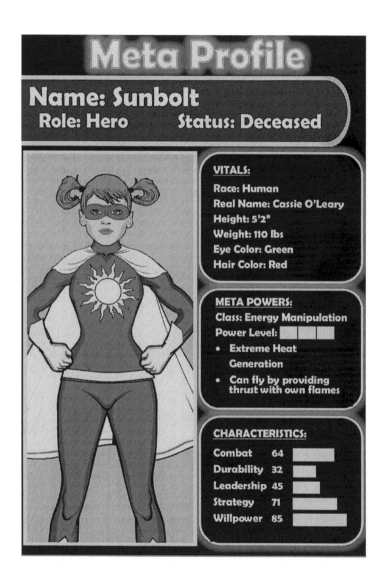

Meta Profile

Name: Sunbolt
Role: Hero   **Status: Deceased**

VITALS:
Race: Human
Real Name: Cassie O'Leary
Height: 5'2"
Weight: 110 lbs
Eye Color: Green
Hair Color: Red

META POWERS:
Class: Energy Manipulation
Power Level:
- Extreme Heat Generation
- Can fly by providing thrust with own flames

CHARACTERISTICS:
Combat   64
Durability   32
Leadership   45
Strategy   71
Willpower   85

SEVEN

I MAKE A STARTLING DISCOVERY

By the time I reach ArmaTech, I'm a sweaty mess.

Since I didn't have the luxury of traveling by Freedom Flyer, I literally had to cut through half the backyards in Keystone City to get here. But I'm lucky I made it at all. I mean, who knew there were so many dogs guarding their owners' properties?

Note to self: never become a mailman.

The whole time I was kicking myself for not borrowing Sunbolt's flight power. But then again, she took off so fast I probably wouldn't have had time to do it anyway. Nevertheless, I'm here for my second run-in with a T-Rex.

And what sane person would want to miss that?

As I approach ArmaTech, I take cover in some nearby woods. The sky is pitch black and the only sounds I hear are crickets chirping and my feet crunching through the underbrush. So, in other words, it's pretty darn creepy out.

Awesome.

I look up at the ArmaTech building. It's a tall, windowless building sitting high atop a rocky cliff overlooking a lake. The only way in is a long, winding, single-lane road that leads right into a twenty-foot high chain-link fence covered in barbed wire. Next to the front gate is a guard station, but it looks empty.

In fact, the whole place seems empty.

But that's not all that's odd.

Why is it so darn quiet?

I mean, I was expecting to walk into a raging battle scene, but I don't see anyone.

Where's the T-Rex?

And where are Sunbolt and Dynamo Joe?

Did they finish fighting already? I mean, I guess it's possible. It did take me a long time to get here. And if that's the case, I probably missed out on my one shot to nab the Time Trotter.

But something feels off.

I need to get closer, but there's a ton of open space between me and the chain-link fence. As soon as I step out of the woods, I'll be exposed for at least a hundred yards. So, I can either stay here safe and sound and wonder what happened, or I can go check it out for myself.

Whenever I'm faced with situations like this, I always ask myself: 'What would Shadow Hawk do?'

And then I usually wish I subbed in Dog-Gone.

Well, here goes nothing.

I take a deep breath and then bolt as fast as I can up the winding road. I pray no one is watching from above because I figure I'm pretty hard to miss right now. It feels like forever, but when I finally reach the guard station I dive beneath the window.

I stay there for a few minutes and catch my breath. Since no one has attacked me yet, I figure I was right and the place is empty. But I need to be sure, so I pop up, peek inside the guard tower, and duck back down.

The coast is clear, and the side window is cracked open. If I'm going to get inside, I need to open the front gate. So, I lift the guard tower window, hoist myself up, and roll inside, nearly landing on my head.

Well, that wasn't graceful.

I shake myself off and look at the control panel. There are two buttons, a green one and a red one. I don't think it's possible to overthink this, so I bash the green one. The front gate slides open with the loudest SCREECH I've ever heard in my life.

So much for the element of surprise.

Now I've got no choice but to go full throttle. I leap out of the guard station and run through the open gate when I realize something. There's no damage. I mean, normally you'd expect to see massive damage in a battle between Metas and a T-Rex. You know, things like crushed trucks, shattered windows, fallen lampposts.

But there's nothing.

It's like there was no fight at all.

I'm about to round the corner when I suddenly hear voices. I freeze.

"Did you find anything on your side of the building?" Dynamo Joe asks.

"Nope," Sunbolt says. "But the Nerve Center said a T-Rex was here. This is ArmaTech isn't it, Dad?"

"It sure is, dear," Dynamo Joe says.

Peering around the corner, I find Dynamo Joe and Sunbolt standing side by side. Dynamo Joe has his hands on his hips, while Sunbolt twirls one of her pigtails.

Well, I guess I'm not the only one confused around here. I mean, believe me, it's not like I want to see a T-Rex again, but I was hoping to find the Time Trotter. He may be the only person who really knows what's going on.

So, now what?

I mean, I know I'm not supposed to interfere in events from the past, but now I've hit a total dead end. And the more I think about it, the more it seems like there's only one move left to make. I just may need to tell these heroes my true identity, otherwise, I'll never figure out how to fix my problem.

I'm about to reveal myself when—

"Dad!" Sunbolt says, pointing in the opposite direction. "I see something."

"Where?" Dynamo Joe says, moving next to her.

"Over there," she says. "In the bushes."

"Are you sure?" Dynamo Joe asks, racing towards the brush. "Because I don't see any—"

FZOOM!

Suddenly, there's a massive burst of light.

I turn away, just as a heatwave blankets my skin.

What's going on? No T-Rex I know can breathe fire.

But when I look back, I can't believe it.

Dynamo Joe is lying face down on the ground, and flames are dancing wildly around Sunbolt's fingers.

"Sorry, Dad," she says.

Wait, what?

I-I'm in shock.

Did she just take out her own father?

But... why?

And then it hits me.

The Trickster!

Sunbolt is the Trickster?

But it makes no sense. I mean, she just saved my life.

Why would she do this?

Then, Sunbolt looks my way and I pull back just in time. I can't let her see me. But when I peek around the corner I'm in for another shock, because Sunbolt scoops up Dynamo Joe and throws him over her shoulder like he weighs nothing!

How'd she do that? I don't remember reading anything about her having Super Strength.

But the surprises don't end there, because instead of flying away, Sunbolt carries Dynamo Joe towards the ArmaTech building. Suddenly, there's a loud CLICK, and a garage door slides open right in the side of the building, bathing them in light! Then, she walks inside, taking Dynamo Joe with her!

Huh?

Why is Sunbolt going inside ArmaTech? But before I can puzzle that one out, I hear another CLICK, and the door starts closing!

This time, I know exactly what Shadow Hawk would do. I sprint for the door and slide headfirst. My body hits the pavement hard, my momentum carrying me just beneath the door before it slams shut. I made it! But there's no time to pat myself on the back. I scramble to my feet and duck behind a large piece of equipment, hoping beyond hope she didn't see me.

I stay silent as I listen to Sunbolt's footsteps fading in the distance. My heart is beating a mile a minute, but I don't dare move a muscle. I wait until I'm sure she's gone, and then I wait a few minutes more.

This was a huge risk. But I can't just let her take Dynamo Joe. Who knows what she'll do to him? Or what she's done to all the others.

Finally, I stand up and take a look around. To my surprise, it looks like I'm standing in a factory. The space is large and sterile-looking, with stark-white walls and white concrete floors. In the center of the room are several large vats with thick pipes running into the walls. Each vat is labeled with strange ingredients like: Nitric Acid, Chemical X, and Gamma Rays.

Note to self: stay clear of those.

I only see one way out, a corridor on the other side of the room. Clearly, that's where Sunbolt went. For a second, I consider turning back. I mean, who knows what I'll find in there? But I can't just leave Dynamo Joe.

So, I take a deep breath and cautiously enter the corridor. The white motif continues inside. I guess ArmaTech got a great deal on white paint. The corridor goes on for a while, and then I hit a fork in the road.

One passageway turns right and the other left. They both seem to go on for a while with no end in sight. I've got no clue which way to go, so I play eeny meeny miny moe. Left wins and fifty yards later it dawns on me that eeny meeny miny moe is probably not how Shadow Hawk makes his decisions.

Suddenly, the space opens up, and I'm standing in a huge chamber without windows or doors, except for the one I came in through. At first, I think I'm alone. But then I realize I'm not.

Not by a longshot.

That's because the room is filled with animals—caged animals! There are dogs, cats, guinea pigs, and all sorts of other creatures. The weird thing is that none of them react to my presence. I look more closely into a dog cage and notice the animal is wearing a white tag around its neck.

But instead of a name, it says: #1374X.

Another dog has: #3721X.

That's strange.

What are those for?

I walk past a cage filled with mice. Actually, these guys look pretty big, so they're probably rats.

Then, I notice metal tables clustered in the center of the room, flanked by rolling carts filled with surgical equipment. My first thought is that this must be a veterinary hospital.

But then I remember I'm inside ArmaTech.

So, this isn't a hospital.

It's... a lab!

My stomach turns.

They're experimenting on these animals!

My instincts tell me to throw open the cages and free them all, but I can't. I mean, who knows why they're here? Maybe they hold the secret to curing some future disease. I desperately want to believe that, but deep inside I know it's not true. These animals aren't here to help humanity. They're here for weapons testing.

I walk past another cart holding an array of vials. I read the labels: *Muscular Cell Decomposer. Molecule Reverser. Brain Growth Serum.*

I feel sick to my stomach.

As I continue, I look at the animals more closely.

Cats are missing tufts of fur, and the dogs are so lethargic they don't even look my way.

I'm heartbroken.

There's nothing I can do, and I still have to find Sunbolt and Dynamo Joe. I need to get back on track. I wipe my eyes and get ready to split when I hear—

"H-Help… m-me…"

I jump out of my skin. What's that?

As I spin around, I see a three-fingered hand wrapped around the cell bar of a prison door.

O.M.G!

There's… a small person on his knees, staring at me with a pair of big, blue eyes!

"Help… me," he pleads.

And then I realize he's not a person at all.

He's an alien!

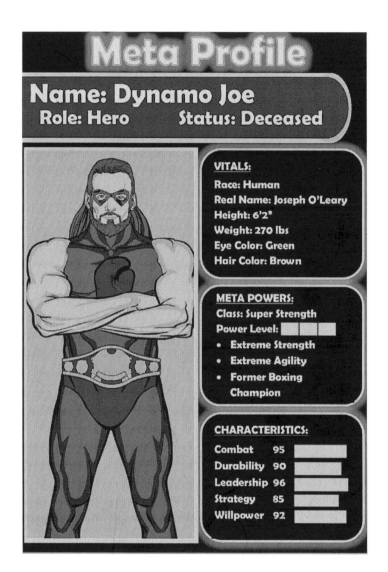

Meta Profile

Name: Dynamo Joe
Role: Hero   Status: Deceased

VITALS:
Race: Human
Real Name: Joseph O'Leary
Height: 6'2"
Weight: 270 lbs
Eye Color: Green
Hair Color: Brown

META POWERS:
Class: Super Strength
Power Level: ▮▮▮
- Extreme Strength
- Extreme Agility
- Former Boxing Champion

CHARACTERISTICS:
Combat   95
Durability 90
Leadership 96
Strategy   85
Willpower   92

EIGHT

I GET SOME KEY INFORMATION

"**H**elp… me."

I'm stunned.

There's an alien in a cell talking to me, but I'm so shocked I can't register a word he's saying. I mean, a minute ago I was looking for a T-Rex. Then, I discovered Sunbolt was the Trickster and followed her inside of ArmaTech where I stumbled upon an animal laboratory. The next thing I know, I'm face to face with an alien!

An alien, right here on Earth!

An alien from the past!

And that's probably not a good thing.

The poor guy is bent over, his pink, three-fingered hand wrapped around the cell bars. He's looking up at me with big, blue eyes, struggling to breathe. He's small, smaller than me, and dressed in a tattered blue uniform with yellow stripes on his shoulders. His outfit sort of reminds me of the army, where the number of stripes on a uniform signifies rank.

"P-Please...," he pleads. "F-Free me."

"Free you?" I say, finally managing to find my voice. "I don't even know you." He doesn't look like any alien I've seen before. And trust me, I've seen lots of aliens. But before I'd even consider helping him, there's one thing I need to know—is he a good guy or a bad guy?

"I-I am from far away," he says, peering up at the ceiling. "I must get back... get help." Just then, his hand slips and he tumbles to the ground.

He lands hard, coughing like a maniac. That's when I spot red slashes on his ribs, like he was scratched by a tiger, and a horrible thought crosses my mind.

"Are they experimenting on you?" I ask.

"They can do as they wish," he spits. "But they will learn the will of an Intergalactic Paladin is unbreakable."

"An Intergalactic what?" I ask.

"Not 'what,'" he wheezes, struggling to sit up. "But 'who.' The Intergalactic Paladins are...," then he bends over and hacks again.

Man, he doesn't look so good.

"Pardon me," he says, wiping some gunk from his chin. "I am an Intergalactic Paladin from Paladin Planet. We are the protectors of the cosmos. We patrol the farthest regions of space, defending the innocent from the direst of threats."

Paladin Planet? Hang on, I remember Scorpio mentioning Paladin Planet. That's where he was going to drop Leo. Well, maybe this alien is one of the good guys after all.

"My name is, um, Eric," I say. "What's yours?"

"I am called Proog," he says.

"Nice to meet you, Proog," I say. "But, if you don't mind me asking, how did you end up in here? I mean, what were you protecting Earth from?"

"I was not just protecting Earth, young one," Proog says, looking me dead on. "But saving the universe."

"The universe?" I say. "Wow, that's a pretty tall order. And what exactly were you saving it from?"

But instead of answering, he looks me up and down with his bug-like eyes, and suddenly I feel uncomfortable. It's like he's reading my soul, determining if I'm worthy of being told or not.

Finally, he leans forward and says, "from Krule."

"Krule?" I repeat. "Who is Krule?"

"He is known by many names," Proog says. "Krule the Tyrant, Krule the Wretched, but most notably, Krule the Conqueror."

"Well, he sure sounds like a man with many talents," I say. "Please, send him my congrats on that, but let him know there's no need to thank me in person. Like, ever."

"Hopefully, you will never meet him in person," Proog says. "Because before I was ambushed and trapped in this filthy prison, I ensured his fate by hiding the key to his freedom."

I clean out my ears.

"Um, sorry," I say, "But I couldn't help but notice you said the word 'key.' Do you mean, like, a Cosmic Key kind of a key?"

"Yes!" Proog says, his eyes bulging out of his skull. "How do you know of the Cosmic Key?"

"Well, it's kind of a long story," I say. "But to cut to the chase, I saw an image of a man with three-eyes and red skin. He said he wanted the Cosmic Key."

"But that's not possible," Proog says, clearly alarmed.

"Okay," I say. "But I'm positive I saw what I saw."

"Then the person you describe was no ordinary man," Proog says. "It was Krule the Conqueror himself. But how did he know the key was here?"

"Beats me," I say. "But if that was Krule, why is he after the Cosmic Key anyway?"

"Because he is also a prisoner," he says. "Trapped with his army of ingrates in the 13th Dimension. And only the Cosmic Key can let him out."

Then, it hits me.

The Cosmic Key!

Everything that's happened to me revolves around this Cosmic Key!

I mean, that's what Krule was using the Time Trotter to find. That's the reason my timestream is all screwed up! That's the reason I'm stuck here in the past!

But I feel like I've been in this movie before. I know there's got to be more to the story.

"Can we rewind a second?" I ask. "What the heck is the 13th Dimension, and how come the Cosmic Key is the only thing that can let him out?"

"The 13th Dimension is a special pocket in space," Proog says, "existing outside the space-time continuum. It was discovered centuries ago by my forefathers, and we have used it ever since to humanely contain the most dangerous criminals in the universe. You see, the Intergalactic Paladins are sworn to protect, not to destroy. Using the 13th Dimension as our prison allows us to remove criminal threats without ever breaking our vows. Once inside, the powers of the prisoners are neutralized."

Wow, that's pretty wild.

"The Cosmic Key is the only object that can unlock the door to the 13th Dimension," he continues. "But using the 13th Dimension is also a double-edged sword. It will trap criminals forever, but once inside, they will never grow old."

"Whoa!" I say, my mind blown. "So, you're saying all of the criminals in there will live forever? Like, they'll never die?"

"Precisely," he says.

Well, scratch that family vacation to the 13th Dimension! Then, I remember Krule saying he knows the Cosmic Key was once here on Earth. In fact, he said he could feel its energy. So, he was right!

Suddenly, an image of the Orb of Oblivion flashes in my mind and I shudder. I've had enough run-ins with crazy extraterrestrial objects to know that this Cosmic Key is probably more than it seems.

"So, let me get this straight," I say. "Krule, one of the most heinous dudes in the galaxy, is trapped in the 13th Dimension looking for the Cosmic Key. And, for some reason, you decided to hide this puppy right here on Earth? Why us? Aren't there, like, millions of other planets you could have stuck it on?"

"Yes, but very few have the Meta energy of Earth," Proog says. "You see, the Cosmic Key has a conscience of its own."

Of course it does.

"The Cosmic Key is attracted to Meta energy," Proog continues, "and your planet emits one of the highest concentrations of Meta energy in the galaxy. We believed that if we buried it here it would stay here, instead of wandering through space in search of Meta energy where it could fall into the wrong hands. Fortunately, I succeeded in the first part of my mission, but I could not escape before being ambushed and losing my Infinity Wand."

Infinity Wand? What's that?

But before I can ask, I hear voices!

It's Sunbolt! And a man!

"Run," Proog whispers.

I can't just leave him here. I look around for something to unlock the cell door, but I don't see anything. The voices are getting closer! I'm too late!

"I've got to hide," I whisper. "Don't give me away."

As I look around for somewhere to hide, I hear—

"You collect more heroes," the man says. "I'll see what I can learn from our special guest."

Uh oh! He's coming in here! I'm trapped!

I duck behind the dog cages. This is not good. I mean, how am I going to get out of here?

"Don't worry, Fairchild," Sunbolt says. "I've got three more in mind."

Fairchild? Isn't that the founder of ArmaTech? And did Sunbolt just say she'll get three more heroes?

O.M.G!

She's going for Rolling Thunder, Madame Meteorite, and Robot X-Treme! I've got to warn them!

Suddenly, I hear footsteps running the opposite way. That's got to be Sunbolt! I have to stop her!

But before I can move, Fairchild enters the lab!

I hold my breath.

Suddenly, I hear CLANKING. Peering over the cage, I see Fairchild. He has his back to me, but I can make out some of his features. He's tall, with dark hair and broad shoulders. It looks like he's assembling some kind of a pole with a sharp tip on it, like a spear.

"Good afternoon," Fairchild says. "Shall we continue our interview?"

He must be talking to Proog!

I'm not sure what to do. I could help Proog, but I'll lose time warning the others about Sunbolt.

But I can't just let Fairchild hurt Proog.

Decision made!

But as soon as I stand up, Proog meets my eyes and shakes his head from side to side. What? Is he saying he doesn't want my help? But I can't just leave him here. And even if I wanted to go, there's no way to sneak out without being seen.

Then, I feel something tugging my leg!

I look down to see a gray-and-black German Shepherd appear out of thin air!

It's that invisible dog!

And he's pulling my bell-bottom pants!

What's he doing here?

The dog looks at me, and I mouth: *'What?'*

"Now," Fairchild says, approaching Proog with his spear. "Let's pick up where we left off. Tell me where you hid the Cosmic Key?"

I want to help Proog, but the dog is pulling me across the room! Then, the mutt releases me and runs to the back wall. And that's when I see the hole behind a loose panel.

It's an escape route!

So, that's how he got inside.

The dog nods his head, and then squeezes through, disappearing from view.

I hear a SCREECH.

Fairchild opened Proog's cell!

If I'm going to help Proog, it's now or never.

"Go!" Proog commands.

I freeze. Wait, is he yelling at me, or Fairchild?

"So, he speaks," Fairchild says. "This is a much better start than our last session."

"Go!" Proog yells again.

This time there's no mistaking it. He's yelling at me!

I want to help, but he's clearly telling me not to.

I'm paralyzed. I don't know what to do.

"Now!" Proog orders.

Why doesn't he want my help?

I feel crummy, but I drop to my hands and knees, crawl through the hole, and I'm gone.

Meta Profile

Name: Proog
Role: Hero   Status: Deceased

VITALS:

Race: Unknown
Real Name: Proog
Height: 4'5"
Weight: 96 lbs
Eye Color: Blue
Hair Color: Bald

META POWERS:

Class: Magic
Power Level:

- Member of the Intergalactic Paladins
- Extreme Meta energy manipulation powered by an Infinity Wand

CHARACTERISTICS:

Combat	96	
Durability	40	
Leadership	99	
Strategy	87	
Willpower	96	

NINE

I MAKE A QUICK CHANGE

By the time I reach the woods, I'm a total basket case.

My furry companion is waiting for me by a tree, but as soon as I catch up, I collapse onto the grass. I can barely catch my breath, but that's not why I'm so upset.

I mean, what kind of a hero am I? I basically just left Proog behind to get tortured. I feel lower than low. But what choice did I have? Proog ordered me to leave. And there's nothing I can do about it now.

But I can't just leave him there. I swear I'll be back to help him if it's the last thing I do. But first I need to take care of some other business—like stopping Sunbolt.

I still can't believe she's the Trickster. It just doesn't make sense. I mean, she saved my life, so why is she doing this?

But I can't figure that out now. I need to warn the other heroes before it's too late. After all, if she took down her own father, there's no telling what she'll do to them. Then, I hear scratching by the tree.

I'm such a heel. I forgot to thank my rescuer.

"Hey, thanks," I say, looking over at my new dog buddy. "I appreciate you—"

Then, I realize something.

My furry companion isn't a 'he.' She's a 'she!'

Well, that's awkward.

But she doesn't seem to mind because she lowers her head and nuzzles my arm. She's a little shorter than Dog-Gone, but with gray-and-black fur. I look at the tag on her collar. It reads: *GG*.

GG?

There are no numbers on her tag. And her tag is black, which is different from the white tags the other animals had in the lab.

"You're not from the lab, are you?" I ask.

She shakes her head from side to side which I'm taking as a firm 'no.'

"So, what were you doing in there?"

She bares her teeth and growls.

"Whoa, it's okay," I say, trying to calm her down. "There's nothing dangerous here. It's cool."

She stops growling, lowers her head, and whimpers.

Clearly, something at ArmaTech agitated her. I wonder what it could be?

"Do you need a hug?"

She comes close and I wrap my arms around her. It's nice to feel the warmth of a furry friend again, even if it's not my own.

"I guess I should call you something. Your tag says GG. Hey, how about Gigi?"

She licks my chin, making me laugh.

Okay, that's settled. But then I realize something.

Invisible dogs aren't a dime a dozen.

This pooch must be one of Dog-Gone's ancestors!

I'm too far back in history for her to be his mom, but maybe she's his grandma or great-grandma. I'd love nothing more than to tell her all about her descendent, but I know I can't do that either. After all, I'd hate for something to happen to my future furball.

"So, I'm guessing you made that hole we escaped from, didn't you? You sure are a brave one. Clearly, your gene pool got diluted as it went down the line."

She licks my nose.

As nice as it is to just hang out and take a breather, I know we can't stay here. I've got to find the other heroes before Sunbolt does. Unfortunately, Sunbolt blindfolded me when she took me to their secret headquarters. So, I've got no clue where to go. But maybe my new companion knows.

"Gigi, do you know where to find Rolling Thunder, Madame Meteorite, or Robot X-treme?" I ask.

But she just looks at me and scratches behind her ear. Okay, that's a negative.

Time to think. Even though I was blindfolded, were there any clues that could help me pinpoint the location of the Nerve Center? Well, I remember Sunbolt unlatching a bunch of locks to the outside door. But there must be millions of doors with locks in Keystone City.

I try to remember any other clues, but I come up empty. It's time to face the music, I've got no idea where—

Wait a minute!

Music!

There was music playing when we entered and left the Nerve Center! Disco music!

Then, I realize something.

Disco music was also playing when I entered Groovy Threads. And Dynamo Joe was the shopkeeper at Groovy Threads.

Coincidence?

Maybe. But maybe not.

"Follow me, Gigi," I say, scrambling to my feet. "It's time to boogie!"

***

It's morning by the time we reach Main Street.

The air is chilly and the sun is rising slowly, like it's deciding if it wants to wake up or hit the snooze button.

The street is empty, except for a few shopkeepers busy opening their stores. In other words, the conditions are perfect for breaking into a fine clothing establishment.

Gigi and I stay out of sight as we make our way to Groovy Threads. I've had plenty of time to map out our strategy, and I'm pretty sure the secret entrance to the Nerve Center won't be through the front door. So, if I were a gambling man, I'd say our best bet is around back.

We sneak down the alleyway to the rear of the store when I find something I'm not expecting.

The back door is wide open.

In fact, it's blown completely off its hinges!

Looking down, I see broken latches scattered at my feet. I bend over for a closer look and realize the latches aren't just broken, they're gnarled and twisted like they've been melted. Well, I don't need to be a detective to figure this one out.

Sunbolt was here!

"Hey, girl," I whisper to Gigi. "I'll understand if you don't want to stick around."

But, to my surprise, Gigi lets out a low growl, steps inside the building, and turns invisible. How Dog-Gone is related to her is beyond me.

I follow her inside and hear the faint sound of music—disco music! Yep, we've come to the right place.

We're standing in a small hallway facing two closed doors. The door to our left reads: *Groovy Threads Storage*

Room. The door to our right reads: *Electric Room. Danger: No Entry.*

Bingo. Right it is.

I turn the knob and the door swings open with ease.

But when I look inside, my eyes pop out of their sockets, because I can't believe what I'm seeing.

The Nerve Center looks like a war zone!

Monitors are shattered, consoles are crushed, and the giant conference table is split in two. There's debris as far as the eye can see, from computer parts to coffee mugs. But Sunbolt and the heroes are nowhere to be found.

Gigi runs over to a pile of rubble and barks. We dig through it until we uncover something long and metallic. At first, I don't know what it is.

Then, I recoil in horror.

It's Robot X-treme's arm!

I plop down on the ground with my head in my hands. I'm too late! Sunbolt got them!

I feel terrible for Rolling Thunder, Madame Meteorite, and Robot X-treme. They had no clue Sunbolt was the Trickster. I remember Dynamo Joe saying: *all of the people we trust are right here in this room.*

So much for trust.

Now they're all captured.

I feel totally deflated. Like I let them all down.

Sunbolt has probably taken them back to ArmaTech by now. But why? What is Fairchild doing with them?

And what am I supposed to do now?

I wish my family was here.

Wait.

My family!

If I can find Mom and Dad, they can help me break into ArmaTech and figure out what's going on. But how am I going to do that? Then, my eyes land on a squat computer that somehow managed to survive the carnage.

It's their Meta Monitor!

I hop over the shattered conference table and check it out. The screen is cracked, but it still looks operational! I type into the keyboard: *Display Meta Signatures*.

The console spits back: *Error*.

Error! Okay, don't panic. I've got to remember this isn't the sophisticated system I'm used to. Let's try something simpler. I type: *Meta Powers*.

Error.

Okay, now I'm getting annoyed. How am I supposed to find Mom or Dad if I can't track their power signatures? This computer may be advanced for this timestream, but it's nothing like TechnocRat built.

Then, I remember something.

This system wasn't built by TechnocRat.

It was built by Robot X-treme.

I type in: *Find Meta 3 Units*.

Suddenly, the screen comes alive with blips.

Yes!

Except there are hundreds of them, scattered all over the globe. Since every blip represents a Meta 3, I need to narrow the scope. So, I move the cursor over the United States, find Keystone City, and click. The monitor zooms in again, pulling up a digital map of the city.

This time there are way fewer blips—five to be exact. I click on them one by one. With every click, I get a brief description of the power signature identified.

Meta 3 Unit: Super-speed. Nope.

Meta 3 Unit: Meta-morph. Nope again.

Meta 3 Unit: Psychic.

Psychic!

I home in on the signature. It's coming from the Keystone City Library. That's right! Mom told me she used to work at the library before becoming a full-time Meta hero. That's across from the police station.

Okay, let's check out those two other blips.

Meta 3 Unit: Super-Intelligence. Clearly not Dad.

Meta 3 Unit: Super-Strength.

Winner, winner, chicken dinner!

The signal is coming from the Keystone City Police Station. Well, Dad was on the police force before becoming the Warden of Lockdown.

"Come on, Gigi!"

We dash out of the Nerve Center and back into the hallway. But before we step out, I stop myself. I can't go rushing over to my parents like this. I was lucky my folks didn't study my face the first time, but this time there's no way to avoid it—and that could destroy the future!

Then, my eyes fall on the door across the hall: *Groovy Threads Storage Room*. Hmmm. Maybe there's something in there I can use to cover my face. Like a hat.

The door opens into a dark room. I fumble along the wall until I find the light switch and flick it on, revealing racks of clothing. Yes, I was right!

But as I step inside, I do a double take, because they aren't regular clothes at all. They're Meta costumes!

I move down the line, running my hand through dozens of backup uniforms for Dynamo Joe, Rolling Thunder, and Madame Meteorite. At the end of the rack are a bunch of smaller costumes in different colors—blue and red, black and gray, red and white. There's a paper pinned to one of the costumes that reads: *New Sunbolt Designs—Must be Tailored*.

Then, I get an idea.

I put down my Groovy Threads bag and look through the selection. If I can fit into one of these costumes, then I can hide my real identity from my parents! The black and gray one looks the largest, so I pull it off its hangar. I'm about to try it on when I find a pair of eyes staring at me.

"Um, do you mind, Gigi?"

Gigi rolls her eyes and spins around.

I take off my clothes and step into the costume. It's a little tighter than I'm used to, but it fits. I jump up and down a few times, trying to stretch it out.

Now I just need shoes and a mask.

I spot some cardboard boxes across the room. I open the first one which is filled with boots. I sift through, looking for my size, but the only ones that look close are neon green. I try them on and they fit perfectly.

Well, I won't be winning any Meta fashion awards.

I open another box filled with gloves, and another stuffed with belts. Still no masks. One box left.

I say a prayer and pop it open.

It's filled with helmets. Loads of freaking helmets.

My heart sinks. This isn't what I wanted at all. I pull a few out. There's one shaped like an army helmet, and another like a construction helmet.

I'm about to close the box when I spot something interesting. One of the helmets looks like it's from the medieval ages. I always loved knights, but as I pull it out, the visor slams down on my fingers. Ouch!

I'm about to toss it when I realize something. The visor could cover my face. If my noggin fits into this thing, my parents won't see my features at all!

I put the helmet over my head and push it down, lowering the visor. Wow, it's snug. But it's also really hard to see out the sides. I don't know how knights fought in these things. It's not ideal, but it's my only option.

"Let's go, Gigi," I say. "We've got heroes to save!"

But as we run out, I smash headfirst into the wall.

Freaking visor!

Meta Profile

Name: Rolling Thunder
Role: Hero   Status: Deceased

VITALS:

Race: Human
Real Name: Dane Rowdee
Height: 6'5"
Weight: 262 lbs
Eye Color: Brown
Hair Color: Black

META POWERS:

Class: Energy Manipulator
Power Level: ▮▮▮▮

- Extreme Sound Wave Manipulation
- Can Intensify and Silence Sound Waves

CHARACTERISTICS:

Combat	86
Durability	77
Leadership	84
Strategy	70
Willpower	82

TEN

I AMBUSH MY PARENTS

Guess who is back at the police station.

I don't know why I keep ending up here, but maybe somebody's trying to tell me something—like I'd be better off behind bars. I have to admit, right now it sounds appealing. You know, like playing Monopoly where you can just chill out in jail until you roll doubles.

Unfortunately, I don't have time to relax. If I'm going to save Proog and the other heroes, I need to get moving. So, this trip to the police station isn't exactly a social visit. I'm here for serious business.

I'm here to recruit Dad.

The good news is that I'm well-disguised, especially wearing my helmet. I've also rehearsed what I'm going to say about a million times. So, I'm as prepared as I'm going to get. Now it's time to execute the plan. Gigi and I just need to walk in, grab him, and go.

This should be a piece of cake.

But as we push open the double doors, I realize finding Dad might be a lot harder than I thought. That's because the inside of the police station is a zoo. Every inch of the ginormous space seems to be occupied by someone—from cops booking criminals to a grandma filing a missing cat report. The noise level is deafening, like a loud buzz, but you can't really make out a single conversation. The whole scene is pure sensory overload.

And to top it off, I don't see Dad anywhere.

As Gigi and I approach the front desk, an officer with glasses looks up from his paper and says, "The Wizard of Oz is playing up the street, kid. This is the police station."

"Yes, we know it's the police station," I say. "We're looking for Officer Harkness."

"Officer who?" he says.

"Officer Harkness," I repeat. "Officer Tom Harkness."

"Tom Harkness?" he says, confused. Then, the lightbulb goes off. "Oh, you mean, Tommy Harkness?"

"Yes," I say. "Is he here?"

The cop chuckles and calls over his shoulder, "Hey, Sal! Get this. This kid wants to see 'Officer' Tommy Harkness! Isn't that a riot?"

"What's so funny?" I ask.

"Nothing," the cop says, wiping tears from his eyes. "Go ahead. You'll find him in the back. He's on official mop-up duty."

But as we pass by, he's still laughing to himself.

"Official mop-up duty," he says. "I kill myself."

What's his problem?

Gigi and I head for the back of the station. I don't remember the police station being this crowded before. It's like all the whackos came out at once.

Suddenly, there's RAPPING on my helmet.

I spin around to find a skinny man with a thin mustache sitting in a chair. He's wearing a green suit and his left arm is handcuffed to a desk.

Gigi bares her teeth and growls.

"Easy, girl," I say, putting my hand on her neck.

"Riddle me this," the man says, "Why were the Middle Ages called the Dark Ages?"

"Um, I don't know," I say.

"Because there were too many knights!" he finishes and then bursts out in maniacal laughter.

"Good one," I say. "You have a great day."

"You too," he says.

Note to self: stay out of prison.

Finally, we reach the back of the station, but I don't see Dad anywhere. In fact, there's nobody here but us and a blond-haired janitor, who is... mopping up the floor.

No. Way.

"Um, excuse me," I say. "Are you Tom Harkness?"

The janitor lifts his head and I'm staring into a pair of familiar blue eyes. It's Dad!

"Yeah," Dad says. "Who are you? And why are you dressed like that?"

Great questions, but ones that I'm ready for. All I need to do now is unleash my brilliant speech and Dad will be on our side.

"I'm a superhero," I say confidently. "And here's the deal. I know who the Trickster is, and I know where she's holding the missing heroes. But it's a dangerous mission and I can't rescue them alone. You're one of the greatest Meta's alive and I'll need your help."

Dad stops mopping and looks me up and down.

"Get lost, kid," he says. "I don't know what you're talking about."

Well, I wasn't expecting that.

Clearly, speechwriting isn't in my future.

I've got one shot to lay it all out there.

"Look," I say, "I know you're Liberty Lad, a Meta 3 Super-strongman who is nearly invulnerable. I also know you're a champion of justice and a major germaphobe."

Dad looks down at his mop and back at me. "How do you know all that stuff about me?" he asks. "Are you a psychic, because I hate psychics?"

"Um, no," I say. "Let's just say I have my methods. And I thought you were a police officer?"

"I will be," he says. "I'm working to save enough

money to take the police academy exam."

"Ah," I say. "Right." Then, I look at his young face again. I totally forgot he probably just graduated from high school! "Well, I'm pretty sure you'll be a great cop when you get there. So, what do you say? Will you help me? Pretty please with sprinkles on top?"

"Help you," he says. "I don't even know you. What's your name anyway?"

Great question. Hadn't thought of that one.

"I'm… the Nullifier," I say. "And this is… Fur-Begone."

"The Nullifier and Fur-Begone?" he says. "And you say you know who the Trickster is, huh? So, tell me, who is it? Maybe it's you?"

Here comes the moment of truth.

"No, it's not me," I say. "It's Sunbolt."

"Sunbolt?" he says skeptically. "Really?"

"Really," I say. "And she's captured Dynamo Joe, Rolling Thunder, Madam Meteorite, and Robot X-treme."

"Hang on," he says. "Blue Bolt told me she was meeting up with Sunbolt and Master Mime."

"Aren't Blue Bolt and Master Mime missing also?" I ask.

"Yeah," he says. "They are. Okay, kid. Meet me out back in two minutes. I've got to put away my cleaning supplies." Then, he shoots us a determined look and heads off.

As Gigi and I exit through the rear door, I'm feeling pretty good about myself. It actually looks like part one of my plan might be a success. But I'm not so sure about part two.

Dad said he hates psychics, so if I tell him we still need to recruit Mom, he might bail on me. After all, they weren't exactly BFF's when those thugs held me hostage. I'll need to handle this very, very carefully. But I don't have much time either.

Speaking of time, where's Dad? We've been standing out here for more than a few minutes, and by the way Gigi is tapping her tail, she's clearly losing her patience.

Suddenly, a figure leaps out of the bushes, scaring us silly. It's Dad, in full superhero costume.

"What took you so long?" I ask.

"Sorry," he says. "Changing in the car is harder than I thought. Where are we going anyway?"

"To ArmaTech," I say.

"ArmaTech?" he says. "Don't they produce military weapons? If our friends are trapped there, it could be bad news?"

"Yeah," I say. "So, we've got to be ready for anything. Which is why we need to stop by the library."

"The library?" he says. "Don't you think now isn't the best time to check out a book?"

"Oh, no, we're not checking out a book," I say. "We're borrowing a superhero."

***

I spot Mom in the stacks, unloading a cart of books onto the shelves. It's weird seeing her so young. I mean, she looks so different, but I'd recognize those eyes anywhere. She clearly doesn't see me, because as soon as some kids go by, she furrows her brow and the books fly into place all on their own.

I feel like I made the right decision coming here alone. Based on how she and Dad bickered the last time they were together, bringing him along would be risky. So, since dogs aren't allowed in the library, I asked Dad to keep an eye on Gigi for me outside. I can't say Gigi was thrilled about it, but I'll deal with that later.

I take a deep breath. I have the feeling recruiting Mom is going to be a lot harder than recruiting Dad. Plus, she's a psychic which means she could potentially read my mind at any time.

Fortunately, I've got powers of my own.

I concentrate hard and project an aura of negation around me. That should block her from penetrating my mind. I just need to stay on my toes because if my concentration slips for a second, she could find out I'm her kid from the future, blowing the whole thing.

I hide behind a bookshelf until some students leave the area. Then, I lower my visor and make my move.

"Excuse me, Kate," I say.

"It's Katie," she says absently. "How can I help—,"

but when she looks my way, she does a double take. "Um, do I know you?"

"No," I say. "But I know you, and I need Brainstorm's help."

"Brainstorm?" she says, looking around nervously. "What are you talking about?"

"It's okay," I say. "I didn't mean to startle you, but there's no time for games. We need to act fast. Lives are in danger—including Blue Bolt and Master Mime."

"Really?" she says. Then, she grabs my shoulders and pulls me into the stacks. "Okay, pipsqueak," she commands, "spill it. Who are you and what do you know about Blue Bolt and Master Mime?"

Then, her eyebrows go up.

"Why can't I get a read on you?" she asks. "Are you a psychic?"

Whew! My powers are working.

"No, I'm the Nullifier," I say, mustering up more confidence this time. "Look, it doesn't matter how I know you. You don't have to worry. Your secret is safe with me."

"And why should I trust you?" she asks. "Blue Bolt and Master Mime trusted the Trickster and look where it got them. Maybe you're the Trickster?"

"No," I say. "I'm a hero, just like you. And you're just gonna have to trust me. Look, I know who the real Trickster is, and I'll tell you, but I need you to join me… and a few other heroes… to save our friends. Deal?"

"Okay, kid," she says, crossing her arms. "I'll do anything to save my friends. Now tell me, who is the Trickster?"

***

Yes! After explaining everything to Mom, which took way longer than even I expected, she's on board! Now I've got both parents helping me. The only wrinkle is that each doesn't know about the other. So, this could either be great or the biggest disaster since Dog-Gone found my secret stash of bubble gum.

I told Mom I'd meet her outside while she changed into her costume. That's where I find Dad and Gigi sitting on a bench. For some reason, Dad doesn't look very happy.

"You know," he says, "you forgot to mention your dog can turn invisible."

"Well," I say, "she's not really my—"

"I turn around and she's gone," he says. "I didn't know if she ran away or what. So, I'm running around looking for her like a fool, and then poof, she magically appears sitting on the bench. I'm pretty sure she was watching me run around the whole time."

"Oh, sorry," I say. "Bad girl, Fur-Begone."

Gigi yawns.

"Anyway," he says, "where's this big superhero you needed to get?"

"Okay, Nullifier," Mom says, running down the walkway. "I'm ready to—," then she stops and looks at Dad.

"Seriously?" Dad says. "Her?"

"He's the 'other hero?'" Mom asks.

"Hang on," I interject. "We're all heroes here."

"I can't work with her," Dad says, standing up.

"I refuse to work with that ignoramus," Mom says.

"How dare you!" Dad says. "I'm no ignoramus!"

Then, he leans over and whispers, "What's an ignoramus?"

I have no clue, but this is getting out of hand.

"Guys, stop," I say. "Listen, we need to work together."

"No dice," Dad says. "I'm out."

"Ditto," Mom says, turning away. "Later, pipsqueak."

"Wait!" I call out.

But they don't stop.

They just keep walking away.

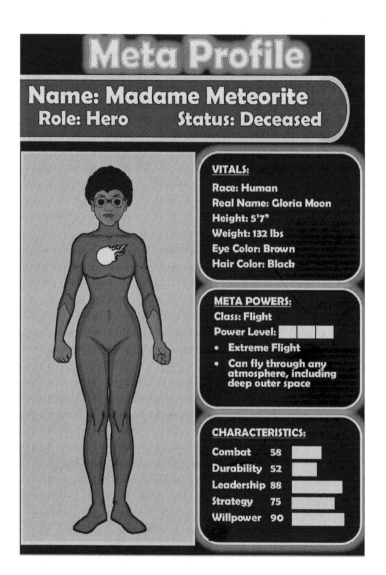

Meta Profile

Name: Madame Meteorite
Role: Hero   Status: Deceased

VITALS:

Race: Human
Real Name: Gloria Moon
Height: 5'7"
Weight: 132 lbs
Eye Color: Brown
Hair Color: Black

META POWERS:

Class: Flight
Power Level: ▮▮▮

- **Extreme Flight**
- **Can fly through any atmosphere, including deep outer space**

CHARACTERISTICS:

Combat	58	
Durability	52	
Leadership	88	
Strategy	75	
Willpower	90	

ELEVEN

I GET THE GANG BACK TOGETHER

This is getting ridiculous.

I mean, in my timestream my parents are happily married and spend loads of time together. But here, they hate each other so much they can't even share the same space. And now they're both walking away despite the monumental task before us.

Is this how they really treated each other in the past?

Or did Krule alter things so much there's no hope of bringing them back together?

And if that's the case, what happens to me?

In the future, I won't even exist!

Okay, I know I'm not supposed to interfere, but now I've got no choice. I need to solve this once and for all.

"Stop!" I yell at the top of my lungs.

Surprisingly, they actually stop.

Dad looks over his shoulder, while Mom crosses her arms and taps her foot.

Wow. Okay, the floor is mine.

"Listen," I say. "I know you guys don't get along, but honestly, I don't know why. Liberty Lad, despite your unfortunate hairstyle, you're a good guy at heart who always fights for what's right. And Brainstorm, while you may have the worst superhero name of all time, you're a hero to the core with more willpower in your little pinkie than anyone I know. There's no reason you guys shouldn't get along. In fact, if you worked together, you'd be the best crime-fighting duo on the entire freaking planet."

Dad raises an eyebrow as Mom uncrosses her arms.

They're listening! I need to keep going.

"And let's not forget," I continue, "that Blue Bolt and Master Mime, your mutual friends, need your help. Not to mention all of the other heroes being held captive. I'm telling you, something dark is going on at ArmaTech. And if Sunbolt and Fairchild took out all of those heroes, do you think any of us will be able to tackle this alone? So, if we don't work together, we've got no chance of saving our friends and putting a stop to whatever evil is going on over there."

"Well," Mom says. "Pipsqueak here may have a point. I was heading to ArmaTech on my own, but maybe that's not such a good idea."

"Same here," Dad says. "Could be a mistake."

"This mission does sound dangerous," Mom says. "Maybe we should team up. Just for this one."

"Perhaps," Dad says. "If Sunbolt took down powerful heroes like Master Mime and Blue Bolt, it probably makes sense to go together. But just this once."

They look at each other, and then at me.

"Wait," I say. "So, we're really doing this? Like, together?"

"Yes," Dad says. "We'll tackle this mystery together. And we'll see how it goes."

"Exactly," Mom says.

"Yes!" I say. "I mean, great. Let's do this."

***

Fifteen minutes later I'm back in the woods outside of ArmaTech. But this time I'm not alone. Mom, Dad, and Gigi are with me, and they're ready for action.

"Okay," Mom says. "Where was this secret entrance you were talking about?"

"Over there," I say, pointing to the west side of the building. "It leads right into the laboratory. It's going to be a tight squeeze, but once we're inside we should pop out across from the alien captive. Are you guys ready?"

But instead of a response, I get silence.

"What?" I ask.

"Did you just say 'alien' captive?" Dad asks.

"You never said anything about an alien captive," Mom says.

"Right," I say, blushing beneath my helmet. "Sorry, I forgot to mention that part." Well, I guess some things never change, even when you're being grilled by young adult versions of your parents.

"Do you want to fill us in?" Dad asks. "You know, before we risk our lives raiding the place."

"Um, sure," I say. "Well, when I was inside, I discovered an alien guy named Proog who was being held prisoner. Apparently, he's part of some kind of space police force called the Intergalactic Paladins. He came to Earth to hide an alien object known as the Cosmic Key, which is the only thing keeping an extraterrestrial bad guy named Krule the Conqueror locked in the 13th Dimension. But before he could leave Earth, Proog was ambushed by Sunbolt and Norman Fairchild, the owner of ArmaTech, who are searching for the Cosmic Key for some reason. Does that make sense?"

But they don't answer. They just stare at me.

"Sooo," Mom says, finally breaking the silence, "somehow you forgot to tell us all of that?"

"Um, yeah," I say. "Sorry, there's a lot going on."

"Is there anything else being held in there that you forgot to mention?" Dad asks. "Big Foot? A unicorn? Anything?"

"Nope," I say. "I think we're all good now."

"Swell," Dad says. "Well, I've never seen an alien

before. So, this should be... educational."

"I'm with you on that one," Mom says.

Wait, what? In my timestream, my parents have dealt with all sorts of aliens! My mind races through all the extraterrestrial races I've encountered: the Skelton, the Dhoom, my friends on the Zodiac. So how is it that these two have never seen an alien?

Then, I remember how young they are. I mean, they haven't even formed the Freedom Force yet. So, I guess it makes sense.

"Okay," Dad says. "Enough talking. Let's get in there and do some damage."

"Whoa, slow down, cowboy," Mom says. "Let's take it nice and easy."

"Great idea," Dad says. "How about we knock on the front door?"

Oh no. Here they go again. I'm about to interject when Dad says, "Um, where's your dog going?"

My heart stops as I look over to find Gigi headed straight for ArmaTech! What's she doing? Then, she turns invisible.

Well, she'll make it undetected, but how will the rest of us... OMG! I'm such a nitwit sometimes.

I concentrate hard, pushing my Meta Manipulation powers towards Gigi's location. Then, I pull them back, capturing her power of invisibility.

Seconds later, I turn it on.

"Hey," Dad says, "where'd you go?"

"I'm still here," I say. "I'm invisible, just like you."

I reach out and grab my parents' arms.

"Where'd Brainstorm go?" Dad says.

"I can't see you either, genius," Mom says.

"Stay calm," I say. "We're all invisible now. Just don't let go of me."

"How'd you do that?" Dad asks.

"Long story," I say. "But now we can get inside without being seen. So, grab my hand. I'm not sure if I can keep this up if we're not connected."

They each grab one of my hands.

"Ready?" I ask.

"It's Fight Time!" Dad says.

"Seriously?" Mom says.

But I don't wait for Dad's response. Instead, I take off with my parents in tow. As we bolt across the terrain towards ArmaTech, I'm smiling the whole way. I'd like to say it's because we're about to solve this mystery. But I know it's because I've been homesick for so long that it feels great to have my parents with me, even if they're barely older than Grace.

A minute later, we reach the hidden entrance. I whisper Gigi's name, but she doesn't respond.

"Your dog is super annoying," Dad whispers.

"Well," I say, "she's not really my—"

"Shhh," Mom whispers. "I can sense our friends are inside, but I'm only getting faint readings. We should move before someone realizes we're out here."

"Okay," I say, "follow me."

I drop to my hands and knees and lead them through the opening. When we pop out the other side, I whisper Gigi's name again but there's still nothing. I scan the room. All of the other animals are here, but not her.

Then, I look up and my stomach sinks.

Proog's cell is empty.

Where is he?

"What's all this for?" Dad whispers.

"It's an animal testing center," I whisper back.

"That's horrible," Mom whispers.

"So, where's the alien?" Dad whispers.

"I… I don't know," I whisper back. "He was right there, in that cell. But he's gone." I try sounding calm, but deep inside I'm panicking. I mean, what happened to Proog? Did they move him? Or… worse?

"I sense our friends are close," Mom whispers. "They're down that hallway."

That's the corridor I came through the first time. It leads to that other passageway I didn't take. The one that ran right instead of left.

"Stay connected," I say. "And follow me."

Mom puts her hand on my shoulder and we move, running single file, down the stark white corridor. While my eyes are looking straight ahead, my mind is elsewhere. I mean, I shouldn't have listened to Proog. I should have saved him while I could. But instead, I took off like a coward.

And now it's too late.

We approach the intersection.

"Stay straight," Mom whispers.

I follow her instructions and head down the hallway. This one is just as white as the others, but for some reason, it feels like it's narrowing with every step. Of course, I'm so distraught by now my mind could be playing tricks on me.

Then, everything opens up and I stop short.

Mom crashes into me, and Dad into her.

No one says a word.

That's because we're standing in an unusual room. The space is cavernous, with a ceiling that looks a hundred feet high and walls that are smooth and curved. But the shape of the room is not what has us speechless.

Along the walls are dozens of glass-domed pods, each one perfectly equidistant from the next. And they're all connected to a grid of metal pipes that are running towards a central location—a sealed, metal chamber with a chair in the center.

What's that for?

"Look!" Mom whispers, pointing straight up.

I glance up and squint, and to my surprise I find a face staring right back at me! It's the face of a masked girl with pigtails!

It's… it's… Sunbolt?

But how could she be up there?

Then, I scan the other pods and find more faces.

It's the heroes!

They're inside the pods!

What's going on?

I'm about to ask my parents when I realize I can see them. Which means my invisibility powers have worn off somehow!

"Uh oh," Dad says, looking at us. "What happened?"

I have no idea.

"Welcome…" comes a deep, familiar voice.

We spin around to find a large frame filling the corridor, blocking our exit.

It's Fairchild!

And he's huge! In fact, he's so huge I don't think I realized how huge he was when I saw him in the lab. He's wearing a suit and tie, and for some reason, the only thing on my mind is where he got a suit that big.

"… and good night," he continues, waving something in the air that looks like a stick.

Then, it glows orange.

And I'm out.

Meta Profile

Name: Robot X-treme
Role: Hero   Status: Deceased

VITALS:

Race: Robot/Human Brain
Real Name: Carlton Musk
Height: 7'0"
Weight: 598 lbs
Eye Color: Blue
Hair Color: Inapplicable

META POWERS:

Class: Super-Intelligence
Power Level: ▮▮▮

- Extreme Analytical Skills
- Extreme Data Processing
- Robot body contains multiple weapons

CHARACTERISTICS:

Combat	91	
Durability	86	
Leadership	81	
Strategy	95	
Willpower	65	

TWELVE

I FLUNK MY INTERVIEW

As soon as I open my eyes, I know I'm in trouble.

I'm lying on my back, staring at a bright, white ceiling. On either side of me are cages and there's a cart filled with surgical instruments by my feet. I don't need Super-Intelligence to know where I am.

The animal testing lab!

I try sitting up, but my arms and legs are strapped to a table, and my helmet is so heavy I can barely lift my head. But from what I can gather, other than the lab animals, there's no one here but me.

Where are my parents?

I flex my muscles, but the straps hold firm. It's no use, I'm tied down tight. This is not good.

I don't know what I'm doing here, but I certainly

don't plan on staying long. After all, I don't want to end up like these poor animals. I've got to get out of here, and fast, before—

"Excellent," comes a deep voice. "You're awake."

—that.

Suddenly, a man's face appears overhead, startling me. He has dark brown hair and crystal blue eyes. I know him immediately.

"F-Fairchild!" I stutter.

"Yes," he says. "I'm flattered you know me, but unfortunately, I don't know you. And that doesn't seem fair, does it? So, tell me, who are you and what are you doing here?"

I don't know what to say. I'm certainly not going to tell him my real name or that I'm from the future.

"None of your business," I snap.

"Perhaps I should warn you that now isn't the time for games," he says, grinning ear to ear. "Because when I play games, I never lose. Now, let's try this one more time. Who are you and what are you doing here?"

"Where's Liberty Lad and Brainstorm?" I demand.

"Enjoying a deep sleep," he says. "Like the others."

"What are you doing to them?" I ask. "Why are you capturing all of these heroes?"

"That's simple," he says. "They are subjects for an experiment I'm conducting."

Experiment?

"What kind of experiment?" I ask.

"An experiment in power," he says. "Which is why I find you so interesting. You seem to possess a lot of power, don't you?"

Huh? How does he know I have powers?

"I'm not telling you anything," I say.

"You won't have to," he says. "Not while I have this."

Then, he waves a long, thin object in front of my face. At first, it looks like a silver baton. But upon closer inspection, I see white dots twinkling inside, like... stars?

Then, it hits me.

I know exactly what that is.

"The Infinity Wand!" I say.

"Ah, I see you've heard of it," he says, staring into it. "It's a fascinating object, isn't it? I thought they were just a myth, but when I learned they were real I had to have one for myself. They're quite powerful. I believe they detect and amplify Meta energy, just like this."

He tilts the Infinity Wand over my head and an orange spark flashes out the end.

"I imagine that in the right hands," he continues, "it would be quite a powerful weapon."

"That's Proog's Infinity Wand!" I yell. "Where is he?"

"Proog?" he says, furrowing his brow. "Oh, yes. Proog. Was that the name of the alien? Well, unfortunately, he expired. I guess his heart was not as strong as his resolve."

"Wait," I say. "Y-You mean, he's dead?" I ask.

"Oh, yes," Fairchild says, waving the wand. "Very dead. But don't worry, I'll take good care of his toy."

"You don't deserve that!" I yell. "Proog was a hero!"

"He was, wasn't he?" Fairchild says. "But he's gone now. So, I guess I'll have to stand in for him. Fortunately, I won't be distracted by any pointless hero obligations."

This guy is nuts! But I can't break free.

"By the way," he continues. "I must thank you for completing my hero collection. I knew if I let you escape, you would come back with others in tow. And that's exactly what you did."

What's he talking about? And then, my blood runs cold. He knew I was watching him with Proog!

"Y-You mean, you knew I was there? And you just let me go?"

"Of course I knew you were there," he says. "The Infinity Wand told me so."

I feel like such a heel. I mean, I led my parents right into his trap! Some son I am.

"I may not be a hero," he continues, "but I'm certainly no fool. So, let's get back to you, shall we? Tell me, who are you?"

But I clam up.

"I completely understand if you don't want to volunteer information," he says, moving out of view. "But by now I hope you realize I will get to the truth… one way or another."

I hear CLINKING noises by my feet. I look out of the corner of my eye and see him by the surgical cart. What's he doing? Then, he lifts a syringe into the air!

He's going to stick me with something!

I try busting out again, but I can't.

Suddenly, he appears overhead again, syringe in hand!

"Shall we begin?" he asks.

RUFF!

Fairchild turns.

What's that? It sounded like it came from far away.

RUFF! RUFF!

That's a dog barking!

Gigi! And she sounds really upset.

Fairchild puts down the syringe.

"Excuse me," he says. "It appears one of my specimens escaped from its cage. We'll continue later."

Then, he disappears, his footsteps echoing down the hall. Relief washes over me. Man, Gigi is the best. I just hope she disappears before Fairchild shows up. Now I've got to get out of here before it's too late. But how?

"Shhh!" comes a voice to my left.

I jump out of my skin.

"Relax," a man says. "I'm going to free you."

Then, a masked face appears overhead.

But it's not just any mask, it's... a hawk mask?

"Shadow Hawk?" I say.

"Shhh!" he whispers. "Quiet, kid. Let's get you out of here."

I hear RIPPING, and suddenly my arms and legs are free! They feel totally numb, so I shake them out to get some circulation going. But even though I can barely feel my limbs, my heart is pumping fast with excitement, because standing before me is one of the greatest heroes of all time. Except, he's unusually thin.

Then, I remember I'm back in the past. So, this skinny guy is a younger version of Shadow Hawk!

"How did you find me?" I ask.

"I wasn't looking for you, kid," he says, folding his hawk-knife and placing it into his utility belt. "I was looking for the Gray Ghost."

"The Gray Ghost?" I say, totally confused. Who is that? Then, everything clicks. The Gray Ghost. GG. Those were the initials on Gigi's tag! "Hang on, you mean the dog is a superhero? The invisible dog, right?"

"That's the one," Shadow Hawk says, helping me to my feet. "And believe me, keeping tabs on her isn't easy."

"So I've heard," I say. "But why are you following her?"

"Because she's Sunbolt's dog," Shadow Hawk says. "Before Blue Bolt and Master Mime disappeared, they told me they were working with Sunbolt. Since then, all sorts of heroes have vanished. Yet, Sunbolt is still around. So, I got suspicious. Clearly, she's up to no good."

"You've got that right," I say. "Sunbolt is the Trickster."

"Yeah," he says. "I figured. The problem is that I've

had a hard time tracking her down. Then, I found her dog running loose around Keystone City. So, I put a homing device inside a piece of bread, hoping she'd bite, and she did. But she never led me to Sunbolt. That is, until she teamed up with you. So, that's how I got here. Now, I don't know you, but I'm guessing anyone Fairchild has tied to a table has to be one of the good guys. What's your story?"

I desperately want to tell him, but I can't.

"I'm the Nullifier," I say. "I... sort of got swept up into this mess."

"Pleased to meet you, Nullifier," Shadow Hawk says, shaking my hand. "But I hope you're ready because this mess is only going to get messier."

"Yeah, I'm sure," I say. "Listen, our friends are stuck in these strange pods in the other room, but I've got no clue why. And now Fairchild has the Infinity Wand."

"Yes," Shadow Hawk says. "I heard him talking about it, although I'm not sure what it does. But it belonged to a friend of yours, huh?"

"Proog," I say. "I can't say we were friends, but we certainly felt like kindred spirits. And based on what Fairchild did to him, we're going to have to move fast to save the others."

"I'm with you," Shadow Hawk says. "Let's end this."

But just as we're about to get going, my eyes fall on the rat cage. It seems like there are hundreds of them in there, milling about, stepping all over one another.

But then something odd catches my eye.

At the top of the pile is a teeny, tiny rat.

He's clearly the runt of the litter, yet he's super determined, fighting to stay on top of the pack. As he balances precariously on top of another rat's head, his paws are flailing, like he's waving at me.

"Hang on," I say.

"Now may not be the best time to pet the animals," Shadow Hawk says.

But I scoop up the little rat anyway. He fits perfectly in my palm. Strangely, he's not putting up a fight. In fact, he looks like he wants to be held. What gives?

But then, my eyes land on the surgical cart. There's a bunch of syringes laid out, including one labeled: *Truth Serum*. Well, I guess Fairchild was going to use that one on me.

But then I see a syringe marked: *Brain Growth Serum #2324*. That's weird, why does that number seem so familiar?

Then, I look at the rat's tag. It reads: *#2324B*.

B? For Brain Growth Serum?

Suddenly, a particular Meta profile springs to mind, and I look into the little rat's pink eyes.

O. M. G!

This is no run-of-the-mill rat!

It's baby TechnocRat!

Meta Profile

Name: Gray Ghost
Role: Hero   **Status: Deceased**

VITALS:

Race: German Shepherd
Real Name: Gray Ghost
Height: 2'0" (at shoulder)
Weight: 81 lbs
Eye Color: Dark Brown
Hair Color: Gray/Black

META POWERS:

Class: Meta-Morph
Power Level:

- Considerable Invisibility
- Can turn all or part of body invisible

CHARACTERISTICS:

Combat	54
Durability	14
Leadership	20
Strategy	18
Willpower	70

THIRTEEN

I SEEM TO ATTRACT BAD NEWS

I think my ears are gonna fall off.

Ever since we injected the Brain Growth Serum into that tiny rat, he's been talking a mile a minute. But I guess I shouldn't be surprised, after all, we've just created TechnocRat.

"—about time," he says. "I've been cooped up in that cage with those squeakers for way too long. Do you have any clue what they blabber about all day? Cheese! All day it's 'cheese this,' and 'cheese that,' and 'where's the cheese?' There are one hundred and seventy-three rats in that box and not a single one has an original thought. Trust me, after about two seconds you'd want to—"

"Does he ever shut up?" Shadow Hawk asks.

"Do you really want the answer?" I respond.

"—and here's another problem—," TechnocRat

drones on.

Then, a strange thought crosses my mind. I mean, I knew TechnocRat came from ArmaTech, but I never thought I'd be the one bringing him to life! Maybe I was too impulsive, but the syringe was sitting right there. If I didn't do it, who knows if Fairchild would have ever gotten to it. I mean, this timestream is screwy enough.

Well, I certainly can't take it back now. What's done is done. I just hope creating TechnocRat hasn't destroyed my future. Or my hearing.

"—and rats just don't work well together. Never have, never will. I told those bozos that if we got on the same page, we could open the cage ourselves. But you know what they said? 'Where's the cheese?' I'll tell you, they have the collective intelligence of a rock. In fact—"

I can't take it.

"—don't think they could find their way out of a maze if they were given a map. In fact, I'm going to give them a map and—"

"Quiet!" I blurt out, covering his tiny mouth with my index finger. "Please, can we just have some peace and quiet for a second?"

"Mmmmkay," he mumbles, looking at me with his wide, beady eyes.

I'm about to start talking but stop myself. I need to be careful. I can't tell him too much, otherwise, I may compromise the timestream. I'll have to choose my words carefully and only tell him what he needs to know.

"Listen, we need your help," I say. "You may not know it yet, but you're the smartest creature on the planet. In fact, you're a Meta hero, a big-time hero, and we need your help to save a bunch of other heroes who are in trouble. Capeesh?"

TechnocRat nods slowly.

"Great," I say, removing my finger. "So, let's stop talking about cheese, and let's focus on what needs to be done right now. Are you with us?"

"Completely," TechnocRat says, sniffing the air. "But before we save the world, I've got two questions."

"Shoot," I say.

"First, who are you and the guy with the beak?"

"I'm the Nullifier," I say, "and that's Shadow Hawk. We're the good guys."

"Got it," he says, his ears perking up. "So, if I'm a hero, I need a superhero name too! Like..." then he strikes a pose, raising his claws over his head, "... Attack Rat!"

"How about ir-RAT-ating?" Shadow Hawk says. "Can we go now?"

"Hang on," I say. "What was your second question?"

"Oh, yeah," TechnocRat says. "Why is your finger fading in and out like that?"

My finger? What's he talking about? But when I look down, I see that he's right! My finger is pulsating—from solid to see-through and then back again! What's going on? I mean, I lost Gigi's invisibility power a while ago.

Then, it hits me.

O.M.G.

I'm... disappearing from existence!

If I don't solve this fast, it'll be the end of me.

"You okay?" Shadow Hawk asks.

"Yeah," I say, lying. "I-I'm fine. Let's get moving."

Shadow Hawk nods and takes off. I cup TechnocRat in my hands and follow.

"How about 'IncinerRat?'" TechnocRat rambles on. "Or 'ObliteRat'. Or 'The PiRat King?'"

But I've got so many things running through my brain I can't even respond. I run down the list. Fairchild has captured my parents and the others for some kind of experiment. Sunbolt is the Trickster, but she's in one of the pods too. So, how's that possible? Proog is dead, and Fairchild has his Infinity Wand, which probably isn't good news. I haven't heard Gigi bark in a while. And there's been no sign of the Time Trotter anywhere.

Oh, and to top it off, I'm fading into nothingness.

It's been a great day.

Then, I look down and nearly faint.

Now the top of my left hand is transparent!

It's spreading!

If I don't figure this out, I'm toast!

Thankfully, I've got Shadow Hawk with me, one of the greatest heroes of all time. And now we've got TechnocRat, the greatest brain on the planet.

"How about... 'The eRaticator?'" TechnocRat asks.

Although you wouldn't know it by listening to him.

But if anyone can figure out this mess, it'll be him.

I hope.

We charge down the hallway, passing the intersection. To say I have a bad feeling about this is an understatement. But there's no turning back now. It doesn't help that it's nearly impossible to breathe through this helmet. I want to rip it off, but I can't let them see my face. It's too risky, even though it feels like I'm going to hyperventilate.

Suddenly, the space opens up and we skid to a halt.

We're inside Fairchild's chamber!

I scan the circular room to find all of the pods still in place. Then, I look to my left and find two pods occupied with new faces. It's Mom and Dad!

Then, I look up.

It's Sunbolt! She's still inside!

"Whoa," TechnocRat says, pointing straight ahead. "Look at that guy."

It's Fairchild! He's sealed inside the chamber, wearing a helmet and harness connected to a mess of wires. What's he doing?

"Allow me," Shadow Hawk says, pulling out a Hawk-a-rang.

But as soon as he throws it, it's engulfed in flames and disintegrates before our eyes. What gives?

"Sorry," comes a girl's voice. "But this isn't a fire-free zone."

I turn, and my jaw hits the floor.

It's Sunbolt!

I look up again, and there she is, unconscious inside her pod. But when I look back down, she's standing right in front of us. That's just not possible.

Unless.

Unless...

Oh, no.

I think I'm gonna hurl.

"Move it!" TechnocRat yells, leaping out of my hands.

I hear his voice, but I don't react. I'm staring at Sunbolt, but my brain is a step behind. It's not until my eyes focus that I realize her hands are pointed right at me.

Uh-oh.

Fire blazes from her fingertips.

I can't react!

But before it hits me, I'm bowled over.

FWOOSH!

There's a huge explosion, followed by an ear-piercing YELP!

I'm lying on the ground stunned, but when I sit up Gigi materializes out of thin air. She's lying beside me and the fur on her back is singed black. She saved me!

"Gigi!" I yell.

I put my hand on her stomach. She's still breathing, thank goodness. But she's hurt. I can see large blisters forming on her back. She needs medical attention.

"Well, at least I got that annoying dog," Sunbolt says. "She wouldn't leave me alone."

"That's because she knows you're a fraud!" I yell.

"I am?" Sunbolt says. Then she wheels around and fires a blast at Shadow Hawk, who barely somersaults out of the way. "You don't know anything about me."

"Not true!" I yell. "I know exactly who you are!"

I focus my negation powers and then push them towards Sunbolt. Suddenly, she begins to flicker, and then her body begins to morph into something else.

Something big and muscular.

And my greatest fear is realized.

"Holy guacamole," TechnocRat whispers.

"What is that?" Shadow Hawk asks, alarmed.

In Sunbolt's place stands a yellow-skinned, pointy-eared creature—staring me down with neon green eyes.

"That is a Blood Bringer," I say.

"And what is a Blood Bringer?" TechnocRat asks.

"An elite warrior from a bloodthirsty race of alien shape-shifters known as the Skelton," I answer.

"Well, that's disturbing," TechnocRat says.

But my back tenses up, because I know this is no ordinary Blood Bringer. All of the other Blood Bringers I've seen can transform into an unlimited number of forms. But this Blood Bringer is different. This one not only copied Sunbolt's form but also her Energy Manipulation powers.

"Who are you?" I ask.

"My true name is inconsequential," he says. "But I am impressed, for it seems you do know of me. Or, at least, my kind. But you demean me by calling me a mere Blood Bringer, for I am so much more than that. Within the Skelton Empire, I am known as the Blood Master. Now prepare to die!"

But as he tries to power up, nothing happens.

"What have you done?" the Blood Master demands. "I cannot activate my powers."

"Sorry about that," I say. "Well, not really."

"No matter," the Skelton says, pulling a long sword from behind his back. "I won't need powers to destroy the likes of you." Then, he twirls the sword effortlessly, like he's starring in a karate movie.

I swallow hard. He's probably right.

Suddenly, there's a blinding FLASH of white light.

I block my eyes, but not in time.

Where'd that come from?

But as my vision returns, I realize the light is coming from Fairchild's chamber. I shield my eyes and squint in his direction. And that's when I see it.

Held high in Fairchild's hands.

The Infinity Wand!

"Stop them!" Fairchild barks. "I must concentrate. Don't let them interfere with my experiment."

"Experiment?" the Blood Master scoffs. "This is no experiment, fool. The fate of the universe is in our hands!"

"Yes," Fairchild says. "But it will all have been for nothing if I fail."

"Failure is not an option," the Blood Master says. "Now get on with it. I'll handle these vermin."

"Um, did he just call me vermin?" TechnocRat says. "Because I've never been so insulted in my life."

With sword in hand, the Blood Master lunges at Shadow Hawk, who dodges it with ease. But I don't know how long this can last. I mean, Shadow Hawk is an amazing fighter, but the Skelton are ruthless.

Then, Fairchild pulls a lever inside his chamber, and all of the pods radiate with orange energy.

"What's going on?" I ask.

But before anyone can answer, the orange energy transfers from the pods to the metal pipes, and then runs towards Fairchild's chamber.

"Based on what I'm seeing," TechnocRat says, "I'd say he's built a Meta conductor."

"A Meta what?" I say.

"A Meta conductor," TechnocRat says. "Typically, conductors are used to transfer electrical currents. But this one looks like it's designed to transfer Meta energy. What I haven't figured out yet is how he's actually pulling the Meta energy out of the heroes' bodies."

Great, if he can't figure it out, we're doomed.

I look back at Fairchild to find the orange energy crackling around his helmet and harness. Then, he lifts the Infinity Wand higher, and the intergalactic weapon releases a huge burst of orange energy! It whips around the room, shattering everything it touches! Shadow Hawk and the Blood Master duck beneath an energy tentacle, which lashes into the wall behind them.

This is nuts! The Meta energy is destroying everything it touches! We've got to stop it before it wipes us out! And the heroes stuck in their pods are helpless!

But before I can react, the wild energy is suddenly sucked back over Fairchild's chamber, forming a giant orange ball.

What's happening?

I look at Fairchild's sweaty face. He's concentrating hard. It looks like he's focusing, trying to control it!

Then, the ball loses its shape.

It's too strong!

But to my surprise, it re-forms and then morphs into a giant, upside down 'U.'

"What's he doing now?" I ask.

"No clue," TechnocRat says.

Suddenly, the ground RUMBLES beneath us, sending us flying like popcorn kernels. I land hard on my backside. That's gonna leave a bruise.

But as I look back, the ground beneath the orange 'U' has completely separated. Debris is spewing up everywhere. It's like he's created some kind of a giant vacuum cleaner, sucking up the earth below!

But why would he do that?

Then, I remember Proog's words: *"We believed if we*

buried it here, it would stay here instead of drifting aimlessly through space where it could fall into the wrong hands."

Buried?

O.M.G!

"I know what he's doing!" I say. "He's using the Infinity Wand to create a Meta magnet! He's—"

BOOM!

There's a massive explosion, and suddenly I'm flying through the air. I hit the wall hard, followed by TechnocRat who slams into my stomach. Then, we drop to the floor.

I pick myself up, but it feels like I've been run over by a truck. I have a funny feeling this is far from over.

And when I look up, I know I'm right.

Because attached to the bottom of Fairchild's Meta magnet is a strange purple object.

It's the Cosmic Key!

Meta Profile

Name: Blood Master
Role: Villain   Status: Active

VITALS:

Race: Skelton
Real Name: Unknown
Height: 6'11"
Weight: 330 lbs
Eye Color: Green
Hair Color: Bald

META POWERS:

Class: Meta-morph

Power Level: ▮▮▮▮

- Extreme Shape-Shifting—can assume endless forms
- Can mimic the powers of those he assumes the form of

CHARACTERISTICS:

Combat	100	
Durability	91	
Leadership	85	
Strategy	88	
Willpower	92	

FOURTEEN

I FUMBLE THE KEY TO SUCCESS

I can't believe it.

I'm staring at the freaking Cosmic Key!

My first thought is that it's way bigger than I imagined. In fact, it looks like one of those giant 'keys-to-the-city' you always see the mayor handing out on the six o'clock news. Except this one is deep purple and has a strangely celestial glow around it.

My second thought is that I'm pretty sure this key is much more than just a key. I mean, the Orb of Oblivion was a living entity that fed off of the desires of its host. I still shudder just thinking about it! Plus, it took absolutely forever to get that thing out of my life.

So, my instincts are telling me to stay as far away from that key as possible.

But my gut is telling me that ain't gonna happen.

After all, I can't just sit here and watch it fall into the wrong hands. According to Proog, the Cosmic Key is the only thing keeping Krule the Conqueror and his band of bad guys prisoner in the 13th Dimension. I'd love to stay on the sidelines, but if they ended up terrorizing the universe, I couldn't forgive myself.

So, I've got to do something.

But what?

Both Fairchild and the Blood Master seem to have forgotten all about us. They're totally fixated on the Cosmic Key. It's like they're stranded on a desert island and the Cosmic Key is the only piece of food around.

One thing I still don't understand is why Fairchild has partnered with the Skelton? Doesn't he realize how dangerous they are? Or is something else going on here?

"Finally!" the Blood Master exclaims. "The Cosmic Key is mine! With Krule's only means of escape from the 13th Dimension in my possession, there will be no one left to challenge the Skelton Empire! We will rule the universe unopposed!"

"Will you?" Fairchild says matter-of-factly. "Because I don't remember agreeing to that."

"You?" the Blood Master says. "What are you talking about? We had a deal, human. I brought you an Infinity Wand, and you were to deliver me the Cosmic Key."

"Yes, and thank you," Fairchild says looking at his Infinity Wand. "But perhaps you misheard me. I said I would deliver the Cosmic Key. But I never said I'd give it to you."

"Traitor!" the Blood Master screams, pointing his sword at Fairchild. "We promised you Earth in exchange for the Cosmic Key. If you renege on our deal, we will destroy you and your pathetic planet."

"Tell me, Skelton filth," Fairchild says. "Why would anyone settle for Earth, when they could rule the entire universe?"

"Filth?" the Blood Master says, his eyes wild. "You will regret that remark."

"Um, guys," I whisper to TechnocRat and Shadow Hawk. "I think now would be a good time to free the heroes. Because this is about to get ugly. Like, really ugly."

They nod and move to opposite sides of the room.

I'd love to help them, but something tells me to hold my spot. I mean, I'm still negating the Blood Master's powers, and that's important, but for some reason, I can't take my eyes off the Cosmic Key.

It's mesmerizing.

"You will pay for your disloyalty," the Blood Master spits, holding out his sword. Then, he charges Fairchild, yelling, "Prepare to die!"

But Fairchild simply smiles and says, "You first."

There's an earsplitting KRAKOW as a tremendous bolt of orange energy splinters from Fairchild's Meta magnet, and I'm blown backward by its enormous force.

I slam into the wall behind me, and for a second, I'm

seeing stars. But as my eyesight returns, I realize my head feels lighter. That's when I reach up and realize my helmet is gone! It's been blown to smithereens!

But that's not the biggest surprise.

When I look over at the Blood Master, he's lying face-down, his body smoldering with orange smoke.

That Meta blast totally leveled him.

He... he isn't moving!

"Fool!" Fairchild crows victoriously.

Suddenly, I feel guilty. I mean, I essentially made the Blood Master defenseless against Fairchild. But maybe I made a huge mistake? What if Fairchild is actually the greater evil?

"You okay, dude?" comes a familiar voice.

I turn to find Dad standing next to me!

He's free! But he looks totally confused.

Then, other heroes start dropping from the ceiling.

Rolling Thunder! Madame Meteorite! Blue Bolt! Dynamo Joe! Master Mime! Robot X-treme!

Shadow Hawk and TechnocRat did it!

They freed the heroes!

But they all look pretty dazed. I guess being stuck in those pods for so long really affected them.

"Ghostie!" comes a girl's voice.

I turn to find Sunbolt running towards Gigi.

"What happened, girl?" she asks, dropping to her knees. "You poor thing!"

Now that's the Sunbolt I remember!

I'm so relieved they're all free.

Except, someone is missing. Where's…

"Hey," comes a female voice.

I feel a hand on my shoulder, and when I turn my eyes meet Mom's eyes.

Her eyebrows go up.

Oh no! Without my helmet, she recognizes me!

"Hey!" she says. "Aren't you that kid those thugs held hostage? And you knew my secret identity. But… but how?"

I lower my eyes. I don't know what to tell her. I mean, how can I possibly explain any of this?

But when I look back up, her face says it all.

She knows everything! With all of the chaos going on, I let my guard down. I forgot to shield my mind from her!

"Y-You're… my… my…," she stutters.

"Please," I say. "You can't tell anyone. You shouldn't know any of this. It might destroy everything."

"With… with… *him*?" she says, looking at Dad, who is busy picking pieces of debris out of his long tresses. "I think I'm going to be sick."

"Trust me," I say. "He's not so bad. Give him a chance."

"What's happening to you?" she says, her eyes bulging wide. "You're… you're vanishing."

What? I look down to see my green boots disappearing and reappearing again. Oh jeez!

"You shouldn't be here," she says. "You need to get back to your timestream."

"Yeah," I say. "That's what I've been trying to do. Except I can't. I-I think I'm supposed to be here for some reason. I just don't know why."

"Come back!" Fairchild calls out, snapping me back to reality.

As I look over, I'm shocked. The Cosmic Key is drifting away from Fairchild's Meta magnet. And it's heading straight for the fallen Blood Master!

And Fairchild's Meta magnet looks like it's shrinking!

What's going on?

And then I remember Proog's words.

"The Cosmic Key cannot be contained. It is attracted to Meta energy."

That's it!

When Fairchild blasted the Blood Master he transferred so much Meta energy the Cosmic Key is following it!

"Get back here!" Fairchild demands. He pulls the lever inside his chamber once again, but this time the pods holding the heroes are empty. There's no Meta energy left for him to siphon.

But Fairchild doesn't stop.

He throws off his helmet and points the Infinity Wand at the Cosmic Key. Suddenly, a huge blast of Meta energy shoots from the Infinity Wand, engulfing the Cosmic Key.

The cosmic entity stops in mid-air.

O.M.G!

The Infinity Wand amplifies Meta energy!

And he's using it to pull back the Cosmic Key!

"We've got to stop him!" Dad declares.

"We're in," Dynamo Joe says.

But just as the heroes unite, there's a loud BOOM, followed by a swirling green vortex—a vortex I know all too well. And when it disappears, it leaves behind two giant figures.

"Um, are those T. Rex?" TechnocRat says.

Are you kidding me right now?

At first, the behemoths look confused. Then, they get their bearings and realize there's plenty of appetizers all around them. They ROAR.

"We'll need to work as a team," Blue Bolt says.

"If we're going to be a team, we need a catchy name," Rolling Thunder says. "How about… the Freedom Force!"

"Surprisingly, I like it," Dad says.

"Thanks," Rolling Thunder says. "Although I feel like I've heard it before."

Well, I guess I won't be getting credit for that one, but that's the least of my problems. Because as the heroes engage the giant lizards, it dawns on me that if dinosaurs are here, the Time Trotter can't be far behind!

But where is he?

Then, I realize Fairchild nearly has the Cosmic Key.

I can't let that happen.

Fortunately, Fairchild isn't the only one who can manipulate Meta energy.

I focus on the Blood Master, who is still crackling with Meta energy. I concentrate hard and then draw all of that energy towards me.

It hits me with a wallop—like a massive power surge.

My body feels electric. Super-charged.

Here goes nothing. I turn towards the Cosmic Key and open my arms, emitting Meta energy all around me.

The Cosmic Key stops.

Then, it heads towards me.

It's working!

I'm pulling it away from Fairchild!

But Fairchild doesn't give up. He pulls harder, and it's like we're playing a game of tug-of-war, with the Cosmic Key in the middle!

"You are powerful," Fairchild says. "But not powerful enough."

Then, he points the Infinity Wand at the heroes.

Uh-oh.

Suddenly, a huge blast of orange energy explodes from the wand's tip, and as it touches the heroes, they freeze! Then, Fairchild pulls their Meta energy back into the Infinity Wand. It's absorbed their powers!

"Now, it ends," Fairchild says, pointing the Infinity Wand at me! But it's shaking violently—like it's holding too much power.

He's going to obliterate me.

I have seconds to act.

So, I do the first thing that comes to mind.

I gather all of my Meta energy, and push it at the Infinity Wand, sending a giant orange ball straight at Fairchild.

"NO!" Fairchild yells, his eyes growing wide.

I look for somewhere to hide, but there's no time.

"Duck!" Mom yells, pulling me to the ground.

There's a massive explosion.

Everything goes black for a second, and when I open my eyes, I find myself lying next to Mom.

We made it! But how?

Then, I notice someone kneeling in front of us.

"You... you blocked the blast," Mom says. "You saved us?"

"Of course," Dad says. "I may be an ignoramus, but I'm an invulnerable ignoramus. Besides, we agreed to team-up for this one, didn't we?"

Mom looks at me and smiles.

"I told you to trust me," I say calmly. But inside I can barely contain my excitement. My parents are finally getting along! This might actually work out!

"The dinosaurs took the brunt of it," Dad says.

And he's right because when I look around the dinosaurs are nowhere to be found. Fortunately, the other heroes seem to be okay. A little worse for wear, but okay.

Poor Fairchild.

I wish I had another option, but he left me with no choice. It was either him or me.

But as the smoke clears, there's a figure still standing.

My jaw drops to the floor.

It's Fairchild!

But… he's even bigger than before.

And his skin and hair are bone-white.

Then, he opens his eyes, which are blazing with energy—a familiar, orange energy…

Meta Profile

Name: Norman Fairchild
Role: Villain   Status: Deceased

VITALS:

Race: Human
Real Name: Norman Fairchild
Height: 6'6"
Weight: 285 lbs
Eye Color: Brown
Hair Color: Brown

META POWERS:

Class: None
Power Level:
- Meta 0
- Brilliant Scientist
- Founder of ArmaTech Weapons Laboratory

CHARACTERISTICS:

Combat	65	
Durability	43	
Leadership	28	
Strategy	73	
Willpower	85	

FIFTEEN

I CAN'T BELIEVE WHAT I'VE DONE

I'm speechless.

I close my eyes and then open them again, hoping beyond hope that what I'm seeing isn't real. But unfortunately, everything matches up perfectly. The massive frame. The bone-white hair and skin. The wild, orange energy blazing around his eyes.

I'd know him anywhere.

The greatest monster to ever walk the planet.

Meta-Taker.

And he was created by me.

"Who is that?" Dad asks. "And what happened to Fairchild?"

I want to tell Dad that Meta-Taker and Fairchild are one and the same. I want to tell him that I caused the Infinity Wand to explode, infusing Fairchild with its powers. But I just can't form the words. I feel devastated. I just want to scrunch into a ball and cry.

I mean, is this why I'm here? Was it my destiny to create the most heinous villain in history? Is this how I was supposed to fix the past so I could return to my present? After this, I don't think things can get any worse.

But, surprise, I'm wrong again.

Because when I look at Meta-Taker, I realize he's holding the Cosmic Key.

"Are you okay, Elliott?" Mom whispers.

Hearing her say my real name snaps me back to reality. I desperately want to tell her I'm not okay. In fact, I want to tell her no one here will be okay.

But I can't let her know what happens next. I can't let her know that half of the heroes standing here are about to die. So, I use my Meta powers to shield her from reading my mind.

"Elliott?" she repeats. "Are you blocking me?"

"I'm sorry, Mom," I whisper back. "But there's stuff you just can't know."

To our left, the heroes are gathering.

"Let's get that guy!" Rolling Thunder shouts.

"No!" I call out instinctively. "You don't understand! He's too dangerous!"

But they don't listen.

Rolling Thunder and Dynamo Joe attack from the sides, but Meta-Taker holds his ground. And then, he uses Master Mime's powers to conjure up a giant purple hammer and clobbers both heroes with one swing.

They CRASH into the wall behind us.

Somebody tugs my arm.

"Eric, what are you doing here?" Sunbolt asks, looking at me with a puzzled expression. "You mean, you're a hero? Why didn't you tell me?"

I… I want to answer. But I can't.

"Okay," she says. "We'll discuss this later. But clearly, you know this guy. How do we take him down?"

But again, I'm torn. I want to tell her everything, but if I do, it could destroy my timestream.

But if I don't, she'll die.

"And by the way, what's wrong with you?" she says. "You're fading in and out! Is that your power?"

I look down at my body, which is now blinking rapidly like a strobe light! I'm feeling light-headed. Is this it? Am I about to disappear from existence?

I look over at Meta-Taker, who is still holding the Cosmic Key in his outstretched hand. The only thing running through my brain is that I'm responsible.

I'm responsible for creating him. I'm responsible for unleashing him on the world. I'm responsible for the deaths of Sunbolt, Dynamo Joe, Rolling Thunder, Madame Meteorite, Robot X-treme, and countless others.

I'm responsible for everything.

But as my eyes fixate on the Cosmic Key, images of other cosmic entities fill my mind.

The Orb of Oblivion.

The Building Block.

The Orb of Oblivion 2.

All of them are gone now. Destroyed.

Blown to pieces.

Blown to…

Then, I get an idea!

If I can blow up the Cosmic Key, I can destroy Meta-Taker before his reign of terror ever begins! I can save my friends and redeem myself! I can erase the mistake I've made!

Even if it costs me my own life.

Suddenly, I have absolute clarity.

I know what I've got to do.

"Get out of here!" I yell to the heroes. "All of you!"

"Elliott, wait!" Mom calls out.

But I'm already gone.

I've borrowed Blue Bolt's speed and Dad's strength.

I'm running so fast, everything around me seems like it's moving in slow motion.

I'm five feet away.

I just need to snatch the Cosmic Key and rip it in half. Then, all of this will be over.

Four feet.

I think about Dog-Gone and Grace.

Three feet.

Hopefully, they'll still make it.

Two feet.

Because after this, I'll be finished. But it's worth it.

One foot.

Meta-Taker looks up, his eyes growing wide. I'm nearly on top of him. But as I reach for the Cosmic Key, something huge swoops across my line of sight, taking the key right out of the monster's hand!

No!

I barrel into Meta-Taker and we both go tumbling to the ground. But when I look up, I'm shocked, because a Pterodactyl is flying through the air—with the Cosmic Key in its mouth!

Then, the prehistoric dinosaur is swallowed up by a green vortex, Cosmic Key and all!

"Finally!" comes a booming voice from above.

And that's when I see him, his red, three-eyed head floating above us all. It's him! It's Krule the Conqueror!

"The Cosmic Key is mine!" Krule says, his voice echoing through the chamber. "And now the universe will be mine as well!"

Then, there's a huge flash of white light and his image is gone, taking my only chance of destroying Meta-Taker with him.

I'm broken. I don't know what to do next.

But I don't have to wait long for an answer, because I'm suddenly lifted into the air. The next thing I know, I'm face-to-face with Meta-Taker!

All of my nightmares from our first encounter come racing back. The penetrating stare. The rotten breath. The evil grin. I look into his eyes. There's absolutely nothing left of Fairchild in there.

My hatred swells, and I swing at him, but it's no use.

I've exhausted every option possible.

But then, there's a huge blast of fire, and Meta-Taker ROARS in pain. As he tries to protect himself, he drops me to the ground. But the fire is so intense it pushes him into the wall!

"Hands off my friend, creep!" Sunbolt yells.

I land on my back. I want to stand up, but I can't. My vision is getting blurry, and I-I can't feel my legs!

Suddenly, I hear, "Let me go!"

I look up to find Mom and Gigi standing over me. I'm so happy Gigi's okay. But they're holding someone captive. It's a man, with a green costume and a cone-shaped helmet.

It's the Time Trotter!

"I sensed him lurking in the corner when that flying lizard showed up," Mom says. "So, I took him down with a psychic blast. And then the Gray Ghost pulled this off his wrist."

She holds up a watch.

His time-traveling watch!

Mom kneels over me and puts it in my hand.

"You've got to leave now, Elliott," she whispers urgently. "I looked inside your mind and set the watch to where you need to go."

"No," I say. "I-I have to stop Meta-Taker, you don't understand."

"You're wrong, son," she says, with a sad smile. "I do understand. I'm so proud of you. You're a real hero. But now you have to leave."

Suddenly, there's a ROAR!

Meta-Taker!

"N-No," I say, panicked. "I-I can't."

"Elliott," she says. "If you die here, there's no telling what could happen to the future. When I looked into your mind, I saw you save the world—several times over. This time you need to trust me. If you're not there, billions could die. You've got to go now. I'll cover your tracks here."

I look into her eyes and I know she's right.

I've done all I can do.

This may be my last chance.

I look at Gigi and say, "Bye, girl."

I close my eyes and tap into the watch.

"Goodbye, son," Mom says. "I love you."

"Love you too," I say.

And then, I'm gone.

EPILOGUE

I GO BACK TO THE BEGINNING

When I open my eyes, I'm totally disoriented.

Somehow, I'm back in my bed, on the Waystation.

But how is that possible? Was I dreaming?

Then, I realize I'm holding something. It's the Time Trotter's watch! Suddenly, it all comes spinning back.

Sunbolt!

Gigi!

Meta-Taker!

The picture!

I look over at my nightstand, and the photo of my family is back! There's no crazy cat!

I drop the watch, throw off my covers, and run out of my room.

Seconds later, I crash into someone coming around the corner.

"Grace!" I yell, throwing my arms around her.

"Whoa," she says, nearly dropping her plate of jelly doughnuts. "What's gotten into you?"

"You're here!" I say. "On the Waystation!"

"Yeah, so," she says. "Did you hit your head or something? And what's up with your pajamas?"

Pajamas?

I look down to see I'm still wearing the black uniform and neon green boots I got at Groovy Threads.

"Oh," I say. "It's just a Halloween costume."

"A little early for Halloween," she says.

"Yeah," I say. "Hey, where's Mom and Dad? And Dog-Gone?"

"Some people are in the Galley," she says.

"Great!" I say, running down the hall. "Oh, and you can watch all the cat videos you want!"

"Gee, thanks," I hear her say. "Weirdo."

I book down the hall and enter the Galley. Dad and TechnocRat are having lunch at the island. I run over and give Dad a big hug.

"Hey, buddy," Dad says. "Nice to see you too."

"Same here," I say. "By the way, the shorter hair is a huge improvement."

"Um, okay," Dad says confused.

Then, I pick up TechnocRat and squeeze him.

"Easy, kid," he says, dropping his cheese stick.

"I'm so sorry for earlier," I say. "I know you did everything you could to help me. You're a great hero. I just wanted you to know that."

"Aw, thanks, kid," TechnocRat says, turning red.

Then, a brown-and-black creature emerges from beneath the table.

Dog-Gone!

I run over and tackle him. We roll over each other and he licks me on the nose.

"Take it easy with him," Dad says. "He had a rough night. Apparently, someone gave him an entire bag of cookies. You wouldn't happen to know who it was, would you?"

"I'm so sorry," I say to Dog-Gone. "I promise I won't do that again, no matter how stubborn you are. You were just trying to do the right thing. I realize now it's in your nature."

Dog-Gone licks my nose again.

"Hey, where's Mom?" I ask.

"I don't know," Dad says. "She's around here somewhere. Do you want some lunch?"

"No," I say, even though my stomach rumbles.

I'm hungry, but there's something I have to do first. Apologizing to TechnocRat felt good, but it wasn't enough. I have more apologies to deliver. Lot's more.

I give Dog-Gone a belly rub and then head out of the Galley. I make my way through the Waystation, to the one place I know I need to go.

The Hall of Fallen Heroes.

As I enter, a chill runs down my spine.

I flick on the switch and the spotlights come on.

They're all here: Rolling Thunder, Madam Meteorite, Robot X-treme, Dynamo Joe, and Sunbolt.

But then, I'm shocked.

Because instead of five statues, there's six!

"Hey, pipsqueak," comes a familiar voice.

"Mom!"

I turn around and hug her tight.

"It's so great to see you again, Elliott," she says, rubbing my back. "I knew you'd make it home okay."

"You knew?" I ask. "But how?"

"Because it just felt right," she says. "Elliott, I know how hard this was for you, but some things are just destined to happen. It wasn't your fault Meta-Taker was created. He would have existed one way or another, and these heroes would have suffered the same fate."

I look at the statues.

Although I hear what Mom is saying, I can't help but feel like I failed them.

"Try not to be so hard on yourself," she says. "You did amazing things back there, but the situation had to play out the way it did. That's why I left you that note."

"Wait?" I say. "That note was from you?"

"Yes," she says. "After reading your mind in the past, I knew that one day you would need it in the present. So, I taped it to TechnocRat's Time Warper right after you were born. But I couldn't tell you about it. Otherwise, things may have unfolded very differently."

"Well, thanks for that," I say. "But how come I was the only one who wasn't affected? Why did I have to go through all of this?"

"I would say thank goodness it was you," she says. "But my theory is that your negation powers shielded you. At least for a while. But eventually, even time started to catch up with you. I guess the saying is true, 'time waits for no man.'"

Yeah, I guess that sort of makes sense.

Then, I get a strange thought.

"Mom, do you think it's really over?" I ask. "Could this time mix-up thing happen again?"

"No," Mom says. "I think we're past this loop now. All of the things that had to happen have happened. And maybe a few things got added that were better than expected."

"You mean, like that?" I say, looking over at the sixth statue.

"I told you I'd cover your tracks," she says with a wink. "I think I accomplished that."

"Yeah, I'd say so," I answer.

"It's nice coming up here and visiting these true heroes, don't you think?" she asks.

"Yeah," I say. "I'll be coming up here more often. It feels nice to remember them."

Speaking of remembering, suddenly the image of a three-eyed man pops into my mind.

"What about Krule?" I ask.

"I don't know," she says. "We haven't heard a thing about him since he took the Cosmic Key all those years ago."

Well, that's a relief. But then again, he's got the Cosmic Key. So, I wonder if he ever escaped from the 13th dimension? I shudder at the thought. I sure hope not, but deep down I feel unsettled just thinking about it.

"Want some lunch?" Mom asks.

"Sure," I say. "I'll be down in a few minutes."

"You got it," she says. Then, she kisses my cheek and leaves.

It's just me and the statues.

"I'm so sorry, guys," I say, tears running down my cheeks. "I-I wish I could have done more for you. But I'll never forget you. You are all a part of me now. So, whenever I do anything heroic, it'll be like we're all doing it—together."

I wipe away my tears and take one last look at the statues.

Rolling Thunder.

Madame Meteorite.

Robot X-treme.

Dynamo Joe.

Sunbolt.

The Nullifier.

Then, I flick off the lights and head for the Galley.

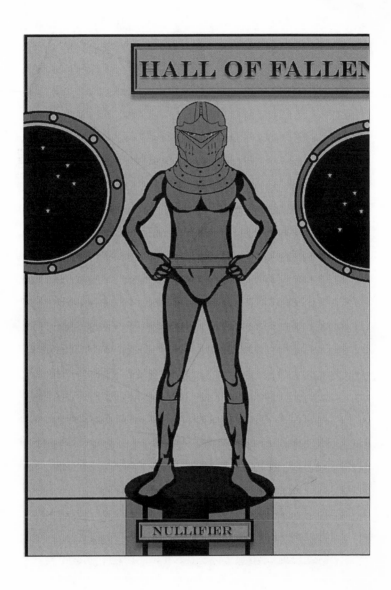

Epic Zero 5: Tales of an Unlikely Kid Outlaw

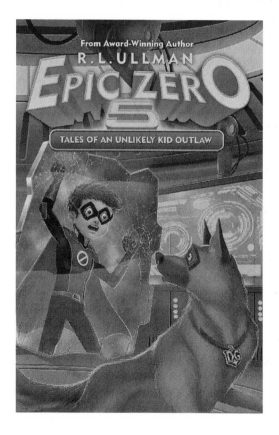

ONE

I GET ROCKED

I'm running through a subway tunnel in hot pursuit.

My prey this time are a brother-sister Meta villain team called Mover and Shaker. Apparently, they broke into the Keystone City Museum and walked out with millions of dollars in precious gemstones. Then, they made their escape through the subway system.

It was a great plan, but unfortunately for them, they're not the only brother-sister Meta team down here.

"Can you possibly move any slower?" Grace barks, zipping over my head with a flashlight in hand. "They're getting away!"

Of course, they're probably the more united brother-sister Meta team down here.

"I'm going as fast as I can," I call out, my voice

echoing through the tunnel. But deep down I realize she's right. Maybe I am dogging it a little. After all, I've barely worked up a sweat.

I mean, normally I'm geeked up for a chance to wrangle up some rogues. But right now, I'm feeling a little cautious. Maybe I should explain.

Up until about ten minutes ago, Grace and I were stuck on the Waystation doing homework while the rest of the team was out on a mission. So, I pretty much resigned myself to an evening of algebra and ice cream.

That is, until the Meta Monitor started blaring.

Even though our parents told us to stay put no matter what, they couldn't really expect us to ignore the alarm, could they? I mean, we're superheroes for Pete's sake. Sometimes you need to sacrifice math to save the day!

I was thinking this would be awesome.

Then, I found out the crooks went underground.

That's when things got a little less awesome.

You see, if there's one thing I hate, it's going underground. And it's not because I'm afraid of the dark. Trust me, I moved past that stage years ago (and no, nightlights don't count). And it's definitely not because I get claustrophobic. I've been in plenty of tight spots before and managed to hold my own.

So, what's my beef with going underground?

Well, in my experience, nothing—and I mean NOTHING—good ever happens underground.

Take Meta-Taker for instance. The first time I laid eyes on that monster was when he popped out of the hole the Worm dug for him. Then there was my nightmare encounter with Alligazer in the sewer system.

See the pattern here?

Yet, where do I find myself now?

Running through Keystone City's subway system—underground.

Yep, you'd think I'd have learned by now.

Of course, I could have opted out. In fact, I pretty much convinced myself I wouldn't be going on this little subterranean adventure. Then Grace called me a 'chicken.'

So that pretty much explains what I'm doing here.

"Come on, slowpoke!" Grace yells, flying around the bend. "You should rename yourself Molasses Boy!"

Well, that was rude. But when I shine my flashlight in her direction she's already gone. Man, I sure wish I had her confidence right now. But I guess I've been burned too many times underground before.

Nevertheless, I pick up the pace. Other than Grace's barbs, the only sounds I hear are my footsteps sloshing through puddles and my heart beating way too fast.

Sometimes I can't believe I'm doing this stuff.

In retrospect, I guess I could have copied Grace's flight power. After all, running through a subway tunnel is risky business. In particular, you want to avoid the third rail. That's the one that supplies power to the train's electric motor. One accidental touch could fry you to a crisp.

So that's pretty unnerving.

Speaking of unnerving, I barely had time to read the profiles of Mover and Shaker before we got here. What I did catch is that Mover and Shaker are Meta-morphs who can change their molecular structures into stone and sand, respectively. I suppose if their criminal careers don't work out, they could open a half-way decent landscaping business.

I flash my light along the walls. Boy, it's depressing down here. Everywhere I look is gray concrete and black mold. Yuck! The sooner we get out of here the better.

The problem is that I'm not even sure we're going the right way. Grace picked this direction and I wasn't going to argue with her, but the subway system is massive. We've probably been heading down this tunnel for five minutes without finding any—

"AHHH!"

That scream!

It's Grace!

Without thinking, I sprint towards her voice, shining my flashlight everywhere but I don't see her. After about fifty yards I stop and catch my breath.

Where the heck is she?

Suddenly, my flashlight is knocked out of my hand and I hear it CLANKING onto the rails.

Great. It's pitch dark and someone is next to me!

Did I mention I hate going underground?

"Well, well," comes a female voice, echoing through the tunnel. "We must be the Pied Pipers for Meta children because it seems like we're being followed by all of these annoying costumed kids."

I reach into my utility belt and activate my flare. It lights up like a sparkler and I suddenly find myself face-to-face with a woman. But she's no ordinary woman.

My jaw drops as I watch her features shift around on her face—her left eye moving to where her nose should be, and her nose moving up to her forehead. For a second, I think I'm going to be sick, and then I remember I'm staring at Shaker, whose entire body is made of sand.

"Where's Glory Girl?" I demand.

"Right here, kid," comes a deep, gravelly voice.

I spin around to find a massive pile of rocks standing behind me. It's Mover—and he's holding Grace! I crane my neck to take him all in because he's at least seven feet tall with muscles the size of boulders.

Then, I realize he's standing right on the third rail—with Grace in his arms! But why isn't there any crazy electricity? Then it hits me. He's all rock, so he's grounded—the electricity can't affect him. But if he drops Grace, she'll be electrocuted!

"Take it easy, rockhead," I say. "Or you'll be sorry."

Laughter echoes through the tunnel.

"Well, I didn't think it was funny," I mutter.

"You're cute, kid," Shaker says, her body shifting

from the shape of a woman into the shape of a giant hammer. "But we've got places to go. So, I think it's time to pound sand."

Um, what?

Then, she swings down at me!

I dive out of the way before—

BOOM!

Dirt and steel explode all around me. I look back to find a giant hole right where I was standing. Wow, she completely smashed through the rails!

That was close, but with Grace down for the count, it's all up to me. Luckily, I've got some tricks of my own.

But just as I'm about to negate their powers, there's a RUMBLING behind me, and my legs start shaking.

I wheel around to see two lights heading our way, growing larger by the second. Uh-oh. Those are headlights. Which means… a subway train is coming!

"Catch, kid," Mover says, throwing Grace at me.

I catch her, but she's so heavy I tumble backward. I hit the tracks hard but squeeze Grace tight, preventing her from rolling onto the third rail.

Then, Mover throws a large sack over his shoulder and jumps, busting through the thick, concrete ceiling. I shield Grace with my body as chunks of debris crash down onto the tracks.

"Sorry, kid," Shaker says, grabbing a sack of her own. "But you two picked a really crummy way to die."

Then, she morphs her body into a spring and

bounces out of the tunnel.

No! They're getting away!

SCCRREEEEECCCCHHHH!

The train!

It's braking, but it's coming in too fast!

I'm about to copy Grace's powers and fly us out of here when I notice the hole in the tracks. When the subway reaches it, it'll derail the train and injure all of those people!

I've got seconds to do something. But what?

Then, I notice sand particles on the ground.

Shaker's particles! That's right! Her Meta profile said she loses sand particles from her body, but they always find their way back to her!

That's it!

I put my palm over the sand and concentrate hard, activating my duplication powers.

But when I look up, the train is nearly on top of us!

I need to time this perfectly!

I concentrate hard and then watch in amazement as my right arm turns to pure sand. Boy, that's itchy, but there's no time to scratch. Instead, I encase Grace inside my sandy appendage and then push it out of the tunnel like a water plume, sending Grace to safety.

One job done, one left to do.

HOOONNNKKK!

It's here!

I look up and meet the terrified eyes of the subway

driver, whose handlebar mustache is drooped over his wide-open mouth. I focus hard, transforming my body into millions of sand granules. Then, I drop them all to the ground, filling in the massive hole in the tracks.

Instantaneously, the wheels of the train press down on me, and I harden my molecules, pushing back up with all of my might. The train is heavy, maybe two tons heavy and at least ten cars long, but I hold my ground, focusing all of my energy on supporting its weight.

Then, after what seems like an eternity, it finally rolls off of me and keeps on chugging.

H-Holy cow! I-I did it?

But there's no time to pat myself on my back, not that I have one right now anyway, because I need to find Grace! I pull my molecules together, forming the shape of a sand spring just like I saw Shaker do, and then propel myself out of the tunnel.

I land with a bounce, relieved to be topside again. It's still night out, but at least there are streetlights. But when I finally come to a stop, I get a surprise.

Someone is pointing a TV news camera at me.

Well, this isn't the best time for an interview. Plus, it won't be long before Shaker's powers wear off and I still need to get myself back together! After all, some of my sandy arm is still with Grace. But where is she?

Then, I feel a pulling sensation to my right.

I follow the feeling, which leads me to a large dumpster. Could it be? I concentrate again, and suddenly, a fountain of sand comes flying out of the dumpster, reattaching to my body!

Whew, I'm whole again! I don't waste any time transforming back to my natural self before my powers wear off. That was certainly a strange experience, but if my sandy arm was inside that dumpster, then that must mean—

"Yuck!" comes a familiar voice.

Suddenly, Grace pops up from inside the dumpster, covered head-to-toe in greenish slime. It takes everything I have not to burst out laughing as a banana peel slides off her forehead.

"One peep and I'll kill you," she says, wiping more banana chunks off her costume. "Now, where's Mover and Shaker? We've got to stop them!"

"Relax," I say. "They got away."

"What?" she says. "How'd that happen?"

"Well, you were unconscious for one," I say. "And then—"

"Um, excuse me," comes a voice from behind.

I turn to find dozens of cameras pointed at us. It's more news people. It's like they all showed up at once.

"Whoa!" Grace says, throwing a leg over the dumpster. "Step back, people. Do I look camera-ready to you? Everyone, please turn off your—"

CRASH!

I look down to find Grace lying on her face.

"Smooth," I say.

"Shut it," she mumbles.

"Excuse me," a female reporter asks, shoving a microphone in my face. "But are you planning to pay for all of this damage?"

"What?" I say. "Um, no. We're with the Freedom Force."

"It doesn't matter if you're an Avenger," she says. "You've probably cost taxpayers millions of dollars in repairs."

"Um, I was just trying to save the day," I answer.

"Do you take responsibility for nearly injuring all of those subway passengers?" a man asks.

"What?" I say. "No. I—I saved them. If it wasn't for me, they could have—"

"Do you believe the Meta population is a menace to society?" another woman asks.

"A… a menace?" I stutter, totally confused.

"I think we're done here," Grace says, finally standing up and blocking the microphones.

"Will you be turning yourselves in for questioning?"

"Excuse me?" I say.

"Grab on," Grace whispers. "We're going back to the Freedom Ferry."

"Do you think you're above the law?"

"Will you be revealing your true identities?"

"Do you think all Metas should be licensed?"

But as the questions keep pouring in, I wrap my arms around Grace, and we take off.

Meta Profile
The Freedom Force

Captain Justice
Class: Super-Strength
Meta: ▪▪▪

Ms. Understood
Class: Psychic
Meta: ▪▪▪

Glory Girl
Class: Flight
Meta: ▪▪

Shadow Hawk
Class: None
Meta:

Epic Zero
Class: Meta Manipulator
Meta: ▪▪▪▪▪

TechnocRat
Class: Super-Intellect
Meta: ▪▪▪▪

Blue Bolt
Class: Super-Speed
Meta: ▪▪▪

Master Mime
Class: Magic
Meta: ▪▪▪▪

Makeshift
Class: Energy Manipulator
Meta: ▪

TWO

I GET BLAMED FOR EVERYTHING

Well, I'm feeling less than heroic.

I still don't understand why those reporters were coming after Grace and me like that. I mean, it's not like we were trying to put people in harm's way. We were just doing our jobs—jobs we don't even get paid for!

Plus, Mover and Shaker got away.

So, today has pretty much been an epic fail.

I can tell Grace is miffed as well, because as soon as we got into the Freedom Ferry she barely said two words to me. And when we reached the Waystation, she headed straight for the showers. Not that I blame her. She was buried up to her eyeballs in garbage.

If she wasn't in such a crummy mood, I would have

busted her for stinking up the entire shuttle. But I figured she'd had enough humiliation for one day. Besides, as soon as she left I hung four of those pinecone-shaped air fresheners on the rearview mirror.

And just to keep the bad news coming, one of the Freedom Flyers was already parked in the Hangar when we got back, which means some of the team had returned from their mission before we did.

My only hope is that Mom and Dad aren't with them, because if they find out we skipped out to go on a mission of our own, we're going to be in even more trouble. And after today, more trouble is the last thing I need. So, come to think of it, the safest place for me to be right now is probably in my room.

I tiptoe out of the Hangar and head towards my bedroom. Truthfully, Grace isn't the only one that could use a shower—after all, I was hanging on to her smelly body—but my stomach rumbles in objection. It's late and I haven't eaten anything since dinner. No wonder my legs feel shaky. It might be risky, but I need to grab a snack from the Galley.

Using my best stealth moves, I make it there without being seen. But as soon as I step inside my luck runs out.

I hear his scrambling feet before I see him, and then I barely sidestep Dog-Gone like a matador in a bullfight.

"Easy, boy," I whisper, as he slides past me into the hallway. "Quiet!" I plead as he regains his footing. "No, boy. Take it easy. I'm trying not to—oof!"

Suddenly, that mangy mutt is on top of me, pinning me to the floor. I brace myself for the inevitable barrage of slobber, but after the first lick he makes a funny face and starts spitting and sputtering like he's tasted glue.

"Shhh!" I whisper. "Relax, you're not going to die. I've just got Grace's dumpster goo all over me. It's not like you gave me a chance to warn you."

Dog-Gone runs to his water bowl and starts guzzling like he's been wandering through a desert for days. Oh well. I guess now's my best chance to grab some chow and make a quick getaway. I open the fridge when—

"Hey, Elliott."

I jump out of my skin.

Standing behind me is Makeshift!

"Oh, hey," I say casually, leaning against the fridge. I need to stay cool. I can't let him think anything is wrong. "So, you're back, huh? How'd it go?"

"I was going to ask you the same thing," he says, grabbing a bag of tortilla chips from the pantry. "Because the last time I saw you, you were doing your homework—in regular clothes."

I look down. I'm still in my costume. Busted!

"Oh, yeah," I say. "We went out."

"Grace too, huh?" he says. "Anything big?"

"Mover and Shaker," I say. "But they got away. How about you?"

"Strange one," he says. "The Meta Monitor picked up four unknown Meta 3 signatures at the edge of the

Ozone layer. But when we got there, they were gone."

"That is strange," I say. "Well, I guess we both struck out. Um, Mom wasn't with you, was she?"

"Nope," he says, opening the bag of chips.

Yes!

"But your dad was," he says.

Dad? Uh-oh.

"Um, Makeshift," I say, "you wouldn't mind not mentioning anything about—"

"Me?" he says, munching on a chip. "Nah, I never saw ya."

"Thanks," I say. I'm about to bolt when I hear—

"Elliott!"

My back tightens. It's Dad!

"Good luck," Makeshift says.

"Thanks," I say. "I'm gonna need it."

"Elliott!" Dad calls again.

Dog-Gone looks up at me and whimpers.

"See you in the next life, buddy," I say.

"Elliott!"

"Coming!" I yell back.

It sounds like he's in the Lounge. As I make my way over, I run through possible excuses in my head. Maybe I'll blame it on Grace. Yeah, that's it! After all, I just wanted to finish my homework. She's the one who called me a chicken. Or maybe I'll—

"Elliott," Dad says.

Huh? I look up and realize I'm already standing in

the Lounge—right in front of Dad!

Oh, boy. What am I going to say?

He's still in costume with one hand on his hip and the other holding the remote control. Then I see Grace sitting on the couch in her pajamas with a pink towel wrapped around her head. She looks really mad.

"Um, am I about to be grounded until I'm a teeny, tiny old man?" I ask.

"Probably," he says. "But right now, take a seat next to your sister and watch this."

Wait, what? My punishment is to watch TV. Really?

"Is he for real?" I ask, sitting next to Grace.

"Yep," she says, staring straight ahead. "It's pretty horrible."

Horrible? Is she crazy? From now on I want Dad to hand out all of my punishments. I slide back on the sofa and throw my feet up on the ottoman. I hope they're watching a movie.

But as I get cozy, I see the TV is tuned to a news station. It's CNC, the popular cable news channel. There are two talking heads on the screen, a blond-haired woman and a very white-haired man with a mustache. I've seen the woman before. Her name is Sarah Anderson, the popular news anchor who hosts the CNC Morning Newsflash. But I've never seen the man before.

He looks kind of intimidating with his piercing blue eyes, military crew cut, and square jaw. Then, titles appear beneath his face with his name.

It reads: *General William Winch.*

"For those viewers just tuning in," Sarah Anderson says, "I'm here with General William Winch, former Chairman of the Joint Chiefs of Staff. So, General, you're serious about this?"

"Dead serious, Ms. Anderson," General Winch says. "Who gave these Metas the right to do whatever they want? It's not in our Constitution, it's not in our Bill of Rights, and I certainly don't know of any laws passed that give Metas special authority to wreak havoc on our society, do you?"

"Well, of course not," Sarah Anderson says. "But not all Metas are bad guys. Take the Freedom Force, for instance. They've saved our planet too many times to count. Surely, you aren't lumping them into that category, are you?"

"Of course I am!" he barks. "Why should they get a free pass to terrorize America?"

"Who does he think he is?" Grace says, slamming her fist into the sofa. "I'd like to see him do what we do!"

"Quiet, dear," Dad says. "Let's see where this goes."

Now I realize why Grace said this is horrible.

This guy is attacking us on television!

"Because they're heroes, General Winch," Sarah Anderson says. "Without them, we probably wouldn't even be sitting here to have this discussion."

"I'm not convinced of that!" General Winch says. "Your network captured what happened this evening.

Run it again and tell me what you see. Because what I see are Meta-humans putting ordinary citizens in danger."

"Yes, sir," Sarah Anderson says, raising an eyebrow. "In fact, we do have that footage and we'll run it one more time for those of you who missed it. This happened tonight in Keystone City's subway system…"

Keystone City's subway system?

Oh, jeez. I drop my head in my hands.

The footage starts, accompanied by the voice of a male reporter. "Today, on the 'L' line in Keystone City's subway system, two Meta children playing superhero attempted to stop a pair of Meta villains from making off with millions of dollars in stolen gemstones. Not surprisingly, the villains got away, but not before the foursome caused an incredible amount of damage to the infrastructure and nearly derailed a subway train filled with innocent passengers."

"Hang on!" I say. "That's not what happened!"

Suddenly, the screen cuts to a grainy, black-and-white image of Grace and I running through a subway tunnel. Then, it switches to Shaker in the shape of a giant hammer smashing the tracks. And then it cuts to Mover busting a hole in the tunnel ceiling. Suddenly, a piece of debris flies towards the camera, and the screen goes black.

"Hey!" I blurt out. "The camera got smashed before it showed me saving all of those people!"

Just then, the image switches to a closeup of Grace

inside the dumpster with the banana peel on her head.

"OMG!" she shrieks, shriveling into a ball. "This is so embarrassing!"

I'm about to laugh, but the next thing I know my face is plastered on the screen. Microphones are pointed at me and reporters are peppering me with questions. I look totally clueless, like a deer in headlights. Then, it cuts to Grace and I flying away.

"Well, that didn't look good," I mutter.

"Quiet," Dad says firmly.

Sarah Anderson and General Winch are back.

"The evidence is right there," General Winch says. "You know what Meta heroes do? They escalate situations. If those inexperienced children hadn't interfered, those crooks would have gone away peacefully. But instead, they put hundreds of lives in danger while costing taxpayers millions of dollars in repairs. We have laws restricting ordinary citizens from carrying weapons in public. Shouldn't we have laws restricting Metas from using deadly superpowers in public?"

"I hear you," Sarah Anderson says. "But I'm not sure most citizens would agree with you."

"Public opinion is changing, Ms. Anderson," General Winch says, staring right at the camera. "And I won't rest until something is done about it."

Suddenly, Dad turns off the television.

Well, that was disturbing.

"I'm ruined," Grace mutters, slumping into the

couch. "That'll never come off of social media."

"Grace, that's not important," Dad says.

"Of course it's important, Dad!" Grace says. "I'll be a GIF forever!"

"Okay, okay," he says. "I get it. But you heard that General. He's on a crusade against Meta heroes."

"But why?" I ask.

"I don't know," Dad says. "But what I do know is that neither of you asked for permission before jetting off to save the day. I think now would be a good time to discuss proper punishment."

"Punishment?" Grace says. "Don't you think I've suffered enough? Believe me, I'm sorry. This horror show will haunt me for the rest of my life."

"And what about you, Elliott?" Dad asks.

"Well, honestly, I'm totally confused," I say, crossing my arms. "I mean, I get it that we took off against your wishes, but we were only doing what heroes are supposed to do. Should we really be punished for that? Yeah, I get there was some damage and stuff. But doesn't that just come with the territory?"

"Elliott..." Dad starts.

But suddenly, the phone rings.

That's weird. Ever since we got rid of the Prop House, the phone never rings. Who could it be? I mean, we live in freaking outer space!

Dad picks it up.

"Hello?" he says into the receiver. "Yes, this is

Freedom Force headquarters. Yes, we are in space. Yes, that is pretty cool. This is Captain Justice. With whom am I speaking?"

Grace and I look at each other.

"CNC news?" he says, raising his eyebrows. "The two kids on the footage? Yes, they are members of the Freedom Force. Yes, the girl with the banana on her head is Glory Girl."

"See!" Grace exclaims, burying her face in a pillow.

"The boy?" Dad says, looking at me. "Yes, he's here. Yes, I'm sure he's a member of the Freedom Force. His name is Epic Zero. Epic... Z-E-R-O. Yes, he really is a hero. You'd like to speak to him?"

Wait, what?

"Epic Zero," Dad says, "it's for you."

"Him?" Grace says, lifting her face. "Why him?"

"Um, hello?" I say, taking the phone.

"Is this Mr. Zero?" a female voice asks.

"Yes," I say.

"Great," she says. "Listen, I'm the Production Assistant for the CNC Morning Newsflash, and Ms. Anderson would love to interview you on tomorrow morning's broadcast. What do you say?"

"Um, what?" I say.

"I know this may come as a shock," she continues, "but you're trending as the hottest topic in the country right now. Of course, some people are defending what you did, but others are questioning your motives and the motives of all superheroes. This is your opportunity for people to hear directly from you. This is your chance to represent all caped crusaders."

"What do they want?" Grace asks, waving her hand impatiently in my face.

"They want to interview me," I say, covering the receiver. "They want me to talk about what happened."

"What?" Grace says, throwing her pillow to the ground. "Why does he get all of the luck?"

"Mr. Zero, are you still there?"

"Um, yes, I'm still here," I say.

"So, are you interested in appearing?" she asks. "Or do you want people to be against superheroes?"

"Against?" I say. "Well, no, of course I don't want that."

"So, you will appear?" she asks, more as a statement than a question.

"Well... I... I guess I have to," I say.

"Great!" she says. "We'll start promoting it now. And don't worry, millions of people will be tuned in to your every word. Get a good night's sleep because we'll see you bright and early at CNC Headquarters. We tape live at seven o'clock. Goodbye."

Uh, did she just say, 'millions of people?' And 'live?'

You know, maybe this isn't such a good idea.

I'm about to pull out when I suddenly hear a CLICK followed by a dial tone.

The phone is dead.

And apparently, so am I.

Meta Profile

Mover and Shaker

Name: Mover

Class: Meta-Morph

Power Level: ▮▮▮

- Body made of rock
- Considerable Strength
- Considerable Invulnerability

Name: Shaker

Class: Meta-morph

Power Level: ▮▮▮

- Body made of sand
- Considerable Shape-Shifting
- Can harden or disperse body into sand grains
- Sand particles always return to core form

THREE

I MAKE A FOOL OF MYSELF

In about ten minutes I'm going to look like a total goober on live television.

What a nightmare.

I mean, it's way too early in the morning, and I'm stuck in the green room at CNC headquarters, pacing back and forth like I'm about to be sent to the principal's office. There are millions of thoughts running through my brain, but none of them are clear because I didn't sleep a wink. Instead, I spent the entire night tossing and turning, freaked out of my mind.

Believe me, I'm kicking myself for not backing out of this in time. Of course, Dad tried to reassure me by telling me everything would be fine. According to him, it's moments like this that build character. I told him I don't need more stinking character!

At least Mom was on my side. When she got back to the Waystation and found out what happened, she was clearly concerned. And based on the number of strange facial expressions Mom and Dad were making at one another, it looked like they were having some pretty intense telepathic arguments. Unfortunately, despite how Mom may have felt about the situation, she told me I had to follow through on my commitment.

So, I tried the next best thing—pawning it off on Grace. After all, she's the one who wants to be the big-time celebrity—not me.

But she wasn't having it.

Even though she was clearly jealous when I first got the call, she claimed her reputation was shattered and she needed to lay low for a while. She called it something like 'image crisis management.' She said she wasn't going to do any public appearances until her fans forgot about her banana-on-the-head footage.

Good luck with that!

So here I am.

Just. Freaking. Wonderful.

Honestly, being on camera isn't my thing. Just knowing millions of people are watching my every move makes me want to hurl. To say I'm not looking forward to this is a gross understatement.

Suddenly, there's a KNOCK and the door opens.

"One minute, Mr. Zero," says a woman wearing a headset. Then, she shuts the door.

Awesome. I can't wait.

"Relax," Dad says. "You'll do fine."

"You sure about that?" Grace says. "Because he looks like he's gonna puke."

"Then why don't you do it?" I offer.

"No dice," she says, buffing her nails. "I'm on a temporary hiatus. Besides, they wanted you."

"You've got this," Dad says. "Just remember what we talked about. Be honest about how you feel and everything will be fine. Remember, you're representing all Meta heroes out there."

"Gee, that'll help me relax," I mutter.

I sure wish Mom was here, but she thought it would be best if she stayed behind. When she kissed me goodbye, she looked more nervous for me than I was. So that's probably not a good thing.

"Hey," Grace says, "your mask is crooked."

As I adjust it, the door pops open.

"It's time," the woman says.

"Well, it's been a great life," I say. "Say goodbye to Dog-Gone for me."

"Don't be silly," Dad says, patting my back. "You've got this."

"Break a leg," Grace says.

"I wish," I say, following the woman into the hall.

As we walk, I try not to hyperventilate. The woman

starts talking to me, but I'm so busy thinking about what I'm going to say I only catch a few words, like:

"Two segments—Debate—Questions—Okay?"

"Um, what?" I say.

"Are you okay?" she asks.

"Yeah," I say, lying through my teeth. "I'm fine."

"Great," she says, pushing me forward. "Because it's showtime. And whatever you do, don't drink from Ms. Anderson's mug. She hates that."

Suddenly, I realize we're on set!

It's a real TV studio, with bright lights, big cameras, and tons of people milling about. A man with a clipboard appears and attaches a microphone to the front of my costume. Then, he grabs my arm, and pulls me onto the stage, placing me in the center of three chairs behind a desk. I look over my shoulder at the big monitors filled with floating CNC logos.

"Eyes this way, kid," the man says, now standing in front. Then, he holds up his fingers and starts counting down. "And five, four—"

Suddenly, a blond-haired woman in a dark business suit plops into the seat on my right. She looks strangely familiar. Then, I realize it's Sarah Anderson herself!

OMG! This is about to happen!

"You look much smaller in person," she whispers.

"—one!" the man says.

I stare straight at the center camera and realize millions of people are watching me right now. I'm gonna hurl.

"Welcome to the CNC Morning Newsflash," Sarah Anderson says. "I'm Sarah Anderson, and as promised, our lead story this morning is the highly controversial topic being debated nationwide. Meta heroes—good guys or dangers to society? We're fortunate to have with us one of the Meta heroes responsible for the massive destruction that occurred yesterday in Keystone City's subway system. Surprisingly, he is an actual member of the Freedom Force who goes by the name of Epic Zebra. Welcome to the hot seat, Mr. Zebra."

"Um, thanks," I say. "But my name is Epic Z—"

"Mr. Zebra," she interrupts, "several prominent citizens are calling Meta heroes a menace to society. In your opinion, is that true?"

"W-What?" I say. "Oh no. We're heroes."

"Interesting," Sarah Anderson says. "But how can you call yourself heroes when your actions result in so much collateral damage?"

"Well," I say, "we don't mean to cause damage. We're trying to stop the bad guys who will do anything to get what they want. Without us, who would stop them?"

"Good point," Sarah Anderson says.

Gee, this isn't so bad. Maybe it'll be okay after all.

Suddenly, a figure sits down to my left.

I turn and do a double take.

It's a man with a crewcut wearing a dark suit.

I feel like I've seen him before. Then, it hits me!

It's General Winch!

What's he doing here?

"I see the other member of our panel has finally arrived," Sarah Anderson says. "Welcome, General Winch. You are the most outspoken critic of Meta heroes like Mr. Zebra here. What do you say to his response?"

"My apologies for being late," he says politely. "I was just speaking with the President." Then, he looks at me and his face turns bright red. "This child is asking who would stop those Meta criminals if superheroes weren't around? That's easy. Law enforcement professionals, that's who! The police. The Air Force. The Army. Highly trained professionals who follow proper safety procedures, unlike these costumed vigilantes who constantly put the public at risk."

Wow! He's so angry he's spitting everywhere.

"Your response, Mr. Zebra," Sarah Anderson asks.

"I—I—um…", I stammer. My mind is racing. I don't know what to say. I wasn't prepared to argue with this guy!

"Perhaps we should roll the footage again," Sarah Anderson says quickly. "That should help you out."

Suddenly, the video of yesterday's subway debacle starts playing on the monitors behind us.

"You okay, kid?" Sarah Anderson whispers. "You're slowing down the show here. This is a debate program. That means you actually have to debate him."

"Um, sorry," I say.

My throat feels really dry. I need some water or something. Then, I notice a mug in front of me. I grab it and take a sip, but as soon as the liquid goes into my mouth, I spit it back out.

"Yuck! What's that?"

"My coffee," Sarah Anderson says, clearly annoyed.

Then, the video ends on a frame of Grace with the banana peel on her head.

"And we're back," Sarah Anderson says. "Mr. Zebra, after viewing yesterday's battle in the subway station, how do you respond to General Winch's accusations that all Meta heroes are untrained vigilantes?"

I open my mouth but nothing comes out. Suddenly, my skin feels super warm. Boy, those stage lights are hot. I wipe beads of sweat from my forehead. Then, I notice the clipboard guy waving at me, encouraging me to say something. But I feel like I'm going to pass out.

"How about some statistics then?" Sarah Anderson jumps in. "According to the accountants, your actions will cost Keystone City over thirteen million dollars in repairs. And the 'L' line is scheduled to be out of service for up to six months. What do you have to say about that?"

Wow, that's a lot of time and money.

"Not to mention innocent lives were nearly lost," General Winch adds. "There's no price tag for that."

"Mr. Zebra?"

"I… um," I mutter. "C-Can I use the bathroom?"

"Okaaay," Sarah Anderson says. "This sounds like a

great time for a commercial break. We'll be right back with this stimulating debate about Meta heroes."

"And cut," the guy with the clipboard announces.

"Listen, kid," Sarah Anderson says. "You've got to pull it together. He's eating you alive out there. If you're going to defend superheroes, you've only got one more segment to do it."

"Okay," I say, standing up.

But as I move past the General, he smirks and says, "Are you really the best they've got?"

I brush past him and head off-stage. The woman with the headset meets me and points me to a nearby room. It's the bathroom!

"Um, you should probably give me your microphone before you go in there," she says.

"Oh yeah," I say, popping it off and handing it over.

Then, I push open the door and lock it behind me.

Thank goodness I'm alone! Truthfully, I didn't have to go to the bathroom, but I needed to get out of there. I mean, what am I doing? I can only imagine what Dad and Grace are thinking. I'm making a total fool of myself!

Why am I letting that guy get under my skin? What does he know about facing Meta villains? I'd like to see him take down Mover and Shaker.

But why can't I tell him that?

I lean over the sink and look into the mirror.

Yep, I look exactly like I feel. My skin is red, my eyes are puffy, and my hair is an absolute mess.

I splash cold water on my face to cool down. I need to speak up. I need to—

"Elliott Harkness."

Huh?

My head nearly hits the faucet, because when I look into the mirror, I'm not alone!

Standing behind me are four men.

But by their faces, they aren't men at all!

In fact, they're not even human!

One has a face like a bug, another looks like a horse, and the other two... well, they don't look like anything I've ever seen before. Then, I notice they're all wearing blue uniforms with yellow stripes on their shoulders.

Wait, I know those uniforms!

"Y-You're Intergalactic Paladins!" I say.

They don't answer but I know I'm right. Their uniforms are just like the one Proog was wearing when I met him at ArmaTech—in the past! Poor Proog. He never stood a chance against that slimeball Norman Fairchild. Man, that was one of the hardest missions I've ever had.

Then, I realize they're all holding silver wands—Infinity Wands—and I shudder. The last time I saw an Infinity Wand, I accidentally destroyed it, giving birth to Meta-Taker!

"Meta readings are confirmed," horse-face says, waving his wand over my head. "He's an exact match."

An exact match? To what?

"Listen, fellas," I say, "I'd love to help you out, but now's not a good time. See, I've got to get out of this bathroom here and go finish a TV show. You do realize we're all standing in a bathroom, right?"

"Elliott Harkness, you are being placed under arrest for aiding in the escape of a notorious intergalactic felon," bug-head says. "You will stand before the Interstellar Court of Law to defend your crimes."

"The Interstellar what?" I say. "What crimes?"

Suddenly, it occurs to me I should probably get out of here. And fast.

"Now," horse-face says.

But before I can move, the four Paladins raise their wands and there's a blinding flash of light.

And we're gone.

Meta Profile

Name: General Winch
Role: Citizen   Status: Active

VITALS:

Race: Human
Real Name: William Winch
Height: 6'1"
Weight: 210 lbs
Eye Color: Blue
Hair Color: White

META POWERS:

Class: None
Power Level:

- Meta 0
- Former Chairman of the Joint Chiefs of Staff

CHARACTERISTICS:

Combat	23	
Durability	15	
Leadership	98	
Strategy	95	
Willpower	90	

FOUR

I FACE JAIL TIME

When I open my eyes, we're no longer in the bathroom.

In fact, I don't think we're even on Earth!

That's because other than the four Intergalactic Paladins surrounding me, there's nothing else I recognize.

We're standing inside a massive stadium that's open to a purple sky with two moons! Beneath my feet is a red track encircling a fifty-foot wide gray disc sitting smack dab in the center. And to add to the weirdness, there's a big black cube floating twenty feet above the disc.

Yep, we're definitely not on Earth anymore.

I'm about to ask my captors where they've taken me when I realize we're not alone. The stadium's stands are filled with people. Except they aren't people at all.

They're more aliens!

Aliens wearing Paladin uniforms!

Then it hits me. I know exactly where I am.

I'm on the home planet of the Intergalactic Paladins!

"Turn and face the Council," horse-face demands.

Council? What Council? It's not until I spin around that I see seven more aliens sitting on a platform behind me. Huh? Where'd they come from?

But unlike the Intergalactic Paladins, these guys are all wearing robes—black robes—like judges.

I don't know what's going on, but by the glum expressions on their faces, I'd say we're not off to a good start. Then, the green, scaly guy in the middle pulls himself up with his large staff and shuffles to the edge of the platform, his fishy eyes fixed on me.

I take a deep breath. Okay, I'm sure this is just a big misunderstanding. I'll be back home in no time.

"Elliott Harkness of Earth," he bellows, "welcome to Paladin Planet. I am Quovaar, Supreme Justice of the Interstellar Council, and you are accused of committing unspeakable crimes against the universe!"

Then again, maybe not.

"The charges against you are serious," he continues, "and you will stand trial for your actions."

"Stand trial?" I blurt out. "For what?"

"Heed my warning, Elliott Harkness," Quovaar says, "ignorance will not serve you well here. But to ensure there are no flaws in our proceedings, I shall formally state the charges against you. First, you stand accused of unlawfully destroying an Infinity Wand. Second, you are charged with aiding and abetting the escape of Krule the Conqueror from the 13th Dimension. The prosecution will demonstrate that you committed these crimes willingly and with malicious intent, endangering the lives of billions who wish to live in peace."

Wait, what?

Did he just say Krule escaped from the 13th Dimension? And for some reason, they think I helped him? That's nuts!

"Um, pardon me," I say. "But you've got this all wrong. That's not exactly what—"

"Tell us, Elliott Harkness," Quovaar interjects, pointing his staff towards the center of the arena. "Does this look familiar?"

My eyes follow his sweeping arm to the hovering black cube. Suddenly, it splits in half, exposing a purple object. My jaw drops.

"The Cosmic Key!" I exclaim as a chill runs down my spine. Supposedly, the Cosmic Key is the only key that can open the 13th Dimension.

"Yes," Quovaar says. "Your positive identification of the Cosmic Key is noted for the record. But by your reaction, I assume you are surprised to see it in our possession? After all, it has taken decades for us to recover it. But recover it we have, although too late to prevent Krule's escape."

My mind is racing. I mean, the last time I saw the Cosmic Key was like, thirty years ago when I used TechnocRat's Time Warper device to go back into the past to fix my present. In fact, I was about to destroy the Cosmic Key and rid the world of Meta-Taker forever, but at the last second one of the Time Trotter's Pterodactyls appeared out of nowhere and snatched it away. Then, Krule's ugly, three-eyed mug appeared and he bragged about how he'd take over the universe.

Now that he's free, is that what he's doing?

And why do they think I helped him? How are they even coming to that conclusion?

"Listen," I start. "I—"

"I recommend saving your arguments for your defense," Quovaar says. "Your trial will commence tomorrow upon the rising of the three suns. Per the Order of the Paladin, you will be permitted to call upon one witness to support your testimony, and the final verdict of guilty or not guilty will be revealed by the power of the Paladin's Pulse."

The power of the Paladin's what?

Suddenly, Quovaar raises his arms, and a giant, pulsating egg rises from behind the platform. The thing is huge, nearly the size of a hot-air balloon. But as I look closer, I realize that the big egg is made up of hundreds of smaller eggs, each white in color.

What is that thing?

"This is the Paladin's Pulse," Quovaar continues,

"the most unbiased legal system in the universe. Each individual sphere on the surface of the Paladin's Pulse is perfectly attuned to the inner conscience of one Paladin present. If the majority of spheres turn red at the conclusion of your trial, you will be found guilty. However, if the majority of spheres are green, you will be declared innocent."

"Hang on a sec," I say, cleaning out my ears. "Do you mean this huge egg thing is gonna reveal if everyone thinks I'm innocent?"

"Or guilty," Quovaar says, narrowing his eyes.

Now I'm totally confused. I mean, the way Proog talked about the Intergalactic Paladins made them seem like noble, peace-loving heroes. Yet, I'm getting the feeling these guys are thirsty for blood. It's like they're ready to send me down the river no matter what the truth may be.

"Look," I say, "I'm not sure what's going on here, but I'm a hero just trying to save lives, and occasionally the universe. I'm not sure you've got the right guy."

"Maric?" Quovaar says. "Your reading?"

Suddenly, horse-face steps forward.

"Yes, Supreme Justice," Maric says with a low bow. "This child's Meta signature corresponds precisely with the Meta signature from Proog's Infinity Wand."

Proog's Wand? What's he talking about?

But then it all comes back to me. When I was trying to stop Norman Fairchild, I absorbed a tremendous amount of Meta energy from the unconscious Skelton known as the Blood Master. And that Meta energy came directly from Proog's Infinity Wand!

Holy cow!

It must have stuck to me!

"Then it is confirmed," Quovaar says. "Elliott Harkness, tonight you will have ample time to build your case while in our prison. Be forewarned that here on Paladin Planet it is useless to use your Meta powers. You are surrounded by hundreds of Intergalactic Paladins, all of whom have been granted the authority to take whatever actions are necessary to subdue you if you try to escape—including your death."

I swallow hard. As I look into the stands, I see hundreds of bright lights. All of the Paladins have activated their Infinity Wands in a show of force!

"Consider wisely who you will call upon as a witness," Quovaar continues. "That individual will provide the only testimony used for your defense. Tomorrow, upon the rising of the three suns, your trial will begin. If you are found innocent, you will be cleared of all charges and returned to your home. But if you are found guilty, you will be punished."

"P-Punished?" I say. "What does that mean?"

"Per the Order of the Paladin," Quovaar says, "if you are found guilty you will be banished to the 13th Dimension."

Suddenly, the disc in the center slides open and I'm

staring into a circle of swirling, purple energy.

No. Freaking. Way.

That must be the 13th Dimension!

"Try to get some rest," Quovaar says. "Because what happens tomorrow will determine your fate forever."

***

Well, I certainly didn't see this coming.

Somehow, I went from flunking a debate on live television to sitting inside an alien prison being charged with crimes I didn't commit. I couldn't have predicted this one with a crystal ball.

I wonder what Dad and Grace are thinking. I'm sure they think I ran away from the CNC building and went into hiding. Not that I blame them. I know I made a fool of myself up there. Unfortunately, that'll be the last memory they'll have of me because I'll probably never see them again.

I take in my bleak surroundings. It's me, a concrete floor, and a whole lot of prison bars. And to add to the ambiance, the whole place smells like gym socks.

Lovely.

I sit down on the floor and stretch out my sore arms. Boy, those Paladins who carried me down three flights of stairs were rough. Of course, I'm sure all of the other prisoners they carted me past are even rougher. I hope I'm in solitary confinement because I don't want to run into any of them.

I mean, I'm no criminal. At least I don't think I am.

Technically, I did destroy Proog's Infinity Wand, but I was only acting in self-defense. If I didn't blow it up, Fairchild would have used it to obliterate me. Of course, I also ended up creating Meta-Taker in the process.

So, who knows? Maybe I should be sent to the 13th Dimension for that alone.

I think back to my conversation with Proog. He said the 13th Dimension is where the Intergalactic Paladins put the most dangerous criminals in the galaxy. And once you're sent there you not only lose your powers, but you also live forever.

Wonderful.

I get to spend eternity with Meta villains who will never die.

That is, unless I can prove my innocence.

Quovaar said I can call upon one witness, so I run through my options. Of course, Mom and Dad come to mind first, but since they're my parents I'm not sure they'd be considered objective. Grace? Nah, she might actually want me banished to the 13th Dimension. There's Dog-Gone, but all he has to offer is slobber.

I go through the rest of the Freedom Force.

TechnocRat is so annoying they'd probably throw the book at me. Makeshift started as a villain, so that won't work. Blue Bolt talks too fast. Master Mime can't talk at all. Shadow Hawk is a possibility, but he'd probably lecture everyone on right versus wrong which wouldn't work in my favor.

So, my options are pretty limited.

I wonder how I'll look in an orange jumpsuit.

"Pssst," comes a sharp whisper.

I look through the bars and see some alien dude staring at me from the cell across the hall. He's bald, with white skin, and big red eyes. He's sitting on the floor cross-legged and wearing a red uniform.

"Pssst," he repeats, this time standing up and wrapping his fingers around his cell door. "Are you deaf, kid?"

"No," I say. "What do you want?"

"To pass the time," he says. "My name is Caliban. What's yours?"

At first, I'm reluctant to tell him. But then I remember I'm in prison, so what do I have to lose?

"I'm Epic Zero."

"Epic Zero, huh?" he says. "You're a little young for this place, aren't you? Must be a good story as to why you're here."

"It's a long story," I say. "Honestly, I'm still trying to figure it out myself."

"Ha," he says. "Well, we've got plenty of time for stories around here—long or otherwise. How about if I tell you mine first?"

"Sure," I say. "Why not?"

"Okay, then," Caliban says, leaning against his cell

door. "You see, I'm no crook. I was the captain of a cargo ship. We prided ourselves on making deliveries on time. If it absolutely, positively had to be there by the next lunar cycle, you'd call us. Life was good until we took a job in the Trans-Neptunian region. Everything was going smoothly until we picked up a bunch of strange readings on our radar. At first, we thought it was a taxi fleet, but then we realized we were being chased by warships."

Warships?

Like, Skelton warships?

"We tried outrunning them," he continues, "but we had no chance. They were first-class vehicles, top of the line. Of course, we sent out a distress signal, but as they closed in, we knew we were doomed because on their hull was a symbol—a three-eyed skull and crossbones."

"Three eyes?" I ask.

"Exactly," Caliban says. "These weren't just any warships. These were pirate ships, manned by Krule the Conqueror and his Motley Crew."

Krule? So there's my proof. He did escape!

"Honestly, I thought I was seeing a ghost," Caliban says. "Last I heard, Krule and his men were trapped in the 13th Dimension, yet it was clearly him. He overtook us in no time, but instead of shooting us down, he boarded us. I'll never forget that strange third eye. As soon as it lit up, my crew walked onto his ship like they were robots!"

Yep, that's him all right.

"Yet, for some reason, he didn't hypnotize me," Caliban says. "Krule said my men were his now. Then, he had them load a giant black box into my cargo hold and told me to head straight for Paladin Planet. He said 'they' would always be on his tail as long as he had this box in his possession. I asked him who 'they' were and what was in the box, but he said it was none of my business. He warned that if I didn't do as he said, my men's lives would be at risk. After that, he took off with his fleet."

Hang on. Did he say a 'giant black box?'

Does that mean—?

"I knew he was a man of his word, and if I disobeyed, he would punish my men. I couldn't live with myself if something happened to my lads, so I followed his instructions. But as soon as I entered Paladin Planet's atmosphere, I was intercepted by a squadron of Paladins who took over my ship. When they opened the black box. I'll never forget what was inside. It was this strange purple key. They called it the—"

"—Cosmic Key!" I blurt out.

"The very one," he says. "They accused me of helping Krule hide evidence of his escape and dumped me in here. My trial was set for tomorrow but for some reason, it's been delayed. But I don't plan on sticking around."

Then, he looks suspiciously from side-to-side and whispers, "Because we're busting out of here. Tonight."

"Um, excuse me?" I whisper back. "Did you just say you're busting out of here... tonight?"

"Yeah, tonight," he says. "Do you think anyone around here really has a shot at a fair trial? I'm not going into the 13th Dimension. We're breaking out at midnight. Do you want to come along?"

"Wow," I say. I mean, I wasn't expecting that. Then again, I wasn't expecting to be here at all. But Caliban's words echo in my brain. *Do you think anyone around here really has a shot at a fair trial?'*

What if he's right? I mean, I know I'm innocent but what if the trial is rigged? What if they're planning on setting me up? I could end up banished to the 13th Dimension no matter what I say!

But something is holding me back.

"Um, I'll think about it," I say. "But how are you gonna do it? I mean, Paladins are crawling all over the place."

"Oh, don't worry about that," Caliban says, nodding towards the cell to his left. "We've got him."

Him? Who's him?

But as I stoop down to get a better look into Caliban's neighboring cell, I see a hulking figure sitting on the floor—a figure with long, curved horns on his head.

OMG!

I-I know him!

It's... Aries?

Meta Profile

Name: Quovaar
Role: Hero   Status: Active

VITALS:

Race: Unknown
Real Name: Quovaar
Height: 6'0"
Weight: 190 lbs
Eye Color: Green
Hair Color: Bald

META POWERS:

Class: Magic
Power Level: ▇▇▇▇▢

- **Supreme Justice of the Interstellar Court**
- **Member of the Intergalactic Paladins**

CHARACTERISTICS:

Combat	98	
Durability	51	
Leadership	100	
Strategy	100	
Willpower	100	

FIVE

I BUST A MOVE

Midnight comes way faster than I expected.

Ever since I learned about Caliban's crazy plan I've been pacing back and forth in my cell like a caged animal. I mean, is he serious? How's he going to bust out of here? This place is swarming with Paladins!

Just thinking about it freaks me out.

But Caliban doesn't look worried in the least.

According to him, his plan is foolproof. He said he's been watching the guards closely for days now, and there's a one-minute window where they leave the prison to switch shifts—right at the stroke of midnight. That's when he's planning to make his move.

That sounds great in theory, but honestly, I'm not so sure that's the best idea. But then again, what other options do I have? Based on Quovaar's tone, my trial is probably just a formality. If I were a betting man, I'd say

I'm destined for a date with the 13th Dimension!

And that's the last place I want to be!

The only part of Caliban's plan giving me any shred of hope is having Aries on our side. After all, Aries and I fought together on Arena World, and I know he's as tough as they come. Plus, we're both members of the Zodiac which is a pretty unique bond.

So, you'd think I'd be feeling more optimistic, but there's one teeny-tiny thing making me uneasy.

Aries won't talk to me.

I don't know why, but every time I try getting his attention he doesn't respond. Instead, he just sits there like a brooding rock. I've got no clue what's wrong.

After all, the Aries I remember had major swagger. When I asked Caliban about it, he said Aries has been like this ever since he arrived, but not to worry because Aries is aligned with the plan. That's great news, but it also raises a question:

What is Aries even doing here?

I mean, he's a big-time Meta hero. I'm here because of a big misunderstanding. But why is Aries on Paladin Planet? I couldn't imagine him committing a crime.

But I guess I'll have to wait for that answer, because just then Caliban walks up to his cell door, looks up and down the hall, and declares: "Now!"

Now?

Wait. Does he mean, like, 'now, now?'

RIP! CLANG!

There's an ear-splitting noise to my right, and when I turn Aries is tossing the front door of his cell to the ground! Seconds later, he's in the corridor, and with two more ear-jarring yanks, he's ripped off the doors to Caliban's cell, and mine too!

Suddenly, SIRENS wail.

"Let's go!" Caliban says.

They take off, but for a split second, I'm frozen. I mean, am I really going to do this? As soon as I step out of this cell, I'll look totally guilty.

"Come on!" Caliban yells. "It's your only chance!"

Caliban falls in behind Aries who is bulldozing his way down the hall. But my mind is still spinning. If I go with them, I'm basically telling the Interstellar Council I'm guilty. But if I stay and lose the trial, I'll be doomed forever!

I-I don't know what to do.

I lean forward. Caliban and Aries are nearly gone. Suddenly, my heart starts racing. I can't stay here. I mean, I shouldn't even be here. This may be my only chance.

"Wait for me!" I call, catching up to them.

I brush past the outstretched arms of other prisoners, but I ignore their pleas. There's no way I'm stopping to free them. I mean, who knows what they did to get put in here?

"What do we do now?" I ask.

"Now we get my ship," Caliban says. "Then, I can fly us off of this planet. We just have to break into the impound yard where they keep the confiscated vehicles."

"Great," I say, "where's that?"

"Next to the stadium," he says.

"Oh," I say. "You mean the stadium where all of the Intergalactic Paladins hang out? Great plan."

Seconds later we're in the stairwell.

I figure this little jailbreak will go one of two ways. Either we're clobbered and somehow manage to escape, or we're clobbered and thrown back in jail. Either way, a clobbering is coming.

Why does this stuff always happen to me?

"Hey!" comes a shout from down the hall.

I look up to find three Paladins heading our way! I stop dead in my tracks, ready to retreat, but the next thing I know, Aries rears back his giant fist and pummels them with one punch, sending them flying like bowling pins!

Let the clobbering begin!

"Move!" Caliban yells.

Aries leaps the entire staircase in one bound, while Caliban takes the steps three at a time. I'm huffing and puffing behind, stair by measly stair.

Man, I really need to do more cardio!

I hear more commotion, and by the time I reach the top level, I step over six more unconscious Paladins. I'm impressed. I remember Aries being tough, but I don't remember him being this tough! As I step outside, I find Aries and Caliban getting their bearings.

Caliban is pointing left and I see the stadium in the

distance. Then, I see a bunch of ships parked behind a tall gate next door. That must be the impound yard!

More SIRENS blare.

But this one sounds different. Caliban stops to listen.

"That signal means 'all-hands on deck,'" Caliban says, "They're calling the entire force into action. Let's go!"

But we're too late.

Because when I look up into the sky, dozens of bright lights are heading our way.

If I have any chance of surviving this pummeling, I can't rely on my own physical prowess. So, I concentrate hard, pulling in Aries' powers of Super-strength, and then I'm ready to go.

"Stick with me," I tell Caliban, grabbing his wrist.

"Wait," he says, "what are you—"

But before he can finish, I tuck him under my arm like a football and jump, hurtling a ridiculous distance. I stay close behind Aries, who is clearing a path in front of us, knocking Paladin after Paladin out of the air.

Seconds later, the impound yard is within range. There must be hundreds of ships in there. I can't believe it, we're actually going to make it!

BOOM!

Then, Aries gets creamed.

I shield my eyes as we fly through the debris, but Aries isn't so lucky. He drops to the ground like a bomb, sending up tons of rubble. As soon as I touch down, I put on the brakes, kicking up a huge dust cloud.

"Don't stop!" Caliban demands. "Keep going!"

"But Aries is back there," I say. "We can't just leave him."

"Do it!" Caliban yells. "Or we're dead!"

I look up and I know he's right. The Paladins are gaining in number, circling above us like vultures. But I can't just leave Aries. He's my friend.

"I just need a second," I say, putting Caliban on his feet before running towards Aries.

"Fool!" Caliban says, bolting towards the impound yard, drawing half of the Paladins with him.

But I can't stop to help him, I need to get to Aries.

I stumble down the newly formed crater with Aries lying at its center.

"Are you okay?" I ask.

"Better than him," Aries grunts, sitting up.

"Nooooo!" comes a scream.

Looking up, I see a squad of Paladins blasting Caliban into submission.

"Caliban!" I yell.

"No," Aries says, standing up. "He's not Caliban. His real name is Xenox Xanth. He's one of Krule's key lieutenants."

"Wait, what?" I say. "You mean, he lied to us?"

"No," Aries says. "He lied to you. I knew who he was the second I laid eyes on him. Now stay alert. Here comes trouble."

I look up to see the rest of the Paladins heading our way! I'm about to grab more of Aries' power, when—

THOOM!

Suddenly, the Paladins are blown miles away!

I turn to find Aries with his arms outstretched and palms together.

"Thunderclap," he says. "Let's get to the stadium."

"The stadium?" I say. "But what about the impound yard?"

"That was Xenox's plan," he says. "My plan was always the stadium. I only told him I was following his plan because I figured he might be a useful distraction. Looks like I was right."

I look over to find Caliban, or rather Xenox, being arrested. But I'm totally confused. Why is Aries going to the stadium? But before I can ask him, he says—

"Follow me," and he's off.

Well, unless I want to be captured by the Paladins, I have no choice, but my mind is totally mixed up right now. I have no clue what's going on. And that's not a great feeling.

Aries leaps over the stadium wall and I'm right behind him, landing on the dirt infield. This time, there aren't any Paladins around, but I'm sure that won't last long. My eyes immediately go to the black box floating over the gray disc. Is what Caliban—or Xenox—or whatever his name is—told me about the black box also a lie? Did Krule really ambush his ship, or did Krule intentionally send Xenox to Paladin Planet with the Cosmic Key on board?

I shudder. Just being near the Cosmic Key makes me nervous. Then, I get a bad thought. Is Aries after the Cosmic Key? Is that what he wants?

I don't know, but I do know one thing, I'm sick and tired of not getting the full story. I mean, why didn't Aries tell me Xenox was a phony?

And what else hasn't he told me?

"Okay," I say. "Spill it. What are we doing here?"

"I'm on a rescue mission," Aries says.

"A rescue mission?" I say. "Um, sorry if you haven't noticed, but aren't we the ones who need rescuing around here?"

"No," he says. "I'm here to save Wind Walker."

My eyebrows hit my hairline.

Wind Walker?

The last time I saw Wind Walker was when he saved me from the Rising Suns and worm-holed me into Elliott 2's universe. After that, he said he was going to try to solve the riddle of the Blur, but I never heard from him again. In fact, I even tried calling for him in the Hydrostation but he never appeared. I always wondered what happened to him.

"Are you saying Wind Walker is here?" I ask. "On Paladin Planet?"

"No," Aries says, pointing down. "He's not here. He's in there."

But as I follow his finger my jaw drops, because he's pointing right at the gray disc.

But—But that's the cover to the… the…

"Wind Walker is trapped inside the 13th Dimension," Aries continues, "and I'm going to get him out."

Say what? I'm in total shock. Two minutes ago, I thought we were getting off of this planet to avoid going into the 13th Dimension! Now, he's telling me he wants to go inside the 13th Dimension voluntarily! Is he nuts?

"Sorry," I say. "But how do you know he's actually in there?"

"Because he haunts me in my nightmares," Aries says matter-of-factly. "He comes to me every night, begging for my help."

For a second, I'm speechless.

I mean, is he serious?

"Um," I say, "are you sure about this? I mean, everyone has bad dreams now and then. I have a recurring nightmare where my sister is the leader of the Freedom Force, but I know it's not true."

"I understand your skepticism," he says. "But I'm certain he's reaching out to me. Look, I won't tell you what I had to do to get the Paladins to lock me up here. But now that I'm here, I'm not turning back."

He looks so determined I can't deny he believes it.

But do I?

"We fought together as teammates on Arena World," Aries says. "Will you join me in my quest to save Wind

Walker?"

As I look into his brown eyes, they flicker with a strange blue energy. But just as quickly, it's gone.

That's weird. Am I imagining things now?

"Well?" Aries asks.

I take a deep breath. I mean, I could never walk away if Wind Walker needed my help, no matter how crazy the circumstances.

"Of course I'll help," I say, shocked to hear my own words. "But how do we get inside?"

As Aries looks up, I feel like a bonehead.

The Cosmic Key!

"Stop them!" comes a voice.

I turn to find hundreds of bright lights in the sky.

The Paladins!

RRIIIIPPPP!

I look back over at Aries who is now holding the huge, gray disc. Peering down, I'm suddenly staring into a swirling abyss of purple energy.

It's the 13th Dimension!

"Grab the Cosmic Key!" Aries yells.

What? The last time I touched a cosmic entity, I couldn't get rid of it!

"Now!" he yells. Then, he tosses the gray disc like a Frisbee, striking the black cube so hard it splits in half, exposing the Cosmic Key above us.

"Halt!" a Paladin yells.

They're nearly on top of us! I don't have time to grab

the Key now, even if I tried!

So instead, I go to plan B.

I concentrate hard, pushing my energy towards the Cosmic Key. Then, I pull it back in and the power surge hits me like a Mack truck.

There's a tremendous rush of power.

Like my body feels electric.

But it's more power than I can contain.

"Q-Quick!" I stammer, reaching out. "Grab me!"

I feel him wrap his large hand around mine, and then we jump into the circle of nebulous purple energy, slipping like ghosts into the 13th Dimension.

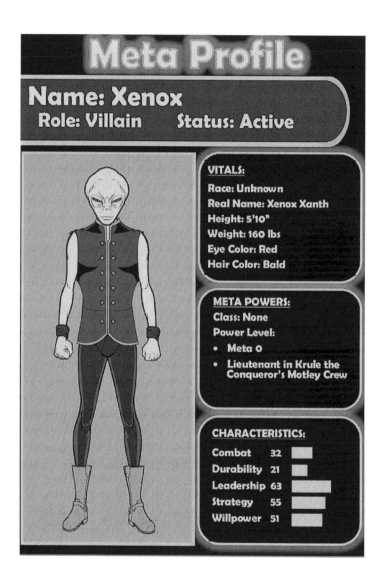

Meta Profile

Name: Xenox
Role: Villain   Status: Active

VITALS:

Race: Unknown
Real Name: Xenox Xanth
Height: 5'10"
Weight: 160 lbs
Eye Color: Red
Hair Color: Bald

META POWERS:

Class: None
Power Level:
- Meta 0
- Lieutenant in Krule the Conqueror's Motley Crew

CHARACTERISTICS:

Combat	32	
Durability	21	
Leadership	63	
Strategy	55	
Willpower	51	

SIX

I HATE THE NUMBER THIRTEEN

It's funny how your mind wanders when you're falling to your doom.

I mean, even though I'm plunging into the 13th Dimension, strangely, all I'm thinking about is how I could use a vacation right now. From what I've heard, most kids get to go on a few cool vacations, like Disney World, the Grand Canyon, or Niagara Falls.

But me? No siree Bob.

According to Mom and Dad, superheroes don't take vacations. Instead, we're supposed to be on call all the time. You know, just in case the world needs saving.

I get it, but don't superheroes deserve a break too? I know we do exciting work, but I'd trade relaxing on a beach for falling into the 13th Dimension any day of the week.

But I'm not sure Aries would agree with me. Based on his steely expression, he looks like he's actually excited to enter the 13th Dimension. Which is impressive because I'm downright terrified!

I mean, what are we thinking? Aries said he's sure Wind Walker is in the 13th Dimension, but what if he's wrong? Then we just dove in here for nothing!

But I guess it's my fault we're in this situation to begin with. Instead of absorbing the power of the Cosmic Key, I could have just let the Paladins capture us. I'm guessing that would have been a lot less painful than whatever's waiting for us when we hit the bottom of this thing.

If we ever hit the bottom of this thing.

It feels like we've been falling through purplish matter forever, but suddenly we break into a thick layer of gray fog. I'm still holding Aries' hand, but I can't see him anymore! I'm about to call out when we enter a beige sky and then—

"Oof!" I exclaim, slamming into something hard.

Aries and I disconnect, and my back is killing me from whatever I just smashed into, but I don't have time to lick my wounds because I'm suddenly tumbling down a rocky mountainside! I'm picking up speed fast, but there's nothing to grab to slow my fall. All I can do is shield my head as my body fumbles end-over-end like a football until I finally hit the bottom. A plume of dirt kicks up into the air and lands back on my face.

I sit up, spitting out a mouthful.

Just. Freaking. Wonderful.

"Are you okay?" Aries asks, standing heroically in front of me like he just stepped out of a toothpaste commercial.

"Yeah," I say, wiping my chin. "Did that rock monster nail you too?"

"No," he says. "I landed on a sand dune."

"Of course you did," I mutter, getting to my feet. "Where are we anyway?"

"Somewhere in the 13th Dimension I presume," he says. "If we're going to find Wind Walker, we'd better move fast. The longer we stay out in the open like this, the easier a target we'll become."

Speaking of out in the open, all I see is desert for miles around, but it's not smooth and flat. The terrain varies widely, with dips and valleys offset by the occasional sand dune. Way off in the distance are giant, craggy mountains, like the one I crashed into.

Great. The 13th Dimension is a giant wasteland.

I shiver. And boy, it's cold. Then I look up and realize there's no sun. That gray fog blankets the entire sky. And there's a strange black dot moving—

Suddenly, Aries grabs me and pulls me against the mountain.

"Hey!" I say, "why'd you—"

"Shhh!" he whispers.

When I look back up, I realize he's right. That little black dot has become a large black creature, with giant wings and a long tail. Thankfully, it doesn't seem like it noticed us, but it's looping around in circles.

We stay still for what seems like an eternity until the creature finally disappears.

"Okay," I say, "how about we speed this rescue thing up? Did Wind Walker tell you where to find him? Because there's pretty much a whole lot of nothing in every direction."

"No," Aries says. "This is going to be a huge guessing game. Maybe there's a landmark or something I'll recognize."

"You mean, like her?" I ask.

I do a double take because standing behind Aries is an old woman who simply wasn't there before. She's hunched over, wearing a black robe with a hood that covers most of her face, except for her hooked nose and blue eyes. Her very, very alert-looking blue eyes.

"Who are you?" Aries asks, taking a step backward.

"Well, I should ask the same of you, shouldn't I?" she says, with an unnerving smirk.

"We're just passing through," he says. "Our names aren't important."

"Yes, names aren't important, are they?" she says, waving dismissively. Then she looks at Aries and says, "My what large horns you have." Then, she looks down at me and says "And you are but a child. It is so rare to find a child here. Did you just arrive?"

"Yes," Aries says.

"Oh, you poor, unfortunate souls," she says, sympathetically. "I've lost a bit of hearing in my old age, but did you just say you were passing through? If so, I'm sorry to tell you that those who enter the realm can never leave."

"The realm?" I ask.

"Oh, yes," she says, with a sweep of her arm. "This is the realm. And those who enter never leave. Unless, of course, you know of a way out?"

Aries and I look at one another and I swallow hard.

No, we don't know a way out. I mean, I didn't have time to grab the Cosmic Key like Aries asked, and I don't feel its power inside of me anymore. Plus, we've fallen so far from Paladin Planet I couldn't duplicate it again if I tried. Now we'll be stuck here... forever.

"I thought as much," she sighs, her crooked body deflating. "I always ask anyone new if they know how to get out. I've been here for so long it would be nice to escape this drab world and allow these weary bones to finally expire somewhere more colorful."

For a second, she looks so sad I feel bad for her. But then I realize I can't let my guard down. I mean, we're in the freaking 13th Dimension! If this grandma is stuck here, I'm guessing it's for a good reason.

"Well," she says. "Perhaps I could offer you some help? I know so much about the realm. Oh, I used to be so good at helping."

"And what would you want in exchange for that help?" Aries asks.

"Oh, nothing," she says. "Nothing at all. Helping is a reward in itself. My father used to say that. Once upon a time I so enjoyed being helpful. But no one seems to want my help anymore. It's a shame really. I can be very helpful if I want to be. Very helpful indeed."

Aries looks at me and I nod.

"Okay," he says. "We're looking for someone."

"Aren't we all?" she says glumly. "But isn't it always the case that when you're most in search of a friend, none can be found?"

"Well," I say, "We're looking for—"

"Yes, friends are hard to find," Aries says, cutting me off and throwing me a look that says 'stop-talking.' "Tell me, who is in charge of the realm?"

Huh? Why'd he interrupt me like that?

"Oh, ho, ho," she snickers, wringing her hands. "Cutting to the chase, aren't you? Yes, the realm always has a ruler. Especially of late. First, there was Broote the Barbaric. But he was dethroned."

"Broote?" Aries asks, his voice rising. "Broote is here? In the realm?"

"Um, who is Broote?" I ask.

"Later," Aries says. "So, tell me, who is powerful enough to dethrone the mighty Broote?"

"A man of three eyes," she says. "He was known as

Krule. Krule the—"

"—Conqueror!" I blurt out.

"Yes," she says. "Krule the Conqueror drove Broote from power and ruled the realm with an iron fist. But he and his army have gone missing."

Missing?

Okay, I know for sure Krule isn't missing. He somehow escaped from the 13th Dimension by getting the Cosmic Key. But maybe she doesn't know that. Well, I'm certainly not gonna tell her.

"Hold on," Aries says. "So, if Krule is missing why isn't Broote back in power?"

"Because there is another," she says. "And he is even more powerful. Very powerful indeed."

"And does this powerful man have a name?" I ask.

"As you said, names aren't important," she says. "But as the ruler of the realm he demands to be called 'King,' and all must bow down before him. If you refuse, he can be quite ruthless—more ruthless than even Krule. But the King knows everything about the realm and its inhabitants. Maybe even more than me."

"And where can we find this King?" Aries asks.

"Well, isn't it obvious?" she says. "The King is in the castle. Aren't all Kings in a castle?"

I look around, but I don't see any castles towering over the horizon.

"Oh, you will not see the castle like that," she says like she's reading my mind. "This castle is underground."

Underground?

Seriously?

"Would you like me to take you there?" she asks. "I can be very helpful if I want to be."

"Um, no thanks," Aries says. "But maybe you could point us in the right direction?"

"Oh, I do enjoy being helpful," she says. Then, she spins around three times, finally stopping with her arm pointed towards the biggest mountain on the horizon. "It is that way. You must pass through the Narrow Chasm and the entrance will be just on the other side. But be careful, there are those here who will try to harm you. Oh, and there is something else. But no, I mustn't. Please forgive me, there is a child present. Maybe I should…"

"Wait," I say. "What is it?"

"Oh, no, I don't want to upset you any further," she says, backing up. "I have so enjoyed being helpful."

"It's okay," Aries says. "He can take it. You've been very helpful so far. We would appreciate any additional help."

"You would?" she says, her eyes widening. "Oh, well that's wonderful."

"Yes," I say. "Please."

"Very well," she says, her eyes narrowing, "you should know that something else lives in the realm. Something evil."

A chill runs down my spine.

"It is known only as 'the Shadow,'" she continues.

"It has lived in the realm since the very beginning—seeing all, hearing all, understanding all. It is ever-present. And it is waiting."

"Um, waiting for what?" I ask.

"For its chance to escape," she says.

Okay, now I'm creeped out.

"Thanks for your ghost story," Aries says quickly. "But we're going to head off now."

"Oh, of course," she says frowning. "I... I... understand. Shame on me. Sometimes I can be too helpful. Remember to follow the Narrow Chasm and be very, very careful. I wish you all the best in finding your friend Wind Walker."

I look at Aries.

D-Did she just say Wind Walker?

How'd she know we were looking for Wind Walker?

We never mentioned his name.

But when I turn back to ask her, she's gone.

Meta Profile

Name: Aries
Role: Vigilante   Status: Active

VITALS:

Race: Ani-man
Real Name: Ramm V'kkar
Height: 6'5"
Weight: 325 lbs
Eye Color: Brown
Hair Color: Bald

META POWERS:

Class: Super-Strength
Power Level:
- Extreme strength
- Invulnerability
- Limited super-speed
- Power-Charge

CHARACTERISTICS:

Combat	100	
Durability	100	
Leadership	62	
Strategy	65	
Willpower	95	

SEVEN

I MIGHT BE CRAZY

We've been wandering in the desert for hours.

Or at least it feels like hours because I can't tell what time it is. Apparently, there's no way of knowing whether it's day or night in the 13th Dimension because every time I look at the sky it's always the same color—dull gray.

I'm also starting to think the mountain that old woman directed us towards is one big mirage because no matter how far I think we've traveled, it never seems to get any closer. It's like we're walking aimlessly on some invisible treadmill, racking up tons of miles without really getting anywhere.

Truthfully, I'm not sure how much longer I can go on. My legs are aching and if we don't find this Narrow

Chasm soon, I'm gonna collapse. Aries, however, looks like he could run a marathon.

Maybe he's saving his energy by not talking to me.

I mean, I tried making conversation, but he just doesn't seem interested. And it's not like we don't have a lot of things to talk about. The last time I heard his voice was when I asked him why he cut me off in our conversation with the old woman.

"I got a bad vibe," he said. "When I told her we were looking for *someone*, she knew we were looking for a *friend*. That made me suspicious."

"Okay," I said. "I get it now. And what do you think about that 'Shadow' business? Do you really think there's some evil force out there?"

"Nope," he answered.

And that was it.

It's been radio silence ever since.

Which is a shame because I've been dying to learn more about that Broote guy. I'd love to know why Aries was so alarmed when the old woman mentioned his name. I've never heard of 'Broote the Barbaric' before, but Aries clearly has, and he didn't seem happy about it.

Since Aries wouldn't answer my straightforward questions, I tried approaching the subject more subtly. Like: "I bet that Broote guy owes you a lot of money, right?" Or: "Hey, I forgot, was that guy's name Broote or Boot?"

Okay, maybe that last one wasn't so subtle.

But no matter what angle I took, Aries wouldn't bite. So, I tried changing the subject to stuff we have in common, like our mutual friends on the Zodiac. After all, I'd love to know what the old gang was up to—including Gemini. Well, especially Gemini. But when I asked him about the team, he didn't respond either.

What's with him?

But even though he's been quiet, my mind hasn't stopped spinning. I mean, how did that old woman know we were looking for Wind Walker anyway? It doesn't make sense. Neither of us mentioned his name. I'd say she was a Psychic, except for the fact that Meta powers don't work in the 13th Dimension.

So, what gives?

Not that I have the brainpower to figure it out right now. At this point, I'm hungry and delirious. I wipe my bleary eyes when Aries whispers—

"Hit the deck!"

His words sound like sweet music to my ears, and I drop to the ground like an anchor, happy to be off of my feet. We're lying on the side of a sand dune and I'm wondering if my cape would make a serviceable pillow when I look up and freeze.

That's when I realize Aries isn't stopping for a rest.

Someone is running right towards us.

My heart skips a beat for two reasons.

First, the man heading our way has blue skin like Wind Walker, and for a split second, I think we're the luckiest fools alive. But then I realize he's bald and way too tall to be Wind Walker. Second, the guy is yelling at the top of his lungs. And what he's saying gives me pause.

"Stay away!" he screams. "Leave me alone!"

He's hightailing it like he's being chased by a pack of wolves. But the thing is, there's no one behind him.

"Stay low and go to the other side," Aries whispers.

I nod, my heart beating a mile a minute. As I shift over, I keep my head below the top of the dunes so I can't be seen. But when I look at Aries, he's crawling into the center, directly in the guy's path!

He's going to intercept him!

"Stay back!" the man yells.

Although I can't see him, I can hear him getting closer. I swallow hard. I mean, is tackling this guy a good idea? This would be our first real fight down here. And without our powers who knows what could happen?

Suddenly, a figure leaps over the dune.

And that's when Aries pounces!

"Ugh!" the man exclaims, as Aries slams into him.

They roll down the side of the dune, a tangle of arms and legs. I want to help Aries, but first I can't help peeking over the dunes to take a look around. I scan the barren wasteland, looking for any sign of movement, but I still don't see anything. There's absolutely no one coming. Then, the sounds of Aries and the man scuffling snap me back to reality.

By the time I slide down the dune on my derriere, Aries has done all of the hard work. He has the man pinned, lying face-down on his stomach with his arms pulled behind his back.

Now, Aries is a tall dude but this guy is even taller—like, pro-basketball-player-tall. And he's breathing hard like Aries knocked the wind out of him. I kneel to ask him what his deal is when he suddenly turns his head to face me and our eyes meet.

My jaw drops.

I'd know those cat-like eyes anywhere.

This isn't just any tall guy.

It's the Overlord!

Instinctively, I spring to my feet. I mean, the Overlord is a major Meta 3 villain who can control gravity! My stomach turns just thinking about what he did to us back on the Ghost Ship. How come I didn't recognize him? Then, I realize he's not wearing his helmet.

"Be careful," I warn Aries. "That's—"

"—the Overlord," Aries says. "Yeah, I know. I was on Arena World too. Fortunately, he's powerless down here."

Speaking of Arena World, the last time I saw the Overlord, he was operating as one of Chaos' combatants in pursuit of the Building Block. How the heck did he get down here? He must have escaped Arena World before the whole planet exploded. I guess the Paladins picked him up at some point and threw him in here.

"Let me go!" he demands, his eyes wild with panic. "They'll catch me! I can't let them catch me!"

"Relax, big guy," Aries says. "There's no one following you."

"You idiots!" the Overlord says, his eyebrows raised. "They're right there! Don't you see them? They're floating right there!"

Aries and I both look up to the top of the dune, but there's nothing there. Not a person. Not a floating thing.

Nothing.

What's going on? He's not making any sense. But then it dawns on me.

Maybe he's crazy.

I mean, this place could make anyone crazy.

"I hear you," I say calmly. "But we can't see them right now so maybe you can fill us in. Who, or what, is chasing you?"

"The Wraiths!" he says. "They scour the realm looking for hosts to possess. They have no bodies of their own, and if they catch you, they'll take over your soul!"

"Well, that does sound disturbing," I say.

"Do not mock me," the Overlord says. "I can tell you don't believe me. But you'll see."

"Okay," I say. "So, tell us. Where did these, um, Wraith-thingies come from?"

"The castle," the Overlord says. "They came from the castle."

"The castle?" I say. "You don't mean the underground castle, do you?"

"It's haunted," he says. "Cursed!"

Right.

Of course it is.

"I just want to go home," he babbles, tears running down his cheeks. "Please, I just want to go home."

I'm taken aback. I mean, not too long ago, the Overlord was one of the most feared crime lords in the galaxy. And now he's a driveling mess.

"So," I ask Aries. "What do we do with him now?"

"Now?" Aries says. "We let him go. We can't take him with us, and I don't think he's in any state to provide useful information anyway."

"Yes, let me go," the Overlord begs. "Please, I'm not useful. I must go. They're… they're coming!"

"Get lost," Aries says, releasing the Overlord.

"Get away from me!" the villain yells, springing to his feet. As he bolts, he screams, "Leave me alone! Please, leave me alone!"

"Let's go," Aries says, walking the opposite way.

But as I watch the Overlord disappear into the distance, shouting and flailing his arms, I get a terrible thought.

If this place can turn one of the most dangerous villains in the multiverse into that, who's to say it won't happen to us?

I catch up with Aries.

"Hey," I say. "You don't think that thing he said about the Wraiths is—"

"No," Aries says, cutting me off. "I don't."

But as we walk across the sand in silence, I'm not so sure.

Meta Profile

Name: The Overlord
Role: Prisoner   Status: Inactive

VITALS:

Race: Dhoom
Real Name: Unknown
Height: 6'9"
Weight: 546 lbs
Eye Color: Yellow
Hair Color: Bald

META POWERS:

Class: Former Energy Manipulator

Power Level: 0

- Former powerful crime boss
- Now a prisoner in the 13th Dimension
- Powers are negated

CHARACTERISTICS:

Combat	55
Durability	30
Leadership	22
Strategy	24
Willpower	12

EIGHT

I GRAB THE BULL BY THE HORNS

Our prospects seem to be dimming by the second.

We're still wandering aimlessly through the desert, we have no idea when we'll stumble across the Narrow Chasm, and we have no clue how we'll get out of here even if we find Wind Walker.

That pretty much makes us 0 for 3.

One big strikeout.

Not to mention our encounter with the Overlord is still freaking me out. I mean, I simply can't match up the person I just saw with the person I once knew. Somehow, this place turned him from a major powerhouse into a hopeless wreck.

Not to mention that thing he said about the Wraiths.

I shudder.

The faster we finish this mission the better.

The problem is, we don't seem to be getting very far. It's like we're walking in ultra-slow motion without even knowing it. I stare at my feet. They're definitely moving.

At least, it seems like they're moving.

Suddenly, Aries stops and says, "We're here."

Huh?

When I look up, I realize we're standing in the shadow of a giant mountain. Wait a second, how'd that happen? A minute ago, we were miles away. Did some invisible hand pick us up and drop us here in the blink of an eye?

This is too weird.

Something isn't right.

But before I can figure it out, Aries points to the center of the mountain and says, "There."

Zeroing in, I notice a sliver of light running north to south down the middle of the rock monolith. At first, I'm not sure what it is, but then I realize it's a jagged fissure, letting light through from the other side.

What is that?

Then it hits me.

It's the Narrow Chasm!

We found it! I reach up for a high five but I'm left hanging because Aries is already gone, running towards it.

Well, that was awkward.

I sprint to catch up, and as I reach the base of the mountain I marvel at the natural wonder before me. It's like someone took a knife and cut straight through the mountain itself like it was a seven-layer cake. And I can see how it got its name because the chasm itself is narrow alright. I watch Aries turn himself sideways and wedge himself in, tilting his head up to prevent his horns from scraping the other side. Then, he's off.

I'm not sure where this thing lets out, but it's not like I'm planning on waiting here for him to ring me when he gets to the other side. So, I take a deep breath and follow. Fortunately, this is one time it pays to be small because I've got plenty of elbow room.

We make our way through slowly, but it's not exactly smooth sailing. While the chasm is open to the sky, it's definitely darker at the bottom versus the top. Plus, there are plenty of spots where the mountain juts out and we have to maneuver ourselves either over or under to keep going. At one point, my concentration lapses, and I nearly eat a face full of rock.

But hopefully, all of this effort will be worth it, because the old woman said the entrance to the underground castle is just on the other side of this mountain. Supposedly, that's where we'll meet the King who may be our only shot at finding Wind Walker.

Unless, of course, she was misleading us.

Regardless, I'll be happy to reach the end. Tight spaces like this just aren't my jam. Once, Dog-Gone and I snuck out of bed for a midnight snack and got stuck hiding in the pantry for two hours until Dad finished a late dinner. That wasn't fun, especially since I had to give my snack to Dog-Gone just to keep him quiet. Boy, I'd give anything to be back in the pantry with that mutt again.

Just thinking about him makes my eyes well up.

But as much as I miss him, I need to stay focused.

This chasm goes on forever, but I have to admit, it does make a perfect secret passageway.

"We've reached the end," Aries says suddenly.

What? Yes!

I look up just as he squeezes through the final section and pops out the other side. Light streams in and my heart swells with joy. I skip gleefully out of the Narrow Chasm, hop over a pile of rocks, and SLAM into the muscular leg of a very large man, bouncing me onto my backside.

Ouch! And who is that?

I take in the figure of the man I crashed into. He's big and muscular and wearing a black costume with the insignia of a ram on his chest. But that's not all. He has two large horns protruding from his forehead—just like Aries!

Just then, two other lunkheads step out of the shadows behind us, blocking any escape back through the Narrow Chasm.

We're trapped!

"Broote," Aries says.

My jaw hits the floor.

Broote? That's Broote?

"Little brother," Broote says, with a menacing grin.

My jaw hits the floor again.

Did he just call Aries... brother?

"I never expected to find you here," Broote says. "What happened? Did you get caught stealing someone's lunch credits?"

"Step aside, Broote," Aries says. "I'm on an important mission. I don't have time for you."

"You haven't changed at all, have you?" Broote asks, cracking his ginormous knuckles. "Still the arrogant fool. You may not have time for me, but I have plenty of time for you."

"I'm warning you, brother," Aries says, the veins on his neck bulging. "We aren't in the coliseum anymore, and you aren't half the gladiator you think you are."

"You're partially correct," Broote says, looking around. "This isn't the coliseum, but unfortunately for you, I'm still twice the gladiator you'll ever be. This should be fun. And to think, I haven't had a good battle since Ravager destroyed our homeworld and all of the people you once loved."

"Like our parents?" Aries yells, his face flushed. "You couldn't rule our world, so you sold it out to Ravager like the traitor you are. You betrayed everyone out of spite. All you ever craved was power and look what it got you. No wonder father never loved you."

"Perhaps he didn't," Broote says casually. "But I'm alive and he's dead. So, guess who is on top now?"

"Fool," Aries scoffs. "You call this living? You're a shell of your former self, trapped in a prison you can't escape from. You're so pathetic you can't even hold the throne of this wasteland."

"Don't belittle me, brother," Broote says. "If you consider me a failure than what are you? I watched you try to avenge our people against Ravager—failing time and time again—until Ravager was destroyed, but not at your hand." Then, he looks at me and says, "You needed this child to do the job. You're pathetic."

Hang on. If Broote was stuck here in the 13th Dimension, then how did he see me beat Ravager? It doesn't make sense.

"Enough!" Aries yells. "Perhaps I have time for you after all. Maybe we were destined to meet again. Maybe it's time for you to pay your debt to our people—to our parents—once and for all."

"That's the spirit," Broote says. "Soldiers, subdue my brother's pet. I will deal with him after I've won."

Pet? What pet? Wait, is he talking about—

"Hey!" I yell as the two goons grab my arms!

I try pulling myself free but it's useless, they're too strong. But when I look back over, Aries and Broote are facing off, measuring each other as they walk in a slow, deliberate circle.

"This ends here," Aries says.

"Correction," Broote replies. "You end here."

OMG!

They're going to fight each other!

To the death!

Then, before I can blink, the brothers charge one another with their horns out first, just like rams!

CRASH!

Their collision kicks up a massive dust cloud that covers everything. Instinctively, I shut my eyes, protecting them from the storm. When the dust finally settles, the brothers are locked in close combat, their arms and horns interlocked! The two warriors push against one another, trying to use their horns as leverage to knock the other off balance. Suddenly, Broote finds an opening and delivers a swift uppercut to Aries' jaw, sending him flying into the side of the mountain.

"Still falling for that one, brother?" Broote says. "A shame. I wonder, will you beg for mercy?"

"I don't beg," Aries says, spitting out blood as he rises to his feet. "Never have, never will."

Then, Aries charges again and Broote lowers his horns just in time. My ears ring as the two collide once again, pushing against each other with all of their might. This time, Broote sweeps Aries' right leg and pummels him with a roundhouse kick, sending Aries stumbling to the ground.

This is not good.

Aries is a great fighter, but Broote is even better! If this is going to the death, Aries doesn't stand a chance!

"Do you want to continue, brother?" Broote says, a smug expression on his face. "Or would you rather surrender to the inevitable?"

Without a word, Aries rises to his feet.

But this time there's something different about him.

His eyes...

They're flickering again with that strange blue energy. Just like I saw before!

"What are you doing?" Broote asks.

"Enough distractions," Aries says, his eyes flaring. "You are keeping me from my goal."

Suddenly, Aries morphs into a gray blur, and there's an ear-splitting BOOM that rattles my teeth. The next thing I know, I'm engulfed in an even bigger dust cloud that makes my eyes water.

The goons drop me to the ground, and I rub my eyes to clear the sting. But when I can finally see again, Aries is standing in Broote's spot, and there's a massive hole in the side of the mountain itself.

Where's Broote?

Then, I see a limp, black-costumed body lying inside the hole. It's Broote! But what happened?

And then I realize...

Aries has Meta powers!

Aries turns and my former captors take off through the Narrow Chasm. Aries rubs his eyes, and when he's finished, they're brown again.

"What happened?" he asks.

"What happened?" I repeat. "You just used your Meta powers to pummel Broote. Don't you remember?"

"Broote?" he says, and then he sees his brother's body. He runs over and hops inside the hole. Kneeling, he checks Broote's pulse and then closes his sibling's eyes.

"Is he…?" I ask.

"Yes," Aries says, coming back out. "He's gone."

"I'm sorry," I say. "But how did that even happen? I thought you couldn't use Meta powers in the 13th Dimension? I thought everyone here lived forever?"

"I… I don't know," Aries says.

Aries looks at his brother's body and lowers his head.

"Are you okay?" I ask.

"Yes," he says. "I did what needed to be done. I just don't remember doing it."

"You mean, you seriously don't remember?"

"No," he says. "I have no memory of what happened."

Wow, that's scary.

"Do you need a minute?" I ask.

"No," he says. "Broote finally got what he deserved. But this doesn't change why we came here. We need to resume our mission. We need to find the underground castle and see if this 'King' knows where we can find Wind Walker."

I nod and we both start scanning the area for an entrance, but there aren't any obvious openings anywhere. What did that old woman say? Something about it being just on the other side of the Narrow Chasm? But where?

Wait a second, 'just on the other side?'

I run over to the Narrow Chasm and look straight down. Sure enough, that pile of rocks I jumped over doesn't look like an ordinary pile of rocks.

There's thirteen of them. And they're arranged in a perfect circle. That can't be a coincidence.

"Aries!" I call out. "I think I found something!"

"That's got to be it," he says, checking it out.

"It's something," I say. "But I don't get why these rocks are arranged in a circle."

"Because it's not a circle," he says. "It's an entrance."

An entrance? But there's just dirt inside?

"Really?" he says. "Follow me."

Then, he hops into the center and disappears!

Oh, jeez, he's right! That circle must be an illusion!

But before I step inside, I hesitate. I mean, why do I keep ending up going underground?

I hate going underground!

But what other choice do I have?

So, I pinch my nose, close my eyes, and jump into the center of the circle.

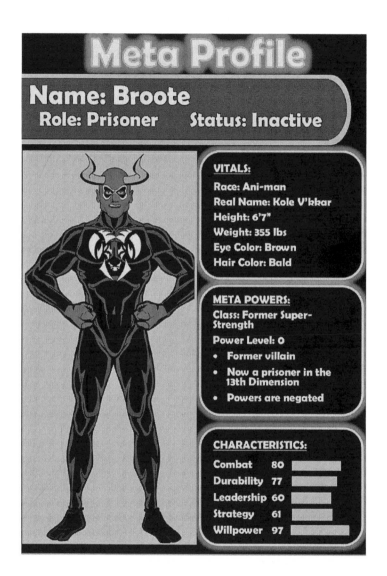

Meta Profile

Name: Broote
Role: Prisoner Status: Inactive

VITALS:

Race: Ani-man
Real Name: Kole V'kkar
Height: 6'7"
Weight: 355 lbs
Eye Color: Brown
Hair Color: Bald

META POWERS:

Class: Former Super-Strength

Power Level: 0

- Former villain
- Now a prisoner in the 13th Dimension
- Powers are negated

CHARACTERISTICS:

Combat	80	
Durability	77	
Leadership	60	
Strategy	61	
Willpower	97	

NINE

I HAVE AN AUDIENCE WITH THE KING

I'm lying face down on a cold, stone floor.

The good news is that I'm alive. The bad news is that I've got no clue how long I've been lying here.

The last thing I remember is jumping into the middle of that rock ring and sliding down a rampway so steep I thought I was going to pass out. I guess I did.

Even though everything feels like it's spinning, I get up onto my hands and knees to take a look around, but it's pitch dark.

Then I realize my cape is flipped over my head.

Genius.

After handling that little embarrassment, the room isn't nearly as dark as I thought, because there's a torch flickering on the far wall giving off some light. From what I can gather, I'm in a small room with rock walls and a high ceiling. Looking up, I see the end of a stone ramp some ten feet off the ground. Well, if that's where I got off, I'm lucky I'm not dead right now.

I bet Aries stuck his landing like an Olympic gymnast. Speaking of Aries, where is the big lug? I mean, I thought we were going to tackle this underground castle together.

Then, I notice an empty torch bracket on the wall.

I'm guessing Aries took that one.

So, where'd he go?

I pull the remaining torch off the wall and wave it around. There must be a passageway around here somewhere? It takes me a little while, but I finally find it.

Tucked in the corner is a creepy stone stairway headed straight down.

Wonderful.

With torch in hand, I descend slowly, the air getting mustier with every step. I do my best not to make any noise, but it's so deathly quiet I'm nervous to even breathe!

As I go down the stairs, I notice strange symbols carved into the wall. They look like Egyptian hieroglyphics, but I can't make out what they mean. What I can tell, however, is that this certainly isn't the vibe I was expecting when I heard the word 'castle.' I mean, where are all of the knights and flowery tapestries?

I step onto a stone landing that connects to another chamber that's slightly larger than the one above. There are all kinds of weapons spilled on the floor, like axes, spears, and swords. By the looks of it, I'm guessing this was a guard post. Thankfully, it's unmanned, but what happened to all of the guards?

Suddenly, I think of the Overlord.

Did the Wraiths get them?

The stairway continues so I go down another level where I find an even larger chamber, but there's still no one around. This one has a bunch of busted open crates filled with ropes and nails and other building supplies. And it's the same story for level four, level five, and so on. The chambers keep getting larger, but more eerily empty.

This is not comforting.

And where's Aries? I never thought he'd leave me behind like this. I want to call out his name, but I don't exactly want to announce I'm here. So, my only option is to just keep looking.

By the time I reach the twelfth level my legs are killing me. Note to self: do more Stairmaster work in the gym. Again, there's no one around. Then, I look down and feel a pit in my stomach.

The stairway ends at the bottom of the next level.

Level thirteen.

Yep, I should've predicted that.

I take a deep breath. If the King is here, I'm guessing that's where I'm gonna find him. I lean forward, listening for any noise, but it's deathly quiet.

No King. No Aries. No nothing.

Truthfully, I'm totally spooked right now. It feels like I'm walking through one of those Halloween haunted house tours where you just know something is going to jump out and scare the pants off of you.

Except those are fake. This is all too real.

My brain is telling me to run back up these stairs to safety as quickly as possible, but deep down I know I can't. Wind Walker needs my help. And by the looks of it, so does Aries.

I take a deep breath and head down the final flight of stairs. I've got to be ready for anything, so when I reach the bottom step I leap off and assume a fighting stance, but thankfully there's no one around.

But this time there's no chamber.

Instead, there's a corridor.

A corridor lined with lit torches.

Which can only mean one thing.

Someone is down here!

I hesitate. I mean, who knows what's waiting for me at the end of this corridor? And without Aries or my powers, I'll be in deep trouble if I run into something I can't handle. But I've come too far to turn back now.

I walk slowly, curiosity propelling me forward.

Of course, didn't curiosity kill the cat?

As I reach the end of the corridor, I can see it opens into a large, circular room. I press my back against the wall and peek inside the door-less frame.

The room is empty, except for a massive crystal sitting in its center! It's purple in color—like an amethyst—but it must be six-feet tall. The front and back are perfectly flat, like the surface of a mirror, while the perimeter is hexagonal.

It's so remarkable I can't take my eyes away.

Without thinking, I find myself walking right up to it. Off to the side is a torch holder, so I set mine inside, leaving both hands free. I stand in front of the crystal, dwarfed by its sheer size. It's only when I'm this close that I realize it's translucent. I reach around and see my hand on the other side. Boy, I bet this baby would fetch big bucks back on Earth.

Instinctively, I reach out and touch it, pressing my palm against the surface. Suddenly, the face of the crystal goes from clear to a dark, swirling mist—and the next thing I know, I'm staring at Dog-Gone's big behind!

Shocked, I pull my hand away and Dog-Gone disappears. Huh? What's going on?

But when I touch the crystal again, Dog-Gone is back. And he's sitting in the Mission Room of the Waystation. Then, everything clicks.

Broote said he was watching me defeat Ravager even though he was trapped in the 13th Dimension. Could he have been using this crystal to do it? Because if what I'm seeing is real, it's like looking through a window into another world!

I keep my left hand on the surface and knock on the face of the crystal with my right, but Dog-Gone doesn't react. Instead, he seems really focused chewing away on something. Wait a minute, that's my slipper!

"Hey!" I yell, banging hard against the crystal. "Drop my slipper you stupid mutt!"

Suddenly, Dog-Gone lifts his head.

OMG! Can he hear me?

"Here, boy!" I yell. "I'm over here!"

Dog-Gone spins around confused.

I can't believe it! I think he can hear me!

"Come on, buddy!" I yell, waving frantically. "It's me, Elliott! I'm standing right here! I need help!"

Dog-Gone stops and sniffs the air like he senses me, but I don't think he can actually see me.

"Get help, boy," I yell. "Get Mom or Dad! Get TechnocRat or Makeshift! Well, don't get Makeshift, but get someone! And fast!"

But instead of following directions, he sits down and wags his tail from side-to-side.

Clearly, he ain't no Lassie.

"Dog-Gone, no!" I yell, pounding on the crystal. "Bad dog! Go get help! Get off your rump and get—"

But just like that, he's gone!

The surface of the crystal turns murky again, and when it settles, I found myself staring at a control panel.

What the—? Where am I?

Then, I look up through a windshield at outer space. Dead center is a large red planet with green rings around it. At first, I think it's Saturn, but Saturn isn't red.

"We are close, Commander," comes a voice to my left.

I turn to find an alien with white skin and big red eyes staring at me. He looks just like Xenox, except it's not Xenox because this guy is just as ugly but way fatter.

"As expected, they have deployed their armada," the alien continues. "We expect the first wave to arrive in twenty point two seconds. Shall we ready the torpedoes?"

"Prepare them, Lieutenant," comes a deep, strangely familiar voice. "But hold fire until I can see the neon green of their eyes."

That voice? I feel like I've heard it before.

But from where?

Suddenly, a huge, red-skinned figure comes into view, and the hairs on the back of my neck stand on end.

OMG!

It's... Krule the Conqueror!

And he's like, eight feet tall!

"First, I will destroy their army," Krule says, grinning from ear to ear. "Then, I will capture their homeworld. And last but not least, I will destroy their Emperor!"

Emperor?

As in, the Skelton Emperor?

"Enemy warships in sight," the Lieutenant says.

"Wait for my command," Krule orders.

Just then, hundreds of Skelton warships appear.

They're coming in fast, getting closer. What's he waiting for? Suddenly, I see the face of the lead Skelton pilot. He's heading straight for the bridge!

He's going to ram us!

But then, the pilot's eyes turn an even brighter shade of green and he veers off at the last second, followed by ship after Skelton ship! What's going on?

I watch as the first wave of Skelton ships loop behind the second wave—and begin firing!

They're blowing up their own ships!

How is that happening?

But when I look over at Krule I have my answer. His third eye is glowing with a strong green light. He's mind-controlling them! He's using Skelton ships to destroy their own army!

"I'm coming for you, old friend," Krule says. "And just like I warned you, the final laugh will be mine."

Then, the whole scene disappears.

I stagger backward, my adrenaline pumping.

That was nuts! Krule is trying to take over the Skelton Homeworld!

I'm about to reach for the crystal again when I notice something out of the corner of my eye. There's a bright light coming from an open doorway that simply wasn't there before.

Was it triggered when I touched the crystal?

This time I leave my torch behind and duck into the shadows. I inch my way over to the opening, walking as softly as possible. When I reach the doorway, I press my ear to the wall.

I don't hear anything, but that doesn't mean there's nothing in there. And if there is something in there it certainly knows I'm here. After all, I *was* yelling at the top of my lungs for Dog-Gone to get help. It's amazing how that pooch gets me in trouble, even out here.

But honestly, I'm sick and tired of tiptoeing around. If I'm going down, I'd rather do it in a blaze of glory. So, here goes nothing.

One… Two…

Three! I jump through the entrance in karate-chop mode, ready for action! But no one attacks. Instead, there's a large, gold throne sitting in the center of the room, facing the other way. And standing stock-still by its side is Aries!

"Bow before the King," Aries orders.

"Excuse me?" I say. Then, I notice his eyes are sparking with that strange blue energy again.

"Bow before the King," Aries repeats.

Suddenly, the throne swivels, revealing a blue-skinned man wearing a crown on his head!

My heart skips a beat.

I-I can't believe it. It's the King!

But the King is… Wind Walker?

TEN

I CAST A LONG SHADOW

I can't believe our luck!

Aries and I came all this way to find the King who supposedly knows where Wind Walker is—and it turns out that Wind Walker *is* the King! I've got to say I'm pretty speechless right now. And since Aries and I risked our freedom entering the 13th Dimension to rescue Wind Walker in the first place, you'd think Aries would be whooping it up right now.

But instead, he's just standing there like a toy soldier, kidding around for me to bow before the King. I'll tell you, that guy's got one strange sense of humor.

"Funny, Aries," I say. "But seriously, now that we've found Wind Walker let's get out of here."

But Aries doesn't crack a smile.

What's wrong with him?

I'm about to ask Wind Walker if he knows what's up when I stop myself. As I stare into his narrow blue eyes, I realize something is off. But what?

Then it hits me.

Doesn't Wind Walker have green eyes?

Suddenly, blue electricity sparks from his pupils.

"Um, Wind Walker?" I say, my alarm bells ringing. "Are you okay?"

Instinctively, I take a step backward when the entrance to the chamber SLAMS shut behind me!

I'm trapped!

"Elliott Harkness," Wind Walker says, his voice a raspy whisper. "I have waited a long time for your arrival."

"Um, what?" I say, totally confused.

"I have exhausted every atom of my being to bring you here," Wind Walker continues. "I have pushed beyond inter-dimensional boundaries, reaching farther than my influence should allow. But now all of my labor bears fruit because you are here and the moment is upon us."

Well, that confirms it. Something is definitely wrong here. The Wind Walker I know doesn't talk like that. And he certainly wouldn't hold me against my will.

So, I figure I need to get out of here—and fast.

"Well, gee whiz," I say. "It's great seeing you too, but unfortunately I need to break up this little reunion. I just remembered I left my hairdryer plugged in and Dad hates it when I do that. So, if you could just open up the door for me, I promise I'll be back real soon."

"No," Wind Walker says. "You are not going anywhere. You are exactly where you are destined to be."

"Riiight," I say. "Listen, I appreciate that you went through hoops just to see me, but don't you think you're crossing the line between super-fan and stalker?"

"I have waited a long time for the arrival of someone with your power," Wind Walker says. "And this time I will not be tricked."

Tricked? What's he talking about?

And then the lightbulb goes off.

Maybe he's talking about Krule?

Maybe Krule somehow tricked him to escape from the 13th Dimension? But then it dawns on me, if this isn't the Wind Walker I know, who is he?

I mean, when the Overlord talked about the Wraiths, he referenced them in the plural, like there's more than one. But Wind Walker is talking in the first person, using words like 'I' and 'my.' So, what does that—

OMG!

My heart sinks to my toes.

Didn't that old woman tell us about something else that lived in the realm? Something that desperately wanted to escape. Something... evil?

I study my friend's face. He looks like Wind Walker, but his mind must have been taken over by... by...

"Holy smokes!" I blurt out. "You're not Wind Walker. You're the Shadow!"

"Indeed," the Shadow says. "But that is just one of my names. I am also known here as 'The Ruler,' or 'The Creator.' My power within this tiny realm is all-reaching. But in your larger realm, my voice is but the faintest of whispers. For between our realms there is a barrier I cannot break. So here I remain, limited in the scope of my power, barely sustaining myself on the energy of those trapped here."

Sustaining himself? On energy?

"Hang on," I say. "Are you saying you live off the Meta energy of others? Like... a vampire?"

"Meta energy is my sustenance," the Shadow says. "The origin of all of my power. But my food sources are limited here. When I finally escape to your realm, my food sources will be infinite. Then, I will rule over all realms, thanks to you."

"Thanks to me?" I say. "What do I have to do with your crazy plan?"

"Because you are rare," the Shadow says. "Only a few in the known multiverse possess the type of Meta energy that can release me from this prison."

"Um, sorry, but no way," I say.

He may be delusional, but I know he's right about one thing. I do have a unique kind of Meta power—Meta Manipulation. The only other Meta Manipulators I know are Meta-Taker and Siphon, but they're long gone. Could there really be others out there with this ability?

"You have no choice," the Shadow says. "Just as I am controlling the mouth of your friend, Wind Walker, I am also controlling his mind. And if you refuse to do my bidding, I will snuff it out like a candle. To prove my point, I will use your other friend for a quick demonstration of my power."

But before I can object, Aries' eyes flare with blue electricity and he begins walking towards me awkwardly, like a marionette on a string! I shuffle aside as he plows past me, only stopping when he slams face-first into the wall.

"Okay, okay," I say. "Calm down. I get it."

Well, that seals it. There's no freaking way I'm letting this monster out of the 13th Dimension. Somehow, I've got to get out of here with Wind Walker and Aries intact. But until I can figure that one out, I need to stall.

"Look, I'm listening," I say. "But first, tell me something. How could anyone trick someone as powerful as you?"

Wind Walker smiles.

"Even creators make mistakes," he says. "I was deceived. A new inhabitant entered the realm and I lured him here to my chamber where I could feed. But my mistake was in assuming he was weak and inept, just like all of the others."

Hold up! Is he saying he only sucks Meta energy here, in this chamber? Then, that would explain why Aries could still use his powers above ground? We hadn't reached the Shadow's chamber yet, so Aries still had his powers the whole time!

And maybe I do too?

"But when he arrived," the Shadow continues, "I learned he was far from weak. His energy was strong, stronger than I had ever encountered before. And when I tried to feed upon him, he surprised me."

"Um, what does that mean?" I ask.

"Instead of taking possession of him," Wind Walker says, "he took possession of me. He bent my will and made me his slave. I could only watch as he used my All-Seeing Eye in ways I had never imagined. And then he escaped from the realm, leaving me behind."

The All-Seeing Eye? What's that?

And then the dots connect.

That giant purple crystal must be the All-Seeing Eye!

Krule must have used it to control the Time Trotter! And then Krule used it again to steal the Cosmic Key right out of Fairchild's hands! It all makes sense now!

But how did he actually project his powers through the crystal? I mean, I couldn't even get through to Dog-Gone.

"Listen," I say, "I get that Krule pulled a fast one on you, but what do you want from me? My powers are totally different than his."

"The manifestation of your powers may be different," he says, "but your energy is the same."

His comment shocks me.

Is he saying Krule is also a Meta Manipulator?

But then I realize something. Why hasn't the Shadow fed off of me? Does he think I'll take him over like Krule did? But I know I can't do that on my own.

I mean, Krule is some kind of a mega-Psychic. My powers don't work like that. But maybe the Shadow doesn't know that? Maybe I can bluff him?

"Sorry, but I still don't get it," I say, a bit more confidently. "What am I doing here?"

"Ever since I spotted you during your fateful encounter with Krule," he says, "I knew you were the one. You are not here by accident, Elliott Harkness. You are here by my grand design, with the help of some outside bargaining."

Huh? What does that mean?

"I see you are still confused," he says. "So, I will clarify things for you. Your arrest by the Paladins was no mistake. It was I who arranged for you to be taken to Paladin Planet."

What?

"Just as it was I who used Wind Walker's voice to cause your friend Aries' nightmares," he continues. "I planted the seed in Aries' mind to commit unspeakable crimes so he would end up on Paladin Planet, in the very cell next to you, only steps away from the entrance to the 13th Dimension."

"Whoa!" I say. "Slow down a sec. Are you telling me you intentionally brought Aries and I to Paladin Planet at the same time? But why?"

"That is simple," he says. "I knew that once your trusted friend Aries informed you of Wind Walker's plight, you could not refuse to save him. Even if you had to travel into my realm—the dreaded 13th Dimension—to do so. That is how I brought you here. That is why you are standing before me now."

My mind is blown.

He used Wind Walker as bait to bring me here. I feel so… so… manipulated. But why?

"Okay," I say angrily. "Congratulations. You got me here. Now tell me what I'm doing here."

"That is simple," he says. "First, you will use the All-Seeing Eye to bring forth an image of the Cosmic Key. Then, you will use your abilities to reach through the crystal and duplicate its power, serving as my key to unlock the door and leave this realm forever."

"No way!" I yell.

"The choice is yours," he says. "You can either help me willingly, or I will take over your mind and do it myself, destroying your soul forever."

Meta Profile

Name: Wind Walker
Role: Hero   Status: Active

VITALS:

Race: Capachee
Real Name: Wohali Staar
Height: 6'1"
Weight: 215 lbs
Eye Color: Green
Hair Color: Black

META POWERS:

Class: Energy Manipulator
Power Level:
- **Extreme Space Manipulation**
- **Can travel across worlds and universes**

CHARACTERISTICS:

Combat	90	
Durability	45	
Leadership	95	
Strategy	91	
Willpower	99	

ELEVEN

I WATCH MYSELF BACK AGAIN

They should really teach kids how to make life or death decisions in school.

I mean, the Shadow just basically gave me an ultimatum. Either I willingly use my powers to free him from the 13th Dimension, or he'll take over my body and do it anyway! Now that's a real problem, unlike those pesky algebra equations that never threaten to destroy anyone's soul. But then again, maybe they do.

"It is time," comes the Shadow's voice through Wind Walker's mouth. "What is your decision?"

"Oh, sorry," I say. "I was waiting for more choices. Are you saying there are no more choices?"

I can't keep stalling him. I've got to think fast.

I'm not exactly in a power position here.

Or am I?

I mean, maybe I'm not as powerless as I thought. As far as I know, he hasn't tried feeding off my Meta energy yet. Which means I may still have my powers.

I could try negating his power, but what if I mess up? The Shadow and Wind Walker are intertwined right now. If I cancel the Shadow's mind link with Wind Walker, would I accidentally cancel Wind Walker's brain functioning in the process? I've gotten a lot better at surgically targeting my powers, but I don't know if I'm that good. It's too risky.

But if I can't cancel his powers, I can always copy them. Maybe that would work? Then again, maybe I'm out of my mind.

Wait a second. That's it!

"Your time is up!" he demands. "Decide!"

"Okay, okay, take a chill pill," I say. "I've decided. Look, as much as I'd love to help fulfill your nutso fantasy of taking over the entire multiverse, I have a pretty strict policy of not working with bodiless parasites suffering from superiority complexes. So, I guess you'll just have to crush my soul. That is, if you can."

"What?" Wind Walker says, his eyebrows rising in surprise. "How dare you defy m—"

But I don't wait for him to stop yapping.

Instead, I go on the offensive.

I concentrate hard, washing my Meta energy over Wind Walker's body. Then, I replicate every iota of the

Shadow's power. Within milliseconds, I can feel his energy swirling inside my body.

Yes! My powers work!

But his energy feels so dark.

Heavy.

And I have an overwhelming sensation of... hunger.

A hunger for even more power.

Immediately, I can tell this was a bad idea.

The longer I hold on to this poisonous energy, the harder it's going to be to control. So, if I'm going to get the Shadow out of Wind Walker's mind, I've got to go in.

I focus all of the Shadow's power and then lash out, penetrating deep inside Wind Walker's mind.

There's a blinding white flash, and then everything goes topsy-turvy. The next thing I know, I'm standing on a clear platform surrounded by millions of gelatinous blobs floating all around me. Boy, Wind Walker's mind is a strange place.

What are those things?

Then, one of the blobs stops right in front of me, and my jaw drops, because inside the blob is the image of a village filled with blue-skinned people. Some are playing drums while others are dancing. It almost feels like a celebration. Then the image moves forward like I'm walking through the scene itself. The drums get louder and the dancers move aside, creating a pathway towards a teepee-like structure.

I push through the flaps of the teepee and enter.

Inside, a wrinkled old man wearing a headdress is sitting cross-legged on the ground.

"Wohali Starr," the man says, "it is time."

Wohali Starr?

Wait a minute, isn't that Wind Walker's real name?

"You have brought great pride to our people," the man continues. "But now it is time for you to leave us in the pursuit of everlasting peace. This is for you."

The man holds up a tan satchel with a shoulder strap. Hang on, I've seen that satchel before. Wind Walker wears it!

"No, Father," echoes a voice that sounds just like Wind Walker. "I am not worthy. The Spirit-catcher has belonged to the Chief of our tribe for generations. It is yours to use for the protection of our people."

And then I realize what's happening. I'm watching Wind Walker's memories through his very own eyes!

"There are none more worthy than you, my son," the man responds. "But you are mistaken. While it is true that the Spirit-catcher has been handed down for generations, it is not to be wielded by the Chief of our people, but by the greatest warrior of our people—and now that warrior is you. Use it with great care," he says, handing it to Wind Walker, "for it is ancient and powerful. Merely opening it will invite great danger."

Wind Walker takes the satchel in his hands. Interestingly, for something so ancient and powerful, it looks pretty ordinary.

"Wohali Starr," the old man continues, "the multiverse needs your courage and wisdom more than ever. I am proud of you, my son. Now go forth and discover your destiny."

Suddenly, the memory blobs shuffle and another scene presents itself. But this time I do a double take because I'm staring at an image of myself! I'm lying face down on the pavement in a place I know all too well—Keystone City! What's going on?

"Are you hurt?" comes Wind Walker's voice, again sounding like an echo.

"Just my pride," I watch myself mutter. "Don't worry, I'll be fine."

"Are you certain about this?" Wind Walker asks.

I cringe as I watch myself get up. It's kind of like seeing yourself in an awkward home movie. But where are we and why does this all seem so familiar?

"Very well," Wind Walker says. "Remember, you are no longer on your world. Places may appear identical, people may look familiar, but nothing is as it seems. For as long as you remain here, your greatest enemy is yourself. If you lower your guard, even for a second, it could cost you your life."

"Okay, okay," I say, smiling awkwardly. "I've got it. I can handle this."

"I hope so," Wind Walker says, "Now, I must try and solve the riddle of the Blur before it is too late. Good luck, Epic Zero. If you need me, call my name.

Hopefully, I will be able to return for you."

"Good luck," I say, as we shake hands.

"Do not forget what I told you," he says. Then, Wind Walker steps backward and is absorbed into one of his black voids.

OMG!

I know exactly what this is from. It's right after Wind Walker rescued me from the Rising Suns and brought me to Earth 2 in search of a second Orb of Oblivion.

But suddenly, the blob goes cloudy, and when it clears, I'm staring at Dog-Gone! That's weird. I don't remember Wind Walker ever meeting Dog-Gone?

"Good boy," Wind Walker says, scratching under Dog-Gone's chin. "There is somebody here who looks like your master but is not. At first, you may not trust him, but the two of you share a common goal—you are both searching for your master. So, remember, it is in your best interest to help him."

The next thing I know, I see myself running down the street to the Prop House. Then, it all comes flooding back. That's where Captain Justice 2 almost killed me! So that must be Dog-Gone 2!

"Follow that boy," Wind Walker says to Dog-Gone 2. "Protect him and keep him safe, at least until your mutual goal is achieved."

Dog-Gone 2 licks Wind Walker's hand and then runs after me, turning invisible after a few strides.

But what is this memory? I don't remember this.

And then it hits me!

Wind Walker didn't just leave me behind on Earth 2.

He must have found Dog-Gone 2 first and sent him to help me at the Prop House before he went looking for the Blur. He saved me from Captain Justice 2.

I-I never knew that.

But just as I'm processing that new info, the memory blobs rotate again and suddenly I'm staring at an image of an old woman sitting on a throne. But it's not just any old woman—it's the same old woman Aries and I met when we first entered the 13th Dimension!

And her eyes are sparking with blue electricity!

"Where am I?" Wind Walker asks.

"You poor unfortunate soul," the old woman says empathetically. "Why, you are in the realm. Now you must tell me how you got here. After all, you did not enter like the others."

"I-I do not know," Wind Walker answers. "I was tracking a great cosmic disturbance called the Blur, but for some reason when I tried cutting across this particular dimensional latitude, my worm-hole collapsed and I fell into this hidden pocket in space."

"Oh, I understand," the old woman says, nodding her head. "But tell me, do you know of a way out? Perhaps you can use those same powers that brought you here to get you out—to get us both out? Do you understand what I am asking? Do you think you can do that?"

"No," Wind Walker says. "I have tried, but I cannot. I seem to be trapped here."

Upon hearing Wind Walker's answer, the old woman's eyebrows furrow and her face turns a deep shade of red.

"Liar!" she screams. "I will not be deceived again! You will use your power to help me escape! You will help me escape at once!"

Then, her entire body dissipates into a black mist.

Huh? What's going on?

But before I can blink, she forms into the shape of a misty arrow and races straight towards us! I gasp, but right before impact, I snap back to reality.

Well, that was terrifying. At least now I know what happened to Wind Walker. No wonder he never responded to my calls. He got stuck here searching for the Blur. I bet he has no clue I solved that mystery when I defeated Ravager.

But more alarmingly, what's with that old woman? I knew there was something strange about her. But based on what I just saw, I think it's even worse. Because I think she may actually be the—

"Elliott Harkness," comes a woman's voice.

I spin around to find the old woman standing on the other side of the platform and I know I'm right.

"Elliott Harkness," she repeats, "you chose foolishly. And now I will crush your soul."

Yep, I was afraid of this.

The old woman and the Shadow aren't two different entities. They're one and the same!

The old woman *is* the Shadow!

But before I can react, she charges me, morphing into a black mist and blowing me backward with such force I land hard on my back! My body slides to the edge of the platform, my head hanging over. I look down and realize there's nothing below us!

If she knocks me off this thing, who knows where— or if—I'll ever land!

But before I can get up, she's on me again, pummeling me with blow after blow. I protect my head with my arms but it's no use. I don't know how to stop her! It's all I can do just to stay conscious!

Then, my brain feels like it's on fire!

OMG!

She's trying to get inside my head!

She weakened me physically so she can attack me mentally. But… I can't give up. I won't give up. I need to respond.

I muster all of the concentration I have left, drawing in all of my power. And then I form a mental barrier between us. If this doesn't work…

She pounds again, but this time I feel less of the blow. But she's relentless, pounding against me over and over again, trying to shatter my shield. I'm holding her back, but I won't be able to keep this up for long. I need a new strategy. I've got to get rid of her once and for all.

I close my eyes and build up my energy again.

I reach deep down inside.

Grabbing all of the dark energy.

I bundle it, squeezing it tight.

It's so powerful it's hard to contain it all.

But I keep it close. Scrunch it up like a ball.

Then, as soon as I feel her coming again, I close my eyes and release it.

There's an ear-piercing SCREAM.

And the pressure stops.

Did I do it?

Please, tell me I did it.

But to my surprise, when I open my eyes I find the old woman standing on the far side of the platform.

"You are powerful," she says. "But not as powerful as the one before you. Do not forget that you are in my realm, playing by my rules. And as I am one with the mind of your friend, Wind Walker, if you destroy me, I will ensure you destroy him as well!"

I swallow hard. That's what I was afraid of! That's why I didn't cancel her powers in the first place. I might turn Wind Walker into a vegetable! But if I don't do it, she'll destroy me!

"Yield!" she commands. "Or die!"

I-I don't know what to do!

"Erase her power," comes a faint but familiar voice.

What? Who is that?

"I believe in you, Epic Zero," the voice says. *"And even if*

you fail, being a slave to her wishes is no way to live."

Wait! I know that voice. It's-It's Wind Walker!

"Do it," he says. *"Erase her power."*

B-But I could screw up. I could...

"Please... for the sake of all... you must..."

Suddenly, I look up to find the old woman morphing into a whirlwind of black mist! She's swirling with such velocity she's scattering Wind Walker's memories all over the place. Then, she rears back and heads straight for me!

It's now or never!

Without a second thought, I fire all of my negation energy directly at the oncoming tornado, engulfing it, swallowing it whole.

But to my surprise, she keeps on coming! I lean forward and push harder, but so does she! Her force is so strong it knocks me backward towards the edge of the platform!

"Yield!" she cries.

"Go suck an egg!" I yell back.

But I don't understand why I can't negate her power.

Suddenly, she thrusts forward.

My left foot dangles over the edge.

She's too strong! I-I can't hold on!

"Enough!" comes a familiar voice.

And then, to my surprise, Wind Walker is standing between us, surrounded by a strange purplish glow.

"Shadow creature," Wind Walker says, "you have preyed upon the souls of others for far too long. Your reign of terror ends now."

Then, he raises his satchel—it's the Spirit-catcher!

But what's he doing with it?

"How did you escape my grasp?" the Shadow asks.

"Begone evil spirit!" Wind Walker commands, opening the flap. "Begone for all of eternity!"

Suddenly, I feel something pulling me in like I'm being sucked into a vacuum cleaner. I try holding back, but I'm losing my footing. Then, I see hundreds of Wind Walker's own memories flying into the satchel.

"Noooo!" the Shadow screams, as she's pulled inside, disappearing through the mouth of the satchel.

I grit my teeth and dig in, but the force is too strong, and the next thing I know, I'm airborne, flying straight towards the Spirit-catcher!

Meta Profile

Name: The Shadow
Role: Spirit Entity   Status: Active

VITALS:

Race: Inapplicable
Real Name: Unknown
Height: appears 5'2"
Weight: Unknown
Eye Color: Blue
Hair Color: White

META POWERS:

Class: Inapplicable
Power Level: Incalculable

- A spirit entity who rules the 13th Dimension
- Survives by feeding off of Meta energy
- Displays immense Psychic power

CHARACTERISTICS:

Combat	Inapplicable
Durability	Inapplicable
Leadership	Inapplicable
Strategy	Inapplicable
Willpower	Inapplicable

TWELVE

I TAKE A RIDE

I'm flying headfirst into the Spirit-catcher!

As I hurtle towards the mouth of the mystical satchel, I can only watch in horror as more of Wind Walker's memories get sucked inside, followed by the last of the Shadow's misty tendrils!

Well, I guess that'll teach her.

But I'm next!

I stick out my arms, hoping to plug the opening like an oversized dust bunny, but I'm not sure it'll matter. Everything is getting sucked into the satchel, regardless of shape or size. I close my eyes.

What an undignified way to go.

Then, all of a sudden, the suction cuts off.

I crash to the floor like a bowling ball.

When I stop rolling, I realize I'm no longer inside Wind Walker's brain. In fact, I'm lying on the floor of the chamber at the foot of the throne—and above me sits Wind Walker!

I scramble to my feet, unsure of which Wind Walker I'm facing when I catch his eyes. They're back to green, his normal color! That's a good sign, until I realize he isn't moving. In fact, he isn't even blinking.

Then, I feel a tap on my shoulder.

"Epic Zero," Aries says, "are you okay?"

Aries? I step back and check out his eyes. They're back to their normal color too. And he's not moving around like a puppet anymore. He seems like his old self again.

"What happened?" he asks. "The last thing I remember is jumping inside that rock ring. After that, I don't remember anything. And what's wrong with Wind Walker? It's like he's in a trance."

"Well," I say. "It's a long story, but here's the quick version...."

As I run through the chain of events, I watch Aries' face fall. I tell him about the old woman being the Shadow, about Krule's escape using the All-Seeing Eye, and about the battle inside Wind Walker's mind. And then, of course, I explain how the Shadow manipulated Aries from afar. By the end of it all, he looks like he's going to be sick.

"Wow, seriously?" Aries says, rubbing his chin.

"That's crazy."

"I know," I say. "I'm sorry. But at least the Shadow is gone. But I'm not sure how long Wind Walker's satchel can hold her. She's really strong and she won't stay in there without a fight."

"I don't know," Aries says. "We'd have to ask Wind Walker about that. But he doesn't look like he's in any shape to answer."

"Wind Walker?" I say, shaking his shoulder.

But he doesn't respond. His chest is moving up and down so he's definitely breathing, but other than that, he's just staring straight ahead.

What's wrong with him?

But then I remember what happened.

"Oh no," I say. "When he opened his Spirit-catcher, he not only captured the Shadow, but most of his memories went in there as well. I-I think he accidentally erased a good portion of his own mind."

"What?" Aries says.

"We have to open the satchel!" I say. "It's the only way to fix him!"

"We can't do that," Aries says. "Knowing Wind Walker, this was no accident. He knew exactly what he was doing. He wouldn't want us to risk releasing the Shadow again for anything."

"But if we don't," I say, "he'll never be the same again. He'll be like this."

As I stare into Wind Walker's eyes, I'm totally

freaking out. I mean, did Wind Walker really do this on purpose? Did he really sacrifice his mind to prevent the Shadow from escaping?

"I know this is hard," Aries says, putting his hand on my shoulder. "But we both know there is no greater hero than Wind Walker. If he chose this course of action it must have been the only path he could take."

A tear slides down my cheek and I wipe it away.

I failed him. I mean, Wind Walker has always been there for me. Even in ways I didn't know of before today. And now he's like this because I couldn't defeat the Shadow on my own.

"Hey," Aries says. "It's okay. You did the best you could."

"Unfortunately, my best wasn't good enough," I say. "I don't even know what to do now."

"Now?" Aries says. "Now you'll take Wind Walker and go home."

"What?" I say shocked. "What do you mean? Aren't you coming?"

"No," Aries says, looking down. "My journey ends here. This is where I belong now."

"Are you crazy?" I ask. "What are you talking about? You can't stay here."

"I'm no longer a hero," Aries says. "My actions will haunt me for the rest of my life."

"You were being controlled by the Shadow!" I say. "You can't take responsibility for that. It's not fair."

"But I am the one responsible," Aries says. "Whether I was in control or not, my actions were mine and mine alone, and staying here will provide justice to the families of my victims. Plus, someone has to guard Wind Walker's Spirit-catcher. With the Shadow inside, we can't ever let it leave the 13th Dimension. Now, there's only one thing left to do."

"What's that?" I ask.

"Get you out of here," he says. "Maybe the Shadow was right about one thing. Maybe you can leave using the power of the All-Seeing Eye. Then, once you're gone, I'll destroy the crystal, preventing anyone from looking outside this dimension again."

***

A minute later, we're standing in front of the All-Seeing Eye. Aries is carrying Wind Walker, who still hasn't snapped back to normal, and honestly, I'm worried about him. I don't know if he'll ever recover from this.

The other person I'm worried about is Aries. Despite my arguments, I wasn't able to convince him to change his mind. I mean, I understand where he's coming from, but quite frankly I'm still shocked by his decision.

After all, who would want to stay in the 13th Dimension forever? But I guess that's the point. Being a hero means taking responsibility for your actions—no matter the consequences.

I look over at Aries and he nods.

Well, I guess this is it.

The last time I touched the crystal, I thought the images that popped up were random. But now I'm not so sure. Both Dog-Gone and Krule had been on my mind, so if I think hard enough, maybe I can get what I want to appear.

I press my palm against the surface and it changes from clear to opaque. Okay, I've got to focus. I close my eyes and fix an image in my mind, pushing away every unrelated thought. I concentrate on visualizing my goal, seeing it in my mind like it's right in front of my face. Then, when I think I have it good and nailed, I open my eyes, and there, floating before me, is a purple key.

The Cosmic Key!

I-I did it!

Now for the hard part. According to the Shadow, all I need to do is use my powers to reach through the crystal and copy the powers of the Cosmic Key. Never mind that it's in a totally different dimension. Well, this should be interesting.

I take a deep breath and try pushing my powers through the crystal itself, but I feel a wall of resistance. It's like my energy is spreading across the face of the crystal, not piercing through. This is hard, and beads of sweat form on my forehead. But I can't give up, this is our only ticket out of here.

Then, I remember the giant hammer Shaker turned herself into. If I can smash through the barrier, then maybe I can reach the key. So, I gather my energy, pull it back, and then strike down with all of my might!

Suddenly, all resistance fades and my power pours through the crystal. It surrounds the Cosmic Key, latching on to it. Smothering it.

And then, I pull it back.

I feel a rush of power, like electricity.

My body feels like a live wire.

But it's so much power, I'm not going to be able to hold it for long. I'm going to have to let it go!

"Now!" I say.

"Hang on," Aries says, laying Wind Walker on the ground. The next thing I know he runs back into the chamber, and I hear a RIPPING sound. Seconds later he's back, balancing the gold throne on his palm like it's lighter than a feather. "We're going to need this."

Um, okay.

Then, he gently places Wind Walker onto the throne and picks up the chair. "Follow me," he says, bolting up the stairs at a ridiculous speed.

I do my best to keep up but it's not exactly easy climbing twelve flights of stairs while I'm trying to contain an unhealthy dose of cosmic energy. I mean, if I release it before we get to the top it'll all be for nothing!

By the time I reach the uppermost level my thighs are on fire and I bend over to catch my breath. That's when I notice Aries is holding some rope. He must have grabbed it from the third level. But before I can ask him what it's for, he jumps up and busts clear through the ceiling, opening the underground castle to the gray sky.

The light hits my eyes and I squint, just as Aries drops back in, grabs me, and takes me topside. As soon as we clear the hole, I feel a tremendous sense of relief.

Note to self: no more underground missions—ever!

But when my vision adjusts, I find Aries tying Wind Walker to the gold throne.

"What are you doing?" I ask.

"Securing him for your trip," he says, pulling the rope tight. "I'm guessing the only way out of the 13th Dimension is the way we came in."

What's he talking about? But as I follow his eyes, I remember how we got here. We fell into the 13th Dimension—from the freaking sky.

"Hold on," I say. "Are you, like, planning to throw us into the air?"

"Yep," he says. "This will test the limits of my Super-strength, but when you reach the edge of the atmosphere, the power of the Cosmic Key should unlock the barrier."

"Right," I say, "Great plan. But it's that word 'should' I'm worried about."

"Do you want to stay here forever?" he asks.

"Not really," I say.

"Then sit down in the chair," he says.

I hesitate, but I know he's right. This is my only way

out of here, and my only shot to save Wind Walker.

"I can't believe I'm doing this," I say, sitting down next to Wind Walker.

Aries ties my body down, leaving my arms free. Then, I realize something.

"Wait," I say. "Do you have—"

"Wind Walker's satchel?" Aries says, holding it up. "Yes, I've got it right here."

"What are you going to do if the Shadow gets out?" I ask. "Not that I think she will. After all, she is kind of stuck inside a dimension stuffed inside another dimension. Kind of like a turducken."

"A tur-what?" he asks.

"A turducken," I say. "It's a chicken stuffed inside a duck that's stuffed inside a—oh, never mind. It's a silly Earth food invention. Don't ask why."

"I won't," Aries says with a smile. "Look, I promise I'll do whatever it takes to keep the Shadow here. Now let's work on getting you guys out of this place."

Aries picks up the throne.

"Do you have a good arm?" I ask.

"I think so," Aries says. "But I guess we'll find out. Ready?"

"Um, not really," I say.

"Great," he says. "Hold on."

I pull on the ropes to make sure we're tied down tight and they don't budge. Then, he rears back his massive arm.

OMG! This is going to happen! I close my eyes.

"Goodbye," Aries says. "Do good things when you get home."

But before I can respond, we're airborne, rocketing through the sky so fast I can barely catch my breath!

My heart is pumping and I feel a surge of power flare out of my body! Darn it! I don't know where this magic doorway is, but I can't blow all of the Cosmic Key's juice before we get there.

We're soaring higher and higher like we were shot out of a cannon. The wind is pressing hard against my face, blowing my hair back. But as we keep ascending, I can't help but wonder what'll happen when we finally reach our peak. After all, there is that little thing called 'gravity.' Man, that would stink.

Then, I see something out of the corner of my eye, moving between the clouds.

It's a black speck.

Nope, scratch that, it's a black speck—with wings!

And it's flying right for us!

Holy hamburger! It's the winged creature Aries and I saw earlier! Immediately, panic sets in. I mean, it looked big at ground level, but now that it's fast approaching, I can tell it's absolutely ginormous, with a huge snout and red eyes focused directly on me!

I look around but there's nowhere for us to go. We're sitting ducks tied to this chair! And why do I suddenly have the feeling this throne is slowing down?

Meanwhile, the creature is only getting closer. It looks determined, flapping its monstrous wings harder and harder.

Then, I notice purple energy crackling all around me.

Oh no! I'm so freaked out I'm losing the power of the Cosmic Key! I can't control it! And when I look down, the beast has caught up with us!

It opens its mouth, revealing rows of sharp teeth!

This is not good!

I lean back and pull my feet up when—

BOOM!

The throne shakes violently.

THUD!

What was that?

I look down to see the creature's limp body shrinking in the distance as it freefalls towards the ground.

Huh? What happened?

Then, I realize we're no longer flying through gray clouds, but through a field of purple energy.

But that can only mean one thing.

We broke through the atmosphere!

We're heading out of the 13th Dimension!

I-I can't believe it! We did it!

Suddenly, there's a loud POP and our throne skids along a rough surface, generating sparks from the friction until we finally come to a stop. The ropes have come loose and I check on Wind Walker who miraculously is still breathing.

Ugh, for a second the world is spinning, and I feel like I've been run over by a herd of elephants. In fact, I think I might hurl.

But that's fine with me because if I just accomplished what I think we accomplished, I'm going to celebrate like there's no—

"Elliott Harkness!" booms a familiar voice.

—tomorrow?

I roll over on my side to find a pair of fishy eyes staring down at me.

Oh no.

"Elliott Harkness," Quovaar repeats. "Welcome back to Paladin Planet. I am pleased to inform you that your trial will begin now."

THIRTEEN

I GO ON TRIAL

Talk about out of the frying pan and into the fire!

I mean, I just escaped from the freaking 13th Dimension, and now I'm sprawled out in front of the Interstellar Council and they want to start my trial right now!

And who says life isn't fair?

Normally this would be ridiculously traumatizing stuff. Especially because if I'm found guilty, I get a one-way ticket right back to the 13th Dimension. But I can't worry about me right now. I've got more important stuff to check on—like Wind Walker's health.

"Elliott Harkness," Quovaar says. "Perhaps you did not hear me. I said your trial begins now."

"I heard you," I say. "But before we start this ridiculous trial my friend needs medical attention. He's innocent in all of this. He's a hero named—"

"—Wind Walker," Quovaar says, finishing my sentence. "We are well aware of his deeds, as well as his mysterious disappearance. But what I do not understand is how he got inside the 13th Dimension."

"I'll give you all the gory details later," I say. "But right now, he needs help. He's not all here at the moment. He lost his memory helping me defeat the Shadow."

"The Intergalactic Paladins aid all heroes," Quovaar says, signaling to others with his staff. "But what is this 'Shadow' you speak of?"

Um, what?

"Sorry," I say, "but are you saying you've been sending criminals down there for who knows how long and you never knew there was a lunatic spirit-lady in there who is trying to get out and conquer the entire multiverse?"

"We know not of what you speak," Quovaar says matter-of-factly. "And the Council demands that you reveal the whereabouts of your accomplice, Aries."

"He decided to stay behind," I say. "He believed that's where he needed to be."

"A wise decision," Quovaar says. "Perhaps you should have done the same."

Okay, now I've had just about enough of this guy. But I guess Xenox was right. There's no way I'll get a fair trial around here. I mean, he's practically convicting me before it even starts!

Suddenly, a bunch of Paladins drop from the sky. One brushes me back as the others tend to Wind Walker. After a few seconds, they use their Infinity Wands to create a stretcher and then cart Wind Walker away before I can even say goodbye.

I sure hope they can help him. I'm still amazed by what he did down there. I don't know many heroes who would knowingly erase their own memory to save the day—and that includes me.

"Now that we have addressed all distractions," Quovaar barks, "your trial shall commence!"

But then again, now might be a good time to start.

Quovaar moves to the center of the platform and bangs his staff on the floor three times. Suddenly, that jiggly guilt-monitor known as the Paladin's Pulse rises from behind the platform.

According to Quovaar, those globules will read the inner conscience of every Paladin present. They're all white now, but if the majority of them turn red by the end of my trial, I'm considered guilty-as-charged!

I don't know why they do it this way, but I do know one thing—I'll never eat Jello again.

As Quovaar takes his seat, I wonder what kind of damaging evidence they've gathered to use against me. Old report cards? A picture of my bowl cut from third grade? Whatever it is, I'm ready to get this show on the road. But shockingly, nothing happens.

I mean, what's going on? He said my trial was starting now. What are we waiting for, fireworks?

"Elliott Harkness," comes a voice from behind me.

I jump out of my skin.

Not cool.

I spin around to have a word with my surprise guest, but instead, I end up doing a double take. Because standing before me is a slender alien with blue, bug-like eyes and pink skin!

"Proog?" I say. "Is that really you?"

"No," the alien says. "As you well know, Proog is dead. My name is Broog. I am Proog's brother and the appointed prosecutor for your trial."

Wait, what? Proog's brother is my prosecutor? He's the one who will be trying to prove my guilt in front of everyone?

"Whoa, hang on," I say, addressing the Council. "This isn't fair. I mean, how can I possibly convince any of you that I'm innocent when I'm being tried by the brother of the deceased? I think that's called a… a 'conflict of interest?' They'd never allow that on Earth."

"Need I remind you that we are not on Earth," Quovaar says. "Here we govern by the—"

"—Order of the Paladin," I say, this time finishing his sentence. "Yada yada yada. Yeah, I get where this is going. You're setting me up. So, let me guess who is defending me, Krule the Conqueror?"

"I would advise you not to question our justice

system," Quovaar says. "Per the Order of the Paladin, you and you alone will bear the weight of defending your actions. The prosecution will be granted one witness, and you will be granted the same privilege."

One witness? OMG! I never decided on a witness!

"Speaking of witnesses, Honorable Council," Broog begins. "I would like to call forth my prime witness in this unfortunate case. Someone who has firsthand knowledge of the defendant's transgressions. Someone who was at the very scene of the crime."

At the scene of the crime? Who could that be?

"Bring forth your witness," Quovaar says.

"He is presently on his way," Broog says, gesturing towards the sky.

Looking up, I see four Paladins flying towards us, towing a box with their Infinity Wands. As the Paladins get closer, I study their faces, but I don't recognize any of them, so I'm not sure which one is the witness Broog was referring to.

But as they lower the box next to me, I take a step back. I was so focused on the Paladins I didn't register how large the box actually was. It's like ten feet tall and made out of tungsten steel!

What's that for?

Suddenly, the box shakes violently and I hear muffled noises coming from inside. That's when I realize something is in there!

"Open the cage," Broog commands.

Did he say 'cage?'

Just then, the front of the box lifts and my jaw drops, because standing inside is a ginormous, yellow-skinned man whose arms and legs are bound by chains!

It's… a Skelton?

The Paladins gasp, and at first, I think it's just some random Skelton warrior. But as I study his face more closely a chill runs down my spine, because I think I've seen him before. His eyes look familiar, except I don't remember all the wrinkles, or the white hairs sprouting from around his ears.

I'm racking my brain. How do I know him?

And then it hits me.

"Y-You're the Blood Master?" I stammer.

He looks at me with his neon green eyes and spits.

I-I can't believe it! The last time I saw him, he was working with Norman Fairchild to steal the Cosmic Key for the Skelton Empire. But that was thirty years ago when I traveled into the past.

And now he's… here?

"Honorable Council," Broog states. "I present my prime witness in these proceedings. His real name is Mowleg Grawl of Skelton, better known to all as the Blood Master. Of course, his reputation proceeds him. He is a natural-born killer and one of the top fugitives on the Intergalactic Paladin's Most Wanted List. Yet, he has been apprehended and I bring him before you because he has an important role to play in the case against Elliott

Harkness. Will you permit me to examine the witness?"

"Permission granted," Quovaar says.

"Thank you," Broog says with a slight bow. "Please tell us, Mowleg Grawl, do you know the defendant standing before you?"

The Blood Master sneers at me and says, "Yes."

"Excellent," Broog says. "You participated in the battle for the Cosmic Key at the institution known as ArmaTech on planet Earth. Is that correct?"

The Blood Master spits again, and then says, "Yes."

"Did the defendant participate as well?" Broog asks.

"Yes," he answers, his eyes never leaving mine.

"Please, Mowleg Grawl," Broog says, "It would be helpful if you could provide more than one-word answers."

"Then stop asking only one-word questions," the Blood Master says. "And I am called the Blood Master. I know of no other identity."

"Very well," Broog says. "Now tell us, Mow—I mean, Blood Master. What role do you remember the defendant playing at ArmaTech?"

"Before I say anything else," the Blood Master says, looking up at Quovaar, "I want assurances the deal for my freedom is still in place. Because I could break these chains in an instant if I wanted to."

Deal? Wait a minute. What deal?

"Silence, fool," Quovaar whispers through gritted teeth. "Now answer the question."

"I'll take that as a yes," the Blood Master says, looking my way. "Of course I remember him. I remember the whole situation like it was yesterday. That child goes by the name of Epic Zero. But at the battle itself, he was masquerading as a hero called the Nullifier. At first, I thought he was just another human weakling. But he proved me wrong."

"How so?" Broog asks, pacing back and forth. "What did the defendant do?"

"He destroyed an Infinity Wand," the Blood Master says. "I saw him do it."

There's murmuring in the audience.

"That's right," the Blood Master continues. "He sent a massive power surge into the Infinity Wand, shattering it into a gazillion pieces. That's what turned Norman Fairchild into the monster known as Meta-Taker."

The Paladins let out a collective gasp, then they start booing.

"Order!" Quovaar demands, tapping his staff against the floor. "Order, I say!"

The audience grows silent.

"So," Broog says, "you are claiming you witnessed the defendant intentionally destroy an Infinity Wand? Proog's Infinity Wand?"

"Yes," the Blood Master says.

"That's a lie!" I blurt out.

"Objection!" Broog yells. "It is not his turn."

"He couldn't have seen me," I say, ignoring him.

"He was unconscious at the time."

"Silence!" Quovaar orders, "your turn will come."

I look up at the Paladin's Pulse. Half the white globules have already turned red! This is not good!

"Go on," Broog says, nodding to his witness. "What else did you see?"

"What else?" the Blood Master says, taking a dramatic pause. "Oh, right. Well, then I saw him hand the Cosmic Key to Krule the Conqueror."

The crowd explodes.

What? But that's not true either!

"Honorable Council," Broog says. "I rest my case."

"Order!" Quovaar commands. "Order in the court!"

But the audience refuses to settle down.

Over the commotion, Quovaar looks at me and says, "Elliott Harkness, it is now time to hear from you. How do you plead to the serious charges brought against you and who will you call to testify as your witness?"

I-I want to declare my innocence.

But I did destroy an Infinity Wand.

And I don't have a witness.

I-I don't know what to do.

Meta Profile

Name: Blood Master
Role: Villain   Status: Active

VITALS:

Race: Skelton
Real Name: Mowleg Grawl
Height: 6'11"
Weight: 330 lbs
Eye Color: Green
Hair Color: Bald

META POWERS:

Class: Meta-morph
Power Level:

- Extreme Shape-Shifting—can assume endless forms
- Can mimic the powers of those he assumes the form of

CHARACTERISTICS:

Combat	100
Durability	91
Leadership	85
Strategy	88
Willpower	92

FOURTEEN

I MOUNT MY DEFENSE

All eyes are on me.

And I'm frozen!

I mean, this is my one chance to say everything I need to stay to stop this mockery of a trial from going any further. But the problem is, I'm the only one who knows the truth and no one else seems to care!

I try to collect myself, but it's clear everything is stacked up against me. I mean, my prosecutor is Proog's brother, his star witness is in cahoots with the Supreme Council, and nearly the entire Paladin's Pulse has turned red before the trial has even ended!

How can they not find me guilty?

"Elliott Harkness," Quovaar says, "please face the Supreme Council and tell us what you plead."

What do I plead? What can I plead?

For some reason, Aries crosses my mind. Even though he wasn't at fault, he sacrificed his freedom to give the families of his victims the justice they deserve. I don't think I've ever seen anyone step up to the plate like that before.

What should I say?

"Elliott Harkness," Quovaar repeats. "You are trying the patience of the Council. What do you plead and who will stand as your witness?"

I take a deep breath and exhale. All I can do is tell the truth and let the chips fall where they may.

"On the second count of aiding Krule's escape from the 13th Dimension," I say. "I plead not guilty."

There's a commotion in the stands.

"But on the first count of destroying an Infinity Wand," I say, yelling over the crowd. "I can only plead guilty—but I acted in self-defense."

The crowd erupts.

I glance at the Paladin's Pulse. It's all red.

The Paladins are eating this up—booing, hissing, and calling me nasty-sounding names in alien tongues I don't understand.

"Order!" Quovaar commands.

But the Paladins refuse to settle down.

"Drop him in!" cries a voice from the crowd.

"Send him to the 13th Dimension!" comes another.

I feel good about telling the truth. I'm just concerned it's not going to make a difference.

"Now who will you call as your witness?" Quovaar shouts over the crowd. "Order!" he commands, banging his staff on the platform.

But now I'm really in trouble because if I can't produce a witness credible enough to back up my side of the story, I'm toast. But who could I possibly call that could sway this biased audience?

"Order!" Quovaar demands again, this time rising to his feet. "Order in the court! I say order in the court!"

Wait. What did he just say?

Order...?

In the court?

That's it!

But it's a longshot.

And if it doesn't work, I'm doomed.

Finally, the Paladins settle down.

"Elliott Harkness," Quovaar says. "While you plead innocent to one charge, you plead guilty to the other, with a claim of self-defense. These accusations against you are serious, and this case must be carefully deliberated. Per the Order of the Paladin, you are allowed to call before the Court one witness who may try to support your claims. Once named, we will summon this individual to the Court immediately. Do you have such a witness?"

"Yes," I say, mustering as much confidence as I can. "I think I do have a witness."

"You do?" Quovaar says, his voice rising in surprise. "Very well then. Who is this so-called witness? Let us bring this individual before the Court at once."

"Certainly," I say. Then, I take a deep breath and say, "I call before the Court my witness. The one, the only, Order!"

I wave my arms with a flourish, waiting for his grand entrance. I'm expecting smoke, music, fireworks.

But embarrassingly, there's nothing.

Did I just make the biggest mistake of my life?

"Good evening, Elliott Harkness."

I jump out of my skin.

Standing behind me is a tall, purple-skinned man wearing a black suit with a white pocket square and tie.

"Order!" I say relieved. "You came?"

"Yes," he says. "I was not going to interfere in these proceedings, but the more I observed, the more I sensed my presence was required to ensure proper balance in the multiverse."

"Wh-Who are you?" Quovaar asks.

"I am Order," he says. "My purpose is to ensure structure, discipline, and boundaries in all things. And you are Quovaar, Supreme Justice of the Interstellar Council. An Interstellar Council that has presided for millennia based upon the principles of the Order of the Paladin— nobility, justice, and fairness. Yet, I sense an overwhelming darkness guiding these affairs."

"I know not of what you speak," Quovaar says.

"Perhaps not," Order says. "But this child is no mere criminal to be thrown to the wolves. He has proven himself a great hero. A great hero with a great destiny."

Um, what?

"He has been accused of serious crimes," Quovaar says. "He must stand trial."

"Must he?" Order says with a smirk. "Very well then. As I am his key witness, you must now observe."

Order snaps and a scene I recognize in my darkest nightmares repeats itself before everyone.

I'm back in ArmaTech. The Blood Master is lying unconscious on the floor, just as I remembered, while Fairchild and I are in a heated game of tug-of-war for the Cosmic Key.

"You are powerful," Fairchild says. "But not powerful enough."

Then, he points the Infinity Wand at a group of heroes, including Dynamo Joe and Blue Bolt. He zaps them with orange energy, and pulls it back into the Infinity Wand, absorbing their power.

"Now, it ends," Fairchild says, pointing the Infinity Wand at me! But the wand is shaking violently. It looks unstable.

Panic registers in my eyes as I focus all of my Meta energy and throw it at the Infinity Wand.

It causes a blinding explosion.

An explosion that created Meta-Taker.

"That is truly what happened that day," Order says. "Elliott Harkness did indeed destroy the Infinity Wand, but he did so to save himself and his colleagues from certain destruction. He acted the only way he knew how, like a true hero."

"B-But..." Quovaar stammers.

"Silence," Order says. "It is not your turn. Continue to observe."

The image shifts to me running at lightning speed towards Meta-Taker. The monster is holding the Cosmic Key, but just as I'm about to reach him a Pterodactyl swoops across the scene, biting the key right out of Meta-Taker's hand!

As Meta-Taker and I collide and tumble to the ground, the Pterodactyl disappears into a green vortex, taking the Cosmic Key with it!

"Finally," comes a booming voice from above.

And then, the face of Krule the Conqueror appears, gloating over us all. "The Cosmic Key is mine!" he says. "And now, the universe will be mine as well!"

Then, there's a flash of white light and he's gone.

"What do you think now?" Order asks. "Now that you have seen the truth?"

"I... I..." Quovaar mutters.

"This is a lie!" Broog states. "He is lying! That is not what happened! My brother did not die in vain!"

"No," Order says, putting his hand on Broog's shoulder. "Your brother did not die in vain. He died as a hero. But unfortunately, not all brothers are as heroic as yours."

"What do you mean?" Broog asks.

"I will answer your question shortly," Order says. "But first, let us put an end to this."

He snaps and Quovaar and Broog shake their heads.

"What happened?" Quovaar says. "What is going on here?"

"You have been manipulated," Order says.

"What?" Quovaar says. "By what?"

"The answer is not 'by what,'" Order says, looking to the sky. "But rather, 'by who.' Isn't that right, dear brother? I believe this trial has ended, but perhaps yours shall begin?"

Brother? Wait, does he mean—

Suddenly, another man appears next to Order. He looks just like him, but he's wearing sunglasses and a leather jacket!

"Chaos," Order says. "Have you had enough fun at the expense of these poor creatures?"

"Of course not," Chaos says. "But fun has a way of dying whenever you show up."

Chaos? What's he doing here?

Then it hits me.

Chaos must be responsible for all of this.

But why?

"What I do not understand is your motive," Order says. "Why choose this child? Has he not suffered enough?"

"You know me," Chaos says. "In the game of chess, it's always important to be a few moves ahead."

"I understand," Order says. "But there is more in store for this one, and the multiverse will need him."

"Your version of the multiverse needs him," Chaos says. "Not mine. I'll bargain anytime, anywhere, and with anyone for proper disorder."

Bargain? Wait a second. Didn't the Shadow mention she bargained with someone to get me into the 13th Dimension?

"You!" I blurt out. "You made a deal with the Shadow!"

"Yeah," Chaos says, buffing his nails. "I make millions of deals every second. Some work, some don't."

"I think it is time you departed," Order says. "And if you know what is good for you, I suggest you leave this one alone."

"Nah," Chaos says, winking at me. "Remember, he's one of your game pieces, not mine. Goodbye, brother. For now."

Then, he snaps and he's gone.

"Elliott Harkness," Quovaar says. "On behalf of the Intergalactic Paladins, I apologize for this gross abuse of power. We did not realize we were being manipulated. Of course, you are cleared of all charges from here to eternity."

I look over at the Paladin's Pulse and my eyes widen.

It's green!

The whole darn thing is green!

"Yes," Broog says, shaking my hand. "I must

apologize as well. In his final moments, I am sure my brother was thankful to have someone as brave as you by his side."

"He was the brave one," I say. "You would have been proud of him. He sacrificed everything to save the universe."

"Elliott Harkness," Order says. "You have been through a lot. Would you like me to return you home?"

Home? After all of this, I never thought I'd see home again. I mean, I know what I've gone through, but I can't even imagine how worried my parents must be.

But then I remember Wind Walker.

I can't just leave him like this.

"Do not worry," Order says with a smile, showing off his perfectly straight teeth. "I will take care of your friend for you. As my brother would say, he is one of my important game pieces as well."

"Really?" I say relieved. "That would be amazing."

"Very well," he says. "Shall we?"

"Yeah," I say.

"Goodbye, Elliott Harkness," Quovaar says. "We salute you. You are a true hero."

Suddenly, he raises his staff, emitting a bright orange light into the sky. And then, to my surprise, all of the Paladins follow suit, flickering their Infinity Wands in a brilliant display of unity.

I smile just as Order snaps.

And we're gone.

Meta Profile

Name: Chaos
Role: Cosmic Entity   Status: Active

VITALS:

Race: Inapplicable
Real Name: Chaos
Height: appears 7'0"
Weight: Unknown
Eye Color: Inapplicable
Hair Color: White

META POWERS:

Class: Inapplicable
Power Level: Incalculable

- Balances his brother, Order, to cause stress, disorder, and randomness throughout the universe

- Cannot harm other Cosmic Entities

CHARACTERISTICS:

Combat	Inapplicable
Durability	Inapplicable
Leadership	Inapplicable
Strategy	Inapplicable
Willpower	Inapplicable

FIFTEEN

I TAKE THE STAGE

Water runs from a faucet as I stare at myself in a mirror.

No surprise, I look like a train wreck, but that doesn't matter right now. The only thing I want to know is where I am.

It doesn't take long to figure it out.

O.M.G.

I'm back in the bathroom at CNC headquarters!

Well, Order returned me home alright, but he dropped me off at the wrong location. I thought he was going to take me back to the Waystation. I'm bummed, but at least I'm not surrounded by Intergalactic Paladins.

Honestly, it feels strange being back here. I mean, the last time I was here I was making a fool of myself on live television. Who knows how much worse it could have been if I hadn't been abducted by those aliens?

Fortunately, I've probably been gone for days, so I'll never know the answer.

Well, there's no sense hiding in here any longer. I guess I'll head out and let the team know where they can pick me up. I can't wait to see Dog-Gone again, even though he owes me a new pair of slippers.

I turn off the faucet and reach for the door, when—

KNOCK-KNOCK.

"Mr. Zero?" comes a woman's voice. "Mr. Zero, are you okay in there?"

I stop cold.

Wait a minute, I know that voice. It sounds like the woman who was wearing that headset.

But what's she still doing here?

"Mr. Zero?" she calls out again. "We really need you back on set. We're rolling live here. The second segment starts in less than a minute."

Second segment?

No. Freaking. Way!

If she's telling me my cruddy interview is still going on, then that means Order not only dropped me off at CNC, but he also returned me only seconds after I was taken by those Paladins!

I feel sick to my stomach.

Maybe I should go back to the 13th Dimension.

KNOCK-KNOCK.

"Mr. Zero?"

"Um, yeah," I respond. "Be right with you."

Holy horseshoes! I can't catch a break. This is totally the last thing I need right now. I don't want to go back out there. General Winch ate me alive!

I need to get out of here—and fast!

My eyes dart around the room looking for an escape route. Then, I notice a vent in the ceiling. Maybe I can pull myself up? No, it's too high. Then my eyes land on the toilet. Maybe I can escape through the sewer system?

It's messy, but it just might work!

But as I lift the lid, it dawns on me that this is crazy. First, I'll never fit down the drain, and second, if I got stuck and CNC got it on camera, my humiliation would live forever on Grace's screensaver.

So, I guess that only leaves one option.

Finish the interview.

KNOCK-KNOCK.

"Mr. Zero?"

I start pacing. I've got this, right? After all, didn't I just do the impossible? I mean, not just anyone could escape from the 13th Dimension or prove their innocence to a deluded court of Intergalactic Paladins. Compared to all of that, how bad could this be?

But then I remember that millions of people are watching me. I've already made a fool of myself once, so do I really want to do it again? Maybe I'll just tell them I'm not feeling well. Yeah, that's a good excuse.

But then I think of Aries and Wind Walker, and I feel guilty. They didn't make excuses. They did what needed to be done, no matter the personal consequences.

That's what real heroes do.

I rub my eyes. I know what I have to do, even if I don't want to do it. But I came here to do a job, so let's do the freaking job already.

I take a deep breath and exhale. Then, I open the door and march past a very relieved-looking woman.

"Are you okay?" she asks, running behind me.

"Golden," I say, entering the studio.

"Great," she says. "Here's your microphone."

As she attaches it to my collar, General Winch looks my way and flashes a condescending smile. I ignore him and take my seat.

"You okay, kid?" Sarah Anderson whispers.

"Yeah," I say. "I'm fine."

"Great," she says. "Now's your chance to take it to him. Ready?"

I nod and she turns to center camera. The man with the clipboard raises his hand and counts down from five with his fingers. Then, he gives us the thumbs up and the camera light turns on.

I swallow hard. We're live again.

"Welcome back to the CNC Morning Newsflash," Sarah Anderson begins. "We're ready for part two in our debate about Meta heroes—good guys or dangers to society. Joining us is General William Winch, former Chairman of the Joint Chiefs of Staff, and Epic Zebra, a young—"

"Excuse me, Ms. Anderson," I say. "But my name is not Epic Zebra. It's Epic Zero."

"What?" she says, looking down at her notes. "Oh, I'm so sorry. Please, forgive me for the unprofessional journalism, and don't worry, someone's head will roll for that. Well then, also joining us is Epic Zero, a young superhero partly responsible for yesterday's damage to the Keystone City subway system. Mr. Zero, let's start with you. Do Meta powers put the public at risk?"

I look straight at the camera, but this time I don't feel nearly as nervous. In fact, I'm feeling pretty good.

"I think the way you asked the question is important," I say. "But before we talk about Metas, let's talk about regular people. Would you say there are good people and bad people?"

"Well, yes," she says. "Of course."

"Exactly," I say. "Some people are good, but others are bad to the bone. And let's remember, any bad person who gets hold of a weapon can put the public at risk. So, having Meta powers isn't the problem. The problem comes when bad people have Meta powers. That's where Meta heroes come in. We stop Meta villains."

"That's a clever answer," General Winch says, "but it doesn't address the real problem. The real problem comes when some yahoo puts on a mask and thinks he's Captain Justice. Most of these so-called 'heroes' are untrained and risk people's lives and property. They're outlaws!"

He raises his chin, grinning like a Cheshire Cat. But

that won't be the end of this debate. Not on my watch.

"Tell me, General," I say calmly. "Without Meta heroes, who would have stopped Ravager from destroying our planet?"

"Well," he says. "The government, of course. We were prepared to detonate a nuclear bomb right into it."

"Really?" I say. "So, you're saying our government would have detonated a nuclear warhead right over the homes of its own citizens to stop an intergalactic monster with the consistency of a vapor cloud? Do you really think that would have worked, General?"

"Well," General Winch says, turning bright red. "That's not what our intelligence reports said at the time."

"Your intelligence reports were wrong," I say. "Just for the record, I traveled to another universe to find a proper solution to the Ravager problem."

"Wow, Mr. Zero," Sarah Anderson says. "That's truly impressive and I thank you for your work there. But if you don't mind, let's shift gears for a second because we have a special guest we'd like to bring into the conversation."

A special guest? Who could that be?

Suddenly, the screen behind us cuts to an image of a man with a handlebar mustache. For some reason, I feel like I know this guy, but it's not until I read his name and title that I remember who it is.

"This is Mr. Carl Frankel," Sarah Anderson says. "He

was the subway driver operating the L train who witnessed the events involving Mr. Zero firsthand. Welcome to the program, Mr. Frankel."

Oh no! The last time I saw him was seconds before I turned myself into sand to keep the train from derailing. I saved his life, but who knows what side he's on.

"Thank you, Ms. Anderson," he says. "It's a pleasure to be here."

"Mr. Frankel," she says, "you claim to have seen everything that happened down there. Can you tell us what you saw?"

I brace myself.

"Certainly," he says. "I saw what it means to be a hero. That boy right there saved my life and the lives of my passengers. If he wasn't there, I'm convinced those villains would have done something to my subway car and we'd be talking about multiple fatalities."

Wait, what? He's defending me?

"We're grateful you're unharmed, Mr. Frankel," she says. "But tell us, what if he wasn't there in the first place? What do you think would have happened then?"

"I have no doubt those villains still would have done something evil," Mr. Frankel says, "and we would have been defenseless against that kind of power. Listen, as the driver of a subway I've seen all kinds of people, and bad people are bad, whether they have Meta powers or not. I'm just thankful this boy was there and his actions saved a lot of lives that day. Thank you, Epic Zero, from the bottom of my heart."

"Gee," I say. "Thanks."

Then, the image of Mr. Frankel cuts out.

"Well, there you have it," Sarah Anderson says. "I guess the conclusion is that it's not the powers but the person that makes the difference, and we'll always need heroes to deal with the villains."

"Not true," General Winch says, pounding the desk. "Mark my words. Meta powers will be outlawed one day. One day soon."

Then, he stands up and leaves the stage.

"Okaaay," Sarah Anderson says. "Well, thank you, Mr. Zero, for sharing your perspective. It sounds like you are making a real difference in people's lives."

"Oh, no problem," I say. "But I'm not done yet. There's still something I need to do."

"Well, I can't wait to hear about it," she says. "But for now, that's it for the CNC Morning Newsflash. Be careful out there and have a terrific day."

"And cut!" the stagehand yells.

"Nice job, kid," Sarah Anderson says. "You came back strong. You really flustered the General."

"Yeah," I say. "I guess I did."

"Keep doing great things," she says. "And maybe we'll have you back."

"Um, thanks," I say, "but I've had enough of the limelight for a while."

"Fair enough," she says, shaking my hand. "Take

care, Epic Zero."

As she leaves, the woman with the headset takes my microphone and escorts me off the stage.

"Nice job, Mr. Zero," she says. "You handed it to that bully."

"Oh, thanks," I say. "It was nothing really."

As she leads me through a maze of hallways, I'm feeling pretty good about myself. I mean, believe me, I'm glad it's over, but I'm also happy I found my voice. It was a big responsibility to speak on behalf of my fellow heroes and I'm glad I didn't let them down.

Finally, we reach a doorway.

"Your family is right through here," she says.

"Thanks," I say, and as soon as I open the door, Dad wraps me up in a big hug.

"Way to go, champ!" he says. "You killed it!"

"Well," Grace says. "Truthfully, you were nearly killed. After the first part, I thought I'd have to give Dad CPR."

"Don't be silly, Grace," Dad says, shooting her a look. "He did a great job."

"Yeah," she says, hugging me. "You really did. I'm proud of you, bro."

"Thanks," I say.

"But what was that thing you said at the end?" Grace asks. "You said there's something you needed to do."

"Yep," I say. "And the good news is that you can do it with me."

Meta Profile

Name: Order
Role: Cosmic Entity   Status: Active

VITALS:

Race: Inapplicable
Real Name: Order
Height: appears 7'0"
Weight: Unknown
Eye Color: Inapplicable
Hair Color: White

META POWERS:

Class: Inapplicable
Power Level: Incalculable

- Balances his brother, Chaos, to ensure structure, discipline, and boundaries throughout the universe

- Cannot harm other Cosmic Entities

CHARACTERISTICS:

Combat	Inapplicable
Durability	Inapplicable
Leadership	Inapplicable
Strategy	Inapplicable
Willpower	Inapplicable

EPILOGUE

I GET BACK ON MY FEET

"**T**his was a great idea, Elliott," Dad says.

"Thanks," I say, ensuring my goggles are secure as I drill the final nail into my stretch of subway track. "How's the third rail coming?"

"It's been replaced," Dad says, snapping in the wheel that carries power from the rail to the train's electric motor. "With 625 volts of electricity, I'd say I'm the right Meta to handle this job."

"For sure," I say. "How's the debris cleanup going?"

"It's all cleaned up," Mom says, "Between my telekinesis and Blue Bolt's speed, it didn't take long to remove it all."

"Excellent," I say. "And is the tunnel ceiling secure?"

"Just about," Grace says, floating above me. "TechnocRat is still inspecting our handiwork. After that, Master Mime can remove the energy beams holding the place up and we should be on our way. Hey, are you sure you don't want to get this on camera?" she says, fixing her hair. "I think I'm ready to get back in the spotlight."

"Um, no thanks," I say. "I'm not doing this for the publicity. Besides, I've had my fill of cameras."

Apparently, my interview with General Winch went viral. I saw some newsfeed article saying it broke all video streaming records, and there's been an overwhelming outpouring of support for Meta heroes, but honestly, that's not what it's about for me.

I realized that being a Meta doesn't make us better than anyone else. We're members of society too, and we need to take responsibility for our actions. Thankfully, the team agreed.

So, I was thrilled when Shadow Hawk got permission from the Keystone City Transit Authority allowing us to fix the subway line. It took all morning, but it saved Keystone City six months and millions of dollars.

"Well," Dad says, putting his hand on my shoulder, "I think we need to do more of this. I'm proud of you, son."

"Thanks," I say.

Suddenly, a rat with a jetpack drops down between us.

"Everything looks good," TechnocRat says. "This baby is approved to run."

"Great!" I say, pulling a walkie talkie out of my utility

belt. I push the button and speak into it. "Makeshift, we're good to go. Just give us a minute to get out of here and I'll give you the all-clear signal. Then you can tell the police to reopen the line."

There's static, and then an ear-piercing SQUAWK.

"Breaker 1-9," Makeshift says over the walkie talkie. "Mohawk numero uno responding. 10-4. Copy. Roger that. Affirmative. Over and out."

I roll my eyes. Who decided it was a good idea to give Makeshift a walkie talkie anyway?

"Okay," I announce, "let's roll!"

I start packing up my tools when I hear—

"Epic Zero."

I drop my drill and it CLANGS onto the track.

That voice? I'd know that voice anywhere!

It's Wind Walker!

I spin around to find him smiling at me, his green eyes looking alert. I throw my arms around him, squeezing him tight.

"You're okay?" I say, backing up, wiping tears from my cheeks. "I-I can't believe it."

"Epic Zero," Dad says, "who is this man?"

When I look up, the Freedom Force is standing all around us, ready for action.

"He's Wind Walker," I say. "The friend I told you about."

"I wanted to thank you," Wind Walker says. "You saved my life."

"Well, you saved mine," I say. "But wait... you remember?"

"Yes," he says. "My memories have returned. At least, most of them. But your actions were impossible to forget. I am forever indebted to you. And to Aries."

"Did you hear from him?" I ask, hopeful.

"Yes," Wind Walker says. "Order felt it was only fair to offer him the opportunity to leave the 13th Dimension, but Aries decided to stay. He said he had an important job to do making sure the Shadow stayed inside the Spirit-catcher, but he was happy we escaped."

I lower my head.

"I will never forget him either," Wind Walker says. "He demonstrated what it means to be a true hero. I will miss him greatly. But I have a gift for you."

"For me?" I say. "Really?"

"It is a small token," he says. "But when I was possessed by the Shadow, I became a part of her. Therefore, everything inside the realm became known to me, from the moment you entered to the moment you disconnected me from her power."

"Wow," I say. "Really?"

"Yes," he says. "I witnessed everything, including the images you saw through the All-Seeing Eye. Just as you observed Krule the Conqueror attacking the Skelton Homeworld, so did I."

OMG! With everything going on I completely forgot about Krule. But now it's all coming back to me.

"Since recovering, I have used my powers to secretly visit the Skelton Homeworld and I must report that Krule has completed his task," Wind Walker says. "He has conquered their planet. But that will not satisfy him for long. Eventually, he will try conquering more worlds, including this one."

"Boy," TechnocRat says, "that's some gift you've brought him. What are you gonna tell him next, there's a shortage on pizza?"

"I am sorry," Wind Walker says, "but this is a reality and you must be warned. But to respond to your comment, no, that is not my gift." Then, he unties a leather pouch from his belt and hands it to me. "This is for you. I recommend you do a better job of protecting these from your adversary. Be well, Epic Zero. And be aware. Always be aware."

Then, he winks at me and disappears!

"That was odd," Grace says. "What's in the pouch?"

"I don't know," I say.

I loosen the strings, reach inside, and feel two things that are soft with rubber bottoms. Wait a minute? No way! I pull them out and laugh.

Wow, I guess he really could see everything that happened in the 13th Dimension.

"Slippers?" Grace says. "He got you slippers?"

"Yep," I say, admiring them. They're the exact same pair as the ones Dog-Gone chewed up. "And they're absolutely perfect!"

Epic Zero 6: Tales of a Major Meta Disaster

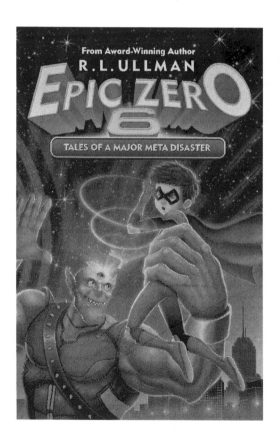

ONE

I CAN'T DO ANYTHING RIGHT

For some reason, I don't have a good feeling about this.

Maybe it's because we're orbiting two hundred miles above Earth on a blacked-out International Space Station. Or maybe it's because there's no sign of the crew, whose last transmission was Code Red, which basically means 'extreme danger.' Or maybe it's because the Meta Monitor picked up a mysterious Meta 3 signature coming from the space station it could only classify as: *Identity Unknown.*

So, yeah, I don't have a good feeling about this.

In fact, I'm pretty darn creeped out.

Fortunately, we have our flashlights so we can see, but the constant BUZZING from the emergency alarm isn't doing much to calm my nerves either. Plus, unlike the Waystation where we have the benefit of TechnocRat's Gravitational Stabilizer, the International Space Station doesn't have artificial gravity. So that means we're floating around like weightless balloons.

Just. Freaking. Wonderful.

Unfortunately, the crummy conditions aren't even the worst part. Not by a longshot. The worst part is that the team decided to put *me* in charge of this rescue mission!

"Me?" I said when they told me. "Why me?"

"Because it's part of your development," Dad said. "Learning how to manage a team in dangerous situations is an important part of being a leader. We've been training your sister, and now it's your turn."

"I see," I said. "But you realize I'm just a kid, right?"

Well, clearly Dad didn't care about that, because here I am, 'leading' Dad and Shadow Hawk—two of the greatest Meta heroes of all time—on this spooky mission.

"What next fearless leader?"

Oh, and Grace, my lovely sister, is here too.

I shine my flashlight on her frowning face.

"Relax," I say. "I've got this."

But honestly, I've pretty much got nothing. I mean, we still have no idea what happened to the astronauts on board, and the Meta Monitor didn't provide much help either. But I do know one thing, I can't fail, because if I do Grace will never let me hear the end of it.

So, that leaves only one option.

Don't screw it up.

There are two exits out of the docking port, left or right. Now, which way should we go? I do a quick round of eeny meeny miny moe—my favorite decision-making tool—and land on left. But as soon as I grab a handhold and poke my head through the airlock, I'm blinded by a flashing light from above.

I stagger backward disoriented. It takes a few seconds to stop seeing stars, but when I do, I find myself staring at Grace's charming face.

"You're such a goober," she says, rolling her eyes.

"Are you hurt, kid?" Shadow Hawk asks.

"Nope," I say. "Just my pride."

I curse under my breath. If I'm going to lead this team to find the missing crew members, I can't make rookie mistakes like that again. I have to do better.

"Follow me," I say. "Oh, and don't look up."

This time I shield my eyes as I float through the airlock into a cargo hold filled with crates tied down by ropes. As I drift past, I read a few of the labels: *Dry Goods, Backup Robot Crane, Extravehicular Mobility Units.* Nothing seems out of the ordinary, but there's still no sign of the crew.

I push through to the next room and scan with my flashlight. It's a small room with a long table bolted to the floor and a pole holding a bunch of I.V. pouches. Okay, I'm clearly in the medical wing. But it's empty.

Then, I notice something floating by my face.

I shine my flashlight and scream in horror!

"What?" Dad asks, floating in. "What is it?"

"It's a… a…," I mutter, completely breathless.

"It's a glove," Grace says matter-of-factly, snatching it out of the air. "It looks like an astronaut's glove." Then, she looks at me with a smirk. "Wait, did you think it was, like, an actual hand or something?"

"Um, no," I say, lying through my teeth.

"Holy cow," she says. "Who put this guy in charge?"

Thank goodness it's pitch black in here, otherwise, they'd see I'm red with embarrassment. Honestly, I don't know why I'm so jittery. I mean, I've handled far worse situations than this. I've got to calm down.

"Follow me," I say, trying to sound confident.

"I'm afraid to," Grace remarks.

I ignore her and duck through the next portal, entering into a large chamber filled with scientific equipment. This must be the laboratory. Part of the crew's mission is to conduct research experiments, so everything here looks normal. I even recognize a few things I've seen in TechnocRat's lab, like an incubator and a centrifuge.

But then, I notice something odd.

In the center of the room is a metal table with four straps lying across its surface. Strangely, the straps are fastened, but they aren't holding anything down. It's only when I take a step closer that I see a big, uneven hole in the middle of the table like something chewed its way through the metal itself.

I kneel to look beneath the table when my flashlight catches a strand of something long and translucent. It looks like... a spider web? Except, it's purple. And as I bend over, I see even more webbing stretched across the legs of the table.

I poke it with my finger. It's taut and sticky, just like a spider web, but a whole lot thicker.

Did I mention that I hate spiders?

Then, I remember something. I didn't see spiders on the space station's inventory list. I guess it could be a stowaway. But why would its web be purple? Unless...

A chill runs down my spine.

"We're in the research lab," I say.

"Yeah, Captain Obvious," Grace says. "So?"

"So," I say, pointing my light down at the webbing. "Do you know any spiders that spin purple webs?"

"No," Grace says, kneeling to look.

"Or eats through metal?" I add, pointing to the table.

"Nope," she says.

"Exactly," I say. "I think we found the source of the problem. I bet the crew caught something they shouldn't have and brought it on board. Something alien."

"What?" Grace says. "Are you serious?"

"Dead serious," I say.

Who knows? Maybe I'm wrong. But when I turn to get Dad's opinion, I realize Grace and I are all alone.

"Hey, where are the other guys?" I ask.

"What?" Grace says, turning around. "They were right behind me a second ago."

"Captain Justice?" I call out, pushing myself back to the entrance. "Shadow Hawk? Where are you guys?"

I shine my flashlight all around but I don't see them.

"I can't believe it," I say, turning back to Grace. "It's like they vanished without a—"

But suddenly, I'm talking to no one.

Because Grace is gone as well.

"Glory Girl?" I call out, my voice echoing through the chamber. Where'd she go? I shine my flashlight all around. "Okay, guys, this game of hide-and-seek isn't funny. Come out, come out, wherever you are."

But no one shows up.

Suddenly, my skin feels all goose-pimply.

I'm alone.

But the problem is, I'm not alone, because whatever nabbed them is probably watching me right now!

Then, something catches my eye.

On the far side of the chamber is a light. That's funny, I don't remember seeing a light there before, but it's clearly there now. And a door is cracked open!

Okay, I've got two choices. Either I can leave now and get reinforcements, or I can press on and see what's behind door number one. I swallow hard.

Why did I have to be the leader?

I float carefully towards the door and grab a

handhold to steady myself. Then, I hang there, pressing my ear against the door. But I don't hear anything. Now what?

I mean, I've got no clue what's happening on the other side, but I'm pretty sure it's bad news. And even though every bone in my body wants to flee, I can't just leave my team behind. What's that old saying—the captain always goes down with the ship?

I take a deep breath and exhale. Okay, here goes nothing. I grab the door handle, pull it open, and float inside. Immediately, I see a giant windshield, a navigation control station, and a captain's chair and I know I've reached the command center.

But then I do a double take because stretched across the twenty-foot windshield is a gigantic purple web—and stuck to it are three large objects wrapped head-to-toe in purple webbing!

At first, my mind tells me there must be some really massive flies on this ship. But then I realize one of the flies is much smaller than the others, and it hits me.

Those aren't flies at all.

That's Dad, Shadow Hawk, and Grace!

If I don't get them out of there, they'll suffocate!

I reach into my utility belt for something sharp, when I notice a large shadow expanding beneath my feet.

I freeze, petrified by what could be hovering overhead. And when I look up, I'm not disappointed, because lowering itself from the ceiling is a grizzly, refrigerator-sized spider-creature with multiple eyes, purple hair, and a gaggle of spindly legs all ending in razor-sharp tips.

Did I mention that I hate alien spiders?

"Oh, sorry," I say, trying to keep from passing out. "Didn't mean to bug you."

But it just narrows its eyes and keeps on coming.

"Not a talker, huh?" I say. "Well, how about you relax and stream the latest Spider-Man reboot off the web while I free my friends here?"

But instead of laughing, the creature swings its front leg! I barely duck out of the way before it slices a monitor clean in two.

Well, now I know where to go for my next haircut. But I still have no clue what its Meta powers are. Unless looking creepy is a new kind of Meta classification.

I've got to keep it off balance. But when I open my mouth to offer yet another witty barb, no sound comes out. Huh? That's weird. I try talking again, but I can't hear my own voice. What's going on?

But it looks like I won't have time to figure it out because the beast floats to the ground and I realize I'm in for the gravity-defying fight of my life!

Then, its long legs hit the tile, and it launches at me!

I push hard off the nearest computer terminal and drift away, bumping into the wall behind me. But strangely there's no sound when I make contact.

Huh? What happened to all of the noise?

And then a lightbulb goes off.

Grace, Dad, and Shadow Hawk didn't make a peep when they were captured. And now I can't even hear myself talk. I connect the dots and realize this thing must have the power to squash sound!

Well, that's clever. I bet it uses its power to mute the cries of its victims. That's perfect for a predator like him.

But the thing is, I've got powers too.

I concentrate hard, duplicating Dad's Super-Strength. And none too soon, because seconds later, the spider attacks! I sideswipe a barrage of slowly swinging legs and counter with a slow-motion roundhouse kick of my own, sending the creature drifting into a wall of computers.

Not bad.

Who knew I was a zero-gravity Kung Fu master?

But when the creature connects, sparks fly from the computer bank behind it, and the entire station tilts forward and then takes off in reverse!

Oh no! That spider must have crashed into the thruster propulsion control panel!

Luckily, I manage to grab the arm of a chair that's bolted to the floor, but everything not tied down is being thrown towards the windshield!

Fortunately, Dad, Grace, and Shadow Hawk are still stuck to the web, but the spider isn't so lucky. For a second, I chuckle to myself as the creature slowly plummets with everything else. But my glee quickly turns to horror as one of its razor-sharp legs pierces the windshield and a giant crack begins to crisscross the glass pane.

Um, that's not good.

The windshield could—

SHATTER!

Suddenly, an incredible force pulls everything towards the opening—including me! I wrap my arms around the chair as my feet lift off the ground! I've got to hold on! If I get sucked out of here, I'll die in deep space!

Out of the corner of my eye, I see the spider get vacuumed right out of the space station! That's great news, but this isn't exactly how things were supposed to go!

The force is pulling me hard!

I grip tighter, but I can feel my fingers giving way!

Then, I remember I can end this.

I just need to say the words.

I try calling out, but somehow the spider's noise-canceling powers are still in effect! And the creature is too far gone for me to negate its power!

I feel my fingers unraveling…

I'm… going… to…

"GISMO!" comes a female voice. "End program!"

"Training module ended, Ms. Understood," Gismo says.

I hit the floor hard, knocking the wind out of me. And when I roll over, the International Space Station is gone.

I'm back in the Combat Room, and boy am I relieved. I hope the team is okay. OMG! The team!

I pop back up to find Dad, Grace, and Shadow Hawk lying on the floor behind me, catching their breath.

Thank goodness they're alive!

"Elliott Harkness!" Mom says. "What's going on down here?"

"Well," I say, "Dad put me in charge, and—"

"He did, did he?" she says, wheeling on Dad.

"Well," Dad says sheepishly. "We did agree we wanted him to become a better leader."

"Yes," Mom says. "But we didn't agree we'd kill him in the process."

"Hang on," Grace says. "Can I get a vote on that?"

"If I hadn't come looking for you," Mom continues, ignoring Grace, "who knows what could have happened? That was an advanced module. He's not ready for that."

"Well," Dad says, "I guess you're right."

"I'm still here," I say. "I can hear you."

"Sorry, son," Dad says, standing up. "Your mother is right. You've done some great things, but leadership is a completely different skillset. Next time we'll start with a more basic training module."

"Next time?" Grace says. "Next time leave me out of it. He may be powerful, but he ain't no leader."

"Enough, Grace," Mom says.

I want to tell her off, but she's right. I'm a terrible leader. A terrible leader who nearly got everyone killed.

"Thanks for the save," Shadow Hawk says to Mom. "But what *are* you doing here? Is something wrong?"

"Oh no," Mom says, the color draining from her face. "I got totally distracted. We've got to get upstairs. We just received a message from the White House. The president needs to speak with us urgently."

Meta Profile
The Freedom Force

Captain Justice
Class: Super-Strength
Meta: ▪▪▪▪

Ms. Understood
Class: Psychic
Meta: ▪▪▪▪

Glory Girl
Class: Flight
Meta: ▪▪▪

Shadow Hawk
Class: None
Meta:

Epic Zero
Class: Meta Manipulator
Meta: ▪▪▪▪

TechnocRat
Class: Super-Intellect
Meta: ▪▪▪▪

Blue Bolt
Class: Super-Speed
Meta: ▪▪▪▪

Master Mime
Class: Magic
Meta: ▪▪▪

Makeshift
Class: Energy Manipulator
Meta: ▪

TWO

I RECEIVE AN EXECUTIVE ORDER

By the time we reach the Mission Room, TechnocRat has the video feed ready to go.

"What took you guys so long?" he asks, typing on a keyboard with his white tail.

"There's no time to explain," Mom says.

"Got it," TechnocRat says, looking at me. "So, what did you do this time?"

"*Me?*" I say. "Nothing."

"Yep," Grace says. "That about sums it up."

"Shut it," I say.

"Make me," Grace says.

"Enough," Mom says. "We're about to speak to the president of the United States. Can the two of you please show some self-control?"

"I can," Grace says, smoothing her cape, "but I'm not so sure about him. By the way, you're not going to let the president see him looking like that, are you?"

"Hey!" I say. "I look fine. Um, don't I?"

"Quiet," Dad says. "Is it on?"

"Yep," TechnocRat says. "We're waiting on them."

"Where's the rest of the team?" Shadow Hawk asks.

"On a mission," TechnocRat says. "But they haven't answered my calls. So, either they're in the middle of a fight or Makeshift lost his communicator again."

"I'd bet on the latter," Grace says.

"Hold on," TechnocRat says. "A signal is coming through. We should have a visual in three... two..."

Suddenly, the monitor flicks on and I stand up a little straighter, excited for my first meeting with the actual president. But when the picture comes in, it's not the president we see, but our friends Blue Bolt, Makeshift, and Master Mime.

"Oh, hey guys," Dad says. "It's great seeing you, but I thought we were talking to the president?"

But the heroes don't answer.

Instead, they just stare at us blankly.

"Um, guys?" Dad says. "Is something wrong?"

But as the camera pans out, I realize something is very wrong, because the heroes are on their knees wearing handcuffs! Except their handcuffs don't look like normal handcuffs, but rather like thick, leather wrappings.

"What's on their wrists?" Grace asks.

But no one can answer her, not even TechnocRat.

Yet, for some reason, that leathery material looks strangely familiar to me.

"What's going on here?" Mom asks.

"They've been captured," Shadow Hawk says.

Suddenly, the camera pulls back even farther and we realize our friends are kneeling on the steps of a super-long, concrete building in front of a large portico. And they're surrounded by a dozen ginormous, armor-plated robots, each painted army green!

"Where are they?" Grace whispers. "And what are those metal bot thingies?"

"They're at the Pentagon," Shadow Hawk answers. "The home of our nation's Department of Defense. But I've never seen those robots before."

"Blue Bolt," Dad says. "Where's the president? Is she safe?"

"Don't worry, Captain Justice," comes a female voice. "I'm right here."

Suddenly, the camera swings left, landing on a steely-eyed woman with gray streaks in her hair. I'd know her face anywhere. It's President Kara Kensington! And standing behind her are a bunch of military officers.

"President Kensington," Dad says. "Are you okay? Do you know what's happened to our colleagues?"

"I appreciate your concern," she says, "but I'm just fine. Your friends, however, aren't feeling so chipper."

"What's going on here?" Dad asks.

"What's going on here is a new direction for America," President Kensington says. "It is my privilege to inform you that Congress just passed a new law called the Meta Restriction Resolution. That means that as of today, all Metas are required to surrender themselves to the government of the United States of America immediately. Therefore, I order you, and all of your Meta friends, to come down to the Pentagon to turn yourselves in at once. The Meta age is officially over."

"What?" Mom says. "Where did this come from?"

But as I scan the crowd behind her, I already know the answer. Because standing to the right of the President is a thin man with piercing blue eyes and a white crewcut—and his name is General William Winch!

The last time I had the displeasure of his company was when I got roped into appearing on the CNC Morning Newsflash to debate the merits of Meta humans. He swore he'd take down all Metas if it was the last thing he ever did.

It looks like he's succeeding.

"President Kensington," Dad says, "is this a joke? The Freedom Force has defended the United States and the world on countless occasions. We've even taken on assignments to protect national security at your request. What you're saying doesn't make sense. And why weren't we notified about this resolution?"

"I'm notifying you now," President Kensington says

firmly. "And I assure you this is no joke. Let me be clear. Our country is run by the will of the people, and the people have decided that Metas are no longer the solution. Metas are the problem."

"But that's ridiculous," Mom says. "What happens when the next intergalactic terror shows up?"

"*If* that happens, Ms. Understood," President Kensington says, "we'll handle it. Just like we've handled your friends here. After all, our new Meta-Buster army is specifically designed to take down Meta threats."

"Interesting," TechnocRat remarks, stroking his whiskers. "I didn't know our government was even capable of developing such sophisticated technology."

"Madame President," Dad says. "We respectfully request that you free our colleagues. They're heroes."

"Really?" she says. "Because our statistics say otherwise. Did you know, Captain, that ninety-seven percent of all crimes are committed by Metas? Or that costs to repair damage from Meta battles have increased over three hundred percent from a year ago? Or that insurance premiums for regular citizens living in Meta-afflicted areas have risen nine thousand percent? America has had enough. The Meta problem stops now."

"Oh, really?" Grace barks. "And what are you planning to do with 'Meta problems' like us who turn themselves in?"

"Glory Girl!" Mom says.

"Hold on," Shadow Hawk says. "That's an excellent

question."

"We have designed a comprehensive Meta rehabilitation program," President Kensington says. "All Metas will be trained to live normal lives as ordinary, productive members of society."

"Trained?" I say. "You mean, like animals?"

President Kensington smiles. "Need I remind you that I am the president of the United States of America? Just as you have dutifully upheld our laws in the past, I fully expect you to comply with our new law now. But if you foolishly choose to disobey, you will face the full power of the United States military. Just like your friends."

The camera pans back to Blue Bolt, Makeshift, and Master Mime who are still kneeling with their hands bound.

"I expect to see all of you at the Pentagon shortly," President Kensington says. "Or else."

Then, the monitor goes black.

"Well," Grace says, "that was unexpected."

"This is no time for jokes," Dad says. "We have to go to the Pentagon."

"What?" Mom says. "Are you crazy? We can't turn ourselves in."

"We're not turning ourselves in," Dad says. "We're rescuing our friends."

"Which is exactly what she is expecting," Shadow Hawk says. "It's a trap."

"Most likely," TechnocRat says. "But that's not the only thing worrying me. I'm still trying to figure out why Blue Bolt and the others are just sitting there like baked potatoes. Whatever is wrapped around their wrists must have some kind of a sedation effect. But I don't know anything that can do that."

Suddenly, green lights start flashing on the console.

"Hang on," TechnocRat says, typing into the keyboard. "We're getting a news alert."

Just then, the monitor flicks on again, but this time we're watching a live broadcast of a street mob. Thousands of people are pushing their way towards the city center, swarming five costumed individuals who are trying to walk down the street. What's going on? Then, a reporter comes into frame and starts speaking Japanese.

"Let me activate the translator," TechnocRat says.

Seconds later, we can understand the reporter in perfect English:

"... have complied peacefully with the request of the prime minister and are now in the hands of our military. Our once great Japanese champions are now prisoners of the government under the new Meta Restriction Resolution. We are not clear what the next steps are, but according to authorities, they will undergo a process called behavior modification. Details are coming in slowly..."

Japanese champions?

OMG! I know exactly who they are.

Suddenly, the crowd parts, and I recognize a masked man holding his arms in the air. It's the Green Dragon! And behind him are Tsunami, Fight Master, The Silent Samurai, and Zen! They're quickly surrounded by armored robots that look just like the Meta-Busters that President Kensington threatened us with, except these robots are painted red-and-white like the Japanese flag.

That's strange.

Why would we share military technology with Japan?

"Who are those guys?" Grace asks.

"They're the Rising Suns," I say. "The best superhero team in Japan. They helped me fight the Herald."

I shake my head in disbelief. Why would the Rising Suns surrender themselves to the government?

"And by the way," Grace says. "Didn't that reporter say something about 'behavior modification?' What's that?"

"Hold on," TechnocRat says. "There's another alert coming. This one is from Spain."

The image switches to another group of heroes surrendering to a different group of Meta-Busters, except these are painted red-and-yellow, like the Spanish flag.

"That's Los Toros," Shadow Hawk says. "The premier Spanish super team."

"The Meta Restriction Resolution has gone global," Mom says. "And heroes are turning themselves in."

"Yeah, the heroes are," TechnocRat says, "but what

about the villains?"

"This is nuts," Grace says. "Why do we bother saving these people if they don't even want us?"

"Because we're heroes," Dad says. "And it's our duty to protect the innocent, even if they're misguided. Now let's go save our friends."

"I can't wait," I say.

"Not you, Elliott," Dad says, putting his hand on my shoulder. "You're staying here."

"What?" I say. "But that's not fair!"

"Sorry, sucker," Grace says, flashing a big smile.

"You too, young lady," Mom says.

"What?" Grace protests, crossing her arms. "That's not fair either!"

"Now is not the time to argue," Dad says. "The political climate is too unstable. Plus, we don't know what those Meta-Busters are capable of. If they took out Blue Bolt, Master Mime, and Makeshift, then it's safer for you two to stay here. For everyone else—It's Fight Time!"

The heroes take off, except for Mom.

"Listen," she says. "This is serious business and we need you to stay put. I don't want to hear any nonsense about intergalactic kidnappings or time-traveling mishaps when I get back. Do I make myself clear?"

Grace and I look at one another.

"Do. I. Make. Myself. Clear?" Mom repeats.

"Yes," we say in harmony.

"Great," she says, kissing us on our foreheads. "I'm

expecting to see you both here, safe and sound, when we return."

Then, she shoots me a final look and leaves.

But as soon as we hear the last of Mom's footsteps fading down the hall, Grace turns and says—

"See ya, squirt!"

"What?" I say confused. "What's that supposed to mean?"

"It means I'm out of here," Grace says, unfolding her arms to reveal a pair of crossed fingers.

"Wait, you lied to Mom?" I say.

"Nope," she says. "I just had my fingers crossed."

"But that's the same thing as lying," I say.

"Is it?" she says, running off. "Oh, well. You snooze you lose!"

"But wait!" I yell. "You can't just—"

But apparently, she can.

Because she's gone.

And I'm all alone.

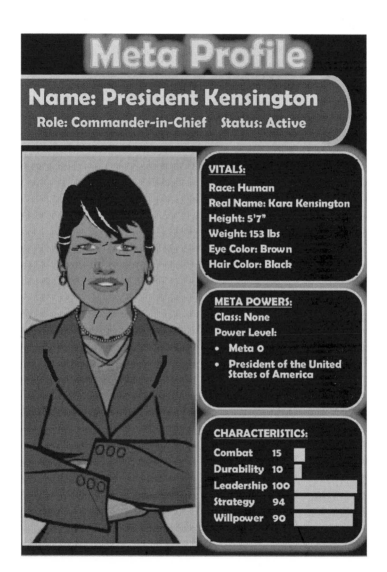

THREE

I GET LEFT BEHIND… AGAIN

Well, I feel like a first-class loser.

I mean, I just stood here flat-footed while Grace raced off to help the team. And even though I want to follow her, I can't. After all, I promised Mom I wouldn't leave the Waystation.

Boy, I wish I crossed *my* fingers.

Oh well, at least I can watch the fireworks when Mom sees Grace on the battlefield. She's gonna flip!

But as soon as I head for the Monitor Room to catch the show, my stomach rumbles. I check the wall clock and realize why I'm so hungry. It's dinner time and I haven't eaten since well before my training debacle. Time sure flies when you're leading your team into disaster.

It should take the gang a few minutes to get to the Pentagon, so I've got time to grab a quick snack. But as I head towards the Galley, I hear noises.

Chewing noises.

Two thoughts hit me at once.

One, I remember I'm actually not alone. And two, I have the feeling I'm about to witness something ugly.

Like, really, really ugly.

When I finally reach the Galley, I brace myself and step inside. And then I wish I hadn't.

"Dog-Gone!" I yell. "Drop it!"

The big mutt is standing on the kitchen counter devouring a chicken drumstick. Diced carrots are scattered everywhere, and a half-eaten chicken carcass is resting comfortably in a fruit bowl.

Ugh! Mom must have just finished cooking when the call from the White House came in, and then she raced off and left everything behind.

The masked bandit strikes again.

"Get down!" I yell.

Dog-Gone looks at me wide-eyed.

"Oh, no you don't!" I warn. "No way! You will not turn invisible right now. Now drop the drumstick and help me clean this up."

But instead of stopping, he cocks an ear—and vanishes! Now all I see is the chicken drumstick, which leaps off the counter and bolts past me down the hallway.

Well, I can't say I'm surprised.

It's been quite a day. Not only did I screw up my chance of ever leading the Freedom Force again, but now I have to clean up after a rude German Shepherd with attitude problems.

I hope that chicken drumstick gives him gas.

I grab a paper towel and start picking up chunks of disgustingness when I suddenly remember what I was doing here in the first place. Ugh, all I wanted was a snack before the team leaped into action. Now I've probably missed the whole thing!

I toss what I'm holding into the garbage and hustle out of the Galley. So much for a bite to eat. Why does Dog-Gone get to feast while I'm still starving? Now I know why they call it 'a dog's world.'

I sprint down the hall and climb the twenty-three steps to the Monitor Room. Before I hop into the command chair, I take my grappling gun out of my utility belt because it tends to chafe my leg. Then, I sit down and punch a few codes into the keyboard. Seconds later, the screen blips on and I'm staring at the most famous five-sided building in the world.

The Pentagon.

Since I don't see any explosions, I'm guessing the team hasn't made their move yet. That's great news because it gives me time to do some reconnaissance. Maybe I can spot something up here that will help them down there.

I start by scouting the perimeter of the building.

Shadow Hawk said the Pentagon houses the Department of Defense, but that's about all I know. So, I query the system for some additional info. Seconds later, a bunch of facts scroll down the screen, like the Pentagon is the largest office building in the world at over six-and-a-half million square feet. Boy, I can't even imagine how many coffee stations are in there.

Of course, the building has five sides—hence, the name Pentagon. It also has five levels above ground and two known levels below ground. My eyes stop on the word 'known' and I wonder: if only two levels are known, how many are 'unknown?'

It's an interesting question, but I don't have time to dig into that now. Instead, I've got more important things to do, like figuring out why those restraints on my friends' wrists looked so familiar. But first I need a visual.

I set the telescopes on auto-zoom and cycle them around the building until I find what I'm looking for.

Ten seconds later, I've got it.

To my surprise, Blue Bolt, Master Mime, and Makeshift are still kneeling on the stairs out in the open. And hiding around the corner is a squad of Meta-Busters.

Yep, I'd definitely call that a trap.

I take a photo of Makeshift's wrists and lean in for a better look. Upon closer inspection, the restraints look rippled. I know I've seen a material like that before, but where?

Well, if anything can identify it, it'll be the Meta

Monitor. So, I feed it the image and hit the 'analyze' button.

This shouldn't take long.

In the meantime, I'd better call Dad and let him know what's going on. I don't want them to be ambushed.

"HQ to Captain Justice," I say, talking into the transmitter. "HQ to Captain Justice."

"Captain, here," Dad whispers back, but he doesn't sound happy. "Epic Zero, what are you doing? End this transmission now!"

"Hold on," I say. "I located the captives. They're on the Northeast side. And they're very well—"

"End the transmission now!" Dad whispers firmly.

"But why?" I ask. "I don't get it."

"Because we're at the Pentagon," Dad says. "And the Pentagon has the most advanced homing equipment in the world. Which means they'll pick up our connection and trace it to—"

"They found us!" I hear Mom yell in the background. "Get ready to fight!"

"Cut off!" Dad orders. "Before they find—"

Suddenly, there's a CLICK followed by STATIC.

Uh-oh.

I think I just got them in trouble. I mean, I was simply trying to help, but I screwed that up too. Sometimes I wonder why I even bother getting out of bed.

And what did Dad say at the end?

Cut off the transmission before they find... what?

"Alert! Alert! Alert!" the Meta Monitor blares.

Great. At least the Meta Monitor finished its analysis.

But when I look down at the screen I see:

MATERIAL ANALYSIS PENDING.

Huh? That's weird. If the Meta Monitor wasn't finished, then why did the alert—

"Waystation breached!" the Meta Monitor blares. "Automatic emergency response system activated! Repeat, Waystation breached! Automatic emergency response system activated!"

Huh? At first, I'm confused. And then my heart sinks to my toes because based on what it's saying, the Meta Monitor hadn't finished its analysis at all. Instead, it's telling me something different. It's saying that someone has boarded the Waystation!

But how?

And then it hits me.

Dad wasn't telling me to end the transmission to only protect *their* location! He was telling me to end the transmission to also protect *my* location!

And the last time the Waystation was invaded I ended up being kidnapped by a talking chimpanzee! There ain't no way I'm letting that happen again!

I've got to get out of here!

I'm about to slide off my chair when I see:

ANALYSIS STATUS: 65% COMPLETE.

I stop.

I mean, I desperately want to know what those restraints are made of, but I can't just stay here like a sitting duck. I glance back down at the monitor.

75% COMPLETE.

It's almost done. If I can just hang on for a few more seconds I'll know what—

BOOM!

Suddenly, the whole Waystation shakes violently and I grip the arms of the command chair for dear life!

That wasn't good! Not good at all!

85% COMPLETE.

I exhale. I just need a few more—

KABOOM!

The Waystation shakes harder this time and a blue wire springs loose from the Meta Monitor's console. Okay, I definitely need to get out of here. Especially since that one sounded way closer! I glance at the screen.

95% COMPLETE.

C'mon! So close!

Then, I hear a BARK.

Dog-Gone!

That does it! I leap from the chair and rush down the steps. Look, I want those results more than anything, but not if Dog-Gone is in danger! But when I reach the bottom I'm blocked by a gate!

The Meta Monitor initiated its response sequence!

I run through TechnocRat's override codes in my head. The first one I remember is for the residential wing.

Then the Combat Room. Darn it! These codes are so similar I'm mixing them up in my head. I'm losing time. C'mon, think!

Maybe this one?

"Override ZY7889ZZ," I yell.

The gate retracts into the ceiling.

Yes! Things are finally going my way. But when I pop into the corridor, I freeze. Because something huge is staring at me from down the hall. Something with red, unblinking eyes.

It's… a Meta-Buster?

Here on the Waystation?

But my powers don't work on robots.

"PRIME TARGET IDENTIFIED," the Meta-Buster says in a deep, mechanical voice. "PER PRESIDENTIAL ORDER, CAPTURE ALIVE. DO NOT DAMAGE."

Um, did it just say, 'presidential order?'

Then, it raises its arm and my alarm bells go off. I press myself flat against the wall just as a net whips past my face. Okay, I'm no zoo animal. It's time to move!

I somersault across the hall into the next corridor, pop up on my feet, and book it. With that bucket of bolts up here, there's no way I can stay on the Waystation.

And then I get a disturbing thought.

What if there's more than—

SMACK!

I stumble backward, my nose throbbing. But before I

can regain my wits, something grabs me by my arms and lifts me into the air. The next thing I know, I'm staring into the electronic eyes of another Meta-Buster!

"Let me go!" I yell.

"PRIME TARGET CAPTURED ALIVE," it says.

I kick it with my foot but it's like kicking a truck. There's no give! Plus, it's squeezing my arms so tight they're going numb!

I can't believe it. How could I give away both of our locations in the same boneheaded move? I try breaking free again but the Meta-Buster is too strong. And even if I did get away, the Waystation is probably crawling with these things.

There's nothing I can do.

I'm caught.

And then I see a chicken coming towards me.

Or rather, a chicken carcass?

At first, I think I'm imagining things, but then I realize what's going on. That's no runaway chicken carcass—it's my invisible pooch Dog-Gone—and he's heading this way!

The next thing I know, Dog-Gone uses the Meta-Buster's metallic backside like a vault and leaps up, jamming the chicken carcass over the robot's head!

"SURPRISE ATTACK!" it says, dropping me hard to the ground as it tries to remove its poultry helmet.

Just then, Dog-Gone materializes in front of me and pulls me to my feet with his mouth.

"Yuck," I say. "Chicken breath."

That's gross, but right now I've got to focus on more important things, like staying alive.

"This way!" I yell, sprinting towards the Hangar.

If my calculations are correct, Blue Bolt took one Freedom Flyer and Dad took the other. So, if those vehicles are gone and Grace followed them in a Freedom Ferry, then that means there should be one Freedom Ferry left. But if I'm wrong, I've trapped us in the Hangar with nowhere to go.

It's a gamble, but it's our only chance.

Suddenly, a laser zips past us, exploding into the wall.

Um, what happened to capturing me alive?

"Keep moving, boy!" I yell.

We round the corner as a barrage of lasers tear up the wall behind us. But suddenly, a massive robot steps out and grabs my cape, lifting me off my feet!

"PRIME TARGET CAPTURED ALIVE," it says.

Not again!

"DESTROY PRIME TARGET," comes a different voice from down the hall.

Um, what?

But before I can react, a laser plows right through the eye of the Meta-Buster holding me, and it falls backward, sparks flying from its eye socket.

I land on my feet next to Dog-Gone and look back.

More Meta-Busters are on our tail! And for some reason, they destroyed one of their own!

"Into the Hangar!" I yell.

We motor inside and I thank my lucky stars because sitting in the very last parking spot is a Freedom Ferry!

"Go for it!" I instruct Dog-Gone.

He's there in a flash—the benefit of four legs—and pops the hatch. I catch up and hop inside, crashing into Dog-Gone who is hogging the seat.

"Move your big rump," I say, taking the controls.

But the Meta-Busters are right behind us! There's no way we'll get this out of here without them spotting us.

Wait a second. Spotting us?

I may not be able to copy the Meta-Buster's powers, but I can copy Dog-Gone's invisibility power. I concentrate hard, pulling in his Meta energy, and then I push it out, covering me, Dog-Gone, and the Freedom Ferry in a cloak of invisibility.

And none too soon, as five Meta-Busters spill into the Hangar looking around confused.

Hah! Those morons will never find us. Time to jet.

But when I turn on the Freedom Ferry, the engine lets out a thunderous VROOOM!

Seriously? Whoever drove this last must have taken it off of 'Silent Mode.' I'm guessing it was Master Mime.

"Um, you don't think they heard that, do you?" I whisper to Dog-Gone. But I already know the answer.

"ACTIVATE INFRARED VISION," a Meta-Buster calls out, its voice echoing through the Hangar.

Infrared vision? As in, heat-seeking vision?

"Get ready!" I warn Dog-Gone, strapping us in.

"DESTROY PRIME TARGET."

I punch it.

The Freedom Ferry blasts off, throwing Dog-Gone and me backward. I press the door opener and grip the steering wheel tight, trying to maintain control as we fishtail left and right towards the slowly opening door.

Then, I look in the rearview mirror.

The Meta-Busters have positioned themselves behind us, pointing their arms in our direction. Holy cow, they're gunning for us! They're going to fire at us!

"DESTROY PRIME TARGET," one repeats.

"Hold on to your biscuits, Dog-Gone!"

I slam the gas pedal, and bash the door opener again, signaling it to close. The Freedom Ferry lurches forward at maximum speed and I hear Dog-Gone's ears snap back.

I'd better time this right or we're roadkill!

I peek into the sideview mirror as smoke rises from the Meta-Busters' hands, but we speed through the opening just as the door SLAMS shut behind us.

THOOM!!!

There's a massive explosion from behind, knocking the Freedom Ferry off course. Something hits the back of our vehicle hard and the dashboard lights up. Great. One of the thrusters is out of order, but the other is okay.

I breathe a sigh of relief.

Wow, that was crazy. I can't believe we made it. I

mean, those Meta-Busters were really trying to kill us. I just hope the Waystation wasn't too badly damaged.

But when I check the rearview mirror, my jaw drops.

Because the Waystation is gone.

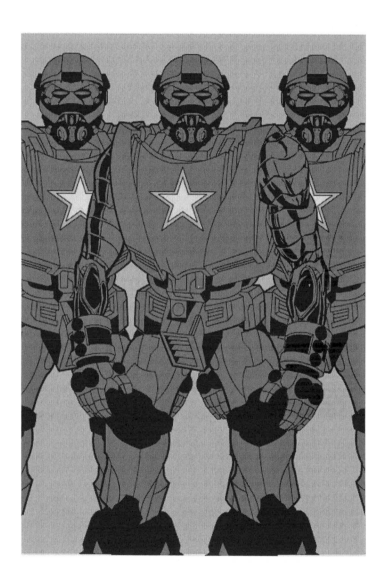

FOUR

I CRASH-LAND INTO ANOTHER FINE MESS

I'm in complete and total shock.

The entire Waystation, our headquarters and home, was just blown to smithereens by a squad of psycho Meta-Busters! Everything we own, everything we care about, is now space dust.

I feel like I'm gonna hurl.

I mean, it's mind-boggling to think about everything we've just lost. The Meta Monitor. GISMO. All of our Meta gear. The memorial statues in the Hall of Fallen Heroes. Dog-Gone's puppy pictures. My comic books.

They're all gone.

And it's all my fault.

None of this would have happened if I hadn't called Dad. And speaking of Dad, he's gonna kill me when he comes home from the Pentagon and there is no more home! And he's not the only one!

I can't even imagine Grace's reaction when she sees that all of her stuff is vaporized. And poor TechnocRat is going to flip his whiskers when he realizes his lab is gone.

OMG!

TechnocRat's stash of Camembert cheese is gone too!

He's gonna nibble me to death!

But just to add more salt to my wounds, it doesn't look like I can even warn them, because the blast that knocked out one of the Freedom Ferry's thrusters also knocked out the communications system. And based on the red light flashing in my face, the landing gear is on the fritz too.

Just. Freaking. Wonderful.

Dog-Gone and I were lucky to get out of the Waystation alive, but we might eat it trying to land this sucker. And since we only have one thruster, I'm not sure we'll have enough juice to make it to the Pentagon. When I enter Earth's atmosphere, I'm going to have to touchdown somewhere closer, like Keystone City.

I plug in the coordinates and rest my head in my hands. I feel like such a heel. Maybe I should have let those Meta-Busters capture me. But then again, the whole thing was pretty confusing.

That first Meta-Buster said it had a presidential order to capture me alive, but the other ones didn't seem to get the memo. Instead, they were clearly trying to kill me, and even destroyed one of their own to do it!

I don't know what to make of that, but I do know one thing. This is, without a doubt, the worst day ever.

The only good thing I managed to do was take Dog-Gone with me. My apologies to TechnocRat, but nearly everything else on the Waystation can be rebuilt. Dog-Gone, however, is one of a kind.

Except right now the poor guy is panting heavily and whimpering under his breath. I need to be brave for him.

"It's gonna be okay," I say, rubbing his back. "Let's just land this Freedom Ferry safely."

But deep down I know that's going to be easier said than done. As soon as I get a visual on Keystone City, I hit the 'Extend Landing Gear' button and pray, but all I hear is WHIRRING. I try again and hear the same result—which officially confirms it. The landing gear is stuck.

Why am I not surprised?

My heart is racing but I need to stay calm. Unfortunately, we can't just eject because the seats on the Freedom Ferry aren't equipped with jets like the seats on the Freedom Flyer. So, this is pretty much going to be a legit emergency landing.

Luckily, I've practiced emergency landings a few times in the flight simulator, but I've never actually done

one for real. Well, I guess there's no time like the present!

"Hold on," I say. "This is gonna get bumpy."

I call up a map of Keystone City to find the best possible landing spot for a 50,000-pound spacecraft without the ability to stop itself. After a quick scan of the topography, I realize I'm going to need a pretty long runway to slow my momentum.

So that only leaves one option: Main Street.

Fortunately, it's well after rush hour so there shouldn't be many cars on the road. At least, I hope not. But as I grip the steering column, I realize my hands are soaked. Yuck, I'm so nervous I'm actually sweating through my gloves.

I glance over at Dog-Gone who is covering his eyes with his paws. Now there's a vote of confidence.

Time to focus.

The streetlamps lining the road light up Main Street like a landing strip, so I just need to stay within the lines and hope there's no traffic. Thankfully, it looks clear as we approach, so I pull back on the column and dive in.

Within seconds we touch down. I angle the Freedom Ferry to land the rear first, resulting in an ear-piercing SCREECH as tungsten steel scrapes against concrete. Then, I lay down the front, throwing Dog-Gone and I forward. Sparks fly all around us as we skid along the street, seemingly forever.

But I have other ideas.

I call up the wing propulsion system and spin the

dial, reversing my one working thruster. Then, I punch the "Thrust" button, and the jet kicks on, slowing our momentum. But because all of our power is on the left side, we swerve off-balance. I counter with the steering column, but it takes another five thousand feet or so until we come to a complete stop.

I breathe a sigh of relief.

"See," I say to Dog-Gone. "That wasn't so—"

HOOONNNKKK!

SCREEEECCCCHHHHH!

My eyes bug out as I see two giant headlights heading straight for us! Instinctively, I grab Dog-Gone's collar, but there's no time to get out! So, I throw my body over Dog-Gone and brace for impact.

PSSSSHHHHHH!

Seconds later, I'm still gritting my teeth.

Huh? Where's the impact?

Dog-Gone and I look at one another, and then I poke my head up to find a huge truck stopped only inches away from the Freedom Ferry.

"What are you doing, kid?" the driver yells, leaning out of his cab. "You could have killed somebody!"

"Sorry," I say. "We just... dropped in?"

"Crazy city drivers!" he yells. And then he backs up his truck and goes around us, shaking his fist at me.

Well, that was lucky. But he's right about one thing, we're sitting in the middle of a four-way intersection. I reverse the wing thruster and motor us over to the side of the road. There, that should handle that, but based on all of the sputtering coming from the engine, this might have been the Freedom Ferry's last ride.

"C'mon, boy," I say, popping the hatch.

We climb out of the Freedom Ferry and look around. Honestly, I've never felt so lost before. I mean, I've got no home, no transportation, and no clue what to do next. Then, I notice we're parked in front of a storefront with televisions in the window. The sign above the window reads: *Keystone City Electronics Emporium.* My eyes drift back to the TVs when I realize they're tuned in to the news. Maybe I can get some info?

I hustle over to the window to find a female news anchor talking to camera with some words scrolling beneath her that read: *Freedom Force Captured!*

Oh. No.

Suddenly, the image jumps to Dad being held down by a group of Meta-Busters. And they're wrapping his wrists with those mysterious leather straps! Then, there's another image showing a group of Meta-Busters carrying away the rest of the team, including Mom and Grace!

Ugh! I was hoping Grace stayed out of it, but it looks like she couldn't help herself. Now they're all prisoners—except for me.

Just then, I feel something wet nuzzle into my palm.

Well, me and Dog-Gone.

But I still can't believe it.

We're the only heroes left.

"Hey, kid," comes a man's voice from behind that makes me jump out of my skin. "Are you taking those?"

I spin around to find a masked, mustached man wearing a blue costume with the insignia of vapor on his chest. Immediately, I know who he is.

"Y-You're Mr. Mister," I say.

"Yeah," he says. "And who are you, the Queen of England?"

For a second, I'm stunned. I mean, Mr. Mister is a Meta 3 villain who can evaporate solid objects into pure mist! I've never faced him before, but I've read his Meta profile and he's one tough customer.

"Now are you claiming those or not?" he asks.

"Um, claiming what?" I say.

"Those TV's," he says. "You got here first so I'm trying to be polite. Now, I'll ask you one last time. Are you looting them or not?"

Looting them?

"You mean, like, stealing them?" I ask.

"Yeah," he says. "There ain't no more heroes around so you can take whatever you want. Everyone's doing it."

Um, everyone?

Suddenly, I hear a CRASH and when I look to my right, I do a double take, because dozens of costumed criminals are stampeding down Main Street! I see Slap Stick and Ferret King and Dark Mind and so on and so forth.

It's like a field day for Meta villains!

"Scoot over," Mr. Mister says, putting his hands on the glass window. Then, he furrows his brow, and seconds later the glass is gone!

He evaporated it into thin air!

"I'm taking this one," he says, grabbing a flat-screen TV. "I accidentally vaporized my last one."

Dog-Gone bares his teeth and I grab his collar before he lurches forward.

"Stay," I whisper.

Believe me, I'd love nothing more than to stop Mr. Mister, but if he doesn't know we're the good guys, then it probably isn't the best time to announce it to the world. Especially if Main Street is crawling with criminals. For the moment, our best option is to lay low. There's no reason to blow our cover over a silly television.

"Return that television, crook!" comes a girl's voice.

Huh?

Suddenly, a heinous odor assaults my nostrils and I cringe. It smells like rotten eggs and spoiled meat all rolled into one barf-inducing package. I pinch my nose, but not before I start feeling queasy.

"What's that smell?" Mr. Mister says, looking like he's about to heave.

Just then, a masked girl wearing a black costume with a white stripe down the center appears on the scene.

"I warned you, creep!" she says. "Now put back that television or face the wrath of Skunk Girl!"

Um, did she just call herself 'Skunk Girl?'

"Go take a bath," Mr. Mister says, ignoring her.

"Get 'em, Pinball!" Skunk Girl yells.

The next thing I know, a round, gray object bigger than a boulder bounces over our heads and SLAMS into Mr. Mister, knocking the TV right out of his hands. The flat screen falls and SHATTERS on the ground.

"My TV!" Mr. Mister cries out.

And that's when I realize that bouncy, round object is no object, it's another costumed kid!

"Whoops," Pinball says. "Sorry."

"Oh, I'll make you sorry," Mr. Mister says, rising to his feet. "By evaporating you!" But just as he's about to grab Pinball, there's a blinding flash of white light and I'm suddenly seeing stars.

"Nice shot, Selfie," Skunk Girl says.

Selfie?

When my vision finally clears, I find Mr. Mister rubbing his eyes and a pretty girl with a brown ponytail and a sleek white-and-silver costume staring at her phone.

"Thanks," she says, looking up at me with her bright, blue eyes. "I can't wait to post it."

These kids look like they're my age.

"Um, pardon me," I say, "but who are you people?"

"Oh, we're Next Gen," Skunk Girl says proudly.

"Next Gen?" I say. "What's that mean?"

"It means we're the Next Gen," she says, "As in 'the Next Generation' of Meta heroes."

"Yeah," Pinball says. "We met in a chat room."

"So," Skunk Girl says, looking me up and down, "I take it you're a villain too. Ready for a bashing?"

"Um, no," I answer. "I'm a hero. But you do know that Meta heroes are banned, right? I mean, I appreciate what you're trying to do, but it's not a great time to be running around in public right now."

"Don't worry about us, buddy," Skunk Girl says. "It may be our first mission, but we can handle ourselves."

Their first mission? I swallow hard.

"Wait a second!" Selfie says. "I know you. I streamed your interview on the CNC Morning Newsflash. You're a member of the Freedom Force. Epic Zebra, right?"

"Shhh!" I whisper. "I am a member of the Freedom Force, but my name isn't—"

"Hey!" Mr. Mister calls out. "Hey, everyone! Get this, that kid in the red-and-blue is a superhero. And he's a member of the Freedom Force!"

Oh, jeez! So much for laying low.

"The Freedom Force?" comes a voice from down the street. "Where?"

"President Kensington offered a reward for bringing in a kid named Epic Zero," comes another voice. "A big one!"

Wait, what? A reward? For me?

Suddenly, there's a mob of villains heading our way.

"Did I say something wrong?" Selfie asks.

"Yeah," I say. "Kind of."

"Sorry," she says.

But her apology comes too late because seconds later, we're surrounded.

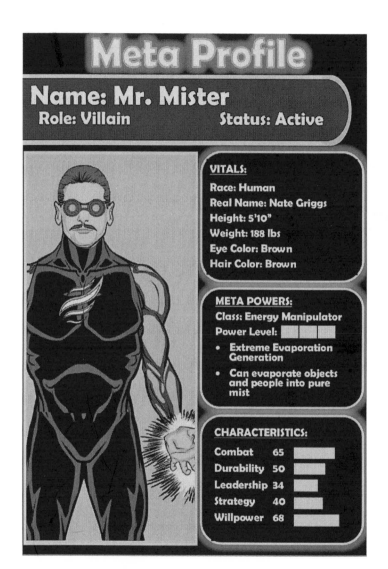

Meta Profile

Name: Mr. Mister
Role: Villain   Status: Active

VITALS:

Race: Human
Real Name: Nate Griggs
Height: 5'10"
Weight: 188 lbs
Eye Color: Brown
Hair Color: Brown

META POWERS:

Class: Energy Manipulator
Power Level:
- **Extreme Evaporation Generation**
- **Can evaporate objects and people into pure mist**

CHARACTERISTICS:

Combat	65	
Durability	50	
Leadership	34	
Strategy	40	
Willpower	68	

FIVE

I GET A BABYSITTING GIG

I really didn't need this right now.

I mean, my bad decisions have already cost me my family and my home. Shouldn't that be enough for one day? But I guess the answer is 'no,' because I'm now surrounded by a mob of Meta villains who want to turn me over to President Kensington for a big reward.

And to top it off, I'm also babysitting—

"Um, where did all of these villains come from?" Pinball asks. "And which one isn't wearing deodorant?"

—three amateur heroes.

"Get that kid," Mr. Mister says, pointing at me. "He must be Epic Zero. He's the one the president wants."

"Whoa, chill," I say, trying to sound calm. "Everyone just relax. You've got the wrong guy here. My name is

Epic Zebra. I know I look just like Epic Zero, but trust me, I'm not. Besides, everyone knows how easy it is to get Metas confused. Remember when Captain Justice took out Devil Head thinking it was Head Devil? Poor Devil Head was just going for a manicure, but cases of mistaken identity happen all the time in our business. So, how about we skip the unnecessary fight scene and jump to the part where we make up and you buy me ice cream?"

"There ain't gonna be no making up," says a short villain with two humungous eyes. "I saw you on that CNC morning news show and I know you're Epic Zero."

"Yeah," Slap Stick says. "Flashback never forgets a face. If he says you're Epic Zero, then you're Epic Zero."

Flashback? That's Flashback?

Uh-oh. Flashback has the ability to retain everything he's ever seen. So, he knows I'm really me—and now so does everyone else!

"So, what are you saying?" I ask. "No ice cream?"

"Oh, I'll make ice cream," Mr. Mister says, raising his hands. "Out of you!"

I do some quick math. There are twenty-one of them and five of us. Even if I negate Mr. Mister's powers, we don't have the firepower to take them all in a fair fight. What's that other old saying—he that fights and runs away, may live to fight another day?

"Guys," I whisper to Next Gen, "grab me if you want to live."

As multiple hands wrap around my arms and a furry body presses against my leg, I get down to business. With all of these Metas around, I've got plenty of options. But I decide to keep it simple.

First, I borrow Dog-Gone's invisibility power.

"Hey!" Mr. Mister says. "Where did they go?"

Then, I grab Slap Stick's adhesion power, making my skin super-clingy so my new friends stick to me like glue.

Finally, I copy Pinball's power, and my body suddenly expands like a balloon, which is accompanied by a loud RIPPING sound as the fabric splits from the bottom of my pants.

Awesome.

But I can't worry about that now because I've got to get us out of here!

"Hold on tight!" I say.

I do a little jump, and when my feet touch the ground, we spring into the air like a super-charged bouncy ball. In fact, we're so high the villains down below look like ants and Selfie lets out a blood-curdling scream, but I think it's kind of fun.

That is, until I realize everyone looking up can see my Batman-logoed underpants. But then I remember we're still invisible and breathe a sigh of relief.

And with my next bounce, we're long gone.

***

Twenty minutes later, we're sitting on the floor of a treehouse in the backyard of a suburban home. It's dark out and the crickets are chirping away, blissfully unaware of the chaos happening in the world around them.

"Cheese puffs?" Selfie offers, holding out a bag.

"Thanks," I say, grabbing a bunch. But as soon as I pull my hand out, a large snout invades my palm and sucks up all of the goodies. Sometimes I wonder if my dog is actually a dog or a vacuum cleaner covered in fur.

"Should he really be eating those?" Pinball asks.

"Definitely not," I say, "but unless you've got dog treats up here, I'll let it go this time. He's had a pretty rough day."

"Me too," Pinball says, adjusting his position. He's so round he can't fit comfortably into any corner. "Hey, Selfie, what's a guy gotta do around here to get some cheese puffs?"

"Don't be rude," Selfie says, offering me the bag again. "We serve our guests first. Besides, you'd probably eat the whole bag all by yourself."

"Hey!" Pinball says, raising his index finger. "I resemble that remark."

I take out another handful and stuff them into my mouth before Dog-Gone has a chance to steal them away. Then, I take a look around.

From the outside, the treehouse looked pretty normal, complete with a rickety old ladder, but the inside is way more sophisticated than I imagined. One wall is covered with floor-to-ceiling computers and giant maps of Keystone City. Another wall holds a large bookshelf with all kinds of supplies on it, like water bottles, tools, and a first aid kit. It's pretty impressive for a treehouse, but it's no Waystation.

"So," I say, talking with my mouth full, "is this, like, your headquarters?"

"Yeah," Skunk Girl says. "Why? Is it not good enough for you?"

"Skunk Girl!" Selfie says.

"It's great," I say. "You've got everything you need here. Speaking of which, do you happen to have a sewing kit? I seem to have split my... I mean, I need to repair my costume."

"Sure," Selfie says, pulling a plastic box off of the shelf. "Here it is. Do you need help?"

"Um, no thanks," I say, my face going flush. "I've got it. But I'd appreciate it if you guys could turn away for a few minutes while I take care of some, um, personal business."

"Oh," Selfie says, her eyebrows raised. "Got it."

"Seriously?" Skunk Girl says. "Fine."

They both turn around.

"I can't move but I'll close my eyes," Pinball says.

I'm all set, except for one last pair of peepers.

"You too," I tell Dog-Gone.

He rolls his eyes and turns away.

Then, I drop my pants and get to work. Yep, just as I

thought, it's a pretty big tear. Thankfully, Dad taught me how to sew. He said Meta heroes have to be prepared for anything, and boy was he right!

"You know," Pinball says. "What you did back there was really cool. You've got some major powers."

"No kidding, Pinball," Selfie says. "He's on the Freedom Force for goodness sake. Of course he's got major powers."

"Well, thanks," I say, threading as quickly as I can. "I'm just doing my job."

"We didn't need him, you know," Skunk Girl says. "We could have taken them ourselves."

"Are you crazy?" Pinball says. "There were hundreds of villains out there."

"Twenty-one," I say. "Not that I was counting."

"Right," Pinball says. "But that's the point. You know because you have more caped crusading experience in your little pinkie than all of us put together. We could learn a lot from you. In fact, Selfie and I were talking, and we think you'd make a great leader for Next Gen."

"What?" Skunk Girl and I say simultaneously.

"Um, I'm no leader," I say.

"But I wanted to be our leader," Skunk Girl says, clearly frustrated.

"You will be," Selfie says, putting her hand on Skunk Girl's shoulder. "But we have to be honest with ourselves and we could have been killed out there. If he can teach us the ropes, then we'll be able to handle any situation."

"Hmph!" Skunk Girl remarks. "I'm not buying it."

"Look," I say, putting my pants back on, "I'm flattered, but I'm really not a good leader. Oh, and you guys can turn around now."

"You're wrong," Pinball says, opening his eyes. "You're not a good leader, you're a great leader. I mean, you saved all of us back there."

"That was dumb luck," I say. "Who knows if I could do that again. Trust me, if you saw the day I've had, you'd pay me not to be your leader."

"Stop pressuring him," Skunk Girl says. "He's clearly not interested. He thinks he's better than us."

"What?" I say. "No, I don't think that at all. I've just got a lot going on. And you shouldn't even be out there right now. President Kensington has banned all Metas, and here's a newsflash for you—that includes you guys. If her Meta-Busters catch you, you're doomed."

"Just like the Freedom Force?" Pinball asks.

My mouth opens but no words come out. I mean, how do I respond to that? The Freedom Force was captured because of me. And if I tell Next Gen it was my fault, what will they think of me then?

"Yes," I finally say. "Just like the Freedom Force."

"But you're going to save them," Selfie says. "Aren't you?"

"Well, of course he is," Pinball says.

"I... I...," I stammer.

"And you want this guy to lead us?" Skunk Girl says.

"Listen," I say, "I am planning on saving them. I just don't know how."

"Why don't you talk to the president?" Selfie asks.

"The president?" I say. "The president of the United States? She's the one causing all of this madness."

"Exactly," Selfie says. "If you can convince her to repeal the Meta Restriction Resolution, then all of this hero targeting will go away."

At first, what she's saying seems ridiculous. But the more I think about it, the more it makes perfect sense. I mean, I could try breaking into the Pentagon to rescue my family, but with all of those Meta-Busters around it would be a suicide mission. But instead, if I can simply convince President Kensington that she's wrong about Metas, I could solve everything once and for all.

"That's a great idea," I say. "But there's just one problem. How am I supposed to get inside the White House? After all, I'm a Meta. Even if I use Dog-Gone's invisibility power, the Meta-Busters could spot me with their infrared vision."

It's quiet for a minute, and then...

"You know," Pinball says, breaking the silence, "they have tours of the White House all the time. My brother's fifth-grade class went last year. If we're lucky, maybe there's a tour we can crash tomorrow."

It's actually not a bad idea, except for one thing.

"I like it," I say, "but there's no *we*. There's just me, and my dog. We'll do this on our own."

"Well, that sounds great to me," Skunk Girl says, gesturing to the ladder. "Why don't I show you the way out?"

"Knock it off, Skunk Girl," Selfie says, taking the sewing kit back. "Look, Epic Zero, you're going to need help. I mean, we've been helpful so far, right?"

"Well, yeah," I admit.

"Great," she says. "Then maybe you could use more help. Tell you what, why don't you think about it tonight? You can sleep right here in the treehouse."

Well, I am tired. And Dog-Gone looks exhausted.

Selfie pulls a blanket off the shelf and hands it to me.

"Thanks," I say. "But wait, where are you guys sleeping?"

"Oh," Selfie says. "We're in my backyard. That's my house right there. Skunk Girl is sleeping over, but don't worry, you won't be alone, because Pinball can bunk out here with you."

"It'll be awesome," Pinball says with a wink. "I've got loads of questions."

Meta Profile

Name: Skunk Girl
Role: Hero   Status: Active

VITALS:

Race: Human
Real Name: Melinda Musk
Height: 5'0"
Weight: 105 lbs
Eye Color: Brown
Hair Color: Black & White

META POWERS:

Class: Energy Manipulator
Power Level:

- **Considerable Stench Generation**
- **Can generate foul odors to repel enemies or knock them unconscious**

CHARACTERISTICS:

Combat	22
Durability	25
Leadership	42
Strategy	61
Willpower	72

SIX

I CATCH THE BUS

Note to self: never, ever, E-V-E-R, sleep in the same room as Pinball again.

The dude talked non-stop until I literally had to pretend I was sleeping. And then, once he finally stopped talking, he snored like a chainsaw all night long! I didn't sleep a wink and based on Dog-Gone's droopy eyes, he didn't either.

But truthfully, I'm not sure it mattered. There are so many thoughts spinning inside my head I probably wouldn't have slept anyway. Of course, destroying the Waystation is weighing on my mind. But the biggest thing I can't shake is how I got my family captured.

If something happens to them because of me I don't know what I'll do. I just hope they're not undergoing 'behavior modification,' whatever that is.

Then, I keep debating if I should go to the White House alone or not. I mean, there's really no reason to drag Next Gen into this mess. Besides, they're rookies. What if they got captured—or worse? That settles it, I have to go solo. I can't risk their lives too.

But as soon as I throw off my blanket, I catch Dog-Gone's tired eyes. The poor lug. If I don't take him with me, he'll probably never sleep again.

"C'mon, boy," I whisper, as sunlight streams through the treehouse planks. Maybe I can make my getaway before anyone wakes up. But just as I tiptoe over to the ladder, Selfie appears.

"Where are you going?" she asks, pulling herself up and into the treehouse. That's when I notice she's wearing a blue backpack.

"Um, Dog-Gone has to use the bathroom," I say, lying through my teeth. "He's got a really small bladder."

"Uh-huh," she says, eyeing me suspiciously. Then, she nudges Pinball with her foot. "Wake up, Pinball."

"Huh?" Pinball snorts as drool rolls down his chin.

"Here," she says, pressing something into my hand. "That's your White House tour ticket."

My White House tour ticket? That's impossible. But when I look down at the ticket, it reads:

- *Official White House Tour Ticket*
- *Name: Bruce Wayne*
- *Age: 12*

- *Citizenship: United States of America*
- *Gender: Male*
- *City of Residence: Keystone City*

Okay, now I'm totally confused. I mean, it looks like a real White House Tour ticket, but I thought you had to write your Congressman months in advance to get one.

"Um, how did you get this?" I ask. "And why does it say I'm 'Bruce Wayne?' That's Batman's secret identity."

"Well, now it's you," she says. "I created them on the computer. Someone posted a picture of what a tour ticket looks like, so I made one for each of us. My mom is a graphic designer, so I used her design software and then printed them on cardstock. Not too shabby, huh?"

"Hey, I'm Clark Kent!" Pinball says, proudly holding up his ticket.

"Right," I say. "Look, these tickets are impressive, but they're not going to fool anyone. I'm sure there's a special hologram or something we're missing. Plus, we're not even signed up on the official White House tour list."

"Oh, don't worry about that," Selfie says with a sly smile. "When we get there just leave it to me. Now get changed."

She tosses me the blue backpack and I open it up to find a bundle of clothing. There's a red t-shirt, blue jeans, socks, and a pair of sneakers.

"Who are these for?" I ask.

"For you, Bruce Wayne," she says, getting back onto the ladder. "What? Did you think we'd just waltz into the

White House in our costumes? We need to look like normal kids. Those clothes belong to my younger brother and you looked about the same size. Get changed and I'll meet you guys on the ground in about ten minutes."

"Younger brother?" I mutter, but she's already gone.

Well, I guess she's right about one thing, no Meta-Buster worth its sensors is going to let us enter the White House dressed as superheroes. But as soon as I start removing my mask, I freeze. What am I doing?

If I take off my mask, these kids will see my face!

That's a major 'no-no!'

But then again, what other choice do I have? The Freedom Ferry is kaput and it's not like I can sneak into the White House using Dog-Gone's invisibility power. Those Meta-Busters have infrared vision! So, I guess Selfie's plan is the only plan I've got.

I breathe deeply and take off my mask.

"Ha!" Pinball chuckles.

"What's so funny?" I ask.

"Well," he says, "with your mask on, I didn't realize you actually had eyebrows."

"Gee," I say. "That's hysterical."

Then, I turn my back and put on Selfie's brother's clothing. Fortunately, it fits, and when I'm done dressing, I stuff my costume and utility belt into the backpack and throw it over my shoulder.

"Let's go, Dog-Gone," I say, descending the ladder.

Dog-Gone follows, but when he looks over the edge

of the treehouse, he suddenly backs up.

"Get back here you big baby," I say. "Climb down backward like I did. Don't worry, I'll support you."

After a few seconds, Dog-Gone extends his business end over the edge, and then lowers a back paw down gingerly until it finds its footing on the ladder. Then comes another paw. And then another. And the next thing I know, his rump is pressed squarely onto my face.

Just. Freaking. Wonderful.

We climb down slowly, and when we finally reach the bottom, my nose is relieved.

"Well, that was graceful," Skunk Girl says, her arms crossed. She's not wearing her mask either and is dressed in all black with a t-shirt that reads: *Punk Rock Rules*. She's also wearing a black-and-white backpack which I assume is holding her costume.

"Hey," comes Selfie's voice from behind.

But when I turn around, I inadvertently gasp, because she's not wearing her mask either and I can see her face—which is, well, really pretty. She's staring at me with her blue eyes and has her hair in a long braid.

"Are you okay?" she asks. "You look really red."

"Um, me?" I stammer. "Oh… yeah. I'm good. Real good." Why am I rambling like a dork?

"Great," she says. "But you do know your dog is peeing on our headquarters, right?"

"What?" I say, turning to find Dog-Gone standing at the base of the tree with his hind leg in the air.

"Dog-Gone!" I yell. "Really?"

"Let's bounce!" Pinball says, dropping from the sky and landing between us. His headgear is off and he's wearing a blue tracksuit with yellow stripes.

"Sounds good," Selfie says. "But this time we're not gonna bounce, we're gonna roll. We've got a bus to catch."

***

"Get your flea-bitten butt off of me," I whisper to Dog-Gone, who is wedged on the floor of the bus between my knees and the seat in front of me.

I feel his weight lift off my feet, but then he plops down again, crushing my toes. Well, he's clearly not going to budge, not that he has anywhere else to go because every seat is taken. Thankfully, he's invisible, otherwise, we never would have gotten him onto the bus in the first place. So, I guess I've got no choice but to grin and bear his weight for our three-hour ride to Washington D.C.

Lucky me.

At least I managed to avoid sitting next to Pinball. Talk about squished! Instead, I'm next to Selfie in the back of the bus, which is presenting, well... different challenges.

I mean, how come my stomach does flips every time I look at her? And why can't I even get up the nerve to talk to her? We've been sitting in awkward silence ever since the bus started moving.

Okay, I've got to say something. Maybe I'll ask her what her favorite color is. No, that's lame. Maybe her favorite food. No, that's really lame. Maybe—

"I'm sorry about your friends," she says suddenly.

"What food is your favorite color?" I blurt out.

"Huh?" she says, staring at me like I have two heads.

"Um, nothing," I say. Why am I such a goober? "Sorry, what did you say?"

"I said I'm sorry about your friends," she says. "You know, the Freedom Force?"

"Oh, those friends," I say, totally embarrassed. "Of course. Yeah, I-I hope they're okay."

As I look out the window at the passing trees, I flashback to the image of my family being carted away by Meta-Busters. I still can't believe it was my fault. And I never did find out what those leathery straps were.

Suddenly, I feel someone tapping on my right arm.

"Huh?" I say, turning to find Selfie staring at me.

"Are you okay?" she asks. "I was calling your name but you kind of zoned out. Well, I *was* calling you 'Bruce,' which isn't really your name, so it's no wonder you didn't respond. Sorry, this fake identity stuff is all new for me. In fact, this whole Meta thing is new to me. I don't think I'm going to be very good at it."

"Hey, don't say that," I say, shifting to face her. "I think you'll be great. I mean, you're the one who temporarily blinded Mr. Mister. And you came up with the plan to see the president. By the way, what's the name on your ticket anyway?"

"Diana Prince," she says, holding her ticket. "It's—"

"—Wonder Woman's secret identity," I finish for her. "Yeah, I know. I'm a big comic book fan."

"Me too," she says.

"See," I say. "Then you already know the deal. With great power comes—"

"—great responsibility," she finishes. "Yeah, I know. I just wish I was better at it. My parents don't think I'm good at anything."

"Really?" I say surprised.

"Yeah," she says, playing with her phone. "They're workaholics. I was pretty much raised by babysitters."

"Well, just think," I say. "You're better off than Tarzan. He was raised by apes. At least you got juice boxes."

She snorts and then shoots me a funny look.

"You're really good at this superhero stuff," she says. "I wish I could be as good as you."

"You will be," I say. "You just need proper training. Look, if I didn't have the Freedom Force, I wouldn't know half the stuff I'm doing. They taught me a lot."

"You're lucky," she says. "The three of us only have each other and we're all pretty new. If we don't have a Freedom Force to train us, how will we learn?"

That's a great question. I mean, I guess maybe I could train them. Maybe in the afternoon and...

Hang on, who am I kidding? I can't train these kids! I mean, I'm a lousy leader. And I'm not even allowed off the Waystation without my parents' permission.

Ugh. The Waystation. I feel sick.

I look over at Selfie who is spinning her phone around her finger. Then, I remember that's no normal phone. She used it to create a massive, blinding light. But as far as I'm aware, there's no app for that, so how did she do it?

"How does that thing work?" I whisper.

"This?" she whispers back, holding up her phone. "Well, honestly, I'm not really sure. I got it for my birthday but as soon as I held it, it sort of, well, spoke to me. I can make it do all sorts of things, depending on what I'm thinking, but I need to point the screen at whatever I'm using it against for it to work."

"It sounds like Magic," I say. "Like how Master Mime uses willpower to control his mystical amulet."

"Really?" she says. "I have powers like Master Mime? That's so cool. See, I'm already learning from you."

"Yeah," I say. "I guess so."

We gab about her powers for a while longer, when the bus finally SCREECHES to a halt. I look out the window, surprised to see we're parked at a bus stop, which means we've reached Washington D.C.

"Wow, that went fast," I say.

"Yeah," Selfie says, standing up. "Time to go."

"Great," I say. "Have fun without me."

"What?" she says confused. "Aren't you coming?"

"I'd love to," I say, "but a two-ton walrus is sleeping on my feet."

Meta Profile

Name: Selfie
Role: Hero   **Status:** Active

VITALS:

Race: Human
Real Name: Crystal Norton
Height: 4'6"
Weight: 85 lbs
Eye Color: Blue
Hair Color: Brown

META POWERS:

Class: Magic
Power Level:
- Considerable Psychic abilities powered by a magic mobile phone
- Vulnerable without it

CHARACTERISTICS:

Combat	16	
Durability	11	
Leadership	50	
Strategy	76	
Willpower	60	

SEVEN

I TAKE A DETOUR OF THE WHITE HOUSE

I've never seen such a show of force.

The bus dropped us six blocks from the White House, and the closer we get, the more guards we encounter. At first, there were just police cars, but the last few blocks were packed with tanks and serious artillery. Not to mention the Meta-Busters stationed on every corner.

Fortunately, Dog-Gone is staying invisible, so we just look like four kids out for a morning stroll. But there's no way I can risk taking him into the White House with us. So, as soon as we hit Pennsylvania Avenue, I give him a stern talking to.

"Listen, Dog-Gone," I say. "It's important you stay invisible and don't move from this spot. I don't care if a squirrel bops you on the head. Stay here until we get back. Got it?"

I feel a wet nose press into my palm.

"Good boy," I say. "Hopefully, we'll be back in an hour. Now remember, stay put."

Then, I nod to the others and we make our way to the White House gates.

"Do you think he'll listen?" Pinball asks.

"Oh, sure," I say. But deep down, I'm not so sure.

When we arrive there's a big crowd of senior citizens funneling through the entrance, so we fall in line behind them. Okay, all we need to do is get through security and we're home free. I just hope Selfie knows what she's doing.

But when I look up, I nearly have a heart attack.

"Um, big problem," I whisper to Selfie.

"What?" she says.

"They're making us walk through a metal detector," I say. "My utility belt will set that thing off like crazy."

"Don't worry about it," she says, moving forward.

Despite her confidence, my instincts tell me to turn and run, but just then, the last old lady waddles through the gate and it's our turn! I take a quick count of the guards. There's one in front collecting tickets, one monitoring the metal detector, and six lining the entry—and they're all holding machine guns.

Suddenly, my palms feel sweaty. I mean, if we get caught, this will be a disaster. Especially after I spot a Meta-Buster standing in the wings.

"Tickets please," the guard requests. "And then step right through the metal detector."

"Sure," Selfie says. "But do you mind if I get a picture with all of you first? It's my first time here and I really want to capture the full experience."

"Sorry, dear," he says. "You can take all the pictures you want inside. I just need your ticket."

"Oh, please?" Selfie pleads. "Just one? It'll be quick. I just need everyone to lean in a bit."

The guard looks back at his colleagues and the guy behind the metal detector shrugs his shoulders.

"Okay," the guard says, rolling his eyes. "Just one."

"Great," she says. "Everyone look at my phone."

All of the guards scooch forward and smile as Selfie points her phone. I turn away before the big flash.

"Thanks," Selfie says. "Here's my ticket. And these guys are with me. You'll let us inside, right?"

"I'll let you inside," the guard repeats robotically like he's in some kind of a trance. And when I walk past, I notice his eyes are glazed over.

"Thanks," Selfie says. Then, she looks at the guard behind the metal detector and says, "Don't worry about our bags. It's all cool."

"It's all cool," the second guard repeats.

As we coast through without a hitch, I make a mental note: never photo bomb Selfie's pictures.

"See," Selfie says with a wink. "Told ya."

"Yes, you did," I say. "Nice job."

Once inside, we have no problem catching up with the other tourists who are ambling their way up the circular driveway. As we walk, I take it all in, amazed. I mean, I've probably seen the White House a million times on TV, but I've never actually been here.

That's when I notice a bespectacled woman heading our way who is wearing a big badge around her neck that reads: *Tour Guide.*

"Welcome to the White House," she says, with open arms. "My name is Lynn Douglas and it's my privilege to once again welcome the finalists from the forty-third Americana Quilting Contest." Then, she spots the four of us bringing up the rear. "Oh, and I see we have some young quilters this year. How wonderful. Please follow me."

"Quilting contest?" Pinball whispers. "No wonder we're surrounded by old people."

"Shhh!" Skunk Girl whispers. "Don't be rude."

"As you know," the tour guide continues, "the White House is the official residence and workplace of every president of the United States since John Adams, our second president, in the year 1800. This building has a fascinating history we'll discuss further inside. But before anyone asks, there are one hundred and thirty-two rooms and thirty-five bathrooms. Of course, we won't be seeing them all, but it's your lucky day because this tour received permission to visit the West Wing."

"The West Wing?" Selfie says. "That's amazing. That's where the Oval Office is located."

"Well, if the oval office is amazing," Pinball says, rubbing his round belly, "then I must be incredible."

"You don't get it, do you?" Skunk Girl says. "The Oval Office is the president's office."

The president's office? That's right! If this tour takes us straight to President Kensington's office, then I can discuss the Meta Restriction Resolution with her.

"Come this way," the tour guide says, ushering us into a long, covered pavilion that opens up to a beautiful garden. "We are walking through the West Colonnade, which connects the main residence to the West Wing. The West Colonnade overlooks the Rose Garden where many official events take place, including receptions and bill signings. Despite its name, you might be surprised to learn there are over thirty types of tulips in the Rose Garden. And to our left are—"

I'm sure what she's saying is fascinating, but the particulars of the Rose Garden are the last thing on my mind. If this tour is going to drop me at the president's doorstep, I need to figure out what I'm going to say!

I mean, how am I going to convince her to change her mind about Metas? Based on her last transmission, she seemed pretty dead set on stopping all Metas no matter what. Not even Dad could convince her otherwise, and he's freaking Captain Justice. So, what can I possibly offer?

Suddenly, I realize we're inside another part of the building. This must be the West Wing, which means I'd better come up with something fast!

"To your left is the Cabinet Room," the tour guide continues. "Here is where the president seeks council from her top advisors. As you can imagine, many spirited debates are held around this twenty-foot table, like the recent ban on Metas."

"I want to break that table," Pinball whispers.

"Shhh!" Skunk Girl whispers, giving him a death stare.

The tour continues into another corridor filled with busy White House staffers. Some are running around carrying files while others are answering phone call after phone call. It's so chaotic I nearly miss seeing a door to our left that's flanked by two men in dark suits who look like Secret Service agents.

"Through that door is the Oval Office," the tour guide says. "But since the door is closed it looks like President Kensington is hard at work running the country. So, we won't have the opportunity to see it today, but there's still more ahead, like the Roosevelt Room. Follow me."

The crowd moans in disappointment, but as they move on, I can't help but linger.

"Hey," Selfie whispers, grabbing my arm. "Come on, you'll never get through. There are way too many people."

But just as she pulls me down the hall, I see a familiar face heading our way. I'd recognize those piercing, blue eyes anywhere. It's General Winch! And he's headed straight for the Oval Office!

Now's my chance!

I take in the scene. The staffers are busy doing their jobs, the tour is heading down the hall, and the Secret Service has their eyes on Winch. No one is looking my way. My heart is pounding fast. It's now or never.

Then, I remember I'm wearing my backpack. I can't risk my utility belt rattling around.

"Take this," I whisper to Selfie, handing her my backpack. But as I pass it over, something falls out of the top and hits the floor with a CLANG.

Great. I guess the bag wasn't zipped all the way.

"What's that?" Selfie says, bending over to pick it up.

"Doesn't matter," I whisper. "Just get ready."

"Get ready?" she whispers. "For what?"

But I don't have time to explain. Instead, I concentrate hard, reaching out for Dog-Gone's power. I extend my scope far and wide like a giant Meta Wi-Fi signal, pushing my power outside the building. I told that pooch to stay put. I just hope he listened.

Come on, Dog-Gone. Where are you? Please tell me you're not chasing some stupid squirrel.

And then, I connect!

Yes! He listened to me! I pull his power back until I can feel it surging through my veins, and then I disappear.

"Hey," Selfie whispers. "Where'd you go?"

"I'm here," I whisper. "Create a distraction."

Suddenly, Selfie starts coughing.

All eyes turn to her.

Perfect!

Just then, Winch approaches the Oval Office. The Secret Service agents step aside and one of them opens the door. This is it! I've got to move!

But I also have to be careful. I may be invisible, but they could still hear me coming. So, I get on my tippy toes and fast-walk my way right behind Winch, matching him stride for stride. I'm so close I can smell his overpowering cologne. Gross!

"Gentlemen," Winch says, nodding to the agents.

I stay as close as I can without touching him, resisting the urge to pinch my nose as we both walk straight through the door. I can hear my heart thumping out of my chest. Please, heart, don't give me away.

And then the door miraculously SHUTS behind us.

Holy cow! I did it! I'm actually standing in the president's office! But then, Winch stops short and I nearly crash into him. Fortunately, I regain my balance just in time and take a quick look around.

We're standing on the edge of a plush, blue carpet with an image of the seal of the United States woven into its center. And it's pretty obvious how the Oval Office got its name because the room is shaped like, well, an oval. There are two cream-colored sofas behind us and paintings of former presidents line the walls.

It's swanky, but I'm not here to admire the décor. I'm here to have a word with the most powerful person on the planet—President Kara Kensington.

Despite our arrival, she's sitting quietly behind a large, mahogany desk with her eyes glued to a file. I'm sure she knows Winch is here, but clearly, she's not planning on acknowledging his presence. I still don't know what I'm going to say, but I guess you can't rehearse things like this. But just as I'm about to make myself visible, she looks up with steely eyes and says—

"I have no patience for idle pleasantries, General. Just give me the update."

"Certainly, my lord," Winch says.

Um, did he just call her 'my lord?' Isn't the whole point of a democracy not to have Kings or Queens?

"We have apprehended three more superhero teams," Winch says proudly. "The Storm Squad, the Watchdogs, and the Marvelous Monsters. The last one resulted in several hundred casualties."

"To be expected," President Kensington says matter-of-factly, closing her file. "It is a small price to pay."

"Yes, my lord," Winch says. "The surviving prisoners have all been transferred to the Pentagon to begin behavior modification and the leeching process."

Leeching process? What's that?

"Excellent," she says. "And the hatchlings?"

"The bio-engineering lab has produced thirty-one more," Winch says. Then, he swallows hard and adds, "but we have lost forty-five due to contamination."

"Unacceptable!" President Kensington yells, pounding her desk.

That's when I notice the surface of her desk is actually cracked like she's done this before.

"Has the root cause of the contamination been identified yet?" she asks.

"No, my lord," Winch says. "The scientists believe it has something to do with the levels of nitrogen in the atmosphere. They are depressurizing the line and—"

"Enough!" she barks. "Please inform them that if this issue is not resolved by tomorrow morning, the only thing that will be depressurized is their hides."

"Yes, my lord," Winch says.

Okay, at this point, I'm thinking I made a huge mistake. I mean, if the president of the United States is acting like a tyrant and making people call her 'my lord,' then there's no way little old me is going to convince her to change her tune about the Meta Restriction Resolution.

I think it's time I made my exit.

I take one step backward when I hear—

"And the Orb Master?" President Kensington asks.

I freeze. Did she just say, 'Orb Master?'

No one's called me that in like, forever.

"He... escaped," Winch says.

"Escaped?" she says. "And what are we doing to find him? Our plan is dependent on him."

"My Meta-Busters are searching for him now," Winch says. "We will not let him escape our grasp."

"You seem to forget yourself, General," she says. "For *your* Meta-Busters are, in fact, *my* Meta-Busters."

"Of course, my lord," Winch says. "A mere slip of the tongue. As long as I am programming them, they serve at your disposal."

"Indeed," President Kensington says. "But it does not excuse the fact that the Orb Master has escaped your robots. Perhaps I..."

Huh? Why'd she stop talking?

And why is she looking down at my feet?

Then, I glance down and my stomach sinks.

Because right where I was standing is an imprint of my foot on the plush carpet. I'm such a fool. I may be invisible, but I'm not weightless!

"Guards!" she commands. "Infrared!"

Uh-oh. Before I can move, two Meta-Busters emerge out of nowhere, their eyes flickering red.

"Seize him!" she yells.

I make a break for the door when I'm suddenly engulfed in a thick, green mist. It smells like rotten eggs, but I've got to keep moving. I've got to get out of here!

But as I reach for the door, the room starts spinning!

My hand misses the doorknob by a mile and I suddenly hit the floor hard.

I try pushing myself up, but I can't move a muscle. My eyelids are getting heavy.

I just need... to... focus.

But... I can't... keep my eyes... open.

And then, everything goes dark.

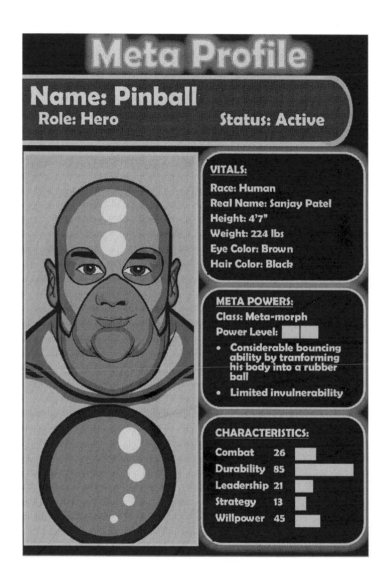

Meta Profile

Name: Pinball
Role: Hero   Status: Active

VITALS:

Race: Human
Real Name: Sanjay Patel
Height: 4'7"
Weight: 224 lbs
Eye Color: Brown
Hair Color: Black

META POWERS:

Class: Meta-morph
Power Level:

- Considerable bouncing ability by tranforming his body into a rubber ball
- Limited invulnerability

CHARACTERISTICS:

Combat	26	
Durability	85	
Leadership	21	
Strategy	13	
Willpower	45	

EIGHT

I NEED A PRESIDENTIAL PARDON

I open my eyes only to wish I hadn't.

I'm in a dark, dingy, concrete room no bigger than an ambulance. The door is bolted shut, and there's a narrow window high on the opposite wall that doesn't look like it opens to the outside. My first instinct is to get out of here, but when I try to move, I'm stuck. That's when I realize my arms and legs are tied to metal posts!

This is not good.

And the room smells like rotten cheese, which may be worse.

"Welcome back to the land of the living," echoes a woman's voice that startles me.

"Who's there?" I ask, my eyes darting all over the place. But there's no one there.

"Don't you remember me?" the woman says, stepping out of the shadows.

"President Kensington!" I say, my eyes going wide.

What's she doing here?

But then it all comes flooding back: the Meta Restriction Resolution. The Meta-Busters. My family.

"Let me go!" I yell.

"You're in no position to be making demands," she says. "None at all."

"Where am I?" I ask.

"In one of the secret sub-basements of this pitiful hovel you call the White House," she says. "It is quite a dump for the supposed leader of the free world. Truthfully, I had expected so much more from your species, but I suppose I have become conditioned to these frequent disappointments."

'Your species?' What's she talking about?

And then I remember she called me 'Orb Master.'

No one from Earth ever calls me 'Orb Master.'

And that's when a chill runs down my spine.

"Who-Who are you?" I ask, fearing the answer.

Then, I watch in horror as her body morphs from the diminutive shape of President Kara Kensington into a towering figure with big muscles and pointy ears.

My jaw hits the floor.

Because she was never President Kensington at all!

In fact, she's not even a she.

It's… it's…

"Bow before your king," the Skelton Emperor says, smiling with glee.

"W-Where's the real president?" I blurt out.

"Let us just say she is my honored guest," the Emperor says. "Along with dignitaries from across the globe."

Across the globe?

"Wait," I say. "Are you telling me those other world leaders are Skelton phonies too?"

"Not phonies," he says, waving his finger. "Skelton operatives. We have taken over your planet by replacing your leaders one by one. It was not difficult. In fact, we assumed complete control of your civilization well ahead of schedule. And your fellow humans are still none the wiser."

Um, what?

He's telling me the Skelton have taken over Earth!

And I'm the only one who knows it!

"B-But I don't get it," I say. "What are you even doing here? What do you want?"

"That is simple," he says. "Earth will become the hub of the Skelton Empire—the new Skelton Homeworld. And all Earthlings will become my servants."

The new Skelton Homeworld?

But that doesn't make sense.

The Skelton already have a—

Suddenly, I remember my conversation with Wind

Walker. It was right after our adventure in the 13th Dimension. I was so happy to see him that I didn't think much about it at the time, but he told me the Skelton Homeworld had been taken over by... by...

"Krule the Conqueror!" I blurt out. "You lost your world to Krule the Conqueror, and now you've scampered here with your tail between your legs to take over mine!"

"Silence, child!" the Emperor yells. "You are in the presence of royalty, and royalty never 'scampers.' Besides, you may believe Earth is rightfully yours, but the truth is, we've been inhabiting this planet for far longer than your kind. Earth is as much mine as it is yours."

"What?" I say confused.

"Oh, yes," he says. "It may be hard to believe, but we had identified Earth as a viable backup homeworld long before humans came into existence. Our scouts have been monitoring your planet for hundreds of centuries, operating as silent observers by blending into the background. If we ever needed to colonize your world, we knew we could easily dominate your kind. But over the last fifty years, new threats started to emerge. A growing sub-population of Earthlings began exhibiting strange new abilities—Meta abilities—and we could not risk this development upsetting our plans."

My jaw is hanging open. I mean, based on what he's saying, Skelton agents have been hiding here in plain sight for, well, forever! Is he serious?

But then I remember K'ami. She could morph into an ordinary housefly. And she told me that flies made their way to the Skelton Homeworld thousands of years ago as stowaways on scout ships that had visited Earth.

So, I guess what he's saying must be true!

It's no wonder the world has flipped out on Metas.

All of our world leaders are Skelton!

"But there's one thing I don't understand," I say. "Why did Krule even attack your planet in the first place? What's he got against you?"

"That is none of your concern," the Emperor says, raising his chin.

"I disagree," I shoot back. "Because if you're here, Krule's gonna follow you here too. And if an entire planet of Skelton couldn't stop him, what makes you think you're going to stop him here?"

"That is simple," he says, "Because here on Earth lives the most powerful weapon in the universe."

"Aaannnd, what's that?" I ask, my eyebrows raised.

"You," he says.

For some reason, I knew it.

That's probably why those Meta-Busters were trying to capture me alive—at least at first. But if he's thinking I'm the most powerful weapon in the universe, he probably thinks I have the Orb of Oblivion. So, now's my chance to rain on his insane parade.

"Sorry to interrupt this ill-conceived scheme," I say, "but here's a newsflash for you. I don't have the Orb of

Oblivion anymore, so I guess you can leave."

There. That should do it.

"Oh, don't worry," he says. "My plan does not require the Orb of Oblivion."

"Um, what?" I say shocked. "I don't get it?"

"Don't you?" the Emperor says. "Amongst all Metas in the known universe, your power is rare. There are but a few Metas who can manipulate Meta energy. And one of them is heading here."

"Hold up," I say. "I've seen this movie before and I'm not going back for the sequel. If you think I'm taking on Krule the Conqueror, then you're even nuttier than I remember."

Okay, I've got to get out of here. I may not have the Orb of Oblivion, but I do have my powers. And since the Emperor is a Skelton, it should be a snap to borrow his.

I concentrate hard, ready to push out my energy.

But I feel... nothing?

That's weird. Maybe I'm tired. I focus and reach out again, but I still don't feel anything.

Suddenly, the Emperor laughs.

"Fool," he says. "Did you think I would risk my own safety in your presence? Clearly, you do not recognize the organisms restraining you?"

Organisms?

I glance up at my left arm to find a leathery, brown material wrapped around my wrist. Holy cow! That's the stuff I've been trying to identify. It's thick, with a rippled hide. I know I've seen it before.

But what could it—

And then it hits me.

I have seen this organism before, but never like this! In fact, the last time I laid hands on one was when K'ami was alive and we were facing the High Commander inside of Lockdown. That didn't end so well either.

"Sheelds?" I say. "You're using Sheelds to dampen Meta powers? But I didn't think they could do that."

"You are correct," the Emperor says, grinning. "Typical Sheelds cannot do that. Due to their unique genetic makeup, Sheelds are the only creatures in the universe who can resist all forms of external stimulation. Fortunately, I am not harvesting typical Sheelds."

"Harvesting?" I say. "What are you talking about?"

"I am talking about genetic engineering," he says. "My scientists are growing a new type of Sheeld right here on Earth. One whose abilities are not wasted on itself but can be transferred to others through physical contact."

Physical contact?

Suddenly, everything makes perfect sense.

That's why Blue Bolt, Makeshift, and Master Mime couldn't fight back! That's why my parents became helpless and got captured! That's why my powers aren't working now!

The Skelton are using these 'super-Sheelds' to suppress Meta powers. As long as these creatures are touching me, I'm powerless!

"But that is not all," he continues. "The harvesting process requires something your planet has in spades."

"And what's that?" I ask.

"Meta energy," the Emperor says. "The process of converting a Sheeld requires an abundance of Meta energy. That is why the heroes of your world are so valuable."

Wait, what? He's using Meta energy to create these super-Sheelds? So, is that what this Meta Restriction Resolution is really about? Is that why he's collecting Meta heroes—to steal their Meta energy?

But if that's the case, there's still something I don't understand.

"If you want Meta energy," I say, "then why are you only focused on capturing Meta heroes? What about all of those Meta villains out there? Why aren't your Meta-Busters going after those guys?"

"Because villains care about nothing but themselves," he answers matter-of-factly.

"Yeah?" I say. "So?"

"So," he repeats, "that makes them much harder to capture. Do you know what makes heroes so vulnerable?"

"Um, not really," I say.

"Self-sacrifice," the Emperor says. "Heroes will risk everything for the welfare of others. Therefore, they are far easier to manipulate. So, until I run out of heroes, I do not have to bother chasing villains."

Wow, I hate to admit it, but he's got a point there. I

mean, my parents dropped everything to save our friends.

But they also flew right into his trap.

"Look," I say. "I don't know what you're expecting me to do, but I'm not going to help you."

"That is where you are wrong," he says. "After all, you too are a hero. Could you really just stand back and watch Krule the Conqueror take over your world?"

Well, he's got me there.

"You will act as my champion," the Emperor continues. "You will use your powers to defeat Krule the Conqueror and save your planet. But first, you must be properly trained."

"Trained?" I say. "Look, I know how to fight. And by the way, I've saved this freaking planet a few times already, including from your kind. Besides, I never agreed to do this. Why would I fight Krule just to leave Earth to you?"

"I thought you might resist," he says, moving towards the door. "So, I brought some added motivation." Then, he swings the door open.

The next thing I know, General Winch enters, pushing a brown-haired girl in front of him. Her head is down and her wrists are bound by a super-Sheeld.

Then, the Emperor lifts her face, and my heart sinks.

"Selfie!" I call out.

She looks at me with terror in her eyes.

"I thought you might recognize her," the Emperor says. "And do not worry, I have your other friends as well. They put up a good fight for ones so young, but in the end, they were no match for my Blood Bringers."

I feel sick to my stomach.

I knew I shouldn't have brought them here.

"Release her!" I demand.

"Now why would I do that?" he says. "You will help me defeat Krule, or your friends will die, starting with this one. Is that motivating enough for you?"

I want to yell out in frustration, but it's no use.

He's got me.

And there's nothing I can do about it.

Reluctantly, I nod in agreement.

"Excellent," the Emperor says. "I suggest you get some rest because the next time we meet I will train you in the Skelton Code of Combat. And then we will see if you have what it takes to survive."

NINE

I STINK AT TESTS

It feels like I've been trapped in this room forever.

My arms have been stuck to these posts for so long it feels like they're gonna fall off. And I can't tell if it's day or night because that little window looks like it goes to another interior room. But who am I to complain? This is probably a fitting punishment for all of the mistakes I've made.

Truthfully, I've resigned myself to my fate anyway. The super-Sheelds have neutralized my powers, and I'm not strong enough to break free on my own. So, I guess all I can look forward to is another visit from the Emperor.

Now that's depressing.

The last time I saw him, he told me he'd be back to train me in the Skelton Code of Combat, whatever that is.

He just never told me when.

Needless to say, I've had plenty of time to torture myself about all of the bad decisions I've made.

Over and over and over again.

I mean, I never should have called Dad from the Waystation, I never should have brought Next Gen to the White House, and I never should have assumed the president was who she appeared to be.

Some hero I turned out to be.

A tear runs down my cheek but I can't even wipe it away. Who knows what's happened to my family? And poor Dog-Gone is probably lost in Washington D.C.

I'm the worst hero to ever put on a mask. Not that I'm even wearing a mask right now.

But despite how crummy I feel, I know I've got to shake it off. Wallowing in self-pity isn't going to get me out of this mess. I need a plan to bust out of here.

The question is how?

BOOM!

Suddenly, the door bursts open and my heart skips a hopeful beat. But instead of the cavalry, it's Winch!

"The time has come," he says, his blue eyes narrowing.

"Um, you sure about that?" I say. "Because I'm good just hanging out here."

But Winch ignores me and unties my left arm from the post. For a split second, I have grandiose visions of a great escape, but as soon as my appendage falls limply to my side, I realize I have no sensation in my arm, and Winch easily re-wraps the super-Sheeld around my wrist. Well, so much for riding off into the sunset. A few minutes later, I'm free from the posts but still wearing my super-Sheeld restraints.

Then, Winch grabs my shirt collar.

"Easy," I say. "These aren't my threads."

My legs feel like jelly as Winch pulls me out of the room, but he doesn't seem to care. Instead, he yanks me through a series of creepy corridors. I have no idea where we are, but I'm pretty sure none of this is on the official White House tour.

He leads me down a steep flight of stairs into a room bigger than a football field—and standing in the center is the Skelton Emperor.

His arms are crossed and his eyes never leave mine as Winch drags me over to meet him. All I want is to slap that big smirk off of his face, but that's not going to get me anywhere. At least not yet.

"Report," the Emperor barks.

"Our scouts have detected Krule's armada entering the Alpha Centauri solar system," Winch says. "Based on his current coordinates, we expect him to enter Earth's atmosphere in fourteen point three days."

"Very good," the Emperor says. "Wait outside."

"Yes, my lord," Winch says, with a bow. Then, he exits, leaving me all alone with the Emperor.

"As you just heard," the Emperor says, "time is of the essence. For you to be victorious in your fight with Krule, you will need to reprogram your weak hero mindset. You must learn to fight like a Skelton: ruthless, cunning, and savage. If you fail to embrace what I teach you, you will perish."

"Sounds awesome," I say. "But just so you know, I'm not great at taking tests. So, if there's like, a pop quiz at the end of this you can just give me an 'F' now."

"Silence!" he barks, his foul breath hitting my nostrils. "You will speak only upon command. Is that understood?"

I nod, not giving him the satisfaction of hearing my answer.

"I asked you a question," the Emperor says. "I expect a verbal answer."

We stare each other down. But then I realize if I'm going to win the war, I may need to lose a few battles.

"Yes," I say reluctantly.

"Excellent," he says, towering over me. "Now you will learn the Skelton Code of Combat. It is more than a battle plan; it is a warrior philosophy designed to give you the upper hand in defeating any enemy. Shall we begin?"

"Sure," I say. Based on his serious expression I feel like I should be taking notes or something.

"Principle number one," he says. "Never show weakness."

Wait? Never show weakness?

That's what K'ami used to say to me. At first, I think it's just a funny coincidence, but then I remember she was a Skelton too. She must have gotten it from the Skelton Code of Combat!

"Principle number two," the Emperor continues. "Always go on the offensive. Principle number three: Use the element of surprise. And finally, principle number four: Show no mercy. These are the four principles that make up the Skelton Code of Combat. These are the principles ingrained in the minds of Skelton Blood Bringers from birth. These are the principles you must learn now."

"Got it," I say. "But I'm more than happy to wait on the whole Krule showdown thing. I mean, I'd still like to get my driver's license one day and—"

"Silence!" the Emperor bellows, his voice echoing through the room. "You will speak only when requested. Now, repeat the Skelton Code of Combat."

"Never show weakness," I say proudly.

The Emperor nods.

See, I was listening. Now for the other three.

Um, what were the other three again? I was so busy thinking about K'ami I missed what he said.

"Repeat," the Emperor commands.

"Hold your horses," I say, trying to remember. "Okay. The second was to be offensive. The third was something about using the element of French fries. And the last one was... What was that last one again?"

But the Emperor doesn't answer me. Instead, he looks like he wants to murder me.

"Let me try again," I say. "I'll nail it this time. Promise."

"If you do not take these lessons seriously," he says, "you will lose. Krule is a killer, and he will dispose of you with the mere blink of his third eye."

"Gee, thanks for the pep talk," I say. "You know, maybe teaching isn't the right career field for you. Maybe you should stick to the stuff you're good at, like ruining people's lives and being generally annoying."

"Enough!" he says. "I have tried to provide you with the tools for victory, but clearly you believe you do not need them. Very well then, let us put your skills to the test."

Okay, now we're talking. I'll do anything to stop his jowls from flapping.

The next thing I know, the Emperor reaches down and removes the super-Sheelds from my wrists and ankles. Well, I wasn't expecting that. And for a moment, I consider using my duplication powers to take him out. But then I remember he's still holding Selfie and the others captive. I don't know where they are and I can't risk anything happening to them, so I'll have to make my move at another time.

"Prepare yourself, child," he says, flashing a strange smile. "Because your enemy is here. Prepare to fight Krule the Conqueror!"

Wait, what?

I spin around and my whole body goes numb because standing on the other side of the room is a giant, red-skinned man with three eyes.

It's... Krule!

But what's he doing here? Didn't Winch just say he's weeks away from Earth? How'd he get here so fast?

"Good luck," the Emperor says.

"H-Hang on a minute," I stammer, backing up.

My heart is beating a mile a minute and my brain freezes up. What should I do? I wasn't ready for this!

"Principle number one," the Emperor says, snapping me back to reality. "Never show weakness."

OMG! He's right. The way I'm fumbling around has got to be giving Krule more confidence. I probably look like I'm going to pass out. I need to get a hold of myself. I may not feel brave, but at least I can look brave.

I stop in my tracks and stare Krule down.

Then, Krule's third eye radiates with green energy.

Uh-oh. Maybe I was better off fumbling.

Suddenly, there's incredible pressure in my brain! It's like he's got my head in a vice and he's trying to crush it!

The pain is so intense I drop to my knees.

"Principle number two," comes the Emperor's faint voice. "Always go on the offensive."

G-Go... on the offensive? Yeah. G-Great idea, if I could concentrate. B-But if I don't act now, I'm dead meat.

Come on, Elliott! Focus!

I grit my teeth and gather all of the negation power I can muster, and then I lash out in Krule's direction. My brain is so on fire I can't even look up. I'm just praying I made contact.

Suddenly, the pressure stops.

Yes, I did it!

I rise unsteadily to my feet and face my opponent. Shockingly, Krule hasn't moved from his spot. In fact, he seems content to simply destroy me from a distance. I don't think I've ever faced a Psychic with this kind of raw power before. Even the Shadow from the 13th Dimension pales in comparison.

I've got to strike while he's out of—

Just then, his third eye lights up again.

—power?

Suddenly, I'm blown off my feet and slam into the concrete wall behind me. My back hits hard, and the next thing I know I'm on my hands and knees, wheezing for air.

This isn't going well.

"Principle number three," the Emperor says. "Use the element of surprise."

The element of surprise? That might work for your average alien mega-menace, but how the heck do you surprise Krule the Conqueror?

I look around for something to use, but the room is empty, except for Krule and... the Emperor!

That's it. I've got a plan.

I cast my duplication powers at Krule and pull them back. There's a massive surge of energy dancing through my veins. But I can't just stand here admiring his power levels. I need to use them to create the element of surprise.

And the Emperor is perfect for that!

"What's happening?" the Emperor says, as I mentally lift his body off the ground using Krule's telekinesis. "Put me down at once!"

But I don't listen. Instead, I turn his flailing body horizontal, and then I launch him straight at Krule like a runaway missile. The Emperor SLAMS into Krule crown-first and they tumble to the ground, the Emperor lying flat on top of Krule.

Yes! Krule wasn't expecting that!

Now is my chance!

But as I hustle over to end the fight and save the universe, my jaw drops. Because when the Emperor rolls off of Krule's body, Krule is nowhere to be found, and in his place is the unconscious body of a girl with dark hair and a white mask with a teardrop painted under her right eye!

OMG! I know her.

It's Zen from the Rising Suns!

What's she doing here? But then I realize she's not moving! Is she...?

I kneel and check her pulse. Whew, she's still breathing. But what's going on? And what happened to Krule?

And then it hits me.

Krule was never here at all.

This was just a test.

After all, Zen is a powerful Psychic in her own right, and the Emperor must have made her use her powers to trick me into believing I was facing Krule. But in reality, I was fighting Zen the whole time!

But why would Zen do that?

And then I feel a knot in my stomach.

This must be what 'behavior modification' means.

The Emperor must have brainwashed her.

"Well done, child," the Emperor says, getting to his feet and dusting off his armor. "You certainly used the element of surprise to great effect, although the next time you employ me as a projectile it will be the last thing you ever do. Now it is time to implement principle number four. Show no mercy. Finish the girl."

What?

"No way," I say. "I can't do that."

"If you are going to defeat Krule," he says, "you must kill him when you have the chance."

I stare at Zen's face.

She looks so young. So innocent.

"Kill her!" the Emperor demands. "End her life, or Krule will end yours."

"Sorry," I say, sitting down next to Zen. "I guess that's just what Krule will have to do."

"Fool!" the Emperor yells. "You will die at his hand. You will—"

But he's just background noise because I've already tuned him out. I drop my head into my hands. Boy, I've really stepped in it this time. I have no idea how to get out of this mess. In fact, I'm not sure there's even a way out of this mess.

Suddenly, Winch appears and slaps a pair of super-Sheelds around my wrists. Then, he picks me up from beneath my armpits and carries me out of the room.

I try to stay alert, but I'm so mentally exhausted I can't keep my eyes open.

My eyelids feel so darn heavy.

"… pay for this…," I hear Winch grumble as he carries me upstairs, but I can't really make out what he's saying.

And then everything goes dark.

Meta Profile

Name: Zen
Role: Hero   Status: Active

VITALS:
Race: Human
Real Name: Mei Nakamura
Height: 4'3"
Weight: 78 lbs
Eye Color: Brown
Hair Color: Black

META POWERS:
Class: Psychic
Power Level: ■ ■ ■
- Extreme Telepathy
- Extreme Telekinesis
- Group Mind-Linking

CHARACTERISTICS:
Combat   35
Durability 22
Leadership 74
Strategy   90
Willpower   95

TEN

I RUN INTO SOME OLD FRIENDS

I wake up in a fog.

My vision is cloudy and I attempt to wipe my eyes clear, but I can't move my arms. What gives? That's when I realize I'm back in my dingy cell. I must have passed out from exhaustion when Winch carried me up the stairs.

I squeeze my eyes tight and then open them again to clear up the cloudiness. Boy, I'd give anything to bust out of here, but with these super-Sheelds restraining me, I couldn't use my powers even if I tried. And it's not like anyone can hear me if I call for help.

Wait a minute. Call... for help?

Wind Walker!

He's rescued me before in situations like this. Like the time the Rising Suns held me prisoner in Japan. I'm such a dufus. Why didn't I think of him earlier?

Fortunately, I'm all alone and the door is closed. So, I take a deep breath and yell, "Wind Walker!"

But he doesn't show up.

Okay, don't panic. Maybe my voice isn't carrying since I'm buried in a concrete sub-basement who knows how many levels below the White House. This time I take a deeper breath and yell Wind Walker's name at the top of my lungs.

But he still doesn't show.

Okay, that's not good. The last time this happened he was trapped in the 13th Dimension. So, either he's in trouble again or these super-Sheelds are blocking our connection. Which basically means I'm stuck.

Fantabulous.

Suddenly, my stomach grumbles. The last thing I remember eating was a granola bar back at Next Gen's treehouse. If I don't eat something soon, I'll probably waste away before I even face Krule.

Hmmm, that might be a good thing.

Who am I kidding? There's no easy way out of this. After all, the Emperor is still holding Next Gen and my family captive. The only shot I have at saving them is to defeat Krule. And if I somehow survive that, then I'll have to deal with the Emperor and his Skelton henchmen.

Sounds like a piece of cake.

Not.

Honestly, I don't think I've ever faced a challenge this big before. Yeah, there was the Worm, and Meta-Taker, and Ravager, but it always seemed like there was a clear path to follow. This time, I don't see one.

I sure wish my parents were here. They'd know what to do. Even Grace would probably know what to do. But me, I'm clueless. Then, I get a scary thought. What if my family isn't my family anymore?

What if they're brainwashed?

I mean, if the Emperor could brainwash a Psychic as powerful as Zen, then what's he done with Mom and Dad? Mom is as powerful as Zen, and Dad is as strong-willed as they come. Are they the Emperor's mindless minions now?

If the answer is yes, then it really is all up to me.

I hang my head in defeat.

This is hopeless.

BOOM!

Suddenly, the door flies off its hinges!

I jolt up, fully expecting to see the Emperor standing in the doorframe, but instead, I'm staring at a slightly overweight German Shephard wagging his tail.

"Dog-Gone?"

I close my eyes, thinking I'm hallucinating, but when I open them again, Dog-Gone is still standing there. And now he's looking down the hall and pointing his nose at me like he's signaling to someone else.

Just then, two costumed characters burst into the room. The guy has red-skin, blue goggles, and a large tail. And the girl is really tall, with blue markings on her face and two swords at her hips.

OMG! I can't believe it! It's—

"Scorpio? Taurus? What are you doing here?"

"Rescuing you," Taurus says. "Now stay still while Scorpio blasts the restraints."

All of a sudden, Scorpio's long tail sweeps past my face and hovers in front of my left wrist. Then, the tip turns bright orange and emits a precise beam of energy that pierces the first super-Sheeld. Instantly, the creature recoils, releasing my arm as it drops to the floor squirming.

Scorpio quickly attends to the other super-Sheelds, and as the last one falls, I flop into Taurus' arms like a ragdoll.

"Thanks," I say. "But how'd you know I was here?"

"We'll explain later," she says. "Because we're not out of the woods yet. Can you run?"

I want to say yes, but when I try to stand up, I feel woozy and collapse back into her arms.

"I'll take that as a 'no,'" she says, hoisting me over her shoulder. "Scorpio, let's go."

Believe me, I want nothing more than to get out of here, but then I remember something important.

"Wait!" I say. "We can't just leave. I have friends here who are prisoners of—"

"Don't worry," Taurus says, "the others got them."

The others? Like, Gemini? Is she here?

But I don't have time to ask Taurus the question because we're already on the move. I can't see much slung over Taurus' shoulder, except for Dog-Gone who is trailing behind, looking at me with concern in his eyes.

"D-Don't worry," I mutter. "I-I'm okay."

But the truth is, I'm far from okay. In fact, I don't think I've ever felt so feeble. Plus, I've got no clue how we're going to get out of here. I mean, the place is swarming with—

"Robots!" Scorpio yells.

THOOM!

There's a massive explosion. I wince as Taurus turns her back, shielding me from a hailstorm of debris. The Meta-Busters! They're right behind us! My heart is pumping fast. Even if I had the strength to help out, my powers are useless against robots.

THOOM!

YIP!

Dog-Gone!

I peer over Taurus' shoulder but I don't see him!

"We need another way out!" Taurus yells.

"Now!" Scorpio calls out.

RIIPPPP!

Suddenly, there's an ear-splitting noise and when I look up, the ceiling is gone! Through the falling debris, I think I spot something that looks like a silver submarine descending from the sky.

But then something hits the side of my head.

Ouch! My... temple...

And everything starts spinning...

***

"Serpentarius?"

I hear a faint voice. A girl's voice.

Familiar. But why?

"Epic Zero, are you okay?"

Huh? That's another girl's voice. A different girl.

What the heck happened and where am I?

I try opening my eyes but it feels like my eyelids are pinned down by toothpicks. It takes everything I've got, but eventually I manage to pry them open. That's when I realize I'm no longer in my cell. Instead, I'm lying on a table staring at a familiar-looking ceiling crisscrossed with wires.

It's the Ghost Ship!

I see Selfie on my left and smile. Thank goodness she's okay. I couldn't forgive myself if anything happened to her. But when I look to my right, I do a double take, because standing there is a pretty girl with green skin, orange eyes, and two antenna stalks poking through her long, black hair.

"G-Gemini?" I stammer. "Is that really you?"

"In the flesh," she says, putting her hand on my arm.

I can't believe it. The last time I saw Gemini was when the Zodiac saved me before Arena World blew up into a gazillion pieces. And when we parted ways, she sort of, well, kissed me on the cheek.

"How do you feel?" Gemini asks. "Taurus said a piece of concrete hit you on your head."

"I'm okay," I say, but as soon as I touch my right temple, I feel a bandage, followed by shooting pain. "Then again, maybe not."

"I patched you up and gave you some medicine," Gemini says. "The pain should lesson soon."

"Gee, thanks," I say, shuffling up onto my elbows. "That was nice of you."

But when I look over at Selfie, she's looking cross-eyed at Gemini. Um, okay. Why is Selfie so upset?

"I wasn't sure I'd ever see you again," Gemini says, looking down. "I was glad you finally called."

"What?" I say. "But I didn't call."

"Apparently, I did," Selfie says, holding up a shiny object shaped like a serpent. "This trinket fell out of your backpack when you handed it to me. I didn't realize it, but I must have activated it when I picked it up."

OMG! That's my official Zodiac communications link! Pisces handed it to me before Wind Walker took me home. There was so much going on I completely forgot about it.

"Serpentarius!" comes another familiar voice.

I turn to find a short girl with spikey hair and gill-like flaps on her neck running towards me. And behind her is a bearded kid who looks half-human and half-horse.

It's Pisces and Sagittarius!

"It's great to see you, Serpentarius," Pisces says, hugging me.

"Serpentarius?" Selfie says confused. "I thought your superhero name was Epic Zero?"

"It is," I say. "Well, I mean, they both are. But Serpentarius is the name the Zodiac gave me when they made me an honorary member of their team. It's the thirteenth sign of the Zodiac."

"Wait a second," Selfie says, "you mean to tell me you joined their team, but not ours?"

"Um," I babble. "Well…"

"See?" Skunk Girl says, appearing behind her. "I told you we didn't need him."

"Yeah," Pinball says. "I guess you're right."

Boy, it's great those guys are safe too, even though they're clearly not so happy to see me.

"Serpentarius," Gemini says. "We never did get to thank you for defeating Ravager. On behalf of all of the members of the Zodiac, past, and present, we thank you for destroying that monster and avenging our worlds. You are truly the bravest hero in the multiverse."

"Um, thanks," I say, blushing. But I sure don't feel like the bravest hero in the multiverse. In fact, I'm pretty sure if they saw me cowering in front of Krule they'd be calling me something else.

Speaking of cowering…

"Hey, where is Dog-Gone?" I ask.

But no one answers me.

And when I look at their faces, no one looks back.

Instead, they're all looking down at their shoes.

"C'mon, guys," I say, laughing nervously. "Enough joking around. He's probably here somewhere just being his annoying, invisible self. Right?"

"I'm sorry, Serpentarius," Scorpio says, coming in from the bridge. "After we escaped, most of the building was completely obliterated. We circled back twice to look for him. We even used our infrared scanners. But we couldn't find him."

Suddenly, it feels like I've been kicked in the gut.

I open my mouth to speak, but nothing comes out.

"He was a brave and loyal companion," Taurus says, appearing behind Scorpio. "When we first arrived, he flagged us down immediately and used his keen sense of smell to lead us straight to your friends, and ultimately, to you. You should be proud of him. He died an honorable death."

The words strike me oddly.

Dog-Gone. Died?

An… honorable death?

Others give their condolences, but I don't hear them.

Instead, all I see is Dog-Gone's face. All I think about are the millions of crazy adventures we've had together. The arguments over dog treats. The belly rubs. The slobbery hugs.

But now… he's gone.

And so is the Waystation.

And who knows what's happened to my parents?

Or Grace.

Or the Freedom Force.

And it's all because of two people.

The Emperor and Krule the freaking Conqueror.

"Epic Zero?" Selfie says. "Are you okay?"

Okay? No, I'm not okay. I'm… numb.

But that feeling is quickly replaced by another. A feeling building inside of me that I can't control.

A feeling of rage.

"Epic Zero?" Selfie repeats.

"I'm fine," I say, matter-of-factly. Then, I rip the bandage off my head and stand up. "It's time."

"Time?" Gemini repeats. "For what?"

"Revenge," I say. "But first I need to call a friend."

Meta Profile

Name: Gemini
Role: Hero
Status: Active

VITALS:

Race: Gallronian
Real Name: Steva Duon 12
Height: 4'6"
Weight: 103 lbs
Eye Color: Orange
Hair Color: Black

META POWERS:

Class: Meta-morph
Power Level:
- Can split into two identical bodies
- Each body can increase in size to 10 feet tall

CHARACTERISTICS:

Combat	45	
Durability	21	
Leadership	72	
Strategy	75	
Willpower	89	

ELEVEN

I UNCOVER MORE PROBLEMS

I'm holding on with everything I've got.

There's a strong force pushing against us and my cheeks are literally blowing backward, but I can't let go, otherwise, I'm pretty sure I'll be lost forever. So, I squeeze even tighter and hang on for dear life. But just when I think I can't hold on any longer, there's a loud POP and I tumble out the other side.

When I finally stop rolling, I see my old friend standing over me with a big smile on his blue face.

"I thought you would be used to it by now," Wind Walker says, extending a hand.

"Clearly not," I say, taking his hand and getting to my feet. "I'm not sure how anyone could get used to traveling by wormhole, including you. But getting inside this place would have been impossible without your help."

"Indeed," Wind Walker says. "I have never seen a facility so well guarded before. What is the name of this place again?"

"The Pentagon," I say.

"Yes," he says. "I am glad my powers allowed us to slip through their defenses undetected."

He's right about that. With all of the Meta-Busters circling, there was no way I'd get within half a mile of here without Wind Walker's help. I'm just glad he answered my call this time.

"I still do not understand why I did not hear you the first time," Wind Walker says. "I was not in any danger."

"Don't worry about it," I say. "It's not your fault. Those super-Sheelds I told you about must have blocked our connection. Anyway, that's why we're here, to get rid of this problem once and for all."

You see, the Emperor made a big mistake. He told me he was genetically engineering Sheelds to control the Meta population. With superheroes out of the way, there wouldn't be anyone left to stop him from taking over Earth.

Unfortunately, he told the wrong person.

Because I'm here to destroy his super-Sheeld lab.

I take a look around to get my bearings. I figured if the White House had secret sub-levels, the Pentagon had them too. And according to my Geo-Locator device, we're actually standing in an 'unknown' level below ground that's not marked on any blueprints. This would be the perfect location for the Emperor's secret lab. And based on what I'm seeing, we've definitely worm-holed to the right place.

That's because everything around us screams laboratory, from the workstations covered with scientific equipment to the blackboards filled with crazy looking math equations. Thankfully, no one else is here at the moment, but the steaming coffee mug on a nearby desk tells me it won't stay that way for long.

"We've got to move," I say to Wind Walker.

I return the Geo-Locator to my utility belt and adjust my mask. It's good to be back in costume. Without it, I felt more like a super spy than a superhero. But now that I'm back in action, the Emperor is gonna pay big time.

I wish we could have brought the others, but it was too risky. Our mission requires stealth and the more people we had with us, the higher the chances of getting caught. That's why it's just me and Wind Walker—there's simply too much at stake.

However, it's not like the others are just sitting around. They're on an important mission of their own. Since Krule also commands an armada of mercenaries called the Motley Crew, we're going to need reinforcements. And with the Freedom Force missing, I tasked the Zodiac with finding help outside of Earth. Thankfully, they agreed to drop Next Gen back at their treehouse before they left.

Needless to say, my three new friends were pretty upset with me. Skunk Girl looked like she wanted to throttle me. But they all knew this mission was way over their heads, and the last thing I needed was for something bad to happen to them—like Dog-Gone.

I feel tears coming on, but I push them aside. I need to keep it together. Besides, he'd want me to stay focused right now. But for some reason, I can't stop thinking about Selfie.

When I tried saying goodbye, she caught me off guard and asked me if I was sending her home because Gemini showed up. I told her that wasn't it at all, but I'm not sure she believed me.

What's wrong with girls anyway?

"Epic Zero?" Wind Walker says. "Are you okay?"

"What?" I say, realizing I've been lost in my own thoughts. "Yeah, sorry."

There's a door on each end of the room, and I'm not sure which way to go. Wind Walker checks out one side while I take the other. When I get to my door, I hold the doorknob tight to prevent anyone from barging through and then place my ear against the surface.

I can't hear anything, but to my surprise, the door is cold. That's when I realize it's metal. But it's not just any metal, it's tungsten steel. I wave Wind Walker over.

"Was your door metal?" I ask.

"No," he says. "It's wood."

"Bingo," I say. "Something is behind this door."

The reason I know this is because TechnocRat always conducts his most dangerous experiments behind tungsten steel doors. So, I'm guessing there is something serious brewing behind this one. And it just might be what we're looking for.

"On the count of three," I whisper, ready to throw the door wide open and jump in.

"On the count of three, what?" Wind Walker whispers back. "There could be guards in there. We must be cautious."

Boy, I hope there are guards in there. I mean, I want nothing more than to avenge my pup. But he's right. If we're discovered too early, it will compromise everything.

"Fine," I whisper. "We'll go in cautiously. Ready? One... two..."

On three, I turn the door handle and pull, but it's so heavy I can't get it open. Fortunately, Wind Walker jumps in to help, and with considerable effort, we crack it wide enough for the two of us to slip through. Then, we lean against it to prevent it from slamming shut.

By the time the door clicks softly closed, I'm a sweaty mess. But before I can even turn around, Wind Walker grabs me and pulls me behind a stack of crates.

"You will be seen," he whispers.

"Sorry," I whisper back, feeling foolish.

I peek around the crates to find we're hiding in a stark, white room with hundreds of vials neatly organized on open shelves—and each vial contains a brown, leathery object floating in a purplish, bubbling liquid.

Super-Sheelds!

Some of them are smaller than my pinky, while others are bigger than a baseball mitt. But in the center of the room is the largest super-Sheeld I've ever seen.

It's thick, bloated, and bigger than an oven, with all of these wires sticking out of it. And next to the giant super-Sheeld is a metal table with arm and leg restraints.

There's no mistaking it.

We've found the genetic engineering lab.

But then I see something I didn't notice before. Sitting on the metal table is a strange-looking helmet. It's gold with mini circuits running all around the rim. It kind of looks like a futuristic motorcycle helmet.

What's that for?

"Now what?" Wind Walker asks.

"Now," I say, "we blow stuff up."

But just as I'm about to stand up, Wind Walker grabs me again and pulls me back.

"Wait," he whispers, "someone is coming."

Just then, a door on the opposite side of the room opens and three people walk in. I see a man and a woman who are wearing white lab coats, and another man who makes my blood boil. General Winch!

"Is everything prepared?" Winch asks.

"The calculations are set," the female scientist says. "We do not anticipate any more errors."

"Is that so?" Winch says, sounding skeptical. "Because your last 'error' resulted in the death of one of the Meta specimens."

My heart skips a beat. Did he say, 'death?'

What if it was Mom or Dad? Or Grace?

I desperately want to charge out there and force Winch to tell me who it was, but I know I can't. If we reveal ourselves too soon, Winch will call an army of Meta-Busters so fast it'll make our heads spin.

"The Emperor will not be pleased to hear the news," Winch continues. "As a result of your idiocy, we have lost another thirty milligrams of Meta energy that could have been used to harvest more advanced Sheelds. I would be surprised if the Emperor lets you live."

"Please, General," the male scientist pleads. "We beg of you, do not inform the Emperor of our mistake. The biochemistry of every Meta is different. It is simply impossible to predict how each one will react to the leeching process. You must protect us. We will do anything you ask."

Leeching process?

Hang on. The Emperor mentioned something about a leeching process back in the Oval Office.

I mean, I know what leeches do here on Earth. They're earthworm-like creatures that can attach to your skin and suck your blood. So, is that what that monster super-Sheeld is being used for? Except instead of blood, it's sucking the Meta energy out of superheroes.

"Anything?" Winch says, his left eyebrow rising. "Very well, but be warned, if I spare you from the Emperor, you must do as I command, no matter what I ask of you. Even if it is against the Emperor's wishes. Do you agree?"

"Against the Emperor's wishes?" the female scientist says. "But that is forbidden."

For a second, Winch looks so angry I think he's going to strike her, but instead, he furrows his brow, and the next thing I know, he transforms from a skinny, regular-sized human into a gigantic armored warrior with bulging muscles, yellow skin, and pointy ears.

OMG!

Winch is… a Skelton?

I'm flabbergasted.

But then again, I guess I shouldn't be, because it makes total sense. Winch always wanted to get rid of Meta heroes, and now I know why!

"Very well," Winch says, turning to the exit. "I was only trying to spare your lives. But if that is your choice than I must go speak with the Emperor at once. As I am the High Commander of the Blood Bringer army, do not be surprised when I return at the Emperor's command to kill you with my own hands. I will leave you now to enjoy your final moments."

The two scientists look at one another, and then—

"Wait!" the male scientist calls out. "Do not go. We agree. We will do as you say."

"You have made a wise decision," Winch says, turning around. "Now bring in our next specimen. I will supervise your work on this one myself. After all, she is critical for the success of my plan."

As the scientists exit the room, I look over at Wind Walker who shrugs his shoulders. Who could Winch be talking about?

But when I turn back my stomach sinks.

Because the 'specimen' the scientists are carrying into the room is Mom!

TWELVE

I CAN'T SEEM TO AVOID DANGER

I can't believe it!

Mom is unconscious, and Winch and the male scientist are hooking her into the table restraints while the female scientist is putting that strange, futuristic-looking helmet on her head!

It takes everything I've got not to jump in to save her, but my instincts are telling me to wait. I don't know why, but I feel like I should trust my gut. So, before Wind Walker springs into action, I put my hand on his shoulder and my finger to my lips.

"She is secure," Winch says, locking the final ankle restraint in place. "And remember the Emperor's orders, do not activate the leeching process for Psychics. They are too valuable to lose if something goes wrong."

"Yes, we remember," the male scientist says, holding up a pair of wires attached to the giant super-Sheeld. "We will set these transfer cables aside."

Okay, that pretty much confirms it. That massive super-Sheeld is some kind of leech, and they're using it to steal Meta powers.

"The B-Mod unit is fully charged," the female scientist says, checking some dials on a computer terminal.

B-Mod unit? What's that?

Then, it hits me! 'B-Mod' could only be short for one thing—behavior modification! And that helmet on Mom's head must be a behavior modification device!

"We can begin the brain override sequence," the female scientist says. "But I must warn you, it is dangerous to employ behavior modification on a Psychic like this without first implementing the leeching process to erase her powers. Anything could happen."

"No leeching!" Winch commands. "Now get on with it. Just ensure you do not accidentally kill this one."

Um, did he just say, 'kill?'

"The Meta-human's biochemistry will determine if she survives the stress or not," the woman says, walking back over to fix Mom's helmet. Then, she reaches for a green button.

Okay, I've heard enough.

"Hands off!" I yell, leaping out from behind the crates. And with one fluid motion, I reach into my utility belt and throw my brand-new Epic-a-rang—which is my E-shaped version of Shadow Hawk's Hawk-a-rang—right at the woman's hand. There, that should put an end to this dastardly scheme.

But the Epic-a-rang whizzes over the woman's head and CLANGS harmlessly against the wall.

"What kind of a fool are you?" the woman asks.

Well, that was embarrassing.

But at least she didn't push the button on Mom's helmet.

"So, we meet again," Winch says, as a strange smile creeps across his face. "I thought you might come here, but I never expected you to succeed."

"Well, I guess it's a day full of surprises," I say.

Speaking of surprises, I quickly glance down at Wind Walker, but he's gone! I swallow hard. I hope he didn't have to use the bathroom.

"Indeed, child," Winch says, stepping towards me. "This day will be filled with more surprises than you ever imagined."

Um, I don't know what he means by that, but I do know one thing, he's way bigger than any Skelton I've faced before. And that's saying something because I've fought more of these buggers than I care to remember.

Maybe I should start wearing alien repellent spray.

But I've got an even bigger problem. I don't have a plan. And based on experience, things don't go well when I don't have a plan.

I'll need to bluff until I can figure something out.

"Let that hero go," I demand, pointing to Mom. "And no one will get hurt."

Laughter fills the room.

"Hey!" I say. "I'm serious."

"The only creature who will be hurt," Winch says, cracking his knuckles, "is you. I have been waiting for this moment ever since our meeting at the television studio. If I had only known then what I know now, I would have eliminated you on the spot. But then again, it appears you are not so easy to kill, because you narrowly escaped from your satellite headquarters before my Meta-Busters could finish the job."

Um, before *his* Meta-Busters could finish the job?

Suddenly, I connect the dots.

When I was on the Waystation, a group of Meta-Busters went rogue and blasted one of their own trying to kill me. And based on what he's saying, Winch must have put them up to that, despite the Emperor's wishes!

But why?

"Um, sorry," I say. "But what did I ever do to you?"

"It is not what you did," Winch says, "but rather, what you could do. You see, the Emperor has put great faith in your ability to defeat Krule the Conqueror. He believes that once Krule is finally out of the way, he will be free to rule the universe with an iron fist. But he has greatly miscalculated."

Suddenly, behind Winch, a black circle appears over

the scientists' heads. And then two blue arms reach down and pull the scientists up into the void!

It's Wind Walker!

"The Emperor does not realize the tides have turned," Winch continues, oblivious to what's happening behind him. "As soon as he gave the order to flee from our Homeworld rather than fight our greatest enemy, Krule the Conqueror, he lost the support of his loyal subjects. Just as I planned."

A second later, the void disappears.

"The Emperor has disgraced the Skelton Empire," Winch says. "Unlike our great leaders of the past who valued strength over cowardice and domination over subservience, the Emperor values nothing but himself. His removal from power is long overdue. But I could never risk acting on our Homeworld. After all, I am not of royal blood, and he was always surrounded by too many minions who could have thwarted my plan. But unfortunately for them, I was in charge of our escape pods, and I ensured that I was the only surviving member of the Emperor's inner circle to make it to Earth alive."

Well, note to self. This guy is way more psycho than I gave him credit for. And that's saying something!

"It is time for a leader who will restore glory to the Skelton Empire," Winch continues, "and I am the one who will do so. Thus, when an unthinkable alliance presented itself, only I was bold enough to take full advantage where others in my position would have run."

Unthinkable alliance? Um, what unthinkable alliance?

"Nothing will stand in my way," he says, raising his right arm, "Including you!"

Suddenly, Winch swings down and I dive out of the way as his giant fist sends floor tiles flying! Okay, he's really strong! And then I remember Winch saying he's the High Commander of the Blood Bringer army.

I'm gonna need help!

Just then, a void opens up next to Winch and Wind Walker leaps out, his fist reared back for the knock-out blow.

Yes!

But just as quickly, Winch leans out of the way and Wind Walker goes sailing past.

No!

Then, with incredible speed, Winch delivers a devastating roundhouse kick, sending Wind Walker headfirst into the wall. Wind Walker hits with a sickening thud and then crumples to the ground unconscious.

"Now it's your turn," Winch says.

I'm about to hit him with a major dose of negation power when Winch grabs a vial from one of the shelves and chucks it at me!

I dive out of the way as the vial zips over my head and SHATTERS into the wall behind me. I cover my head as glass flies everywhere and a super-Sheeld flops to the ground.

Holy cow! He's throwing super-Sheelds at me!

Now I'm not much of a dodgeball player, but if those super-Sheelds touch me, I'll lose my powers! But before I can get up, Winch grabs another vial and winds up for another pitch. I throw myself behind a computer terminal as the vial SMASHES into the wall behind me.

My heart is pounding out of my chest. I've got to stay calm. If I don't handle this wacko now, I might not get a second chance to save Mom.

Then, I realize it's quiet.

Why is it so darn quiet?

RRROOOAARRR!

Um, what's that?

Just then, a massive hairy, white fist reaches around the computer terminal! I make like a pancake, pressing flat against the wall as four giant fingers try pulling me into a death grip! What is that thing? Then, I realize this must be one of the forms Winch can morph into!

I've got to get out of here!

But the next thing I know, six paws wrap around the terminal and toss it aside like it was a tissue box. The terminal SMASHES into another bank of computers and CRASHES to the ground, barely missing Wind Walker's still unconscious body.

Now nothing is standing between me and Winch! Except Winch looks like a cross between the Abominable Snowman and a spider.

Did I ever mention that I hate spiders?

My mind goes through some quick mental

gymnastics. Either I can stick around to fight monster-Winch, or I can go into flight mode and get the heck out of here!

Winch opens his mouth and ROARS!

Well, that settles it. It's flight time! My eyes dart around the room, looking for an escape route. Then, they land on Wind Walker.

Desperate times call for desperate measures! So, I focus my duplication powers on Wind Walker's prone body and copy his powers. Then, just as Winch reaches for me with his six overgrown mitts, I create a void, jump inside, and I'm gone.

Suddenly, I'm standing high above him in a wormhole, looking down as he spins around in circles trying to find me. Boy, it's strange how everything around me looks blurry like I'm speeding past in a subway car. Yet, I'm standing completely still. Winch has no idea where I went, and it would be super easy to just take off, except there's no way I'm leaving here by myself.

As I step gingerly through Wind Walker's wormhole, I realize everything is different. I mean, when Wind Walker pulls me through one of these things it's always a roller-coaster experience. But now that I'm in control, everything seems so much calmer. That's when I look down and see Mom's blurry body.

She's still lying on the table, down for the count. I check on Winch who is still raging on the other side of the room. Now's my chance. I bend down and reach through the wormhole, grabbing Mom beneath her arms. Then, I deadlift her up to safety. Ugh! My back feels like it's broken but I got her. I just hope she's okay.

"Mom," I say, gently patting her cheek. "Can you hear me?"

She moans.

Then, I realize she's still wearing that funky helmet. I try pulling it off but it's stuck. Okay, this will have to wait. I've still got one more person to rescue.

I crawl to the other side of the wormhole and look down. Winch is searching the room more carefully now, even pulling panels off of computers to look inside. After struggling to get Mom, there's no way I'm gonna be able to lift Wind Walker.

But then I realize I don't have to. After all, I've seen him project his voids across great distances to swallow up his victims. So, I concentrate hard, creating a void right over Wind Walker's entire body.

RROOARR!

It's Winch! He's looking up! I need to act fast!

I drop the void over Wind Walker's body like a drape and he disappears. Then, I grab Mom's hand to do the same when Winch jumps up and rips open a swath of ceiling right next to us!

OMG! He knows we're up here!

So, I wrap my arms around Mom and make us disappear!

THIRTEEN

I MAKE THE RULES

We POP out in the woods and I drop to my knees in a jumbled mix of exhaustion and disbelief.

I mean, everything that just happened was nuts!

Winch is a Skelton, there's an entire lab of super-Sheelds sucking away Meta powers, and a Meta died during the leeching process! I'm so overwhelmed I don't even know what to do.

"E-Elliott?" comes a feeble voice.

"Mom!" I blurt out, crawling to her side. She's lying on the ground with that futuristic helmet on her head. "Are you okay? Please tell me you're okay."

"I-I'm fine," she says, sitting up. She looks groggy, but when she finally regains her wits, she wraps me up in a big hug. "Oh, Elliott, I'm so happy to see you."

As I fall into her embrace, tears stream down my

cheeks and I start bawling like a baby.

"Hey," she says, holding my chin. "It'll be okay. Now tell me what's going on."

"I-I…," I stammer, but I'm so choked up I can't even speak. But with Mom, I don't have to, because she looks me in the eyes, and in an instant, she's mind-read the whole thing.

"Oh, Elliott, I'm so sorry," she says, hugging me again. "Dog-Gone was a brave hero and a good friend."

"Yeah," I say, wiping away my tears. "The best. Even though he was really annoying."

"Yes, but he was the best kind of annoying," she says.

We chuckle, and it feels good to laugh again, but the moment is cut short when I hear—

"Epic Zero," Wind Walker says, sitting up with his head in his hands. "What happened?"

"Are you okay?" I ask. "You got clobbered by Winch. But I used your wormhole powers to get us all to safety."

"You did?" he says surprised. "Well done, my friend." Then, he looks up and says, "but I think our troubles are just beginning."

Huh? What's he talking about? But when I look up, I see hundreds of dots in the sky. What are those things? They seem too high to be birds, but then my stomach drops as I realize those aren't birds at all.

They're spaceships!

Krule and his Motley Crew have arrived!

I hear SHOUTING to my left and when I look over,

I can see the Pentagon through the trees. It's total chaos over there as soldiers are running every which way while Meta-Busters are assembling on the roof. It looks like they're trying to mount a defense.

But as I look back up, I realize something is not right. I remember Winch telling the Emperor it would take weeks for Krule to get here. How could he be so wrong?

And then I remember Winch talking about his 'unthinkable alliance,' and a lightbulb goes off.

Winch was lying to the Emperor!

Winch has partnered with Krule the Conqueror!

That's his 'unthinkable alliance!'

"What is this thing?" Mom says, touching the helmet. She tries yanking it off of her head, but it doesn't budge. Then, she twists it and it pops right off.

"That's a Skelton behavior modification device," I say. "The Skelton have been using it to brainwash heroes."

"Not this hero," Mom says, tossing it over her shoulder. "Thanks to you. And if what I learned from reading your mind is true, these spaceships aren't here for a friendly visit. We're going to need help to send them back where they came from. Fortunately, I know where the rest of the Freedom Force is located, but I'll have to sneak back inside the Pentagon. Do you think you'll be safe here until I get back?"

"There is no need to sneak," Wind Walker says. "I can take you there directly."

"Wait," I say. "What about me? I want to come."

"No, Elliott," Mom says, standing up. "We can't... I mean, I can't risk it. Look, getting me out alive was lucky enough, but I'm not sure what's happened to Dad or Grace. And if something did happen... Well, I'm not ready to lose you too. Please, just wait here for me."

The concern in her eyes squashes my soul.

I mean, I get it. I just lost Dog-Gone and I'm absolutely gutted. And I certainly don't want anything to happen to Dad or Grace either, but I just can't sit here twiddling my thumbs while either Krule or the Emperor take over our planet. After all, sitting on the sidelines is what got me into this mess in the first place.

"Ten minutes," I say firmly, crossing my arms.

"Elliott—"

"No, Mom," I say. "You've got ten minutes. If I don't see or hear from you guys in ten minutes, then I've gotta do what I've gotta do. Look, I've more than proven I can take care of myself. I know it's easy to forget sometimes, but I destroyed the Orb of Oblivion, got rid of Ravager, and just saved the two of you. So, I know I'm still a kid and all, but I'm a hero, just like you."

"You're right," Mom says, giving me another hug. "But you're not just any hero, you're a great hero. However, I'm still your mom, so if I'm not back in ten minutes don't do anything stupid."

Then, she takes Wind Walker's hand, and they disappear into a wormhole.

Okay, the countdown starts now.

But as I look back up, the spaceships have gotten way closer! In fact, I can see the first few pretty clearly now and none of them look the same. One is long and thin and shaped like a 'Y,' while another is round and stout and shaped like an 'O.' I guess that's why Krule calls them 'the Motley Crew,' because they're just a ragtag gang of degenerates from across the galaxy.

But that's not all that's happening, because when I look over at the Pentagon, they seem much more organized. Soldiers are standing in formation next to heavy artillery, and the Meta-Busters are rocketing into the sky in well-organized battalions. But then I see something else. There, standing at the edge of the roof, are two figures I know all too well—General Winch and the Emperor!

I reach into my utility belt and pull out my binoculars. Winch is standing behind the Emperor, pointing to the sky, while the Emperor is looking up with his hands clasped behind his back. They look like partners in crime, but the Emperor has no clue Winch has betrayed him.

Okay, I figure five minutes have gone by and there is no sign of Mom or Wind Walker.

I carefully pick my way through the underbrush and hide behind a thick tree to get a better vantage point. But when I peer around the trunk, my foot CLANGS against something solid. Hmm, rocks don't make noises like that.

But when I reach down to investigate, I pull up

Mom's helmet. That's funny, I almost forgot about it. I turn it in my hands, studying it closely. I've got no clue what all of these Skelton symbols mean, but I do recognize the green button that scientist was going to push to turn it on.

For a second I nearly chuck it, but then I decide to hold onto it. Who knows? It may come in handy.

Okay, the ten minutes have to be up by now.

Where's Mom? I hope she's okay. But if she's in trouble I never asked her where she was going in the first place, which means it'll be impossible for me to find her.

I smack my palm against my forehead.

How many other 'great heroes' are idiots like me?

Suddenly, there's a massive explosion overhead and when I look up, parts of a Meta-Buster are raining down from the sky. Uh-oh, it's started! And even though the ten minutes have passed I don't know what to do next.

I look through my binoculars again and do a double take because Winch is still standing behind the Emperor, but now he's pulling a knife out from beneath his armored vest!

He's literally going to backstab the Emperor!

For a second, I hesitate. I mean, would it be so bad if the Emperor was a goner? But then my conscience takes over. I can't just sit here watching a murder unfold right before my eyes. But how can I stop Winch from here?

And then I remember something.

I just used Wind Walker's powers, and if I still have

some juice left, I should be able to get over there in time.

So, I concentrate hard and summon a void.

And then I step inside.

FOURTEEN

I JUST WANNA FLY

I reach the roof of the Pentagon in the nick of time!

I'm about a dozen feet behind Winch, who is still drawing his knife behind the Emperor's back! And even though the firefight above sounds like the Fourth of July, I don't want to give myself away, so I step gingerly out of the void.

For a split second, I contemplate jumping Winch and wresting the knife away, but after taking one look at his broad shoulders I decide against it. Instead, I'm about to call out to the Emperor when I hear—

"My Meta-Busters are failing," the Emperor says.

"What a pity," Winch says, his long knife now fully exposed. "I had designed them to fight."

"And yet, it appears they are giving up," the Emperor says. "Why are they giving up, General?"

Giving up? But as I steal a glance at the sky, I see he's right! The Meta-Busters are actually flying away from the fight, giving Krule's army a clear path to Earth.

"Maybe they no longer want to fight for you?" Winch says, raising the knife over his head.

Oh no! This is really about to happen!

"Emperor!" I yell. "Look out!"

But instead of striking down the Emperor, Winch spins around to face me, the knife still over his head!

"You!" he says, looking at me wild-eyed.

"There you are, child," the Emperor says, turning to face us both. Strangely, he looks completely calm. In fact, if I didn't know better, I'd think he was... grinning? "Thank you for the warning, but it was not necessary. I had the situation well under control."

"You spineless fool!" Winch says, spit flying from his mouth as he turns back to the Emperor. "You have control of nothing! You are the most pathetic leader in the history of the Skelton Empire! Today I will save our people from your cowardly reign! Today there will be a change in power, and my blade will deliver it!"

"Ah, yes, your blade," the Emperor says, eyeing Winch's knife. "It *is* quite impressive. In fact, is it not the Knife of Terrors you wield—the very same knife I bestowed upon you when I appointed you as Head Commander of the Blood Bringer Army?"

"Y-Yes?" Winch says, his eyes growing wide as he looks upon his knife.

"I thought so," the Emperor says, breaking into a sinister smile.

FAZZZZZAAAMMM!

Suddenly, a massive surge of electricity bursts from the hilt of Winch's knife. I shield my eyes from the blinding light and turn away as my body is blanketed by an intense wave of heat. And when it finally subsides, I look back to find a charred body lying where Winch used to be standing.

"You-You killed him," I say.

"I did, didn't I?" the Emperor says, holding some kind of a device in his hand. "But he knew it was coming. After all, he did murder my entire council of advisors. Of course, I respected his ruthlessness for that little maneuver, but I never trusted him. That is why I secretly outfitted the Knife of Terrors with nearly ten thousand volts of electricity before I gave it to him. Fortunately, I keep the activator handy in my belt. Poor Winch. He had potential, but he never quite learned that cunning always beats strength in the end."

"But he wasn't acting alone," I say. "He was working with—"

"—me," comes a deep voice from behind that sends shivers down my spine.

I swallow hard. I don't want to turn around, but I have to. And when I do, it feels like someone sucked all of the air out of my lungs, because standing in front of me is the biggest, baddest villain in the entire multiverse.

Krule the Conqueror.

"I must thank you for disposing of Winch," Krule says to the Emperor. "He was useful but far too needy. Now I can focus on my primary objective, which is ridding the universe of you."

"I am sure you would like that," the Emperor says. "But I am afraid I have other ideas."

The two are facing off like they're in an alien version of an old Western movie—and I'm stuck in the middle!

"You are filled with clever ideas, aren't you?" Krule says. "Like how you tricked me into entering the 13th Dimension."

"You might consider it trickery," the Emperor says. "I would call it masterful plotting."

"You violated our agreement," Krule says. "You were to rule your side of the universe and I was to rule mine. Yet, that was not enough for you, was it? You had to have it all to yourself."

"I am far from naive," the Emperor says. "Did you really think I believed that someone named Krule the Conqueror would settle for half of anything? You see, we are not so unalike. I knew your thirst for power would be your undoing. All I did was plant the seed by bribing one of your underlings to pretend he discovered the coordinates to a new universe. I believe Xenox was his name. He was a shifty character, but once he delivered the coordinates, I knew you could not resist your animal instincts to conquer an entirely new universe.

Unfortunately, those coordinates just happened to belong to the 13th Dimension."

"You hoped to trap me in that barren wasteland forever," Krule says. "But my unrivaled power transcended even that forsaken place. I only wish I could have seen the look on your face when you heard of my escape—when you realized I would be coming to destroy you."

"Well, I admit I was surprised you even wanted to leave," the Emperor says. "I figured the 13th Dimension was a perfect match for your lifeless personality."

"Enough!" Krule says, his third eye glowing green. "No more games. You may have escaped when I conquered your Homeworld, but now there is nowhere left to run."

"Perhaps not," the Emperor says, buffing his nails. "But there is no need to run. Not with my champion here to protect me."

"Champion?" Krule says. "What champion?"

"The child," the Emperor says. "He is my champion."

Um, what?

"Ha!" Krule chuckles. "You must be joking."

"No," the Emperor says. "I am certainly not joking. The child's powers dwarf even yours. In fact, I believe he would beat you handily in a fight to the death."

"Whoa!" I say, stepping forward. "I never agreed to that."

"Forgive my 'champion,'" the Emperor says to Krule.

"He must have forgotten that if you destroy me, you will conquer his planet and turn all of its inhabitants into mindless slaves. Isn't that correct, 'Champion?'"

I want to say, 'no way,' but I know he's right. At the moment, the Emperor is actually the lesser of two evils. If I'm gonna save everyone on Earth, I have no choice but to stand and fight Krule first—maybe even to the death.

"Very well," Krule says, eyeing me up and down in triplicate, "I accept your challenge. After all, I always relish a good appetizer before feasting upon the main course. I will destroy the child, and then I will destroy you."

"Excellent," the Emperor says, backing away. "Good luck, 'Champion.' And do not forget what I taught you."

What he taught me? But suddenly Krule turns his massive frame my way and it's hard to remember anything!

"I know you," Krule says. "You were tangling with the Time Trotter, trying to stop me from obtaining the Cosmic Key."

"Yep, that was me alright," I say, backing up. "I was just, you know, doing what heroes are supposed to do."

"That is amusing," Krule says, "because where I come from, what heroes are supposed to do is die!"

Suddenly, Krule's third eye glows green and I hit the panic button. I mean, this is Krule the freaking Conqueror—the most powerful Psychic ever! If he can take over hundreds of people at once, I'm about to get hammered! I need to protect myself!

I send my duplication powers at Krule and pull them back quickly, but the massive power surge throws my system off balance! Holy smokes! I only grabbed an ounce of his power, so if this is a taste of what's to come, I'm in serious trouble!

Just then, I feel incredible pressure in my head!

Submit.

It's Krule! He's burrowing inside my brain!

I hear a CLANKING noise and when I look down, I see the behavior modification helmet hit the edge of the roof and roll off. Honestly, I forgot I was even holding that thing!

Submit, child.

No! Never!

I push him out, but it's only for a second and the pressure starts building again. He's way too powerful. I can't sustain this. I need to try something else.

That's when I spot the Emperor slinking into the corner. That coward! He's trying to escape!

Not on my watch!

I concentrate hard, pushing Krule out of my head with all I've got. Then, I focus all of my power on the Emperor, bathing him with duplication energy. I need to absorb as much of the Emperor's shape-shifting powers as I can! If I can just morph into one of those crazy creatures like Winch, then maybe I've got half a chance against Krule!

But when I pull the Emperor's Meta energy back, I barely feel anything. Huh? That's weird. And when I cycle through the Emperor's rolodex of bizarre and scary creatures, there's almost nothing!

In fact, all I'm getting are human shapes or... flies?

What's going on? Then, it hits me.

K'ami once told me there are two types of Skelton: regular Skelton, who can morph into a few forms, or Blood Bringers, who can change into anything imaginable. And I did run into that souped-up Blood Bringer called a Blood Master a few times.

But to my surprise, the Emperor isn't a Blood Bringer or a Blood Master! Which can only mean one thing—he's just an ordinary, run-of-the-mill Skelton!

OMG! I wonder if the other Skelton know that, or if the Emperor has been fooling them all of this time?

Now I know why he needed me to defeat Krule for him! The high and mighty Emperor is nothing but a fraud!

But I can't worry about that. Right now, I need to focus on survival! If I can get some distance to regroup, I can come up with a plan. So, I take what I've got and morph into a fly. Then, I buzz off.

Beating my wings is a bit awkward at first, but I quickly get the hang of it. But as soon as I clear the roofline and head towards the woods, I hear—

Nice try, but you cannot escape my power.

Suddenly, my head feels like it's on fire!

Krule is pushing his way inside again! It's... hard to concentrate... on flying. I try forcing him out, but he's too strong.

And then I feel myself turning against my will.

What's happening?

Then, it dawns on me. In fly form, my brain has shrunken to the size of a poppy seed. It's... harder to keep him... out! And Krule is... manipulating the part of my brain that controls my... motor skills!

I've got to... stay strong. Push him... out!

Come. Come back to me.

Just then, my whole body jerks left and my wings start beating even faster. No! Stop it! Let... me go!

I try flying away, but he's bringing me right back up to the roof! And once he sees me, he'll squash me!

I-I need to go...

... down?

Then, a lightbulb goes off.

The only reason I'm flying back towards Krule is because I have wings.

This might not be the best idea, but what other choice do I have? So, I concentrate hard and let the Emperor's shapeshifting powers go. Suddenly, my wings retract and my body morphs back into a full-sized kid.

Then, I drop like a rock.

I need to stop my fall!

I reach into my utility belt for my grappling gun when I realize I left it on the Waystation.

That's not good.
I'm falling to my doom!
Four stories.
I'm picking up speed!
Three stories.
I flap my arms to slow my fall.
Two stories.
Everything goes blurry.
And all I see is black.

Meta Profile

Name: Krule the Conqueror
Role: Villain   Status: Active

VITALS:

Race: Unknown
Real Name: Krule
Height: 8'0"
Weight: 654 lbs
Eye Color: Orange
Hair Color: Bald

META POWERS:

Class: Meta Manipulation
Power Level:

- Extreme Psychic Meta Manipulation Power
- WARNING: No known weaknesses. May possess Meta 4 Power Levels.

CHARACTERISTICS:

Combat	100	
Durability	100	
Leadership	100	
Strategy	100	
Willpower	100	

FIFTEEN

I FACE DOUBLE TROUBLE

"**E**lliott."

I hear a faint noise in the distance.

"Elliott."

Repeating itself. Getting louder. Strangely familiar.

Wait a second. Why does this all seem so familiar?

Suddenly, the hairs on the back of my neck stand on end and my eyes jolt open. It's dark and misty, but I can make out the shape of someone walking towards me in the distance.

It's... a girl?

My instincts are telling me to run, but for some reason, I can't move a muscle. I can blink and breathe just fine, but my limbs are frozen. But as the girl gets closer, the only thing I can make out are her eyes.

Her neon, green... eyes?

Then, she steps out of the darkness, and my jaw drops in disbelief. OMG! It… it can't be!

"K'ami?" I say.

But that's impossible! Except, the girl standing in front of me looks exactly like her. My eyes dart from her pretty face to her pointy ears, to the dark ringlets falling over her shoulders. She's even wearing the same outfit I saw her in last—all white with gold trim!

I must be dreaming, but when I shut my eyes and open them again, she's still standing there.

"K'ami?" I repeat. "Is that really you?"

"Yes, Elliott Harkness," she says, her voice echoing all around us.

"B-But…," I stammer. "You're dead!"

"That is true," she says.

"So," I say, looking around the darkness, "does that mean I'm dead too?"

"No, Elliott Harkness," she says. "Not yet. But if you keep this up, you will be soon."

"Um, okay," I say. "Then, where am I?"

"You are in a place called the 'In Between,'" K'ami says. "A place that exists neither in life nor in death. But we don't have much time. I'm only able to hold you here momentarily."

"Hold me here?" I say. "What are you talking about? I mean, if you're dead, how are you even doing this?"

"You can thank the Orb of Oblivion," she says.

The words send a chill down my spine. I mean, the

Orb of Oblivion is what got her killed in the first place.

"I see your confusion, so let me explain," she continues. "As I lay dying in your arms, I was holding the Orb of Oblivion. As you know, the Orb of Oblivion has the power to fulfill the desires of its host. And although I knew it was too late to save me, I asked the Orb for one final request. I asked it for the power to save you."

"What?" I blurt out. "Are you serious?"

"Yes," she says. "The Orb agreed, but I'm sure it did so only to serve its own selfish needs in case something dreadful happened to you. But it granted me the power nonetheless—the power to save you one time and one time only."

"But that's not possible," I say. "Is it?"

"I questioned it as well," she says. "Especially once I moved beyond the living, but it appears that it has worked because here I am in your greatest time of need."

"K'ami," I say, tears suddenly squirting from my eyes. "I'm so sorry for everything that happened. I-I should have seen it coming. I should have taken the Orb from you. I shouldn't have let you…"

"It is okay, Elliott Harkness," K'ami says, smiling gently. "I am at peace, and I am proud of you. I believed in you in a time when you didn't believe in yourself, and now look at all of the good you have done."

"B-But K'ami," I blubber. "I… I can't do this. Krule is too strong. The guy is a psychopath. And he's—"

"—powerful," K'ami says, finishing my sentence.

"Just like you. Never forget the power you possess. Inside of here," she says, pointing to my head. "But most importantly," she says, now pointing to my heart, "inside of here."

"But K'ami," I plead. "I don't know how…"

"Yes," she says, smiling. "You do. You know exactly how to defeat him. Now it is time for you to return."

Then, she reaches out and touches my temple, but strangely I don't feel any pressure against my head.

Instead, a light breeze tickles my hair.

"Go back, Elliott Harkness," she says. "Go back and use all that you have learned. And remember, never show weakness."

Suddenly, my eyelids feel super heavy.

They start closing, but I don't want to lose her again!

Yet, no matter how hard I fight to keep them open, I can't. I open my mouth to beg her not to leave me again, but no words come out.

And then everything goes…

***

…dark.

I feel groggy like I've been napping for hours. I press my hands down and realize I'm lying on a hard surface that feels like concrete. Okay, I'm probably not splattered all over the pavement. So that means my dream about K'ami must have been real.

Holy smokes, she actually saved my life!

I open my eyes, hoping to gaze upon a peaceful, blue sky, but instead, I find a raging battle being waged overhead. Krule's Motley Crew are scattered all over the sky, but they're no longer fighting Meta-Busters. Instead, they're weaving through a cloud of orange specks that sort of look like … fireflies?

But then it hits me.

Those aren't fireflies.

They're Infinity Wands!

The Intergalactic Paladins are here!

So, that means—

Just then, a silver, submarine-shaped vehicle swerves behind one of Krule's ships and blasts it from behind, sending it towards Earth in a smoking death spiral.

It's the Ghost Ship!

Yes! The Zodiac did it! They actually recruited the Intergalactic Paladins to help! Suddenly, there's a blinding barrage of orange light as the Paladins go on the offensive with their Infinity Wands, knocking ship after ship out of the sky.

I can't believe it. The good guys are finally winning!

And I feel something I haven't felt in a while—hope.

But then my body is shrouded in a dark shadow.

"Stand and fight, 'Champion,'" Krule says in a mocking tone. "Show me this vast power your master has bragged about. Unless, of course, you are afraid."

Oh, jeez. Back to reality!

I scramble to my feet and face Krule, my neck craning back to take him all in. He's an absolute giant, towering over me with his arms crossed and a smirk lining his smug face. Honestly, I don't think I've ever met a scarier looking dude, but for some reason, this time I'm not feeling so scared.

In fact, I'm feeling downright angry.

K'ami's last words echo in my head—*use all that you have learned*—and suddenly, I know exactly what to do.

Principle number one: Never show weakness.

"I'm not afraid of you," I say, my hands on my hips.

"That is a mistake," Krule says, his third eye flickering green. "Most likely, your last."

Principle number two: Always go on the offensive.

I concentrate hard, and then project my powers up into the sky, pushing them further than I've ever pushed them before, reaching out for every single Intergalactic Paladin in flight. And then I duplicate the power of a hundred Infinity Wands at once!

The energy surge is massive!

My body feels super-charged, like pure electricity is coursing through my veins—and when I look down, orange sparks are dancing around my fingers!

I-I've never felt such immense power before. It feels like I'm floating on air, like I'm having an out-of-body experience. It feels like I might be at... Meta 4?

But it's way more power than I could ever hope to contain. Fortunately, I don't plan on keeping it.

I point my arms at Krule, and then I let him have it.
SZZAAAACCCKKKK!

The massive discharge knocks me clear off my feet, but not before I see the blast strike Krule full in the chest, blowing him straight through the concrete walls of the Pentagon. Debris flies everywhere as the entire building buckles and then collapses on top of him, sending a giant plume of dust into the air.

By now I'm lying flat on my back with orange smoke billowing off my hands. Wow, I wasn't expecting that, but I'll take it. I just hope he's down for the count.

Please let him be down for the count.

But as I get to my feet, massive chunks of concrete come flying back out of the hole, followed by a wave of office equipment. I dodge a conference table and duck beneath a stapler that zips over my head. Darn it, he's clearly not down for the count, and I guess he doesn't need to staple anything.

Okay, I'm in serious trouble. I mean, if a blast from a hundred Infinity Wands couldn't knock him out then what will? I need another solution and fast.

But as the dust settles, my heart skips a beat, because standing inside the ruins of the building is an eight-foot silhouette. Krule is coming back for more!

If I'm gonna win, I've got to think outside the box. I need to surprise him. Wait a second. Surprise!

That's principle number three!

Suddenly, I get a wild idea.

It may not work, but it's all I got. So, I bathe Krule in my duplication powers, grab some telekinesis, and then get down to business. I concentrate hard, sending Krule's power deep below the Pentagon.

"I have had enough," Krule says, his voice booming. "Your life ends now."

Well, that certainly sounds bad, but I can't risk diverting my focus. I keep pushing Krule's telekinesis downward, but there's just a ton of earth in the way. But I can't give up. Even though sweat is pouring down my face, stinging my eyes, I need to keep trying.

Then, out of the corner of my eye, I see Krule!

He's striding towards me, his third eye glowing.

Submit.

Aahh! There's a sharp pain inside my brain! He's getting inside my head! I need to… hold him off! But I… can't give him my full attention. I can't stop… doing what I'm doing.

You are strong, but I am so much stronger.

I glance over again and realize he's almost on top of me! He's raising his arms! He's not waiting for his mind control! He's gonna pound me with his fists!

This is it! Focus!

I bend down and give it everything I've got!

RRRIIIPPPPP!

Suddenly, the ground between us bursts wide open and a funnel of dirt spews out like lava from a volcano.

Krule's three eyes go wide and he steps back startled.

But I keep pulling because what I'm going for isn't dirt and rubble—it's super-Sheelds! Just then, the brown, leathery organisms pop out of the hole one by one, hovering in the air as I collect them between us—and then I send them at Krule like an army of killer bees!

Krule staggers back as the giant one slams into him first, latching onto his chest. And then the others pile on, covering every inch of Krule's massive body as they knock him to the ground, draining his power.

I did it! But I'm so exhausted I drop to my knees.

"Well done, Champion," comes a voice.

I turn to find the Emperor standing behind me, smiling like he's just won gold in the Evil-Olympics. Then, he reaches into his belt and pulls out a thin golden rod. What's that for? But with the mere push of a button, it extends on both sides into a long, sharp spear!

"Now it is time to execute principle number four," he says, offering the spear to me. "Show no mercy. Kill Krule before he recovers and kills you."

What? Kill Krule?

"Take the spear, my champion," the Emperor demands. "Finish the job before it is too late."

I stand up, my legs still wobbly. My brain hears what the Emperor is saying, but something doesn't feel right.

"Take it," the Emperor insists. "End his life."

I don't want to do it, but I know he's right. I mean, this might be my only chance to stop Krule for good.

I grab the spear.

"Excellent," the Emperor says. "Now, for the survival of your planet, do what needs to be done."

I walk over to Krule, who is writhing on the ground, trying to pull the super-Sheelds off his body. I approach slowly, raising the spear over my head. Okay, all I need to do is strike. Then, this will all be over.

Or will it?

I look over at the Emperor who is practically salivating. After I deal with Krule, I'll have to face him.

I close my eyes and raise the spear over my head. I just need to do this before Krule knows what's happening. I just need to murder him in cold blood.

But... I can't.

I lower the spear.

"Do it!" the Emperor yells. "Do it now, you fool! Why are you—"

Suddenly, Krule arches his back and yells "GET! OFF!" And the next thing I know, all of the super-Sheelds are blown off his body with incredible force, disappearing into the distant sky.

"No!" the Emperor yells.

"You thought you could suppress my power!" Krule says, rising to his feet. "But that is impossible! Now I will destroy you both!"

I jump back. I think I've just made a huge mistake.

And now Krule is gonna cream me!

But suddenly, a horrible smell hits my nostrils.

"What is that?" Krule says, scrunching up his face.

"Sorry, tri-eyes," comes a girl's voice. "But as the saying goes, 'whoever smelt it dealt it!'"

Just then, a girl in a black-and-white costume bursts onto the scene. It's Skunk Girl?!?

"You won't be destroying anyone today," comes a boy's voice. "Not with a killer headache like this."

And then a big, gray ball SLAMS into Krule's forehead, knocking him off balance.

Pinball? It's Next Gen! They've come back to save me!

"Say cheese!" comes another girl's voice. But this time I know who it is.

"Selfie!" I yell. "Stay back!"

But as she raises her phone, Krule is ready for her.

His third eye lights up and Selfie's eyes flash green!

No! He's got her! She'll be his slave!

Without a second thought, I lift my spear and throw it at Krule! But unlike my Epic-a-rang disaster, this time the spear sails right over Selfie's head and lands true, plunging deep into Krule's third eye!

"AAAHH!" Krule screams, reaching for the spear as green blood pours out everywhere.

"Selfie!" I yell, running over to her. "Are you okay?"

"I-I think so," she says, bending over, her eyes turning back to blue. "But things got really weird for a minute."

Whew! That was close. But with Krule finally out of the way, the first part of this nightmare should be—

"YOU ELIMINATED MY POWERS. AND NOW I WILL DESTROY YOU!"

—over?

Seriously? I spin around and my knees wobble, because standing before us is Krule! Blood is still gushing from his third eye but it doesn't seem to matter.

What's it gonna take to get rid of this guy?

And that's when I notice something.

He's holding the bloody spear, and it's pointed at me! I flinch as the villain rears back his massive arm.

But before he throws it—

FAZZZZZAAAMMM!

"NOOOO!" Krule screams, as the shaft of the spear erupts in a field of electricity. Krule's eyes bulge and his limbs jerk uncontrollably. And then his body falls face-first to the ground in a smoldering heap.

Huh? What just happened?

"Do not celebrate, Champion," the Emperor crows, holding an activator in one hand and a gun pointed at me in the other. "You may think I saved your life, but I am only delaying the inevitable. You see, I had hoped to eliminate the both of you in one shot, but once you threw away my spear, I was left with no choice but to kill you one by one. And since Krule was holding the spear, I could not waste the opportunity. But now it is your turn to die."

For a second I'm confused by what he's saying, but then the pieces come together.

That spear he handed me was booby-trapped with electricity, just like the knife he gave Winch! So, if I had stabbed Krule earlier like he wanted, the Emperor would have electrocuted us both at once! But since I threw the spear away, he couldn't do it.

What a slimeball.

"However, I must congratulate you," the Emperor says. "You fought like a true champion, but now you are expendable."

But as the Emperor raises his weapon at my head, I see a golden helmet bobbing its way towards him. It's the behavior modification helmet! But how?

Then, a German Shephard appears, carrying the helmet in its mouth!

Holy Cow! It's Dog-Gone! He's alive!

"What?" the Emperor cries, as Dog-Gone climbs up his back, knocks off his crown, and slams the helmet over his head.

Now's my chance!

The Emperor drops his gun to remove the helmet, and I spring into action, running straight for him. But he's so tall I'm gonna need help.

"Dog-Gone, sit!" I yell.

As my pooch screeches to a halt, I step on his back and leap up towards the Emperor's head. Then, I reach for the helmet and push the green button. I hear a CLICK as I fly past and land hard on the ground.

Ouch! My right shoulder is on fire, but when I look

back up, the Emperor is standing stock still.

I did it!

"Um, what is that thing'?" Pinball asks.

"That, my friend, is a Skelton behavior modification device," I say, getting to my feet and walking over to the Emperor.

I don't know if I'll ever get a chance like this again, so I need to pick my words very, very carefully.

"Listen up, Emperor," I say. "I want you to order every last one of your Skelton operatives off of my planet and I never, ever want you to return. In fact, I want you to forget that Earth even exists. If you ever see it on a map, you will ignore it like it was a figment of your imagination. Do you understand?"

"I understand," the Emperor repeats robotically.

Wow, this might actually work!

"And that's not all," I say. "Under your leadership, the Skelton will become a peaceful Empire. You will find a new, abandoned Homeworld and never, ever bother anyone again. Is that clear?"

"Yes," he says. "That is clear."

"Great," I say. "Oh, and one more thing. That helmet you're wearing is your new crown. You should never remove it under any circumstances or let anyone ever touch it. Are those instructions clear?"

"Yes," he says. "They are clear."

"Good," I say. "Now go, and don't ever come back."

Then, the Emperor turns and walks away.

"Um, are you sure we should just let him go like that?" Skunk Girl asks.

"Yep," I say. "Someone needs to lead the Skelton Empire, and it might as well be their behavior-modified Emperor. Besides, after this, I don't think he'll be bothering anyone ever again."

Just then, I feel something wet nuzzle into my palm.

"Dog-Gone!" I throw my arms around him and we tumble to the ground. "I'm so happy you're alive!" I say as tears roll down my cheeks. "I thought I'd lost you forever. You big dummy, don't ever do that to me again."

"You won't believe this," Selfie says. "But he was waiting for us back at the treehouse. It probably took him days to get there, but after the Pentagon disaster, I don't think he knew where else to go. But once we arrived, he led us right back here."

"You're too smart for your own good," I say, squeezing him even tighter.

"Epic Zero!" comes a familiar man's voice.

Dad? And when I look up, I see the whole gang. Mom, Dad, Grace, and all of the Freedom Force! And behind them are Wind Walker and a whole bunch of other heroes, including the Rising Suns!

"You're alive!" I say, throwing myself into Dad's arms, as more tears stream down my cheeks. "I'm so sorry. I never should have contacted you. I really messed up. I—"

"It's okay, son," Dad whispers. "You did great. You

saved us all."

"Even I've got to hand it to you," Grace says, hugging me. "You're really amazing. And this time my fingers aren't crossed."

"Well, this was fun," TechnocRat says. "But it'll be great to go home again. I've got a hankering for some Camembert cheese. In fact, I think I'll even break out the good stuff."

Home? Oh boy.

"Um," I say, trying to smile. "I've got something I need to tell you guys…"

EPILOGUE

I START A NEW CHAPTER

I grab my popcorn and settle into the command chair.

As I look around the Monitor Room, I'm amazed at how TechnocRat nailed every single detail of the original Waystation. He's calling our new headquarters 'the Waystation 2.0' and he's right. Everything feels exactly the same, but with some pretty cool upgrades.

For one, he built himself an even bigger laboratory, with an indestructible vault to house his precious Camembert cheese. There's also a swimming pool, which seemed like a great idea until Dog-Gone decided to test it out. Now we have to keep a gate around it at all times so I don't end up blow-drying wet fur for hours on end.

There's also a bunch of other new goodies, including a break-away satellite pod on the other side of the Hangar allowing for a quick getaway in case we're boarded again.

If I didn't know better, I'd think TechnocRat was trying to tell me something.

Anyway, it feels great to be home again. After all, we had to spend two months living in a cramped apartment while TechnocRat rebuilt the place. Being together was awesome, but sharing one bathroom among seven people, a teenage girl, and an irritable rat is not so much fun. And forget about ever getting a hot shower!

Oh, another major upgrade I forgot to mention is the Meta Monitor—or should I say, the 'Meta Monitor 2.0.' This version not only monitors Earth for Meta signatures but it now also monitors outer space! Of course, it still needs to work out a few kinks, like the time it mistook a meteor shower for an alien invasion, but it's using artificial intelligence to get more accurate every day.

But the best part of the new Waystation is the enhanced Mission Room communications system. Now, with the simple push of a button, we can have direct communication with not only President Kensington but also Paladin Planet and the Ghost Ship!

And by the way, thank goodness we found the real President Kensington. After the whole Pentagon episode, I feared the world would plunge into chaos without its leaders. But then Mom picked up a faint mental cry for help, and we discovered all of the world's leaders trapped inside a reinforced steel room several levels beneath the Capitol building. They were a bit shaken up, but with the help of the other Meta super teams like the Rising Suns and Los Toros, we got them all back to their home countries safe and sound.

Speaking of the Rising Suns, the Psychics like Mom were able to team up to reverse the behavior modification job done to Zen and the others. It wasn't easy, and once she was back to normal, I was amazed that Zen had no recollection of our fight! Sadly, we learned that Tsunami was the one who passed away in the Emperor's lab. He was a brave hero and we're planning to go to his memorial service in a few days.

It was also hard saying goodbye to the Zodiac and the Intergalactic Paladins. It was great seeing Broog and Quovaar again, and they said they'd help keep a closer eye on our solar system—which I thanked them for.

As for the Zodiac, well, they're galactic adventurers at heart so they didn't stick around for long. But with our improved communications system I've been able to keep in touch with all of them, especially Gemini—sometimes well after bedtime.

Of course, I've had to bribe Dog-Gone with a million doggie treats not to tip off Mom or Dad. But that's okay. After all, I'm just happy he's still around.

I look at the Meta Monitor 2.0 but nothing is happening. C'mon, we need some action.

But just as I stuff a handful of popcorn into my mouth, the Meta Monitor 2.0 blares—

"Alert! Alert! Alert! Meta 1 disturbance. Repeat: Meta 1 disturbance. Power signature identified as Erase Face.

Alert! Alert! Alert!"

Erase Face? That's perfect!

I put down my popcorn, send three signals down to Earth, and leap off the command chair. But as soon as I take my first step down the stairs, I hear CRUNCHING behind me.

"Dog-Gone?" I yell over my shoulder. "Were you invisible the whole time? Get out of my popcorn!"

The box tips over and popcorn spills everywhere, but I don't have time to stop. Instead, I race down the stairs and make a mental note. Despite TechnocRat's upgrades, he forgot to install the heat-seeking cameras I asked for.

I bolt through the Galley where I find my parents sitting at the table.

"You taking this one?" Dad asks, sipping his coffee without even looking up from his newspaper.

"Yep, it's a Meta 1," I say, jogging through.

"Have fun," Mom says. "And be back by dinner. It's meatloaf."

"I hate meatloaf!" I say, exiting into the corridor.

I turn a corner and nearly crash into Grace.

"I've got it," I say.

"I figured," she says. "Say hi to your friends for me. And let them know I think they're in good hands. You're a pretty great leader, Elliott."

"Gee," I say, stopping for a second. "Thanks."

"Of course, I might have my toes crossed," Grace says with a wink. "Go get 'em, squirt."

I smile and step into the new Transporter Room. I key in the coordinates and feel the unnerving pins-and-needles sensation of my atoms dissipating. Seconds later, I'm pulled back together at the base of a treehouse.

"It's about time," Pinball says. "We got your signal, like, five minutes ago."

"Sorry," I say, "I got... hung up for a bit."

"Are we ready to go?" Skunk Girl says. "I'm dying to stink something up!"

"Yeah," I say, but then I notice someone is missing. "Where's Selfie?"

"Right here," she says, running over. "Hey."

"Hey," I say, unable to stop my big smile.

"Um, awkward," Pinball says. "Can we go now?"

"What? Oh, right," I say. "Okay team, we're about to do battle with Erase Face. He's a Meta 1 with the ability to wipe things away with his nose. Yes, I know it sounds ridiculous, but don't underestimate him. And please, don't approach him from straight on. Got it?"

"Got it, boss," Skunk Girl says, with a salute.

I look them in the eyes. They're eager to learn and want to do what's right. And for a second, it feels kind of weird that they're hanging on my every word. But then I realize I can really help them, and for the first time, I realize I wouldn't want it any other way.

"Okay, Next Gen," I say. "Get ready, because it's Fight Time!"

They nod, and then we're off!

YOU CAN MAKE A BIG DIFFERENCE

Calling all heroes! I need your help to get Epic Zero in front of more readers.

Reviews are extremely helpful in getting attention for my books. I wish I had the marketing muscle of the major publishers, but instead, I have something far more valuable, loyal readers, just like you! Your generosity in providing an honest review will help bring this book to the attention of more readers.

So, if you've enjoyed this book, I would be very grateful if you could spare a minute to leave a review on the book's Amazon page. Thanks for your support!

Stay Epic!

R.L. Ullman

GET MORE EPIC!

Don't miss any of the Epic action!

Get a **FREE** copy of
Epic Zero Extra: Tales of a Superhero Screw Up
only at rlullman.com.

META POWERS GLOSSARY

FROM THE META MONITOR:
There are nine known Meta power classifications. These classifications have been established to simplify Meta identification and provide a quick framework to understand a Meta's potential powers and capabilities. **Note:** Metas can possess powers in more than one classification. In addition, Metas can evolve over time in both the powers they express, as well as the effectiveness of their powers.

Due to the wide range of Meta abilities, superpowers have been further segmented into power levels. Power levels differ across Meta power classifications. In general, the following power levels have been established:

- Meta 0: Displays no Meta power.
- Meta 1: Displays limited Meta power.
- Meta 2: Displays considerable Meta power.
- Meta 3: Displays extreme Meta power.

The following is a brief overview of the nine Meta power classifications.

ENERGY MANIPULATION:
Energy Manipulation is the ability to generate, shape, or act as a conduit, for various forms of energy. Energy Manipulators can control energy by focusing or redirecting energy towards a specific target or shaping/reshaping energy for a specific task. Energy Manipulators are often impervious to the forms of energy they can manipulate.

Examples of the types of energies utilized by Energy Manipulators include, but are not limited to:

- Atomic
- Chemical
- Cosmic
- Electricity
- Gravity
- Heat
- Light
- Magnetic
- Sound
- Space
- Time

Note: the fundamental difference between an Energy Manipulator and a Meta-morph with Energy Manipulation capability is that an Energy Manipulator does not change their physical, molecular state to either generate or transfer energy (see META-MORPH).

FLIGHT:
Flight is the ability to fly, glide, or levitate above the Earth's surface without the use of an external source (e.g. jetpack). Flight can be accomplished through a variety of methods, these include, but are not limited to:

- Reversing the forces of gravity
- Riding air currents
- Using planetary magnetic fields
- Wings

Metas exhibiting Flight can range from barely sustaining flight a few feet off the ground to reaching the far limits of outer space.

Often, Metas with Flight ability also display the complementary ability of Super-Speed. However, it can be difficult to decipher if Super-Speed is a Meta power in its own right or is simply a function of combining the Meta's Flight ability with the Earth's natural gravitational force.

MAGIC:
Magic is the ability to display a wide variety of Meta abilities by channeling the powers of a secondary magical or mystical source. Known secondary sources of Magic powers include, but are not limited to:

- Alien lifeforms
- Dark arts
- Demonic forces
- Departed souls
- Mystical spirits

Typically, the forces of Magic are channeled through an enchanted object. Known magical, enchanted objects include:

- Amulets
- Books
- Cloaks
- Gemstones
- Wands

- Weapons

Some Magicians can transport themselves into the mystical realm of their magical source. They may also have the ability to transport others into and out of these realms as well.

Note: the fundamental difference between a Magician and an Energy Manipulator is that a Magician typically channels their powers from a mystical source that likely requires the use of an enchanted object to express these powers (see ENERGY MANIPULATOR).

META MANIPULATION:

Meta Manipulation is the ability to duplicate or negate the Meta powers of others. Meta Manipulation is a rare Meta power and can be extremely dangerous if the Meta Manipulator is capable of manipulating the powers of multiple Metas at one time. Meta Manipulators who can manipulate the powers of several Metas at once have been observed to reach Meta 4 power levels.

Based on the unique powers of the Meta Manipulator, it is hypothesized that other abilities could include altering or controlling the powers of others. Despite their tremendous abilities, Meta Manipulators are often unable to generate powers of their own and are limited to manipulating the powers of others. When not utilizing their abilities, Meta Manipulators may be vulnerable to attack.

Note: It has been observed that a Meta Manipulator requires close physical proximity to a Meta target to fully manipulate their power. When fighting a Meta

Manipulator, it is advised to stay at a reasonable distance and to attack from long range. Meta Manipulators have been observed manipulating the powers of others up to 100 yards away.

META-MORPH:
Meta-morph is the ability to display a wide variety of Meta abilities by "morphing" all, or part, of one's physical form from one state into another. There are two sub-types of Meta-morphs:

- Physical
- Molecular

Physical morphing occurs when a Meta-morph transforms their physical state to express their powers. Physical Meta-morphs typically maintain their human physiology while exhibiting their powers (with the exception of Shapeshifters). Types of Physical morphing include, but are not limited to:

- Invisibility
- Malleability (elasticity/plasticity)
- Physical by-products (silk, toxins, etc…)
- Shapeshifting
- Size changes (larger or smaller)

Molecular morphing occurs when a Meta-morph transforms their molecular state from a normal physical state to a non-physical state to express their powers. Types of Molecular morphing include, but are not limited to:

- Fire
- Ice
- Rock
- Sand
- Steel
- Water

Note: Because Meta-morphs can display abilities that mimic all other Meta power classifications, it can be difficult to properly identify a Meta-morph upon the first encounter. However, it is critical to carefully observe how their powers manifest, and, if it is through Physical or Molecular morphing, you can be certain you are dealing with a Meta-morph.

PSYCHIC:

Psychic is the ability to use one's mind as a weapon. There are two sub-types of Psychics:

- Telepaths
- Telekinetics

Telepathy is the ability to read and influence the thoughts of others. While Telepaths often do not appear to be physically intimidating, their power to penetrate minds can often result in more devastating damage than a physical assault.

Telekinesis is the ability to manipulate physical objects with one's mind. Telekinetics can often move objects with their mind that are much heavier than they could move physically. Many Telekinetics can also make objects move at very high speeds.

Note: Psychics are known to strike from long distance, and, in a fight, it is advised to incapacitate them as quickly as possible. Psychics often become physically drained from the extended use of their powers.

SUPER-INTELLIGENCE:
Super-Intelligence is the ability to display levels of intelligence above standard genius intellect. Super-Intelligence can manifest in many forms, including, but not limited to:

- Superior analytical ability
- Superior information synthesizing
- Superior learning capacity
- Superior reasoning skills

Note: Super-Intellects continuously push the envelope in the fields of technology, engineering, and weapons development. Super-Intellects are known to invent new approaches to accomplish previously impossible tasks. When dealing with a Super-Intellect, you should be mentally prepared to face challenges that have never been encountered before. In addition, Super-Intellects can come in all shapes and sizes. The most advanced Super-Intellects have originated from non-human creatures.

SUPER-SPEED:
Super-Speed is the ability to display movement at remarkable physical speeds above standard levels of speed. Metas with Super-Speed often exhibit complementary abilities to movement that include, but are not limited to:

- Enhanced endurance
- Phasing through solid objects
- Super-fast reflexes
- Time travel

Note: Metas with Super-Speed often have an equally super metabolism, burning thousands of calories per minute, and requiring them to eat many extra meals a day to maintain consistent energy levels. It has been observed that Metas exhibiting Super-Speed are quick thinkers, making it difficult to keep up with their thought process.

SUPER-STRENGTH:

Super-Strength is the ability to utilize muscles to display remarkable levels of physical strength above expected levels of strength. Metas with Super-Strength can lift or push objects that are well beyond the capability of an average member of their species. Metas exhibiting Super-Strength can range from lifting objects twice their weight to incalculable levels of strength allowing for the movement of planets.

Metas with Super-Strength often exhibit complementary abilities to strength that include, but are not limited to:

- Earthquake generation through stomping
- Enhanced jumping
- Invulnerability
- Shockwave generation through clapping

Note: Metas with Super-Strength may not always possess this strength evenly. Metas with Super-Strength have been observed to demonstrate powers in only one arm or leg.

META PROFILE CHARACTERISTICS

FROM THE META MONITOR:

In addition to having a strong working knowledge of a Meta's powers and capabilities, it is also imperative to understand the key characteristics that form the core of their character. When facing or teaming up with Metas, understanding their key characteristics will help you gain deeper insight into their mentality and strategic potential.

What follows is a brief explanation of the five key characteristics you should become familiar with. **Note**: the data that appears in each Meta profile has been compiled from live field activity.

COMBAT:

The ability to defeat a foe in hand-to-hand combat.

DURABILITY:

The ability to withstand significant wear, pressure, or damage.

LEADERSHIP:

The ability to lead a team of disparate personalities and powers to victory.

STRATEGY:

The ability to find, and successfully exploit, a foe's weakness.

WILLPOWER:

The ability to persevere, despite seemingly insurmountable odds.

DO YOU HAVE MONSTER PROBLEMS?

Half boy. Half vampire. All hero...
Readers' Favorite Book Awards Winner

It turns out monsters are real—and only a half-vampire kid hero can save us all! You'll sink your teeth into this fun, award-winning series.

Get the Monster Problems Series Collection Books 1-3 today!

ABOUT THE AUTHOR

R.L. Ullman is the bestselling author of the award-winning EPIC ZERO series and the award-winning MONSTER PROBLEMS series. He creates fun, engaging page-turners that captivate the imaginations of kids and adults alike. His original, relatable characters face adventure and adversity that bring out their inner strengths. He's frequently distracted thinking up new stories, and once got lost in his own neighborhood. You can learn more about what R.L. is up to at rlullman.com, and if you see him wandering around your street please point him in the right direction home.

For news, updates, and free stuff, please sign up for the Epic Newsflash at rlullman.com.

ACKNOWLEDGMENTS

Without the support of these brave heroes, I would have been trampled by supervillains before I could bring this series to print. I would like to thank my wife, Lynn (a.k.a. Mrs. Marvelous); my daughter Olivia (a.k.a. Ms. Positivity); and my son Matthew (a.k.a. Captain Creativity). I would also like to thank all of the readers out there who have connected with Elliott and his amazing family. Stay Epic!